INDIAN BURIAL GROUND

ALSO BY NICK MEDINA

SISTERS OF THE LOST NATION

INDIAN BURIAL GROUND

NICK MEDINA

BERKLEY
New York

BERKLEY
An imprint of Penguin Random House LLC
penguinrandomhouse.com

Library of Congress Cataloging-in-Publication Data

Names: Medina, Nick, author.
Title: Indian burial ground / Nick Medina.
Description: New York: Berkley, 2024.
Identifiers: LCCN 2023035704 (print) | LCCN 2023035705 (ebook) |
ISBN 9780593546888 (hardcover) | ISBN 9780593546901 (ebook)
Subjects: LCGFT: Thrillers (Fiction) | Horror fiction. |
Paranormal fiction. | Novels.
Classification: LCC PS3613.E314 I53 2024 (print) |
LCC PS3613.E314 (ebook) | DDC 813/.6—dc23/eng/20230830
LC record available at https://lccn.loc.gov/2023035704
LC ebook record available at https://lccn.loc.gov/2023035705

Printed in the United States of America
1st Printing

Book design by George Towne

This is a work of fiction. Names, characters, places, and incidents either are the product of the
author's imagination or are used fictitiously, and any resemblance to actual persons,
living or dead, business establishments, events, or locales is entirely coincidental.

For U.B.

AUTHOR'S NOTE

Indian Burial Ground includes content that addresses issues of addiction, alcoholism, murder, the deaths of children and adults, and suspected suicide. Please read with your well-being and best interest in mind.

INDIAN
BURIAL
GROUND

PROLOGUE

She couldn't feel her feet. Not her knees or her hips either. Running like a Thoroughbred in a race, no one would know that she'd been limping just thirty minutes earlier, from her front door to her Jeep, favoring her left ankle, swollen and plum purple.

Maximus bore the blame for her sprain. If the damn dog hadn't snatched her phone from her hand, she wouldn't have chased him yesterday in the yard, and she wouldn't have rolled her ankle on the knot of wood—probably chewed up by old Maximus himself—hidden in the grass. Pain had made her grimace with each tender step thereafter, but now, despite the force of her wide, rapid strides driving her feet hard against the asphalt, she didn't feel any pain at all.

Just worry and dread.

He might still be alive, she thought. *Please, let him be alive.*

It couldn't have taken her more than a minute to run down the road to the Grand Nacre Casino and Resort, which was glittering in the light of the descending sun. She would have called for help from the Jeep if she could have found her phone. It'd been in the cupholder beside her when she'd set off for work, earlier than usual because the bum ankle would slow her down—thanks again, Maximus—but after she'd swerved the Jeep to the left in a desperate Hail-Mary-hold-tight at-tempt to avoid the inevitable, the cupholder was empty, the Jeep was on its side, and the man she'd tried not to hit was partially wrapped around the base of the tree trunk that'd prevented him from flying into the woods that bordered the road.

Sounds from the impact remained within her. Taylor Swift singing "Anti-Hero," silent now. The deafening crash of the Jeep. The report of the man's ribs meeting metal. The sickening crack of his skull against glass. Its top down, she'd clung to the Jeep's steering wheel as the vehicle, toppling in slow motion, rolled onto its side like her ankle on that knot of wood.

Call an ambulance, she'd shrieked at Caleb Guidry, ragged nails between his teeth, at the security station just beyond the casino's slid-ing glass doors.

What's wrong, Lena? A piece of nail shot from his mouth. Used to her flirty smiles as she enticed high rollers to her blackjack table through the swing shift hours, he'd never seen her so worked up before.

She'd shouted other things at him in response

. . . Man . . .

. . . Hit him . . .

. . . Up the road . . .

HURRY!

before turning right around and pounding the pavement again.

Please don't be dead. She wondered if Caleb had summoned the ambulance yet. The resort had medics on-site. It wouldn't take them long to arrive.

I'm alive, had been her first thought after the toppled Jeep touched down, relief and disbelief swelling within her. Her fingers made quick work of disengaging the seat belt that had kept her head from cracking against the ground, an old commercial surfacing in her mind.

This is your brain on drugs.

2

But it was only half an oxy she'd taken, for the pain in her ankle, and it'd worn off by the time she'd left for work.

Having retched on the road's shoulder upon spying the unmoving man, she'd been too terrified to scurry toward the trees to see if he still had a pulse. The blood was what kept her at bay, spreading through his clothes, his hair.

His heart must have been beating, she thought hopefully as she returned to the Jeep, lying like a murdered elephant in the road. *He wouldn't be bleeding if his heart wasn't beating.*

Feeling the sprint's toll on her neglected cardiovascular system, she slowed to a brisk walk, wheezing all the way. Even when she took Maximus to the park, he did all the running while she stood stationary, throwing sticks and balls for him to fetch.

"Please," she gasped, then, "Why? WHY?" as she tried to make sense of what the man had done, her ears searching for sirens. Still, they didn't come.

Feeling wavy inside, as if her skin were a sack filled with water, she wanted to collapse like the Jeep. Maybe then someone would come along and do the things she couldn't, like put pressure on an open wound or start mouth-to-mouth resuscitation.

His back was broken, his spine curved the wrong way around the tree trunk. Just seeing it again in her mind's eye made her stomach judder. She spat on the road, which was littered with shattered glass, amber bits of a broken side marker, her handbag, empty and half-full water bottles that she'd habitually tossed into the passenger side footwell, the Starbucks cup that had held her Salted Caramel Cream Cold Brew—ordered only minutes earlier—and the cherry-blast-scented Little Trees air freshener that had somehow come loose from the rearview mirror. Still, there was no sign of her phone. And still, she saw no ambulance on the horizon.

Dizzy and defeated, she staggered to the shoulder, then screamed and leaped back toward the middle of the road—much the way the man had seemingly leaped in front of the Jeep—at the sight of a coyote, half the size of Maximus yet far more fearsome, standing over the man's body. Head low, ears up, mouth open, glistening red teeth on display, the canine growled.

Its muzzle was matted with blood.

ONE

Noemi

I'd just given the rolling paper a twist when I thought I heard a knock at the door. My eyes shot to the window. Sure enough.

He looked confused when I pulled the door open, as if he'd expected someone else. His lips moved. I held up a finger, telling him to wait while I went to lower my music.

"You sure like it loud," he remarked upon my return.

"Drowns shit out," I said. "Lookin' for my mom?"

His lips moved again with no sound coming out. And then he said, "Yeah. And you, too."

I felt my forehead wrinkle, my upper lip coming up as my eyes examined him. Short gray hair that matched the patchy stubble on his chin and cheeks. Heavy lines beneath his eyes. Skin that had yet to see the summer's sun, though it was already late July. Beneath those new and unfamiliar traits stood a man I hadn't seen in twelve long years. The scar on his left nostril gave him away.

"Uncle Louie!" I didn't mean to screech, but my voice has a way of doing that. Like a grasshopper, I leaped at him, wrapping him in a hug that pinned his arms to his sides. I was thrilled to see him, the man who wasn't just my uncle but the closest thing to a father and a brother

I'd ever had. At least he had been until distance, I guess, got in the way. But before that, he'd always brought me gifts and given me advice—even when I didn't want it—and he'd practically raised me until the age of five.

"Come in! Oh my god, come in." I yanked him into the trailer he'd once called home. He took two big steps away from me, looking at the TV on the wall, the painted paneling, the leather sofa, the glass end table, the laminate flooring, everything but my eyes.

"You didn't recognize me at first, did you?" I said, immediately wishing I hadn't.

He scratched beneath his collar. "You're not a kid anymore. You must be for—"

"It's been more than a *decade*." I cut him off because I knew what he'd been about to say, and I didn't want him to think of me that way—*forty*.

I pocketed the joint from the coffee table just as his eyes passed over it. There was nothing I could do about the bong other than hope he took it for a vase.

"Putting the per capita payments to good use," he said with just enough sarcasm to make me think it was a joke.

Feeling heat in my cheeks because he'd just discovered one of my vices, and because he didn't know yet how badly I'd fucked up with my share of the casino money, I dropped onto the couch, only to bounce right back up. We were both nervous, no question about that.

"Did my mom know you were coming?"

He shook his head, and I supposed he hadn't told anyone on the reservation he was coming home.

"Wasn't sure I'd go through with it until the tires left the runway," he admitted. "She here?"

I cocked my head toward the bathroom door. He nodded as if he should have known. With a snap of my fingers and a smile—suddenly remembering—I exclaimed, "The pow wow starts tomorrow!" figuring that must explain why he'd chosen now to reappear. He used to visit every summer, proud of the fact that he'd attended every pow wow since the year he was born. That streak, however, ended in 2011, the last time he came home.

"Yeah." He nodded again, in a way that seemed to reassure him more than me this time. "Looking forward to it."

"Still teaching?" I snapped a few more times. "What is it?"

"Folklore and mythology. Yeah, I'm still teaching. And you? What fills your days these . . . days?" An awkward grin blossomed on his face as I felt my own mouth betray me, the corners of my lips sinking toward my chin. Hoping he wouldn't see, I swung my head to the right, making my waist-length hair wrap around my body as my eyes sought comfort in the delicate magnolia on my exposed shoulder, the pink feather on my forearm, the vibrant butterfly on my wrist. "Just living the dream," I muttered.

The bathroom door opened just then, and I'm sure we were both glad it did. From within, black leather boots, skinny jeans, a black tank top with a rainbow heart bedazzled across the chest, shiny lips, and puffed-up hair emerged. Mom.

Her eyes widened. Fear momentarily cracked her made-up face, and a scream of terror in response to the strange man standing in our living room almost rang out, transforming instead into a cry of joy at the last second, right when she recognized him. "Louie!" She did a little hop, her boots thumping against the laminate floor. "Don't do that to me!" A second later, she was in her brother's arms.

"Lula," he cried.

We'd gone years without phone calls, video chats, and greeting cards. Sometimes we'd exchange texts on birthdays and holidays, filled with statements like *Hope you're well*, rather than questions that might encourage conversation.

Mom looked up at him, taking his face in her hands. "You cut off your hair. It's gray." Even though she was three years older than him, Mom's hair has been chocolate cherry my entire life. "Let me turn back time for you." She laughed. "My god, what are you doing here?"

"Pow wow," he said.

"I wish you'd have told me. Everyone's going to be so surprised to see you. But this is perfect!" She clapped her hands. "We're meeting friends at the Blue Gator tonight. You can meet Noemi's boyfriend. My new guy's gonna come by too."

"No he won't," I interjected from the couch. Mom threw a dismissive wave in my direction.

"Say you'll come," Mom said.

"Sure. Yeah." He seemed to reassure himself again. "I'll meet you there after I check in at the hotel."

"Why not stay here? I know it's a little small for—" Mom paused, finally looking past her brother. "Where's Holly? Jill?"

"Can we—?" he started, but was cut off by a trio of stern knocks against the door.

It wasn't Holly or Jill.

"Chief Fisher," Mom and Uncle Louie said in unison the instant I opened the door. Luke Fisher wasn't chief of the tribal police anymore, but he had been for so long that most of us still called him that. Most days, he still acted like he was on the job.

"Noemi." His hands reached for mine as his eyes gave Mom an acknowledging glance. They lingered a little longer on Louie, but whatever he'd come to say took precedence over the friendly reunion that might have otherwise occurred.

"What is it?" I said. Luke wasn't the type to just drop in for visits. He wasn't the type to just stroke the back of your hand either.

"Let's sit," he said.

I didn't want to.

"It's Roddy," he uttered. "I know how close the two of you are, so I thought I should tell you before—"

"Tell me what?"

His old hands, veins stretching the thin skin, squeezed mine. "He was hit by a car."

"What?" I shrieked. Mom did too.

Luke glanced at the sofa, but I hadn't changed my mind about sitting. "I'm really sorry."

Sorry. I'd never known how much weight a word could hold until Luke uttered it.

"No!" Tears appeared as if a magician had waved a wand in front of my eyes.

"Tribal PD will figure out what happened."

"You're saying . . . ?" Though I heard what he was saying, I couldn't grasp it. Didn't want to.

"I'm sorry," he said again.

"How?"

"He was out on Grand Nacre Drive. The driver said he came out of nowhere."

That didn't make sense. I'd texted Roddy a couple hours earlier, confirming our plans for the night. He was going to pick me up at eight. I told Luke as much. "He didn't say anything about driving anywhere else."

"He wasn't driving. He was on foot."

That made even less sense. "It's the height of summer. Roddy hates walking in the heat." There were only two reasons to be along Grand Nacre Drive: to get to the casino or to leave it. "Was he at the casino?" I asked, knowing he had no reason to go there.

Luke's shoulders hitched. "There's a lot to figure out."

I pulled my hands away from his and braced myself against the wall. Reality wasn't yet registering, but I knew what I'd lose if I lost

Roddy. Hopes, dreams, second chances. Without him, all I'd have were memories, regret, and forty years in the rearview mirror. Mom told me the years would go fast, back in my twenties when $130k—the amount of my trust fund, thanks to years of per capita payments I couldn't touch until I turned twenty-one—seemed like a million bucks. And Mom was right, the years came and went like sparks. And, like the money, I'd wasted them all.

"When?" I asked Luke.

"About an hour ago."

I looked out the window. The sun was below the horizon. All that remained of its light was a fiery orange band like the ring around a lit cigarette. "It must have been light when the accident happened." Anger rose within me. "Was the driver drunk?"

"Noemi . . ." Luke threw his head back and cupped his brow. I'd never seen him so unsettled. "It might not have been the driver's fault."

"He's blaming Roddy?"

"*She's* saying . . ." Eyes clenched tight, he slowly exhaled and then, finally looking like the authority he'd always been, as his arms fell to his sides and he gave it to me straight. "The driver said Roddy *lunged* in front of her vehicle. You've already said yourself that Roddy didn't like to walk and that he hadn't mentioned going anywhere today. There's concern"—his voice softened—"that this could have been suicide."

"*What?!*" I shrieked again. "No fucking way. He wouldn't. He *wouldn't*. We had plans. We were gonna get out of here. We were gonna get tattoos!"

"There's a lot to figure out," he repeated.

"What exactly did the driver say about Roddy?" Uncle Louie asked, stepping closer to Luke.

"According to her, he jumped in front of—"

"He wouldn't!" I insisted.

"With the way word travels around here, I might as well tell you everything." Luke exhaled another deep breath. "The driver ran for help. When she returned to Roddy, she saw a coyote standing over his body . . . with blood around its mouth."

My stomach churned. I finally sat. Mom plopped beside me, wrapping me in her arms, while Uncle Louie, paler than before, inexplicably locked the door.

TWO

Louie

I'd shoved Horace Saucier down deep with dead pets, lost loves, and regrets—things too upsetting to think about for more than a few seconds at a time. The words Luke Fisher spoke in the living room of my old home, though, brought Horace back to the surface. The Takoda Vampire too. And everything that happened in the summer of 1986.

Horace had been dead ten years by then. I was six when the vampire got him. He was nineteen, a man to me. He'd lived down the road from my trailer on our tribe's reservation in nowhere Louisiana. I saw him once by the river, alone with rocks in his hands. I didn't speak to him, and he didn't speak to me. We'd barely known each other, but that didn't stop me from thinking about him a decade after his death as I walked to the wake of Aubrey Forstall, another boy I barely knew.

Few on the rez truly believed that a vampire killed Horace, but no one knew who, or *what*, had ended his life. One of us kids must have given the killer its moniker, because of what it'd done. It was we who gave the Takoda Vampire's legend legs—and teeth, so many teeth. Growing up, the Takoda Vampire was what my buddies and I talked about during the day, bravely swinging from branches that hung over the river. The vampire was what we whispered about as the sun singed the horizon upon evening's approach. It was what we refused to openly acknowledge once blackness washed over the sky, and it's what kept us tied to our porches at night.

I didn't go to Horace's funeral, and I might not have gone to Aubrey's wake if it hadn't been for the fact that Jeannie Forstall, his sister, had always been cool to me. She was friends with Lula, who had a job and a toddler at the time. Since Lula couldn't pay her respects, I figured I'd do it for her.

I wore the only collared shirt I had, the one I wore for pictures at school. Baggy and white aside from the yellow stains under the arms, I thought it'd be transparent with sweat by the time I arrived at the Forstalls' front door. I gave thought to unbuttoning it, but only for a second because another Horace-inspired memory bombarded my brain.

I saw him come back from the dead, Lula said, when she was eleven and I was eight. *He looked the way he'd looked before the vampire got him.*

Nuh-uh. I shook my head so fast that Lula looked blurry to me.

Saw him standing by the shed.

I knew exactly which shed she meant. The one rusting and listing to the left.

He was looking right at me. If Lula had been joking, her jest escaped me. Horace was no joke. Neither was the vampire. *He wanted me to go into the shed. He wanted me to go with him.*

He talked to you?

I saw it in his eyes, Louie. They're black and bloody and he never blinks. If he wants you, you'll know.

How'd you get away?

I almost didn't. He tried to hit me with one of his bloody rocks when I ran.

Lula's claims made our trailer cold that day, so I bolted out beneath the scorching sun, sure that it'd prevent anything from sneaking up on me unseen. It was only after the sun set that I'd find myself squinting over my shoulder, wondering what might be behind me and what it would do if it got me in its grip.

Thinking about Horace made me feel sorrier for Aubrey than I had before. Most of us on the rez had felt sorry for Aubrey all his life. Though he was twenty-two when he died, he'd operated on a lower level. Intellectually disabled—what we called "retarded" back then— he'd never lived on his own. He'd barely been mobile, and he'd only mastered a handful of words. An eternal child, I couldn't think about him without thinking about Noemi.

Lula was sixteen when she had her. Lula's best friend, Rosie De- shautelle, gave birth the same year, only months after my sister. And though there'd been plenty of young mothers on the rez, they still got treated like twin dummies with half a brain between them, especially since they'd hooked up with boys who bragged about their conquest rather than men who supported their kids.

Something pegged me between my shoulders just then. The hairs on the back of my neck prickled. I whirled around, thinking a rock had hit me. The sound it made against the ground after it ricocheted off my back called to mind the sharp clicks I often heard against my bedroom window. While none of us knew who or what the vampire was, there was one thing we all believed: Horace and the vampire could come for you.

I wouldn't have admitted it back then, but at sixteen I was still staining my drawers whenever I heard even the gentlest ping against my bedroom window. I'd plug my ears and clench my eyes, but never would I get out of bed to peek beyond the curtain for fear of finding Horace there with his bloody face against the glass, the vampire stand- ing behind him.

It was said that if you were woken by a rock, Horace and his killer had come for you. Horace, some believed, would do you no harm. The vampire he brought with him, however . . .

My feet ground to a stop at the mouth of the Forstalls' street, unmarked like every other street on the reservation. It was unpaved, too, which meant you'd kick up dust when the earth was hot. I stared at the lonesome little house at the end of the street, realizing just how much I dreaded seeing the dead body being waked inside. The house itself looked dead. The street looked dead too. The depressing brown and yellow hue of dirt and sunbaked grass dominated every inch between me and the sad structure. The only sign of life came from the blazing fire burning in the front yard. It would send up smoke until Aubrey's body was in the ground.

My hand released the top button of my shirt from the hole holding it hostage. The shirt, as I'd imagined, was drenched. My long hair clung to my forehead and neck. I slowly started for the house again.

I'd known what I would find within its walls, but the true horror of it didn't strike me until I was within fifty feet. Aubrey. Dead. A toddler's brain in a twenty-two-year-old's body. The thought, combined with the stifling heat, robbed my lungs. I grabbed my knees, inhaled, and wiped my forehead against my shoulder, leaving a gray streak on my white shirt. I didn't want to see him. Not like that.

I hung on to my knees until my back began to ache, then started to walk once more. Sweaty and incapable of taking a full breath, I hoped everyone inside would attribute my condition to sorrow rather than fear. I stopped again on the stoop, feeling foolish for arriving emptyhanded. I hadn't brought a picture book, a model car, a piece of candy, or anything else Aubrey could take on his way from this realm to the next.

My hand went to the doorknob. My gaze dropped to the ground to the left of the door. Camouflaged in the dirt by brown, black, and reddish markings was a canebrake rattlesnake. I jumped back, my breath caught in my throat. The rattler issued no warning. Stock-still, engaged in a standoff with the snake, I kept my eyes on its tail. No movement. No sound. I inched closer, expecting a dry jangle to spin me the serpent's version of "Hit the Road Jack." The sound never came and, as I bowed my head over the dusty thing, I saw why. There was a dent in the snake's head, the likely result of someone fending it off with a rock or a stick. Crusted blood lined its mouth, and a dried trickle extended down into the dirt. Its eyes were sunken and black, telling me the snake was just as dead as Aubrey on the other side of the door.

I huffed at the rattler as if my breath might wake it. The puff of air quickly transformed into a muted scream when the Forstalls' front door flung open so fast I thought it'd fly off its hinges.

My feet carried me backward as faces I should have recognized rushed from the house. Pouring from those faces were screams, pleas, prayers, and tears. Absolute horror made them unrecognizable.

"What's wrong?" I said, as if a dead twenty-two-year-old with a toddler brain wasn't wrong enough. I stumbled to the street where those who'd streamed out of the house had huddled. The women clawed at each other, struggling to fit six bodies into a single embrace, while the men lit cigarettes and plugged them between their lips. Gradually, I recognized Miss Autumn, Miss Vicky, Rosie, Tilly, Ray, Luke, Miss Paula, and Miss Mary Forstall, Aubrey's mother. People I'd known my entire life.

"What's wrong?" My voice trembled.

Luke, stiff as always, pushed words past his cigarette. "They thought they heard something."

I grabbed Miss Vicky's bony shoulder and spun her around so I could look in her eyes. The horror that had distorted her narrow face faded. Her teeth continued to chatter, and her lips quivered.

"Aubrey spoke," she said, then pulled away to rejoin the hysterical mass.

I looked back at the door, still gaping wide. Soft cries came from inside. I couldn't make sense of Miss Vicky's words. How could Aubrey speak? Bracing myself, I took cautious steps up the walk and grabbed the doorframe to steady myself before peering inside. What I saw was something I've never been able to shake. Jeannie, younger than Aubrey but as watchful of him as I was of Noemi, was rocking her big brother, his body hanging halfway out of the casket, undeniably dead.

The sun at my back, I cast a shadow into the house that fell at Jeannie's feet. She lifted her bloodshot eyes. I quickly looked away, dropping my gaze to the left of the door once more. The canebrake's carcass was gone. All that remained was crusty blood and S-shaped marks in the dirt, left by the dead snake that had somehow slithered away.

THREE

Louie

I ran home from the Forstalls' house, my sweat-soaked shirt balled up in my hand. No matter how many times I wiped my face with it, my flesh remained gritty and wet, sticky like the back of a licked stamp. The trailer was silent when I burst through the door. I thumped our finicky box fan to make it whirl, then rinsed my shirt with cold water and swabbed it over my skin, which was gray, like Aubrey's.

Breathless lungs aching in my chest, I ran to my mother's room and pushed her bedroom door open. Noemi, surrounded by a slew of empty beer cans, was asleep on the bare mattress against the wall. My mother was out cold next to her, her hand clutching a can. Even in her sleep, Ma didn't spill a drop. The room reeked of her foul breath, pumped into the air by wet and raspy exhalations. Dizzied by the odor, I stumbled to the trailer door, only to stop before going outside again. Nothing more than dirt, heat, and the opossum-playing snake awaited me out there.

Retreating, I found myself peering into my room as my spiraling mind settled. Two rolled-up swatches of buckskin sat at the foot of my bed. Grandpa Joe had given them to me with orders to assemble an outfit for our tribe's annual pow wow later that summer.

My trembling hands reached for one of the swatches and pulled it to my face. Cool against my flesh, its odor put me at ease. I felt the resilience of the hide between my fingers. The fact that I couldn't rip it gave me a sense of security, making me realize why our ancestors had worn it in war. Clueless, I spread the buckskin across the floor, wishing Grandpa had conceded when I'd begged him to hire one of the rez's experienced regalia-makers to design my outfit. In his knowing way, he'd said, *If you don't do it, you won't learn*—as if I had an interest in that—and so, using worn clothes as a guide, I sketched the outline for a vest and a pair of pants upon the buckskin.

Another gift from Grandpa gleamed on the shelf above my bed. Its four-inch blade had an eye-catching edge, but its deer antler handle made it special; Grandpa had carved my initials into it: L.B.

Other than to thrash it around my room, tearing apart cowboys in my mind, I hadn't picked the hunting knife up with purpose until that afternoon. I stabbed it into the buckskin.

You'll be seventeen soon, Grandpa Joe said upon bringing me the swatches. *You're old enough to dance with the men.*

I'd danced at our pow wows every year since I was two, but the summer of 1986 would mark my first time participating in the traditional warrior dance. A deliberate display in which the tribal men re-enact motions of warriors past, it signifies strength, pride, and honor, making it a momentous part of our pow wows.

The knife slid easily through the resistant leather, the blade practically pulling my arm along. Once the pieces were cut, I punched holes along their edges to indicate where I'd eventually stitch them together. I worked fast, only to punch a hole in my finger when something rattled my window.

My spring-loaded legs unfolded beneath me, propelling me toward the wall. My knuckles went white around the antler handle while my eyes darted to the gap between the curtains. Fearing it was a rock I'd heard, I stood silent—wounded finger bleeding fast between my lips—until the window rattled again.

"Who's there?" Blood on my tongue, I hoped I sounded bolder out loud than I did in my head.

"Get your ass out here, Louie."

My hand loosened around the antler. "Dumbass," I muttered. Approaching the window, I shoved the curtains aside, letting in hot light that would make my muggy room even more unbearable.

"Meet me out front," Jean-Luc said.

I put the knife back on its shelf and went to find my best friend sitting on the top step of our laughable porch. Shirtless, as always in the summer, his sun-bronzed skin glistened with sweat. "Comin' in?" I said.

He jerked his head toward the road. Lula, glowering in black, was almost home from Miss Betsy's Unique Hair Boutique, where she worked in town. Her hair, teased high that morning, looked sticky and flat from the heat of the sun. Her forehead glistened more than J.L.'s biceps.

"Come on," I said.

Jean-Luc slowly stood and walked backward, his eyes clinging to Lula.

"What's up?" I asked once he was inside.

"It's hotter than your sister out there. Wanna cool off at the river?"

"Sure. There's something I gotta tell you." I dipped into my room to change out of the pants I'd worn to the wake.

"Hey," I heard Jean-Luc say to Lula. "You're lookin'—"

"I'm *so* not in the mood for you today." The trailer shook beneath her feet. The bathroom door slammed.

I pulled on some shorts and darted into the kitchen, only a few feet from Jean-Luc in the little living room of our tiny trailer. "For Noemi," I said, retrieving an apple I'd already sliced and smeared with peanut butter. I set it on the counter where Lula would find it.

Unexpected footsteps scraped the carpet just then. I turned to find a malnourished bear emerging from hibernation, Noemi in her arms. Ma, jet-black hair hanging in tangled clumps below her shoulders and bags nearly touching her nostrils from beneath her eyes, looked tired but no less beautiful, the comely *Indian woman with papoose* captioned in our history books.

Noemi was quiet with sleep's touch still upon her. She looked from me to J.L. then back to me. Slowly, she began to slide from my mother's grasp. If Lula hadn't come out of the bathroom to collect her, Noemi would have fallen to the floor.

"Love bug." Lula pecked Noemi on the cheek a second before crinkling her nose at me. "You couldn't change her?"

Noemi's arms stretched in my direction. "I changed her three times today."

Lula huffed and disappeared into her room, kicking the door shut behind her.

"Her snack's on the—"

"Miss Doris called," Ma cut me off.

The call didn't surprise me; the fact that Ma had gotten up to answer the phone did.

"What'd she say?"

Ma took a shallow breath that required alarming strength. A pause passed between us. "Wants you to come by."

I nodded. "Have you eaten today?"

She reached for the cans spread across the coffee table. I could tell they were empty by looking at them, dented where her hand had held them tight, but she shook each one just in case she'd missed a sip. Inspection complete, she shuffled back to her room at the end of the hall, her door closing like Lula's.

"Ready?" J.L. asked.

I licked the last bit of blood from my fingertip. He sprang ahead of me, and, crowing like a righteous bird, leaped from the porch. Dirt billowed around his feet as he shuddered at the sight of the trailer across the field from ours. "Gives me the creeps."

There'd never been much to see across the way, but the trembling blinds in the window of the trailer there sometimes made it feel like a cloud had floated in front of the protective sun, if only for a second. "Don't look," I said. "Works for me."

"What'd you wanna tell me?" He eyed a cluster of wildflowers along the road, vibrant and alive. They thrived in the ditches and out in the fields, breaking up the reservation's disheartening shades of sunbaked brown and yellow, like warm rays of light penetrating a stormy sky.

"Something strange happened at the Forstalls'," I said.

"What were you doin' over there?"

"Aubrey."

"Shit. Thought they were buryin' him tomorrow?"

"Yeah, but the wake was today."

"Why didn't you tell me?"

"You wouldn't have gone."

"I mighta gone. How'd Jeannie look?"

"Her brother just dropped dead. How do you think she looked?"

"Anguished?" he said—a big word for him—and forced a laugh. "Bet I could make her feel better."

"Keep dreaming."

"You gonna tell me what happened or not?"

I described what I'd seen, sheer horror that had rendered people I'd known my entire life unrecognizable. "Miss Vicky said Aubrey spoke. And she wasn't the only one who heard something. They just couldn't agree on what came out of his mouth."

"Freaky," J.L. said.

"That's not all. They said he sat up. They'd been sitting in silence when Miss Mary"—Aubrey's mother—"let out a shriek that, according to Miss Vicky, knocked her to the floor, one hand clutching her chest, the other pointing at Aubrey sitting straight up in his casket. Miss Vicky locked eyes with Aubrey. She said it felt like being stabbed in the stomach. She said he wasn't really looking at her . . . wasn't really seeing.

"There was a lot of screaming after that, which is why no one could agree on what Aubrey said when his lips pulled apart and sound came out. Miss Vicky heard him say, 'Water?' like he was asking for a drink. Rosie Deshautelle heard him burp, which Miss Tilly argued was a whimper. Luke Fisher swore that Aubrey hadn't made a peep, while Miss Autumn said she heard the worst thing of all."

"What?"

"An accusation."

J.L. hummed. "What was it?"

"Miss Autumn didn't wanna say. Luke tried gettin' it out of her after the shock wore off, but she'd begun to doubt her own ears by then, and she didn't wanna make the situation worse by saying something stupid."

"Couldn't Luke have forced it out of her?"

"Maybe. But he hadn't heard anything, and I think he thought everyone else was overreacting. He mostly just stood there taking it all in, his jaw tight, like it was stuffed full of peanut butter."

"That's the law for you," J.L. said. Luke Fisher didn't have a squad car or a fancy hat like the sheriff in town, but he was the go-to guy when trouble broke out on the rez. "What about Jeannie? Did she hear somethin'?"

I shook my head. "No one knows. Miss Vicky said Jeannie didn't say a word. She just cried and clutched Aubrey, probably hoping his death had been a terrible dream."

"So he *is* dead?"

"I guess. He looked dead when Edgar Forstall hauled him out of Jeannie's arms and into the family car. They were taking him to the hospital, I think."

"How did he die? Heard your gramps got the scoop straight from the horse's mouth the day Aubrey bit the dust."

Grandpa Joe had spoken with Mary, Edgar, and Jeannie Forstall shortly after the incident, but I questioned if what he told me was everything they'd told him.

"Aubrey just started thrashing on the kitchen floor," I said, recounting what I'd been told, the muddy scent of the river finally hitting my nose. "Grandpa says it was a seizure. Aubrey had a lot of them because of his condition. Jeannie was making breakfast when it happened. Aubrey was dead before she knew it."

"You don't think the accusation Miss Autumn heard was against Jeannie, do you? Could she have done something to Aubrey the morning he died?"

"No," I reflexively said. Even if Grandpa Joe hadn't told me everything about Aubrey's death, I had no reason to doubt that Jeannie only ever wanted the best for her brother, especially after the way I'd seen her cradling his corpse.

FOUR

Noemi

Mom cradled me on the couch. So tight her Henry Rose Queens & Monsters perfume rubbed off on me. She was crying too, clearly trying to hold back her tears, probably afraid they'd ruin her makeup if she let them spill over her eyelids.

Luke glanced back at Uncle Louie, standing now with his spine stiff against the door as if he were holding it shut, or as if he needed the support to hold him up.

"I'm sorry," Luke said again, to Uncle Louie this time.

"I didn't know him," Uncle Louie muttered.

I squirmed in Mom's restrictive embrace, our skin hot and sticky, shiny from tears, sweat, and snot. I cleaned my nose against my shoulder, unable to reach it with my hands.

Luke's phone buzzed. He unclipped it from his belt and studied the screen, inches beneath his nose.

"What?" I said, expecting another bomb to explode in my face.

"It's nothing." He looked to the door as if he were trapped, as if he regretted coming.

"*What?*" I sobbed, sure he was keeping something from me. My body shook harder than it had before.

"It's only Sue, wondering why dinner's late." His chest swelled. Exhaled air whistled through his nose. "I haven't told her yet." He clipped the phone back onto his belt without responding to the text.

I felt like I had to tell someone too, but who? It was always Roddy I texted a million times a day, telling him how hot he looked on TV, asking what he was having for lunch, reminding him how excited I was to see him later, bugging him anytime I got bored. I texted my best friend Becca a lot, too, but she was in Vegas for a coworker's bachelorette party, and I wasn't about to spoil her fun; the bad news would be waiting for her when she got back. My blurry gaze settled on my phone sitting silent atop the coffee table, its screen black.

"Why isn't anyone calling?"

Mom's troubled face became puzzled. Uncle Louie looked lost by the door. Luke sat on the edge of the barrel chair by the window, his upper body angled toward me.

"Word hasn't spread yet," he said.

That could have been true. It probably was. My distraught mind, though, made me think that someone else's phone might be ringing instead.

"You're sure it's him?" Doubt flooded in. Preposterous hope flared. I'd never known Luke to pull pranks or to be mistaken about serious matters, but why was I just taking his word for it? His eyes were nearly twice as old as mine. Maybe he'd seen someone other than Roddy covered in blood. "You're sure you saw him yourself?"

I didn't wait for an answer. I was already thrashing in Mom's arms, breaking her embrace. "Get off." I shoved her away, reaching for my phone instead. With just two taps, CALLING RODDY appeared on the screen.

"Noemi," Luke said.

I willfully ignored him, focusing on the ringing in my ear.

"It's him," he said.

26

The preposterous hope gave my heart a squeeze when I heard Roddy's voice, promising to return the call as soon as he could.

"I saw him," Luke said. "I wouldn't have come here if I had any doubt."

My hand slowly fell from the side of my face, the voice mail continuing to record.

"I wanna see him." My backside left the couch. My feet brought me to the door. Uncle Louie looked surprised to see me there.

"Let's not rush into that." Luke stood from the chair. Mom stayed seated. She dabbed her eyes with a tissue she'd plucked from a nearby box, preserving her makeup. "The coroner has to assess the scene first. She's probably there now."

I felt greasy and cold inside upon hearing that word—"coroner." It gave me the creeps because I didn't associate it with anything pleasant, just death investigations, pronouncements of death, and dead bodies. I took a step back. Badly as I wanted to see Roddy, I didn't want to see him like that.

"What can I do?" The words tumbled out of me. Never had I felt so helpless. My body began to crumble.

Luke caught me with one hand beneath my right arm. "Take a breath," he said, his voice compassionate yet stern. Clearly he'd been through things like this enough times before. "Focus on your breathing, then go wash your face and find a new shirt. You got that one dirty."

I shouldn't have given a shit, but the strings of snot drying on the front of my tank top mortified me. Snot was crusting on my bare shoulder too.

I lifted my hands to cover my mess and noticed upon glimpsing the phone in my hand that I was still leaving a message. I ended the call and ran to my room. That's when Luke's distraction wore off, broken by all the Roddys around me. On my nightstand. On the dresser.

Below the TV. Each with his eyes on me. I looked from one to the next, turning, crying, telling myself it wasn't true, not all of it.

The mirror reminded me that I hadn't changed my shirt when I finally staggered to the bathroom across the hall. Phone in my pocket, I cupped cold water in my hands and held it to my face. The water soothed my eyes and cleansed my skin, and I imagined it was the cold water making me shiver. What a relief that would have been, to be shivering from cold.

I put on a clean shirt, then went back to the living room a little more stable than before, though the ground felt like foam beneath my feet. Mom was by the counter in the adjacent kitchen, clutching two glasses filled with water. She followed me into the living room and set the glasses on the coffee table.

". . . ran off, I guess," I heard Luke say when I got close.

"Did it—?" Uncle Louie stopped himself, his eyes on me. "The driver . . . what was she in?"

"A Jeep. A Wrangler," Luke said.

Finally moving away from the door, Uncle Louie turned back to glance out the window. "Like that one?" He pointed to my Jeep Wrangler parked beside the porch.

"Yeah. A red one."

"The same—"

"Mine's not red," I said.

Uncle Louie looked out the window again.

"Orange," I muttered. "Punk'n Orange."

Uncle Louie turned to Luke. "The sun was setting at the time of the accident, wasn't it? Right about when orange could be taken for red?"

"I don't understand," Luke said.

I didn't either.

Uncle Louie shook his head. "Did the driver say if she saw his face? His expression?"

"She said it all happened so fast."

"Did he seem like he wanted to hurt her? Or like he was happy to see her?"

The questions were so absurd that we all fell silent for a few seconds.

"What are you *not* saying?" I finally said.

Uncle Louie shrank, his shoulders curling inward. "Nothing . . . It's just that if we take all of Roddy's actions into consideration, we might be able to figure out his motivation for them."

"Or lack of motivation," I said.

"If it was an accident," he agreed, nodding.

"Not *if*," I said, accepting his explanation, though there still seemed to be something he wasn't telling me. I didn't have time to let suspicion grow. My phone rang in my pocket.

"Mike!" I screamed into the phone. Roddy's best friend.

"Noemi!" he cried. Only every second or third word of what he said came through clearly after that.

No matter what he was saying, I had to accept that Luke hadn't made a mistake.

"They're moving him now," Mike gasped.

If he was at the scene, then I thought I should be too. I jumped toward the door and grabbed my bag, my keys.

"Noemi!" Mom cried as I undid the dead bolt. "Where are you going?"

"Just go to the Blue Gator," I shouted back at her.

I hopped into my Jeep. It looked red in the limited early night light.

FIVE

Louie

Aubrey went into the ground the day after his wake. The Forstalls had rushed him to the hospital after he sat up and spoke, only to be dealt the same crushing blow they'd been dealt two days earlier. Their boy was dead.

The hospital medical examiner explained that unexpected things can happen after death. Strong muscle contractions can make a dead body sit up straight. Built-up gases in the belly can escape through the windpipe, creating strange and scary sounds. Aubrey hadn't been whimpering, questioning, or accusing. Miss Vicky and the others had let their imaginations get the best of them. I couldn't blame them. Who knows what I would have heard if I'd been sitting among them, thinking about Horace and the vampire.

Aubrey's mystery appeared to be solved and yet another brewed as I walked the mile to Miss Doris's trailer, wondering what she'd ask of me.

"Sorry I couldn't come by yesterday," I said, letting myself in.

"Have you heard?" The words rushed out of her like air from a burst balloon.

"About Aubrey?"

Johnny, Miss Doris's grandson, ran to me and wrapped his arms around my legs. Ferocious animal sounds rumbled in his throat. I patted him on the head.

"You haven't heard!" Miss Doris jolted forward in the recliner she seldom rose out of. Her back was bad, and her gait was even worse.

"Heard what?"

She took a deep breath, winded as if she'd done a million jumping jacks. "The tribal cemetery. Someone's been digging in it again."

The tribal cemetery, across the river on an expanse of land not far from the pow wow grounds, was a place I rarely visited. My gram was there, but I could feel her spirit at home just as strongly as I could at the cemetery—stronger even.

"Digging? Do you know who did it?"

Miss Doris shook her head, her big red cheeks boxing her ears.

"Is anything missing?" By "anything" I meant anyone.

Miss Doris shrugged. "I just heard the news from Miss Paula, who went to Aubrey's burial, the poor thing. Paula said she saw three mounds of dirt that weren't from the hole they'd dug for Aubrey's grave. Considering there hasn't been a death since Jim passed . . ." She made the sign of the cross over her body. Up until a year and a half earlier, Jim had been her rock, but his heart exploded on his way to work one morning, leading her to call on me after that. "It must mean only one thing."

Johnny, lips spluttering, clawed me, trying to climb my trunk like a tree.

"Has anyone talked to Ray Horn?" Ray kept the cemetery grounds.

"Lord only knows, but I'm sure Ray's loving it. Paula said he sees every horror movie that hits the silver screen. She's going to call if she hears anything else. Oh! She told me about Aubrey's wake. Surely, you heard about that?"

My free hand sprang to my waistband to keep Johnny from revealing more than the first inch of my ass crack. "I was there."

"It's strange, isn't it? I just hope Mary and Edgar are all right and that no one's done anything to Jim in the cemetery. My heart couldn't handle that. Little John!" She slapped a flyswatter on the metal tray table next to her. "Stop that. Get over here."

Johnny kept clawing at me. I hoisted him into my arms.

"He's getting bigger by the day," Miss Doris said.

"So is Noemi."

"Holding him on my lap's about all I can do anymore. Bring him here."

I dropped Johnny into her arms and stood back to adjust my pants. He fought with Miss Doris and her flyswatter for his freedom.

"I'm getting too old for this." She looked at the clock, undoubtedly counting down the minutes until her daughter Rosie got off work. "There's more of that black stuff creeping up the shower wall. Could you give it a good scrape? You did such a nice job last time."

I did what Miss Doris asked and left with my lungs tight in my chest, like adult feet shoved into children's shoes. It could have been the humid air irritating my lungs or, more likely, the noxious spray I'd used to dissolve the mold growing in Miss Doris's muggy bathroom. Or maybe I couldn't breathe right because I couldn't stop thinking about the unearthed graves.

I took deep breaths on my way up our porch steps. The air inside our trailer would be as oppressive as it was outside, heavy, humid, and suffocating, like walking into a hamper full of musty towels.

"Louie." A hollow voice floated on the air. My skin crawled at the sound of my name. I turned and scanned the front yard. No one was in the grass or standing by the road.

"Louie." My eyes reluctantly skimmed the field that separated my trailer from the one closest to it, half a football field away. I shivered and dropped my gaze to the porch planks. The untrained eye would have seen nothing more than a beat-up trailer across the field, boxy and white and streaked with dirt. But if you looked closely, you'd see a speck in the window to the right of the trailer's door. That speck would grow once you spotted it because it wasn't a speck at all. Blurred by a screen, it was a face, large and round with folds of walrus fat hanging off it. I'd always ignored that face, which only made it more startling when I happened to spy it and its eyes trained on me. Like going swimming in the river and spotting a snapping turtle near your toes, or hiking through the fields and suddenly hearing a canebrake's rattle at your side, that gaze always got me when I least expected it. It spooked me every time.

"Yeah?" I called without looking in the face's direction. I hadn't made it a habit to ignore Ernest Mire, the owner of that fat face, just because he unnerved me. I ignored him because seeing him was just plain sad.

"You seen my ma?"

In my sixteen years, I'd never heard Ern speak. I'd only been aware of him watching me, spooking me, from that window. Upon first hearing it, his voice sounded empty and unchanging, like that of a reawakened corpse. The hair on my arms bristled. "Nah." I opened the door to go inside.

"She's missin'."

I'd always had uneasy feelings about Ern, but his mother had always been sweet to me. She'd been sweet to everybody, well-loved on the reservation. I paused in the doorway and peeked at Ern again. He looked enormous in his little window despite the distance between his trailer and mine.

"Missing?" I hollered.

"Come over." It was a command.

I stalled, mind racing. My regard for Miss Shelby, his mother, eventually led me to trek through the thick grass. That and the assurance I gave myself: Ern was only as unnerving as the snapper and the canebrake, not dangerous at all.

He pulled the cord on the blinds hanging in the window when I got close. The slats dropped to cover the top half of his face, making it impossible for me to get a good look at him, not that I wanted to look at him.

"She left?" I said, from the bottom of the steps outside his door. Even from there, I could feel the wonderfully cold air spilling out around him. The air conditioner mounted in the window on the opposite side of the steps must have been set to the lowest temperature, a necessity for a guy his size in summer. There wasn't much I wouldn't have given for a window unit like his. My eyes focused on the stair rail's peeling paint rather than him and the blinds blocking his face.

"She went to sing at Aubrey's wake yesterday like she does for all the dead," he said. "She went down the road a little while after you left."

"You haven't seen your ma since yesterday?" Surprise drew my eyes to the window for a split second, only Ern's mouth and inflated cheeks were visible beneath the blinds. He shook his head, casting his mighty jowls from side to side. I looked at the peeling paint again. Anyone who knew the Mires would consider Miss Shelby's absence strange. Though Ern was nearly thirty, Miss Shelby never left him on his own for long. At more than six-hundred pounds, there wasn't much Ern could do for himself other than watch a very small part of the world go by.

"You didn't see her at the wake?"

Considering how the wake had abruptly ended, I wouldn't have been surprised if no one noticed that Miss Shelby hadn't arrived. "No. I didn't see her at the Forstalls' place or on my way back. You'd think we would've crossed paths at some point."

"I'm hungry."

"Did you call Luke to let him know?"

"This mornin'."

"I'll ask my ma and Lula if they've seen her." Fat chance, though. I knew Ma wouldn't have seen anything and that Lula wouldn't have paid attention if she had. I turned to go.

"Don't leave." Another command.

My eyes flicked up at him. That thick and layered face of his, the half that I could see, was inescapable. Intimidating, too.

"Somethin' strange happened at the wake," he said, knowing.

"It had nothing to do with your ma, if that's what you're thinking."

"Tell me."

I didn't want to go over it again, especially since the explanation given to the Forstalls at the hospital stripped the story of its astounding parts. But then I remembered the horror I'd seen. Horror that'd made everyone who'd run out of the Forstalls' place unrecognizable to me. Their fear had been real, and it was hard to believe that something so authentic could have been produced by misinterpretations.

"Tell me 'bout the wake, and I'll tell you how Aubrey really died."

Ern's offer commanded every bit of me. "What are you talking about?"

He yanked the cord, giving me a quick glimpse of his eyes. They were as empty as the hot tins left over after tea light candles wink out. He dropped the blinds. "Miss Paula came by to talk to my ma since she didn't see her at the wake. Ended up talkin' to me instead."

Paula Bishop again, the biggest gossip on the rez making her weekly rounds. Miss Paula was Miss Shelby's best friend and Miss Mary Forstall's sister. If anyone had insight as to what had happened in the Forstalls' kitchen the day Aubrey died, it was her. I told Ern my version of things.

"All of them trembling on the Forstalls' lawn," I said, at the end of the story. "Hard to believe they were only reacting to muscle contractions. I'm starting to think they really did hear more than just gas escaping Aubrey's windpipe."

"It's not the craziest story I've ever heard." Ern, by birth, was one of the Takoda Tribe's Singers and Legend Keepers, tasked with studying the ancient Takoda stories and songs to ensure they'd endure from one generation to the next. That's why Miss Shelby had been going to

Aubrey's wake, to lead the others in traditional mourning songs. Her father, her father's father, and countless generations before them, had kept our tribe's oral history alive by teaching our people's tales and songs to their children. The Mires knew every origin story. Every chant. Every myth. They could tell you about every old spirit in the sky, on the earth, and below it.

"Can you explain what happened?" I asked.

"I'll tell you what Miss Paula told me. Come to your own conclusion."

I settled on the lowest step and gripped the edge of the plank. Its peeling paint stuck to my palms.

"She said Aubrey did somethin' impossible just before dyin' on the kitchen floor. Jeannie'd been boilin' eggs for breakfast. She had 'em in a pot on the stove. Aubrey was pagin' through one of his favorite picture books at her feet. When Jeannie turned to take butter from the fridge, Aubrey reached up and grabbed the pot's handle. Jeannie saw him do it from the corner of her eye. She reeled around to stop him, but he moved faster than she ever could."

Ern, his upper body bobbing from side to side behind the blinds, struggled to maintain his breath. He swallowed hard, wheezed, then carried on.

"Aubrey hurled the boilin' water at Jeannie. She just barely jumped outta the way to avoid gettin' burned. What I don't understand, and what Miss Paula couldn't understand either, is how Aubrey lifted that pot of boilin' water off the stove. Miss Paula told me how bad his condition was. She said the poor guy couldn't even walk. He was weak. He may have been able to pull the pot down by reachin' up and puttin' his weight on the handle, but the water woulda spilled onto him. He shouldn't have been able to cast the water into the air the way he did. Miss Paula said it arced clear across the kitchen." Ern wheezed some more. "And then Aubrey rolled across the linoleum into the mess he'd made. His hands, which had been holding his upper body up, slipped, causing him to hit his head hard against the floor. He thrashed around in the scalding water and then . . . *pfff.*"

Ern's thirdhand account sat like a boulder in my belly. I wondered if the Forstalls had told Grandpa Joe the same story Miss Paula told Ern, or if they only told him the part about Aubrey's apparent seizure. Sitting there in the shadows of sunset with Ern's wheezy mouth in the window a few feet above me, I felt the rare chill I only ever felt on the infrequent evenings when J.L. and I would be by the river and our conversations would turn toward the Takoda Vampire. But that only happened if there was still a sliver of sun on the horizon. I wrapped my arms around my chest.

"Aubrey really was dead, wasn't he?" My voice sounded fragile against the discordant symphony being performed by countless cicadas and frogs.

"Yeah, Louie, but death ain't the end. It's just a new beginning." His hidden face. His hollow voice. I still didn't know how I felt about Ern. "People around the world believe the spirit . . . essence, soul, whatever you wanna call it . . . goes somewhere else after death, sometimes in another form."

"But what about Aubrey? If his spirit left his body, how the hell did he sit up and speak?"

"Maybe his spirit came back."

"You think it's possible?"

Ern shrugged. "On the third day . . ." he said.

I hugged myself tighter. "What do you think really happened?"

"Maybe the stone floated."

"What stone?"

"The Takoda death legend. You know it."

I shook my head. "Tell me."

Ern took a breath that made him cough. "After the great gators allowed our people to walk on land, the Takoda elders had to make a decision about death because those who had died had not experienced identical fates.

"Some upon death were allowed to return to their families. Others were sent to the sky where the star spirit only allowed them to look down upon their people at night. The elders wanted all to be treated the same upon death, and so they decided that the earth spirit should throw a stone into the river whenever one of the Takoda people died. If the stone floated to the top of the water, then whoever died would return to the Takoda within three days. If the stone sank into the mud, then whoever died would go with the star spirit and watch over the Takoda at night."

"The elders must have known the stone would always sink," I said.

"They did. That's what they wanted to happen. The sinkin' stone, they said, would birth sorrow in the world. It would lead us to have empathy for one another because we'd all experience the pain of loss brought on by death."

Engulfed by darkness except for the thin streams of light leaking through the window around Ern's head, I shivered and swatted at the mosquitoes adding more bites to my already bumpy arms. While I didn't firmly believe that a stone had determined Aubrey's fate, I couldn't rule out other possibilities. Surely, there were things in the universe I knew nothing about. Things related to our Native traditions, our adopted Catholic religion, or other beliefs I'd yet to encounter. Sitting there on the step, looking out at the empty fields that spanned between the trailers and the shanties that spotted the reservation, I wondered what secrets were hidden in the shadows. I knew no literal stone had been cast, yet I asked, "If the stone had floated, wouldn't Aubrey still be alive?"

Ern didn't answer right away. His labored breaths competed with the cicadas' calls. "Sure," he finally said. "But if the stone sank, Aubrey wouldn't have sat up and spoke at all."

That was enough for me. His words made my bladder burn. I rubbed my hands together to cast the specks of paint from my palms and started for home. I heard the blinds go up as soon as my back was to Ern.

"Tell me if you hear anything 'bout my ma," he said. It was an order.

"Anything I hear, you'll hear." I had the feeling he'd been listening in on us for years.

SIX

Louie

The front door opened before I could reach it.

"Gammpa Joe!" Noemi looked up from the coloring book page she'd scribbled over, indifferent to the thick black lines depicting a surprised kitten dangling from a tree.

"Good morning, my beautiful lark." Grandpa stooped to kiss the top of her head. He had a bulging bag in his hand, which he set by the door. His droopy eyelids told me he hadn't slept. I hadn't either after talking with Ern. Grandpa's long hair, snow white for the first five inches and gray after that, hung like ragged curtains around his shoulders. The deep lines above his mouth formed a frown atop the one on his lips.

"Coffee?" I offered.

"Mae?" he said.

I pointed to Ma's closed bedroom door. Grandpa nodded. Of course she'd be in her room. Her nightshifts at Roscoe's Get 'n' Go, the gas station mini-mart just off the rez, would tire a corpse. Or so I thought. "Should I wake her?"

Grandpa did the waking. He didn't knock on her door, he just went in and pulled the sheet tangled around Ma's legs. She moaned. The mattress creaked. A minute went by and then the bedsprings announced that Ma had gotten up. The progression, starting with Grandpa's solemn entry, followed by his mute command for Ma to get out of bed, filled me with guilt, like I'd get in trouble for letting him barge in like that. I knelt next to Noemi on the floor. The brilliant colors she scribbled drew some of the tension from the trailer.

Grandpa stalked back into the living room. "There's something I have to say."

"Something's wrong," I uttered. It was almost a question.

Grandpa rubbed the dark skin under his eyes. His face softened, then transitioned from serious to sad when he saw the aluminum mess in front of him. I pushed the cans to a corner of the coffee table as if clustering them would diminish the amount.

"What is it?" I asked.

Grandpa didn't say a word until Ma was out of her room. Her threadbare T-shirt hung to her knees. Its worse-for-wear neck hole looked like it'd never been round. Grandpa watched her shamble from her doorway to the shallow hall to the living room, where she labored to lower herself into the lawn chair across from the couch.

Tired was all she was. That's what I thought. Once she cast away her groggy haze, she'd be just fine.

"Grandpa?"

He looked at the half-heart-shaped stain on Ma's shirt. "We've been desecrated," he said.

I thought about what Miss Doris had told me. "The cemetery?"

Grandpa nodded. His hair spilled forward. "Three graves have been disturbed."

Again, I wondered if anything—*anyone*—had been taken. My stomach constricted. I eyed the brilliant colors in Noemi's coloring book.

"My grandfather's been unearthed," he said.

Grandpa's grandpa. Chief Hilaire Broussard. The last official chief of the Takoda Tribe. Grandpa Joe was something of a chief himself.

He was the tribal chairman. After Hilaire's death, the tribe opted for the election of a tribal government in which a chairman and five tribal council members were selected to oversee all tribal matters. In 1986, those matters mostly revolved around finding lenders to back the construction of a high-stakes bingo hall on our land, which everyone hoped would make our wallets fat.

"So has my wife," Grandpa continued.

Caroline Broussard. My gram.

"Why?" My voice sounded the way it had when it broke a few years earlier. I cleared my throat to make it deep again.

Grandpa didn't have a reason, nor did he try to offer one. "I'm talking about your mother, Mae."

Ma didn't react to his words. She just swayed in the lawn chair, making it creak. Each time she blinked, her eyelids stayed shut a little longer than they had the time before.

"Do you know who did it?" I leaped to my feet, making up for Ma's lack of emotion. She sat like a silent spirit while I fought back angry and unexpected tears. My grandmother had been like air to me, always around and essential for survival. She'd answered my every call as a kid, fulfilling every need, big and small. She'd walked me to school every morning and back home in the afternoon. She'd bandaged my scrapes and told me it was okay to cry. She'd taught me how to make my own fishing pole, how to braid my hair, and how to play stickball in the field. She'd cooked and cleaned and cared for me and Lula every day until she couldn't care for herself anymore. I couldn't stand what had been done to her. Never had I wanted to break something so badly . . . a window, a TV, a face. "What are we gonna do?"

Grandpa set a hand on my shoulder and squeezed. "Walk lightly, Louie. We'll make things right."

My trembling hands turned into hungry fists. "Why would someone do that? What could they want?" My gram was a poor woman. She hadn't been buried with anything worth a damn.

"I'm holding a meeting at the Blue Gator Grill tomorrow at three," Grandpa said. The Blue Gator was the only place on the rez where you could get a hot meal back then. It was where everyone went to drink their sorrows away. "Bring your mother if you can." He squinted at her, his lips pressed tightly together. I'd never seen him look at her like that. "I have to go next door. Miss Shelby's missing." Grandpa stood and retrieved the bag he'd set by the door. "A little something for Ern," he explained. The bag's swollen belly must have contained enough food to feed a family of four.

"Grandpa!" I followed him onto the porch. "You said three graves were disturbed."

Eyes ahead, he said, "Horace Saucier was the third."

I staggered into the trailer like a lion hit in the ass with a tranquilizer dart. Ma, even in her sleep-like state, knew when Grandpa was gone. She shuffled back to her room. Her door shut behind her, leaving Noemi and me alone with the weight of Grandpa's words squarely on my scrawny shoulders.

Why Horace? Why did it have to be him?

I'd spend hours pondering those questions that day. The more I thought about Horace's unearthed grave, the more troubled I felt. It was as if he'd limped closer once I knew there wasn't any dirt between him and us. As if he no longer only existed in the legend we'd let grow.

Worried and wrathful, I peered past the curtains. Grandpa, like a child with a treat trying to coax a dog into trusting him, waved the swollen bag in front of the blinds hiding Ern in the window. As Grandpa worked to win Ern over, four of the five tribal council members joined him in the sun. Miss Shelby was the missing fifth.

"Sticky." Noemi pulled my attention away from the window. I'd made her a PBJ for lunch and she'd gotten its gooey parts all over her fingers.

"And that's a wrap." I hoisted her from her high chair in exchange for the tub. I cleaned her, diapered her, and put her down for a nap.

"Tell me a *stowry*, Douie." She called me "Douie" because she hadn't mastered my name just yet. Despite how much I wanted to see if Grandpa had lured Ern into opening his window, I sat at the edge of the bed and, instead of grabbing one of the cardboard books from the crate in the corner, I told Noemi the tale Gram had told me a hundred times or more. It was a story everyone on the reservation knew, not just the Mires. It was the story of how we came to be.

"It is said that the Takoda people were born from a sacred hole in the ground. Blocking the hole was a bayou, and blocking the bayou rested two great gators, called 'tamahka' in the Native tongue. One was red. The other was blue.

"The Takoda leader said to the tamahka, 'Let us leave this hole. Let us know the land, the sun, and the water in which you swim.' The tamahka approved because the Takoda were pure of heart and their souls were sincere. They were born without weapons or ill intent. But, the tamahka warned, should the Takoda people become sneaky like the snake when it silently slithers behind its prey, or callous like the bobcat when it kills for its own amusement, then the red and blue gators would swallow the Takoda whole, for alligators only use their teeth to shred and to tear. Tamahka do not chew."

I told the story the same way Gram always told it to me. Noemi undoubtedly understood little of what I said, but that didn't matter. She'd hear the story time and again, and someday she'd tell it the same way. Since she still hadn't fallen asleep, I started it again. Even after her eyes closed and her breathing took on the steady rhythm of sleep, I kept telling it, always ending with the warning, "Tamahka don't chew."

SEVEN

Noemi

His body was gone by the time I got there. The red Jeep wasn't. Perched atop an idling flatbed tow truck, it looked like it was being exalted for what it'd done. Considering the significance of Roddy's death, I'd envisioned countless mourners lining the street, like the thousands I'd seen on TV for Queen Elizabeth's funeral last year, rather than the handful of gapers drawn by flashing lights. At least the queen had lived a full and privileged life. Roddy was only thirty-one and just starting to make it.

My hand reflexively rejected the call that was making my phone ring. It hadn't stopped singing for more than a few seconds since I'd run from the trailer. Luke had been right when he said that word hadn't begun to spread, but now that it had, I didn't want anyone's pity. Did they really think they could make me feel better? Or that I didn't already know? I texted Mike to tell him I was there. His reply came within seconds of tapping send.

Couldn't take it. At the ice
bar now

I glanced in the direction of the casino and resort in response to his reply. I couldn't blame him for running. I might have, too, if I'd seen the white sheet, the stretcher, the body bag. I pulled as close to the yellow tape cordoning off the scene as I could get, my high beams illuminating debris from the accident and a handful of officials milling about.

My phone rang again. "Fuck you!" I nearly chucked it at the windshield. There was only one person I wanted to hear from, and I never would again. Roll your eyes, but Roddy Bishop was the closest thing to a knight in shining armor I could have hoped for. Nine years his senior, aimless, and unhappy, I was an all-around human fucking fiasco defined by a string of brainless bad decisions that had kept me tied to my past. I wasn't the kind of girl a morning news reporter working his way up to the anchor's desk would look at twice.

But Roddy had looked, that night in Baton Rouge at Andrew and Olivia Landry's wedding reception. I'd thanked the booze from the open bar when he beckoned me to dance, then laughed later that night when he asked for my number, only to obsessively check my phone every few minutes—doubting yet hoping he'd call—until I heard his voice on the other end of the line, asking if I'd brunch with him after he got off air the next morning. He was twenty-eight. I was thirty-seven. His acceptance of me added to my meager worth. Suddenly, I felt ten years younger, restarting my thirties, living through him, alongside him, *for* him. Things I thought had been stolen by the hands of time—marriage, kids, happiness—seemed possible again. I'd never been so fucking optimistic.

I opened the Jeep's door and stuck my feet out. A figure came toward me.

"Noemi?"

I recognized his voice before I saw his face. "Where *is* she? I want to talk to her." I wanted to do more than just talk. I wanted to make her feel my futility.

"Stay in your vehicle," Chief Cain Fisher, filling his father's old role, said. He put one hand on the Jeep's door and the other on the roof, blocking me in. "I'm sorry, Noemi. I really am. We're gonna do everything we can to figure out what happened here."

"Where is she?" I demanded.

"She's giving a statement at the station."

"Do I know her?" By that I meant, *Is she from the rez?*

Cain shook his head. "She's a dealer at the casino."

"Did you test her? Make her walk a straight line?"

"Standard procedure," he said, nodding.

"And?"

He didn't reply. He just looked exhausted. Irritated, too.

"He wouldn't have killed himself, Cain!"

"Do me a favor, all right?" He sighed. "Go be with your mom tonight. Get some rest, then come by the station tomorrow. Whenever's best for you. We want to talk to everyone he was close to."

I pulled my feet back into the Wrangler. "I'll head over now." Knowing *she* was there, I had no reason to wait.

"No. Tomorrow," he said again, sternly this time. "We'll get to the bottom of this."

I pulled the door shut and initiated a U-turn, barely giving Cain enough time or space to get out of my way. If I were younger—I already felt older than ever without Roddy—I might have had a smidge more respect for Cain's authority, but to me he was just Crybaby Cain, tattletale extraordinaire, always running to daddy when he detected a breach of the law. If keggers had blood, it'd be all over his hands. Lord knows how many high school parties he'd ruined. If only he'd played it cool, we would have invited him. . . . maybe.

My tires squealed against the asphalt. Cain let out a shout. He must have hit the side of the Jeep with his hand because I heard a thump followed by a loud pop. The latter not caused by him. One of the front tires had blown.

"Goddamn-mother-fuck!" I screamed. Having completed the turn, I eased the lopsided Jeep onto the shoulder.

"There's broken glass and debris all over." Cain aimed his flashlight at the street.

I pounded the steering wheel so hard the bones in my hands cracked. Another torrent was building behind my eyes. Soon it'd rage free.

"Come on," Cain said. "I'll get Dakota to give you a ride."

I killed the engine and clutched my phone. Cain started toward the silhouetted officials when I got out of the Wrangler, but I didn't follow him. I didn't want him or any of the others to see me cry. I ran into the night with Cain calling after me, probably afraid I'd meet the same fate as Roddy. The thought didn't worry me at all.

I ran through the dark, leaving the lights of the emergency vehicles behind, taking random turns down random streets until my lungs were blazing. The Blue Gator Grill came into view.

Approaching it from behind, I glowered at the memorial painted and spotlighted on the back of the watering hole. The large mural depicted a woman I may have met but never knew. Her expression marked her as proud and strong—things I couldn't relate to—though her flecked eyes were in dire need of fresh paint.

The tail of a big white dog thumped against the planks of the wooden walkway when I rounded the building and approached the door.

"Good Boy," I muttered, the back of my hand getting wet against his nose as I staggered past.

I spotted Uncle Louie the instant I stepped inside. He was sitting on a stool at the corner of the bar. Mom was to his right, farther from me and veiled by him. Both were facing Good Boy's owner, standing just a foot in front of them, with their backs to the bar— Uncle Louie's as rounded as a third wheel. None of them noticed when I slipped onto the stool perpendicular to Uncle Louie at the corner.

"The wolf cut would look great on you," Mom, speaking in a somber tone that tried to sound optimistic, said to Good Boy's owner, who wasn't much older than me. "It's one of the hottest styles this year . . . shaggy and a little longer in the back. You could totally pull it off."

"You know I trust you, girl," Good Boy's owner said. Faded marks on her cheek scrunched when she smiled. "I'll be in on Tuesday."

Mom seemed to remember Uncle Louie just then. "Louie's back! My brother."

"The college professor?"

"That's him." Was that pride on Mom's face? "Have the two of you met?"

Good Boy's owner squinted at Uncle Louie. Both slowly shook their heads.

"Grace Hebert." She stuck out her hand.

"Pleasure." Uncle Louie shook with her, barely straightening his back.

"That's her dog outside," Mom said.

"Good Boy!" Grace beamed. "I was gonna DoorDash, but he's been cooped up all day and I couldn't say no to those pleading eyes."

Jade Peltier leaned over the bar just then and handed Grace a brown paper bag, stapled at the top, grease already seeping through the sides. Grace slipped the paper bag into a sturdier canvas sack hanging from her arm, one of its straps digging into a thick scar, as if an emblem had been etched into her skin.

"I'm gonna call Noemi again," Mom said, focusing on Grace. "Do you think you could talk to her?"

"For sure," Grace said. "That is, if she *wants* to talk to me. She might not be ready yet. But even if she isn't, I have some pamphlets and info sheets that might help. It's tragic . . . the rising suicide rate among Natives. It's gotten worse since the pandemic."

Mom tapped her phone screen. The three of them jumped when my phone began to ring.

"Thank god," Mom said, pressing one hand to the bedazzled heart on her chest as she turned toward me. "Where'd you run off to?"

Nowhere. I shook my head.

"I was just talking to Grace," Mom said. "You know she's a mental health therapist at the Resource Center here on the rez. She can help you get through this. And it's free, so you don't have to worry about . . ." She looked back at Grace. "What's it you say over there?"

"No judgment, no charge. Just come in and get the care you need," Grace said to me, quickly adding, "Not just *you* specifically, I mean anyone on the reservation."

Hope shined in Mom's eyes. "Will you?"

Indignation seared me inside, demanding that I scream something at her for telling Grace that Roddy had taken his life.

"Give her time," Uncle Louie said, saving me.

"Yeah," I murmured, glancing at Grace. "Don't let your food get cold."

"Right." She heaved her bag.

"Tell Dave I said hi," Mom muttered.

Grace smiled and waved goodbye. Mom and Uncle Louie swiveled on their stools, turning back toward the bar. Mom took a slow sip of her light beer. She lingered on the swallow. "Noemi?"

I took a deep breath. "I don't wanna talk about it, all right? I just don't wanna be alone."

"Okay . . ." Mom slid me her beer, then turned to Uncle Louie. "So, Holly? Jill? They couldn't make it?"

He stared straight ahead, unmoving for an uncomfortable moment. "Holly and I split," he finally said.

"Shut up!" Mom shrieked, shocked.

He kept silent, letting the news sink in. I liked Aunt Holly. Suddenly, I was sad about losing her even if she hadn't crossed my mind in years. Jill, too, was a sweet kid, but we'd never been close. I was too much older than her for us to hang out.

"Why? I thought you and Holly were—?"

"The relationship just didn't work anymore."

Mom slumped. "Do they ever work?" She looked like she wanted her beer back. "You could've come to me. How long's it been?"

Uncle Louie's face reddened. "Eleven years. I know . . ." he said before Mom or I could react. "I should've told you, but I buried it deep inside myself and I've tried not to look back. It's in the past, so let's just . . ."

Mom understood. "What about Jill?"

Uncle Louie's tongue moved around his mouth. "She's twenty-six now. Moved to Boston two years ago with a boy from college. She calls on Sundays."

"*Twenty-six*," Mom said. "How the hell did that happen?"

Uncle Louie shrugged. "Crept up like fifty-three crept up on me, which makes you—"

"Don't you dare say it."

In some ways Mom and I were very different; in others we were very alike.

She stabbed him with her eyes and leaned in over the bar to flag down Miss Tilly. I noticed how Uncle Louie did a double take before quickly mirroring Mom, only he wasn't leaning over the bar to flag down Miss Tilly. It looked like he was leaning forward to hide behind his sister, shielding himself from her friends on the opposite side of her.

Rosie Deshautelle—her hair dyed a little too dark, according to Mom, and her shoulders getting thicker by the year—was peering straight ahead, presumably ignoring Uncle Louie the same way he was ignoring her. Sitting beside her in a sweat-stained tank top was Jean-Luc Picote, looking stringy, underfed, and shabby, like an old sponge that's been wrung out too many times. He was leaning backward, mouth hanging open, straining to get a better look at my uncle.

I'd always thought Uncle Louie and Jean-Luc were tight, but judging by Uncle Louie's reaction, that clearly wasn't the case. Maybe he wasn't ready to reconnect with everyone from his past yet, just like I wasn't ready to talk about Roddy.

"Louie Broussard!"

The exclamation nearly knocked Uncle Louie from his stool. His wide eyes collided with Miss Tilly, no doubt grayer and more wrinkled than he remembered her.

"Surprised you noticed me." He worked up a smile. "Don't tell me you're still slinging beers and fries?"

She flexed a saggy muscle. "I've hired extra help." She jerked her head toward Jade, sopping up a spill. "But what else would I be doing? And it's not just burgers, fries, and pies anymore," she said as Mom leaned back to whisper with Rosie. "I expanded the menu. Got all sorts of things now. Barbecue wings, fried shrimp, coleslaw, alligator bites. Don't leave without trying the beignets. I'll get you some."

"No more peanuts?" he asked. They used to be all over the place. We'd throw the shells right on the floor.

"Ellie Bloom's daughter is allergic." Miss Tilly leaned in, reducing her voice to a whisper. "I'll bring you a bowl. What are you drinking?"

"Coke, please."

"Good boy." She took Mom's order for a round of beers after that.

"Still?" Mom questioned Uncle Louie.

"Still," he confirmed.

Mom's one word question confused me at first, but then it clicked.

Uncle Louie might have been able to abstain, but I couldn't. Taking a sip of the beer Mom had passed me, I remembered something Roddy used to say whenever we were about to tie one on.

May we be in heaven a half hour before the devil knows we're dead.

Just like that, I was crying again.

EIGHT

Louie

Rain pummeled the rez the day of Grandpa Joe's meeting at the Blue Gator Grill, the fat droplets like hooves of wild horses stampeding from one end of our trailer's aluminum roof to the other. Despite the rain, Grandpa, holding soggy sheets of newspaper in place of an umbrella, darted past our trailer on his way to Ern's a few hours before the meeting's start.

I watched him hop up Ern's steps like an old frog. He knocked on the door, waited a few seconds, then let himself in. Apparently, he'd earned Ern's trust the day before.

Curious, I peeped through the window. Ern's head turned inward, presumably talking to Grandpa Joe face-to-face, uncomfortably, no doubt. Miss Shelby, I took it, was still missing. I was about to turn my attention to the dishes in the sink when the rest of the tribal council members—Eaton Ballard, Thomas Lavergne, Miss Vicky Peltier, and Sawyer Picote, Jean-Luc's uncle—passed by on the road outside. They were all in Eaton's brown 1978 four-door Ford Fairmont, and they were headed for Ern's.

I couldn't imagine what they were up to, especially since they and Grandpa had spent the previous afternoon talking with Ern through the window. I supposed they were feeding him since it must have been a struggle for Ern to even take a leak on his own. Miss Vicky carried a dish that could have contained a casserole or a cake. They squeezed inside the trailer behind Grandpa, bringing the mud on their boots with them.

Ern shifted in the window again, giving me a rear view of his meaty neck, like something on display at the local butcher shop. On the verge of looking away, the mystery deepened. Luke Fisher pulled up in his pickup. He went into the trailer too.

I thought they might have found Miss Shelby. If they had, it meant something bad, and most likely irreversible, had happened to her. Why else would they go to Ern's together? Why was she still not home?

Unable to shake the conclusion I'd come to, I rinsed the dirty dishes while wondering what would become of Ern. Who'd make his meals and scrub his plates? Who'd love him the way his mother had? What would happen to the stories and songs he'd been left to pass along?

I didn't look at Ern again until I left for the meeting. He was all alone by then. So was I, since Ma hadn't answered when I'd asked if she'd come along. My sneakers were muddy and the cardboard I held over my head was mush by the time I reached the Blue Gator. Even my bones felt wet from the relentless rain.

Excitement streamed out of the joint. I could hear voices above the deluge before I opened the door and tossed the cardboard aside. It looked like everyone on the rez was crammed inside. Some sipped beers at the bar, others swapped stories and made bets about what Grandpa would say. It wasn't three in the afternoon, and more than a dozen of the regulars were already engaged in a losing battle with their barstools. Their drunken fingertips picked at free peanuts while their asses slid from their seats. Their mud-streaked children sucked salt off peanut shells on the floor at their feet. The mass huddled around the large tube television in the corner grabbed my attention. It wasn't uncommon for a crowd to gather by the TV on Sundays in the fall when the Saints played at the Superdome, or when there was some other big broadcast, but there was nothing worth watching that day.

"Hey, sugar," Miss Tilly called from behind the bar. She and her husband Mac Langdon owned the joint. She waved her wet rag at me, and I waved back. "Where's Mae? Haven't seen her 'round since I can't remember when."

Ma had been a regular at the Blue Gator, but that was almost a year earlier, before things went from bad to worse. "I'm sure she'll come around again." I wanted that to be true, awful as it was. "What's goin' on?" I pointed toward the TV.

Miss Tilly smiled. "Go take a look."

I pushed into the crowd. Mac, one arm draped over the top of the television, snared my shoulder and pulled me close before I could get a look at what was on the screen.

"Finally got it," he said. Droplets of spit sprayed my face. "Ain't she a beaut?"

I didn't know what he was talking about until I realized his arm wasn't draped over the top of the TV. It was draped over the otherworldly machine sitting atop the television.

"Whoa." The sight of it stole my breath. I felt my eyes widen, turning my face into a giant pair of binoculars.

"It's last year's model, but it can freeze-frame, fast-forward, visual search, and record up to eight hours at the touch of a button. It's got a wired remote too." He hugged it like a father protecting his firstborn. "Got it at a steal. Only thirteen bucks a month for twenty-three months."

Technology that had made its way around the world had finally arrived on the rez. It was the most extraordinary thing I'd ever seen. Black and gray and streaked with silver, it had a small digital screen that displayed the time in tiny blue lights. More than two dozen buttons, each begging to be pressed, spotted its face. The largest depicted an arrow pointing to the right. I leaned close to take the contraption in. Not only did it look like something from the future, it had a mysterious scent as well. The high-tech odor of plastic and metal machinery filled me. I wanted to hold it in as long as I could.

"When'd you get it?" I wheezed, looking around for J.L., knowing he'd be equally blown away by the beautiful box. He wasn't anywhere in sight.

"Let's see it already!" a girl bobbling on her toes at the front of the crowd said. Her braids bounced against her shoulders.

The crowd cheered in agreement.

"All right, Anna, if you say so," Mac said to the girl. He slowly separated himself from his prized possession and reached behind the bar for the videotape that had been on display since last summer. The tape made a whisper as sexy as its jet-black casing as it slid from its cardboard sleeve.

We watched Mac press the silver eject button on the VHS VCR as though he were turning water into wine. A metal basket, slightly larger than the videocassette, sprang from the top of the device.

"Top-loader." Mac's voice reflected the smirk on his lips.

We giggled, inching even closer. The cassette made a satisfying plastic-against-metal scraping sound when Mac inserted it into the basket. An even more satisfying click reverberated when he pushed the basket into the machine.

"Ready?" Mac said.

"Yes!"

He turned on the TV, then pressed the button with the arrow on it. The VCR whirred. Snow crackled on the screen, followed by random bars of color. Then it was there in front of us, the pow wow we'd hosted last July.

I remembered watching the man from town with the giant camcorder on his shoulder, a cinderblock with a lens attached. He'd gone around the dance circle filming our people after Grandpa gave him permission to capture two of the dances. I'd eyed him, wondering where he got the device and how he'd afforded it, not knowing he was a prominent mayor's son until he donated the video to our tribe a few weeks later. Since none of us had a way to play it, the videotape sat in the bar as a reminder that we all owned it even if we couldn't watch it.

The sound of a grand pow wow drum, accompanied by rolling voices singing in unison, floated from the TV's speakers. While the VHS VCR may have initiated our awe, what we saw on the tube quickly overtook it. Men from our tribe, along with men from tribes across the country who'd joined us in our communal celebration, danced across the screen. Dressed in beaded vests, smoked-hide leggings dripping with fringe, bone breastplates, and headdresses made of feathers, porcupine quills, and fur, they looked as unworldly as the VCR. But they were born of ancient practices, not new ones. Everything about them was symbolic, from the movements they made to the war paint on their faces. Red for strength and success. Blue for confidence. Green for endurance. Black for victory in battle.

The men moved slowly, matching their steps with the rhythm of the drum, mimicking the movements of eagles with their arms. Their actions were focused and proud, mirroring those of our ancestors when they came face-to-face with an opponent. The men stomped in semicircles, never turning their backs, keeping their eyes fixed on the enemy before them, just like warriors of old.

The colors, the comradery, the sacred blend of people, history, culture, and tradition. All those things spoke of our pride, which may have been damaged throughout history but never lost.

The dancing warriors looked mighty and impervious to harm. My body wanted to move with the music. It longed to make the assured movements the dancers made. I could only hope that when my time came to perform the warrior dance, I'd be as honorable as the men on the screen.

Three solo strikes of the drum marked the dance's end. The room burst into spontaneous applause.

"Cool, ain't it?" Mac accepted the ovation for himself. He pressed the VCR's stop button and cast a glance at the rear of the Blue Gator where Grandpa had appeared beneath a flickering neon sign, his feet mashed in a heap of damp sawdust and peanut shells, his heavy arms slung across his chest.

I pried myself from the VCR and sat at one of the tables closest to Grandpa. I had to resist the urge to ask what he'd been doing at Ern's earlier. Miss Doris limped in a moment later and dropped onto a chair as though she couldn't bear her weight a split second longer. Squeezing the handle of her cane with one hand, she fanned herself with the other. Face red as rhubarb, her hair fell in drippy clumps around it, probably more from perspiration than from rain. It must have taken every ounce of will she possessed to hobble through the mud; her car had gone with Jim the day he swerved off the road. I knew no matter how painful it must have been for her to cross the rez, it would have been twice as torturous for her to miss the meeting.

Miss Tilly came by and set a Coke in front of me. "On the house," she said, perhaps because Ma had contributed so many dollars to the VCR fund. She left before I could thank her.

"Let's begin." Grandpa dropped his arms from his chest. "Thank you for being here as the sky spirit cries upon us."

Aside from the rain pummeling the roof, nothing made noise, rendering the interior of the Blue Gator as silent as a stone.

"We're here for Miss Shelby," Grandpa said. "It's been two days without a hint of her."

"Have you spoken to her son?" someone called from the bar.

"Ernest has been as helpful as he can be."

"He's still alive?" someone else muttered. "Thought he died years ago."

"Ern welcomed the tribal council, Chief Fisher, and me into his home earlier this afternoon," Grandpa said. "He let Chief Fisher do a thorough search. I can assure you that Miss Shelby is not there. Considering the state Ernest is in, he's going to need our help until we sort this out."

A bottle clinked against the bar. I slid the glass in front of me closer to my chest but didn't take a drink.

"I did something this afternoon that I don't like to do," Grandpa Joe said. "I contacted the sheriff in town. I let him know that one of our own has gone missing. While it's unlikely that Miss Shelby would have gone off the reservation, considering she was on her way to pay her respects to Aubrey Forstall when she went missing, we can't ignore the fact that someone might have taken her away from here. We may need outside help."

"Shoot the shit straight to us, Joe." Beaux Ballard broke the silence in a slurred sort of way, both because he was drunk—as always—and because he was six teeth shy of a full set. "Do you think someone killed her?"

"Missing," Grandpa said.

"There's no evidence to suggest anything else," Luke Fisher stepped in. "Sam and I"—Sam Peltier was Miss Vicky's husband and one of the few members of the tribal police force—"have done our best to search as much of the reservation as possible, but we can't do it alone. We need to pull together. I'm asking that you search the fields around your homes. I might even need volunteers to help us drag the river." He paused, lips clenched between his teeth, making him look like a duck without a bill. "Miss Shelby would have crossed the bridge on her way to Aubrey's wake. If she slipped into the water, there's a chance we might find her in the rocky area where the river bends."

The statement sobered up a few of the regulars. Though Luke didn't say it, we all knew he was talking about finding her dead. I took a sip of my Coke. The bubbles burned the back of my throat.

"Does her goin' away have somethin' to do with what happened in the cemetery?" Beaux Ballard asked, tapping for Miss Tilly to bring him another beer.

"What exactly happened in the cemetery?" Miss Doris said. Drops of water from her hair landed in silent splats against the table. "All we know is that graves were dug up."

"We have no reason to believe that Miss Shelby's disappearance is connected to what happened in the cemetery," Luke said in response to Beaux's question.

Grandpa addressed Miss Doris. "Three graves have been disturbed. I want to assure all of you that—"

"Is it like last time?" Miss Doris asked.

"I've spoken with Ray Horn." Grandpa gestured toward the cemetery caretaker sitting a few feet away. "We've worked out a plan to keep the cemetery under twenty-four-hour surveillance until we identify who committed these crimes. Sam and a few others will rotate shifts over the coming days and nights."

"Is it like last time?" Miss Doris asked again.

Grandpa stalled, perhaps wondering which *last time* Miss Doris was referring to. "Things were taken from the graves," he said. "But it's not like the last time things were taken. Not at all."

The *last time* of which Grandpa spoke occurred two years before I was born, when dozens of warrior graves from the early 1700s were dug up and robbed of the prized possessions the deceased had taken with them into the afterlife. The missing relics came to be known as the Takoda Treasure. For years, no one knew where the treasure had gone. Some thought it would never be found. Greed was our tribe's saving grace back then. When the thief, a security guard from Bienville Parish, tried to sell the artifacts without proof of ownership, our tribe, following a battle in court, recovered what our ancestors had lost. In all, the treasure consisted of hundreds of items ranging from ancient iron tools to musket parts, jewelry, Native pottery, and hundreds of thousands of European trade beads.

"If it's not like last time, then what was taken?" Miss Doris asked.

"And who was it taken from?" Miss Tilly said.

Grandpa didn't stall. "Bones. Bones were taken from the graves."

A collective gasp hit the Blue Gator's ceiling, the thrill of the VCR now gone. Someone dropped a glass. My stomach lurched. The urge to break someone's face returned. Gram. My beautiful gram.

Why'd it happen? Who'd done it? We all wanted those questions answered at that very moment. Well, most of us did.

"What about the bingo hall?" Beaux broke the silence with his slurred, sledgehammer question. "You got any word on that, Joe? You found any lenders to help us get it built?"

Miss Tilly stabbed Beaux with her eyes and shut him up by setting another beer in front of him. "Whose bones?" she said. That was another question everyone wanted answered.

I already knew the names Grandpa would say, but still I listened like my life depended on it.

"The bones were taken from my grandfather Hilaire Broussard, my wife, Caroline . . . and Horace Saucier."

Another gasp went up, then heads turned. There was someone in the crowd I hadn't noticed earlier. George Saucier, Horace's father.

He stood alone by the exit, arms tight around his chest. The dozens of eyes upon him didn't disturb him. He kept his gaze fixed on my grandfather.

I didn't know much about George Saucier. I don't think anyone really did. What I did know was that his wife, June, had passed away nearly two years to the day after Horace's murder. George, it seemed, had little to live for after that. He holed himself away in the trailer he once shared with the two people he'd loved, never opening his curtains, letting the brush around his home grow thicker by the year. We seldom saw him around the rez. Most of us avoided him as much as he avoided us.

I knew better than to stare, but seeing George was like seeing the vampire, especially since some said he'd killed Horace and June. I'll admit his withered arms, sunken chest, deflated face, and weary eyes made him look like nothing more than a sad old man suffering yet another unexpected blow. But while anyone else with his features would have posed no more of a threat than the cracked peanut shells on the floor, I was wary of him. What he said didn't make me feel any better.

"Joe." His voice was rough like bark. "I want to see my son."

NINE

Louie

"I miss her." The hollow voice came from across the darkened field upon my return from the Blue Gator Grill, later than expected, having hung around to marvel at Mac's ability to record regular TV onto a blank tape. "It's lonely here." Ern's lack of inflection made me squirm. He could have been talking to himself as much as he was talking to me. I stiffened and slowly opened the door, hoping if I moved carefully enough I wouldn't attract more of his attention.

"Come over."

I knew I could ignore him, but I felt like there'd be a price to pay if I did, like he'd sock me in the stomach from across the field. It didn't feel right leaving him all alone, either.

Umbrella-less, I approached his window through the rain. The blinds dropped to just below Ern's nose when I got close, turning him into a phantom behind a mask. "I'm sorry," I said. I don't know why the apology fell from my mouth. I guess it was for Miss Shelby.

"The meetin' went all right?"

"Mac bought a VHS VCR." I felt the pleasant kiss of Ern's air-conditioning on my sticky skin. "It's the coolest thing I've ever seen."

I was slowly getting used to Ern's ways. Even so, I bristled in response to how he spoke without any interest for the impressive device, his voice a low rumble. "Good for Mac. What'd your grandpa say?"

I shrugged. "George Saucier was there." I didn't want to talk about the search for Ern's ma with him.

"George. Is he good? He was always good to me."

The rain kept falling, so I pressed myself against Ern's trailer door to take refuge beneath the shallow awning overhead. His assertion took me by surprise more than seeing George at the Blue Gator. "You knew him?"

"He and Miss June used to play Bourré with my ma when I was a boy. They never played for much, but George would always toss me a dime if he won the pot. That was before everything got bad. A million years ago . . ."

"You knew Horace!" I exclaimed, as excited as if he'd handed me a crisp one-hundred-dollar bill.

Ern shrugged his meaty shoulders. "Knew him no better than anyone else on the rez."

"What was he like?"

"Nervous as a worm on a hook. He didn't like bein' 'round people and that made people not like bein' 'round him . . . uncomfortable, I mean. His ma said he was shy, but it was more than that. He'd freak out anytime someone talked to him. I saw it happen. My ma would say, 'Hey, honey, how you doin'?' and he'd start stammerin' like he was speakin' in tongues. I swear, sometimes it looked like he was gonna drop like a fly in a fire. He never could answer when asked a question."

"I guess that's why people thought he was strange."

"People thought he was strange 'cause he was."

Rumors on the rez made Horace out to be more than just strange. Some said he was sick. Some said sinister. "I mean, I guess that's why so many people doubted him. You know some say he brought the vampire upon himself, right?"

Ern scoffed. "People only say that 'cause of what happened in the cemetery. They jumped to conclusions 'bout what he was doin' there, and they got scared. Said he was up to no good . . . said he *was* no good."

In the years between the theft of the Takoda Treasure and the desecration of the three graves in the summer of 1986, Horace himself had been caught digging in the cemetery. Clawing, really. He'd used nothing but his hands to cast the dirt away, which is what Miss Doris had been referring to at the meeting when she asked Grandpa Joe if the latest case of someone digging in the cemetery was anything like *last time.*

"Don't you think people were right to be suspicious of him?" I asked. "He was trying to dig up a two-hundred-year-old warrior."

"No," Ern said. "Mighta looked like he was tryin' to dig up a warrior, but he wasn't. Not at all."

"Ern?"

"You know how Horace liked lookin' at the rocks by the river?"

Standing in the rain, intermittently casting my gaze up at the window and seeing Ern's mouth, outlined by dark lips that looked like they could stretch around my head and suck me in, I felt cold and alone, especially when Ern mentioned the rocks.

"Legend has it that Horace liked to do more than just look at the rocks by the river," I said.

"Yeah, well one day when Horace was lookin' at the rocks, he found somethin' that'd washed up on shore. It was a trade bead like one of the thousands stolen from the graves years before. Horace thought the thief musta dropped it in the river. He wanted to put it back in its proper place. That's the real reason he was diggin' in the cemetery."

"How do you know?"

"He told me."

"He talked to you?"

"When he wanted to. I mighta been the only one who'd listen."

"You believed him?"

"Sure did."

"Why?"

"'Cause he showed me the bead."

"Why didn't he tell the others what he was really doing?"

Ern heaved his shoulders. "Musta tried, but I already told you . . . he had trouble talkin'. Couldn't speak to save himself."

I realized then that Horace and Ern were a lot alike. Horace unable to speak without stammering; Ern unable to speak without blinds in front of his face. Both awkward. Both strange.

"Besides," Ern went on, "everyone else was too busy makin' him out to be a monster. Said he was a weirdo . . . disturbed for doin' somethin' like that. No one other than Miss June and George saw much of Horace from that point on. He stopped comin' to school, which gave the whispers about him room to grow into the rumors you grew up with. Rumors that got worse after Horace died."

I watched raindrops splash into the mud puddle at the bottom of the steps. The scent of the rain mingled with the scent of the earth, filling my nose with a swampy, sweet odor.

"Do you believe a vampire killed him?" I asked.

"Vampires are shit." Ern didn't hesitate. The Mires didn't just know every bit of the Takoda's fabled history, they knew folklore from around the world. I knew from talking to Miss Shelby that her shelves were full of books about all kinds of wondrous things. When Ern wasn't watching life go by, he must have been eating or reading. "The vampire's ever-changin'," he said. "It's been a bloated bringer of death, a gaunt and charismatic charmer, a drinker of blood beneath a full moon. The vampire has always reflected the times, Louie. It's a malleable monster that tempts us as much as it scares us. But no matter its form, the vampire has never been said to do that which was done to Horace."

"Who do you think killed him?" My skin prickled. Storm clouds whirled above, the sky purple and dark.

Ern's fleshy shoulders, each a sow's backside, went up to his ears—not far, considering he hardly had a neck. "Who knows if the mystery'll ever be solved."

The silence that followed must have clued Ern in on what I was thinking. I couldn't voice the words myself.

"I don't think that what happened to Horace has anything to do with what's happened to my ma," he said. "I'm not stupid. Somethin' musta happened to her. There's no reason she'd be gone this long."

"We might drag the river," I whispered.

"Luke told me." Ern raised the blinds, giving me my second glimpse of his eyes. They looked worried, not sad. "Bring me somethin' to eat."

I appreciated the command. "I'll see what I can find." I hopped off the steps, back into the rain.

TEN

Noemi

Barely two and a half hours had passed and everyone already knew. My gaze was on the pint glass in front of me, but I could feel eyes from every angle, snaring me in a net tangled with pity, curiosity, and alarm—a net that threatened to drag me under rather than promising to pull me from the depths. I could hear questioning whispers, too, somehow overpowering the music through the speakers and the excitement of a pre–pow wow Friday night. Part of me wanted to leave. The other part still didn't want to be alone.

I glanced at Uncle Louie, picking at a basket of beignets, getting dusty sugar all over his fingertips. Eyes cast down, he was ignoring Jean-Luc and Rosie. I made the mistake of peeking at the couple. Jean-Luc was staring straight at me.

"Jumped in front of a Jeep, huh?" he said, pausing with the rim of his glass an inch from his mouth. "Someone said a coyote ate him?"

I didn't answer. I didn't even want to wonder about the coyote. The thought of Roddy—was it his fingers, his cheeks, his lips?—going down the animal's gullet brought something lumpy and vile to the back of my throat. I forced myself to swallow and checked my phone again. Notifications were adding up—missed calls, texts, and social media mentions. I opened Instagram only to close it a minute later after skimming several heartbreaking stories shared by Roddy's stunned friends.

"Are you sure?" Mom whispered to me.

Maybe she was asking if I was sure I didn't want to talk, or if I was sure I wanted to be there. I kept my eyes on my phone, my thumbs tapping out a text I wasn't sure I should send. I sent it anyway.

> Do u know what Roddy was
> doing?

A response came almost instantly, much faster than I'd expected.

> No. Do you?

> No idea

> This is so fucked up

I should have censored that last one. Roddy's little sister, Sara, was seven years younger than him, and she didn't care much for me. Never mean or impolite, she just never made me feel like a friend, even when I tried to be one. Roddy said she thought I was loud and—I had to force him to admit it—a little too old.

> Have u heard anything from
> tribal pd?

I wondered if family had been given more info than me.

> Just that they're investigating

I took another sip of beer. A drop splatted across my phone screen. I cleaned it against my shirt. Hands shaking, I felt like a fraud for even thinking about what I needed to ask next.

He wouldn't have, would he?

Why, after I'd so stubbornly proclaimed to Cain Fisher, his father, and my family that Roddy wouldn't have ended his life, did I now need reassurance from someone else? Maybe it was because Sara and Roddy were so tight. She knew him almost as well as I did. If we both believed the same thing, there'd be no denying it.

Idk. I hope not.

I gasped at the response. How could she say that? The answer was *NO!* Roddy and I had sessions booked with Gunn Garver, one of the best tattoo artists in New Orleans. The sessions weren't for another few months because Gunn was always booked, but we were going to make a weekend out of it. Roddy was looking forward to getting his first tattoo. He'd said so.

Maybe Sara didn't know about the tattoos, but she had to know that reporter Roddy was on his way to becoming Roddy Bishop, mid-day anchor for News 11, central Louisiana's number two news outlet. It was almost all he ever talked about, his ultimate goal being to commandeer the morning anchor spot. He swore he'd make it happen before he hit thirty-five, and I didn't doubt that he would. He could use his charm on anyone, and he looked great on TV.

He didn't!

I was welling up again, fighting not to scream. Sara didn't text back. I assumed she was with her parents.

Can I come over?

I knew the answer two minutes before it finally came.

Not rn

Roddy always denied it when I'd ask if his parents disapproved of me. I guess the fact that I felt the need to ask should have been answer enough.

Lmk if u hear anything

I let the phone fall onto the bar, then swiped it up and quickly added:

Please?

"What's wrong?" Mom asked. She was talking to Uncle Louie, not me.

He barely shook his head. "Your boyfriend still coming?"

She checked her phone as if she'd missed something. I checked mine too. "He'll be here," she said. "He just . . . takes his time." She tilted her head back and drained the dregs from her glass. Raising her hand, she waved three fingers at Missy Tilly.

"Don't," Uncle Louie said.

"Life is short, Louie. Why not enjoy it?"

I don't know if alcohol actually brought Mom joy, but I do know it dulled pain. I didn't turn the drink away when Miss Tilly set three drippy glasses in front of us. Mom slid one in front of her brother, pushing his Coke aside.

"I don't want it!" he snapped, the loudest he'd been all night. Half the beer sloshed onto the bar and over the edge, right onto Mom's lap, when he pushed it away.

"Damnit, Louie!" She jumped up, trying to cast the beer to the floor before it seeped into her skinny jeans. "Why'd you even come?"

I don't know if she meant to the Blue Gator Grill or to the rez in general.

In a quiet voice, he said, "Wanted to see if it still looked the same."

"Same as what?" Mom sniped, reseating herself. "You never used to come here."

"I did," he argued. "When we were kids and you were off doing whatever you did."

A text came through from Sara.

> We're going to Roddy's to see if
> he left a note

ELEVEN

Louie

Wearing the impermeable buckskin of my pow wow regalia heightened my sense of power. Still, I was more worm than warrior.

"Looks good, Louie." Lula's compliment from the bathroom doorway yielded wrinkles in my brow. Rarely did she say more than a few rushed words to me as she raced out the door in the morning or when she'd scoop Noemi from my arms after work. Nor were they ever that nice. Not to mention that the outfit I'd stitched together looked no better than if I'd wrapped myself in masking tape.

"Thanks," I said a second before realizing why she'd said it. Holding a brush in one hand and a bottle of poor girl's hairspray—sugar mixed with water—in the other, she wanted the bathroom mirror.

"But—" I said.

"It's flat." She lifted the puff of hair on her head to show that it wasn't standing as high as it could. I took another look at myself in the mirror, wondering if anyone would buy me as a warrior in my getup. Shaking my knotted mane in Lula's face, I stepped out of the way in time to see Jean-Luc, a mere shadow on the opposite side of our screen door, climb the porch steps.

"Get out here, Louie." He sounded muffled, like he had something in his mouth.

I peeled out of the heavy buckskin and made a monkey face at Noemi on my way out the door. She giggled.

"River?" J.L. finished chewing whatever was between his teeth and washed it down with a hard swallow.

"Sure," I said, then thought about Miss Shelby and how she might have died there. "If you've got some dough we could go to the Blue Gator for fries."

"I'm broke as a joke." J.L. dug into his pocket and pulled out a tin of chewing tobacco, bringing some lint along with it. He pried the lid off and offered me some.

"Nah." The scent made my stomach constrict. He pinched a juicy wad between his fingers and stuffed it under his lip. "Won't your old man notice it's gone?"

"He never notices nothin'." J.L.'s voice sounded muffled again, but in a different way. He spat into the mud made by yesterday's rain. The sun, hot as ever, hadn't turned everything back to dust just yet.

"What've you been up to?" I asked because he stank like sweat, stronger than usual.

"Can't say, but it involves your sister." His lips formed a thin grin that pointed up at lustful eyes.

"Shut up." It was the best defense I had. J.L. didn't have a sister. Or a brother. "What about the pow wow?" J.L.'s father had invited him to dance among the men that year as well. "What are you gonna wear for the warrior dance?"

"Not doin' it. No point."

"It's a rite of passage."

"A right-a what?"

"It's what makes us who we are. It's a tradition. Boys become men. Men become warriors."

"Yeah? Well, what have traditions done for me? Or for any of us? Look around, Louie, and tell me how many happy faces you see on this shitty piece of land." He stomped his foot in a mud puddle to punctuate his point. The brown globs that splattered his leg were like little defenders of his cynical stance.

"Noemi smiles."

"She won't for long."

I couldn't argue. There weren't many givens on the reservation, but one I learned from Ma was that hopelessness would wash over us all. Another was that there'd always be a barstool with your name on it at the Blue Gator. It was just up to you to accept it, like Ma did when I was eight.

"Where would you go if you could get away from here?" I said.

J.L. shrugged and spat. "New Orleans. They have strip clubs on every corner. And live sex shows. If we ever get the bingo built . . ." he said, in the same dreamy way everyone else on the rez said it. His sentence could have been finished a million different ways. If only.

"My pop says the Seminoles raked in a million bucks a month last year with their bingo in Florida." He whistled. "Damn, why can't that be us? What would you do with your share of the dough?"

"An air conditioner'd be nice. Or a VCR like Mac's. Man, you shoulda seen it."

"That's stupid." He punched my shoulder.

"What's your plan, genius?"

He spat again. "You seen the new Lamborghini Countach?" He rattled off the model. "If I can keep the babes out, I'll take you for a spin."

"Sure." I slowed my pace fifty feet from the riverbank. The water sat high on the shore, making the river's rush and roar more ferocious than usual.

Jean-Luc went ahead of me. "Goin' in?" he turned to ask. We were at our usual hangout—so far upriver that you couldn't see the bridge that connected the east to the west side of the reservation—but still, I didn't feel comfortable there. My mind dwelled on Miss Shelby. I knew her body would have washed downriver from the bridge, but I didn't like the thought of being in the water with her.

"I'll stay here." I pulled myself up on a branch so that I wouldn't have to sit in the mud. J.L. went forth on his own. He spat the chewing tobacco out as he hurried down the riverbank, rustling up insects as he went. Nabbing a grasshopper right out of the air, he popped it into his mouth. Its abdomen crunched like celery.

"Still grosses you out?" He smiled back at me and my disgust, antennae between his teeth.

"It'll always be gross."

"Like a lemon." He winced, swallowed, and laughed. Already shirtless, he kicked his shorts atop some brush, then dove straight into the river wearing his tighty-whities, which weren't so white.

While the rushing water washed sweat from J.L.'s skin, I thought about what he'd asked. What would I do with money if we built the bingo hall and we all got rich? It was a question I'd never considered because fantasizing could hurt. Bad.

J.L. sent a spray of water high into the air. We'd spent a lot of time in that very spot, attacking each other with Spanish moss and expertly packed mud pies. It was there when we were five that J.L. showed me a snapper he'd caught with his own two hands, proud because he still had all ten digits intact. That's when we became friends. We'd go into the water wearing just the skin on our backs when we were little, not caring who might see, but that changed when we changed. It was after a swim that I was forced to face the fact that my childhood days were numbered, the realization hammered home by the appearance of a single short hair a few inches below my belly button, a hair that made me excited and scared and which stood straight up when I wiped the water away.

J.L. didn't stay in the river long. "Folks've been talking about you."

He hopped up the riverbank and wrung water from his hair, now rich with the musty sweet scent of earth.

"What do you mean?"

"About your family."

I dropped from the tree to face him, my feet plummeting into the mud. His wet skin glistened, his soggy briefs barely veiling his frank and beans. "What have they been saying?"

"Nothin' bad. They just think there might be a connection between you and Horace."

"What?" I shouted.

"Because of what happened in the cemetery. Two Broussards. One Saucier. Why were they the only ones dug up?"

"I don't know!"

"I'm not asking you to explain. You know how people always make shit outta mud around here. They've got nothin' better to do."

"What else have they said?" My left hand found a forgotten scab on my right elbow. My fingers proceeded to pick it.

J.L. tugged his shorts back on. "Nothin' really. Everyone likes a good story, is all. With what happened to Aubrey, Miss Shelby, and the cemetery, there's plenty of gossip going around."

I looked downriver, expecting to see Miss Shelby there. I shivered. "Let's get outta here." The scab broke from my skin. I winced at the sting. J.L. snatched the crusty thing from between my fingers and held it up like a priest presenting a communion wafer.

"If I wanted to keep it, would you let me?"

"What? No. Throw it away."

"It's part of you, Louie. It's your blood."

"You're weirding me out, man." I tried to flick the scab from his hand, but he quickly concealed it in his palm. "What's with you?"

He smiled and said "Nothin'," then cast the scab toward the river. "Now your blood will mix with the mud, and you'll be part of the earth, just like our people have always believed we are. Tradition,

Louie. It's important to you, right? Like the pow wow and the warrior dance." He clapped me on the back and ran up the riverbank. "If I'd kept it, would I be any different from whoever took the bones from the cemetery?"

He confused me. "Whoever took the bones from the cemetery defiled the graves. That's pretty damn different."

"Let's check it out."

"Check what out?"

"The cemetery!" J.L. took off toward the bridge, whooping as he went.

"Wait!" I raced to catch up, only getting him to slow by clasping his shoulder from behind. "We can't go there!"

"Why not?"

"It's a crime scene."

"Exactly! I bet everyone else has already checked it out." He plowed forth, dragging me along.

"But my gram . . ." I neither wanted to see what'd been done to her nor what'd become of her in the ground. "And Sam," I said, remembering he was monitoring the graves.

"I just wanna see. We won't stay long."

Reaching the bridge, I refused to look at its balusters because I knew I'd only obsess over the fact that Miss Shelby couldn't possibly have slipped through into the water below. Something worse must have happened to her. Something like the vampire.

The cemetery was over the bridge, just beyond the pow wow grounds. Both were celebratory spots: the cemetery for death; the pow wow for life. A wide circle sat in the center of the pow wow grounds where the dances took place. An expanse of open land surrounded the dance circle, providing space for spectators to watch and roam among stalls selling fresh-squeezed lemonade and Indian tacos with delicious fry bread as their foundation. Some tribal members relied on the pow wow for much of their year's income. They sold handmade jewelry inset with sparkling stones, beaded moccasins, woven rugs, dolls, drums, blankets, pottery, flutes, pipes, and knives. Most of the wares were made and sold with pride, but some things, like the plastic bows and arrows, the rubber hatchets, and the feathery felt headbands, were sold to make a quick buck.

I didn't look at the pow wow grounds as we breezed by, but I could hear the steady rhythm of a grand drum accompanied by a dozen uplifting voices as the musicians practiced for the upcoming celebration. My chest swelled. The robust music fooled me into thinking I could march into the cemetery on my own.

"There's Sam's truck." It was parked next to the dirt path that led into the cemetery. We could've easily snuck onto the sacred ground. The cemetery was too large for one man to monitor on his own, and there wasn't a gate to keep anyone out, just some patches of overgrown grass. J.L. stopped when we spotted Sam slumped against the truck's bumper. Neon green gas station sunglasses shielded his eyes, and a cigarette hung from his lower lip. Light wisps of smoke fought for visibility against the rays of the late afternoon sun. "He looks bored as shit."

He really did. Sweeping his gaze from one side of the cemetery to the other, he lazily scanned the quiet expanse.

"Horace," J.L. whispered, pointing at a mound of earth about forty feet from the cemetery's entrance.

My mouth went dry. My head started to spin. "Can we go?" I longed for the steady drum back at the pow wow grounds.

"I just wanna see." J.L. ran closer while simultaneously distancing himself from Sam's truck. I followed because it was better than being alone.

J.L. crouched in the grass at the cemetery's border. I crouched next to him. We were closer to Horace then, the closest I'd been since the vampire got him.

"Why hasn't anyone covered him back up?" Jean-Luc said.

"They're probably still looking for clues."

A sharp whistle pierced our ears. I collapsed against the ground.

"Shit." J.L. ripped a handful of sunburnt grass from the dirt and threw it into the air. "Busted."

Sam didn't say anything when I looked in his direction. He didn't even get off the truck's bumper. He just shot a thumb over his shoulder and blew out a large puff of smoke.

"I told you we shouldn't be here, Louie!" J.L. shouted, grinning from ear to ear. He sped off, leaving me on the ground.

"Bastard!" I scrambled to my feet, my eyes landing on what must have been Aubrey's grave, marked with a wooden cross and covered with fresh mud. Had he made any more sounds beneath the earth? I wondered, as the wind began to blow. It brought with it a scent of death so strong that I held my breath until I was halfway home.

TWELVE

Louie

Miss Doris called just after I'd put Noemi down for her nap. She asked me to come over, said it wouldn't take long.

Johnny hugged my knees the instant I walked through the trailer door.

"I'm a gorilla!" he said.

I gripped his shoulders and shook out a growl.

"What's it today?" I hoped the toilet hadn't clogged again. Something bubbled on the stove, garlic filled the air. "Did you leave something off your last grocery list?"

"No, no." Miss Doris shook her head. "I was just wondering about Noemi."

"Noemi?" Had I heard her right?

"You take care of her, don't you? When your sister's not around."

"Yeah, when Lula's at work," I said. "Not that I have much of a choice. There's only me and Ma. Grandpa helps when he can, but . . ." I trailed off.

Miss Doris smiled and clapped her hands. Her recliner jolted backward from the force. "Terrific!"

"What's terrific?"

Johnny kept growling. His usual attempt to scale my legs, like a bear trying to climb a tree, forced me to cup the branch below my waist.

"Don't you think they should be friends?" Miss Doris said. "Who knows, they might even be sweethearts one day."

"Who?"

"Johnny and your niece, of course."

I still hadn't picked up on what she wanted.

"I was just thinking . . . since you take care of your niece during the day, why not look after Johnny as well? I'm sure they'd love each other's company."

My blank stare must have given my reluctance away. I loved Noemi, but I took care of her because I had to.

"I'll pay you," Miss Doris said. "You'd only have him a few hours during the day, and only for the summer. Rosie handles him in the morning, and I'm good for an hour or two after that, but my starch ain't what it used to be. I'm just not built for chasing little boys. And with this"—she shook her cane—"I'm apt to fall and break a hip. Or two!"

"I don't know. . . . I'm only sixteen." Not to mention the ball-busting I'd endure if the guys on the stickball field found out I was the most sought-after babysitter on the rez.

"Sixteen or not, you're more responsible than half the folks on this reservation. Half? Lord, what am I saying? You're as responsible as they come. You've never let me down, Louie. Besides, Johnny loves you."

I looked down at the boy, toes curving around my kneecaps, his hands tight around my waist. I could see that he liked me, and that he was a handful.

"You wouldn't have to do anything other than watch him. I'll pack up some nice snacks for him each morning and everything else he needs. You just spend some time with him, and then I'll send Rosie to pick him up when she's done with work. What do you say?"

"What if he doesn't like it at my house? What if he and Noemi don't get along?"

Miss Doris discounted my worries with a flick of her cane. "Kids are adaptable. It's good for them to be around others their age. Besides, I'm worried about Johnny. He's cooped up with me all day, and then he sits in his mama's lap all night. He has no one to gruff him up. Being around you will do him good."

I took a deep breath. "Okay." Screw the guys on the stickball field. She'd mentioned money.

Miss Doris clapped her hands again. "Now maybe he'll learn all those boy things I can't teach him."

Johnny growled and crashed two toy trucks against the wall. He seemed gruff enough to me. "What things?"

"Oh, you know, like how to throw a ball or catch a frog without squishing it to death." Her lips stretched thin, barely forming a grin. "We still can't get him to pee standing up." She pointed to the potty chair in the corner. My flesh got hot. "Don't worry, he's pretty good about going on his own. You just have to remind him every now and then. Sometimes he gets so wrapped up with toys that he forgets he's a big boy now."

"Big boy!" Johnny echoed. The trucks exploded into the air, narrowly missing Johnny's head on their way down. He latched on to my waistband and curled his toes around my kneecaps again. "I'm a big boy!"

"Yes, you are!" Miss Doris turned her attention back to me. "Be careful with the building blocks." She laughed. "Once he starts stacking, he never wants to stop. Before you know it, you've got a stinker on your hands."

"I don't know a thing about potty training." Noemi, months older than Johnny, had yet to see a training chair. Lula spent more time teasing her hair than anything else.

"Well, don't worry about the peeing thing. I'm sure you'll do just fine. We'll start tomorrow. You can pick him up after breakfast."

"You said you'd pay me?"

Her jowls shook when she nodded. "Ten dollars a day. How's that sound?"

Considering I'd only have the kid for a few hours at a time, I agreed.

Johnny, having slid down my legs, climbed atop the sofa and launched himself at me.

"Little John!" Miss Doris snapped. "Get over here. You'll have plenty of time to play with Louie tomorrow."

Johnny launched himself at me again, then pounced next to one of his tiny trucks and scooted it out of the living room on his knees.

"I guess I'll see you in the morning." I turned to leave.

"One last thing, Louie . . ." Miss Doris's voice had dropped. "It's the toilet again."

THIRTEEN

Noemi

Suddenly, I was afraid to touch my phone. It lay on the bar in front of me, its screen darkened, then turned black. If it vibrated with a message from Sara, I'd nab it, wake it from its slumber, and consume whatever she'd written as if her words would quench a deadly thirst. Hitting Go to complete the search I'd typed into my web browser, though, was even more daunting than when I'd sat down with my doctor to learn the biopsy results of the mole he'd removed from my back. I was afraid of what I might find out.

Leaning forward, I woke the phone. The three words—"native american suicide"—I'd typed into the search bar glowed up at me, thanks to the unsettling notion Grace Hebert had implanted in my mind when I overheard her talking to Mom. Filling my lungs, I jabbed the screen with my index finger. The phone's face flashed and then a list of results appeared. I squinted as I read the links.

American Indian Suicide Rate Increases

Suicide rate worsening among American Indian and . . .

The hard lives—and high suicide rate—of Native Am . . .

High Suicide Rates Among American Indian or Alas . . .

My head spun. Everything abruptly felt too close, suffocating. Slipping off my stool, I staggered out the door. Fresh air didn't fill my lungs outside, only the secondhand smoke from the smokers who'd gathered by the door after Good Boy's departure. It was just as good.

"Bum me one," I said to Germy—real name Jeremy—Forstall, obnoxiously swinging his hips to the music spilling out of the bar.

He held out his pack, and I plucked a smoke stick from it. I felt calmer with it between my lips and even better when Germy leaned forward to touch the tip of his lit cig to the tip of mine. My first in more than a year, I inhaled deeply, only to hear Roddy again, spouting one of his goofy jokes.

Don't make an ash *of yourself.*

He'd helped me kick the habit. Sort of.

Germy tried to dance with me, but I waved him off, separating myself from the smokers around me because I didn't want them to see what was on my phone; I didn't want them thinking that I thought Roddy had done it. I only tapped one of the links because I was curious. That's all.

Making myself small against the side of the Blue Gator Grill, I read the headline in its entirety.

High Suicide Rates Among American Indian or Alaska Native Persons Surging Even Higher

Written by Joan Stephenson, PhD, the article published late last September came from the *JAMA* Health Forum, a peer-reviewed open-access journal, according to the website.

I scrolled down, forcing myself to read.

Rates of suicide among American Indian or Alaska Native persons increased substantially from 2015 to 2020, compared with only a small increase among the general US population, a new study from the Centers for Disease Control and Prevention (CDC) shows.

There were facts and stats, some of which I didn't understand, but I nearly sank when I read *The highest percentage of suicides in American Indian or Alaska Native populations (47 percent) occurred in those aged 25 years to 44 years. . . .*

It all made me dizzier than before. But it didn't sway me. I didn't doubt that thousands of Natives were struggling to find a reason. I just didn't think Roddy was one of them.

I tapped the X to close the browser window. I didn't need those awful truths glowing at me. I just needed to calm down, to take a deep breath, and to remind myself that Roddy hadn't been dealing with any of the issues listed in the article. No relationship problems. No recent losses of loved ones. No substance abuse. He didn't fit the mold, whatever it might be.

I checked for any texts I might have missed from Sara, then turned what remained of the cigarette to ash, flicking the butt out into the lot. I wiped my face against my shirt and brushed my fingers through my hair, wondering why I hadn't just gone to him after he'd gotten off work instead of waiting for him to come to me. I should have been with him instead of sitting at home, listening to songs I'd heard a million times, rolling another joint.

I'd have given anything to change things, anything to do the afternoon over.

FOURTEEN

Louie

As I watched lightning bugs flicker in the field, they showed me that even overwhelming darkness can be broken by little things. Tired, my anxious mind wouldn't let me sleep. I wondered about my place in the world. Was it only on the reservation that I belonged, weathering the humid days until it was my turn to take up space in the tribal cemetery? Two long years of high school remained. What I'd do after that was anyone's guess. I'd seen enough of what awaited everyone else after they crossed the commencement stage—*if* they crossed the commencement stage—to know better than to believe the best was yet to come. Still, I had hope.

I leaned against the trailer and took deep breaths until my worry waned, all the while aware of the shadowy movements coming from the window across the way.

"You awake?" My voice competed with the crickets singing in the grass.

"Anything to eat?"

His question was a knife that deepened the wound opened by what I'd been pondering. Ern exemplified what I feared. If ever there was a waste of life, time, talent, hope, space, and God knows what else, it was Ernest Mire. He was supposed to carry on his family's tradition of storytelling and singing, a tradition the tribe respected and admired, but all he carried was a belly the size of a Buick.

I'd tried to ignore the horror of Ern's life since I was small, but it'd never struck me as plainly as it did that night. He sat. He watched. He ate. His situation possessed no potential. There was no promise of it getting any better. At least I had possibility. At least I could think my existence might amount to something. Ern, in his present state, couldn't have that thought. He lived like a man on death row, waiting out each day until it was time to meet his maker.

Ignoring his request for food, I trekked across the field. He dropped his blinds, putting his mask into place, making me wonder what he had to keep hidden. I sat on the lowest step.

"Still no sign of her," he said.

"You can't give up hope." Trite, but what else could I say?

"Never realized how much I rely on her. She cooks. Cleans. Does things for me I'm too embarrassed to admit. All 'cause I can't do a goddamn thing on my own."

His words settled inside me like something I'd swallowed without chewing enough, like a bite of overcooked meat or a piece of stale bread. "Have you ever wanted anything more than this?" The tortured part of my mind needed to know how he could settle for a life like his.

"What else would I want?" He didn't sound offended.

"Are you happy?"

"I was, up until a few days ago."

"Don't you ever wanna get out of that trailer?"

He considered the question, his glistening lower lip hanging down. "No. Never think about it."

"Aren't there things you wanna see? Things you wanna do? You've been in there all your life and—"

"Not all my life, Louie."

"I can't remember a time when you weren't in that window."

The blinds bobbled. "I saw everything there is to see out there. I don't miss any of it."

"You only saw the reservation." I supposed that was true.

"Went down to New Orleans with my ma when I was seven," he said. "I remember the music and all those neat lookin' buildings. Do you really think life's any different away from here? Seems to me it's all the same no matter where you go."

"It might be different. . . . It could be." I desperately wanted to believe that.

"So what if it is? What good will it do you?"

I couldn't say. "What's the last thing you did outside your trailer?" The thought that Ern could once come and go as he pleased snared me. I couldn't wrap my mind around the fact that he'd had a final day of freedom, that he'd transformed from a kid like me to a giant piece of fry bread at the mercy of his mother.

"Don't remember," he said.

"Think. Did you know it was the last time you'd be outside?"

"No. Just didn't have the energy to get up one day. Before I knew it, I couldn't get up at all."

"So tell me. What was your last day like?"

Ern dropped the blinds completely, perhaps trying to separate himself from that part of his life. "Walked to the Blue Gator, I think. . . . Yeah, for lunch. Ordered one of Miss Tilly's double-stacked burgers with two sides of fries, a bowl of peanuts, a pickle, and two slices of pie. Blueberry and pecan. Miss Tilly put a scoop of vanilla on the blueberry one for me. Had to talk Beaux Ballard into givin' me a ride home after that 'cause it hurt too much to move. That's the last time I saw Beaux. He's never come by."

"He's still at the Blue Gator."

"Figured he would be. Know why? 'Cause men like him don't change. Most men don't. They do what they do until they die, and then new men take their place. You know that's true."

Yeah, it was. I'm afraid it still is.

"So whose place are you gonna take?" he asked. "Beaux won't be on that barstool forever."

"I'm not—"

"You will." His voice was so firm I couldn't argue. He yanked on his cord, bringing the blinds up to his nose. "Heard anything new about the cemetery?"

"Nah," I said, and then, since he knew so much, asked, "Who do you think took the bones?"

"Haven't the foggiest."

"Would a vampire want them?"

"Vampires want blood."

"I know." Horace's murder had made that abundantly clear, even if Ern didn't believe a vampire had killed him.

"Voodoo, on the other hand," Ern said, "that's big in New Orleans, too."

"What about it?"

"I read that human bones are sometimes used in Voodoo rituals. Believers say the bones of one's ancestors possess curative powers when ground up and served with rum. Imagine that, Louie . . . bet it tastes better than cough syrup."

"My gram," I muttered.

"Maybe," he said, failing to make me feel better. "But most of the bones are kept in shrines . . . sometimes with more disturbing things."

"Like what?"

"Like the corpse of a boy."

"Aubrey." I thought of how childlike he was. Goose bumps sprang up on my arms and legs, not from the cold air leaking out of Ern's window. I ironed them flat with my palms.

"Maybe," Ern said again.

And again, I wondered if Aubrey really could have come back from the dead. "Are you saying that the missing bones are connected to what happened at Aubrey's wake?"

"I'm just talkin'."

"Then tell me one more thing. . . . Can Voodoo make a dead man sit up and speak?"

"Some say so." Ern answered fast, making my flesh crawl. "But only if he were drugged with puffer fish poison before his death, and only within three days of dyin'."

"Puffer fish poison?"

"Seems like a long shot, don't it?"

"Yeah." I mulled it all over. Vampires. Voodoo. Who the hell knew what to believe?

"Whatever happened, or is happenin', here," Ern said as if he could hear my thoughts, "doesn't need a vampire or Voodoo to explain it. It's people, Louie. It always comes down to people."

I wanted to accept and reject Ern's assertion. If someone were responsible for the mystery on our hands, I thought I might be able to sleep with my window open some night, assuming the *someone* eventually got caught. But if a human really had birthed the horror on the rez, it more than likely meant that someone among us had torn Horace to shreds.

"You could be right," I half-heartedly said.

Something moved in the shadows of the field. My heart kicked. I looked longingly toward my front porch.

"Go," Ern said.

I dashed across the field, stirring up mosquitoes as I went. The overgrown grass scratched my ankles and sent whispers to my ears. The hissy and sibilant sounds constituted a language foreign to me, and yet the grass's whispers made me run faster because they sounded like warnings that filled me with fear.

The cough of our 1966 Ford F100 yanked me from a restless sleep several hours later. The old Ford belonged to Grandpa. He'd given it to Ma after her sedan crapped out so that she wouldn't have to walk to and from work in the dark. Two-toned red and white with matching interior, the pickup was hard to shift, and it squeaked like an old mattress every time it hit a bump. I drove it into town sometimes, and, despite its age, I wouldn't have traded it for the slickest sports car in the world. Nothing new would have smelled the same. The odor in the cab was a little like Grandpa, a little like Ma. Like motor oil mixed with cigarette smoke and vanilla air freshener, accentuated by a hint of old leather from a reliable pair of work boots. It was the first vehicle I ever drove, and I loved it.

I thought Ma was asleep behind the wheel when I ambled outside, her head hanging forward, her hair all around the steering wheel. I descended the first porch step just as the truck door swung open. Ma lingered on the seat and then got out, the truck's key dangling from one hand, a bulging brown paper bag dangling from the other.

She didn't speak as she swayed toward the porch. Our eyes met, and then mine darted away, landing on Ern, already up and peering out his window like an inverted Peeping Tom, which may or may not have afforded him pleasure. My heart fluttered, a reaction to being spooked though I couldn't identify if it was Ma or Ern that made me feel that way.

"Armadillo." She practically uttered four words instead of one. I noticed the Ford's bloody front bumper just then.

"What happened?"

There was a pause, making it impossible to truly connect with her.

"Damn thing." She put the truck's key in her pocket and pawed for the porch railing. "Rolled right in front of me. . . . Like it was fightin' with itself. . . . Like it wanted to be flattened. . . . Damnedest thing."

She lumbered up the steps and swayed some more. I thought she wanted me to open the screen door, but then her quivering hand grasped the handle and pulled it open. I followed her inside.

"How was work?"

Her pauses were getting longer. I counted the seconds in my head. *One . . . two . . . three . . .*

"Ran out of Swiss Rolls."

"Swiss Rolls?"

She reached into her brown paper bag and pulled out a sweaty can. Then she did something she'd never done before. She gave it to me. My brothers on the stickball field would've chugged the beer before she changed her mind, but I didn't even think about bending the tab. It didn't excite me or make me feel like a man. It lit an inferno inside me instead. How could she think I wanted that? To become like her? I tossed the can into the kitchen sink as she staggered to her room.

"Put your bag down. I'll make breakfast," I said.

One . . . two . . . three . . . four . . .

The hiss of a can. The click of her bedroom door.

FIFTEEN

Louie

The old red wagon, more brown than red, thanks to rust that'd eaten away its paint, tested my strength like so many other things that summer. Its unoiled wheels didn't want to roll. They squeaked like field mice as I pulled Noemi down the road.

"Faster, Douie!"

"*Faster?* You wanna go faster?" I took off at a trot, being careful not to lose her in the dirt that billowed up behind us like smoke from a rocket. Noemi squealed, clapping her hands. I'd already told her twice to hold tight to the sides.

"Faster, Douie, faster!"

I shifted into higher gear and broke into a sprint despite how wiped I was from such little sleep. For the moment—me panting, Noemi laughing, the rusty wagon clanking down the road between rustling fields—everything felt all right. The sun was still early-morning-warm, not yet at its hot noontime height, and the sky was endlessly blue. That was about as good as it got. During those few seconds in which I ran fifty yards, Noemi was happy and so was I. But then we encountered Thomas Lavergne in his front yard and my happiness faded like a candle flame that's run out of wick. Bent over, he was a few feet from his riding lawnmower, grass nearly up to his knees.

Thomas stood and jerked his chin at me. I wiped the sweat from my forehead.

"Find something?" I called across his vast lot of land. The grim thought of what might be moldering in the overgrown grass made it impossible to smile. Only Noemi could keep the dimples in her cheeks because she didn't know any better.

He shook his head, annoyed. "Hit the septic tank lid. I think a piece of it landed over here." He resumed his search as I—relieved— glanced up at the Lavergnes' front window. Miss Autumn, Thomas's wife, was there with her mother, Fay, at her side. Miss Autumn waved. Miss Fay, blank-faced and frail, followed suit. I wondered if she re- membered me. She used to live on her own until dementia demanded that she receive around-the-clock care.

"Faster!" Noemi demanded.

I willed my mind away from what could be in Thomas's grass. "I have to tell you something," I said. "We're going to pick up a boy named Johnny. He's going to be your friend."

The words meant nothing to Noemi. She grabbed the sides of the wagon and thrust her upper body forward, attempting to make the wagon move faster. For a moment, I thought I ought to explain what a friend was, but I didn't because teaching is tough, and I figured she'd catch on soon enough. "You'll have to share the wagon."

We'd talked about sharing after she'd gotten stingy with a bag of gummy bears Grandpa Joe gave us. Her little knuckles whitened along the wagon's rim. "Mine," she said, echoing her cries when I'd tried to take one of the gummy bears. I blew out a breath instead of arguing. Johnny'd be with us on our return whether she liked it or not.

She insisted that I carry her inside once we reached Miss Doris's trailer, where Johnny, wearing one sock and superhero Underoos, was running in circles around Miss Doris's recliner.

"I know what you're thinking," Miss Doris said, "but he tires out after a while. Trust me, you're going to do just fine."

"Maybe someone else would do better?"

Miss Doris shook her head, refusing to let me off her barbed hook. "There's no one Johnny likes more than you."

The little tornado halted at the sound of his name. Curiosity crept across his face upon spotting me with Noemi in my arms. The two toddlers looked like they'd just discovered alien life. Johnny gazed up through dizzy eyes; Noemi glared down with a furrowed brow.

"I hear wedding bells in their future," Miss Doris cooed.

"I'm not so sure about that."

The showdown lasted a minute more, then Noemi put my concerns to rest. "Friend," she said, extending drool-slathered fingers in Johnny's direction.

"Well, isn't that the most precious thing you've ever seen?" Miss Doris beamed. She aimed her cane at the table by the door, upon which sat a large beach bag loaded with Johnny's building blocks, an extra set of clothes, crackers, cookies, something wrapped in foil, a banana, and two five-dollar bills sticking out of the side pocket to remind me why I was taking the kid off her hands.

"I just gotta finish getting him dressed," she said. "Arms up, Little John!"

Johnny stuck his arms straight into the air, his eyes still glued to Noemi and his feet glued to where he'd stopped. Laughing, Miss Doris propelled herself out of the chair and lassoed the boy with a T-shirt as if he were a bull. She dressed him, and I hoisted the straps of his bag onto my free shoulder, only to shake the straps down into the crook of my elbow when Noemi reached for the cookies inside the bag.

"Friend," she said again. "Share!"

She learned quickly. "After lunch." The last thing I needed was a couple toddlers jacked up on sugar. "All set?"

"He's ready." Miss Doris wrangled a kiss from him and gave him a soft swat on the rear. "See you later, alligator."

"While, crocodile!" He showed his teeth and growled.

"Wish me luck." Noemi on my hip and Johnny's bag hanging from the opposite arm, I took Johnny's hand and headed for the door.

"Louie," Miss Doris called. "There's one more thing." I turned to find her cane pointing at the training chair beside the table. "You remember what I said about boy things, don't you?"

I managed to smile while gritting my teeth. I slid the tiny toilet toward the door with my feet and reached back into the trailer to grab it once Noemi and Johnny were seated in the wagon. They barely fit sitting straddle with the bag atop the chair squeezed in behind them.

"All aboard!" I took off down the road. Noemi squealed. Johnny growled. The journey was just one more test I'd face.

The kids were fine for two minutes, and then Noemi's happy squeals turned to whines. Johnny's hands had morphed into claws, pinching her from either side.

"Stop that. Play nice." He pinched her again. She screamed.

"I'm a crawdad!" Johnny said.

I knelt by the wagon. "You know what claws are for?" A dumb question, considering he just pinched Noemi some more. I scooped a handful of crackers from his bag. "They're for eating!" I shoved a cracker between each claw and dropped some more onto his lap. Thankfully, he was happy to reduce the crackers to crumbs. I yawned and continued the journey home.

The increased weight of the wagon had my skinny arms burning long before we crossed paths with Thomas Lavergne again, giving his land a crew cut, a lot of grass to go. Miss Shelby could still be out there.

99

"Douie!" Noemi cried. Almost home, I expected to have to harness Johnny's claws again, but when I turned to look, Noemi was pointing behind us, her mouth open wide. "Uh-oh."

Johnny's bag was on its side about thirty feet back. Slick with sweat, I wiped my brow against my shirt, the dirt on my skin gritty beneath the fabric. "Stay here," I said instead of unleashing the string of profanities that wanted to stream out. "I'll be right back."

I ran to retrieve the bag and discovered that a trail of Johnny's belongings—a shirt here, a sock there, a banana fifty feet back—stretched far down the road. "Shit," I grumbled, then raced to recover what we'd lost. Giggles erupted as I swiped at a five-dollar bill somersaulting on the wind. Looking back, I saw the two toddlers climbing out of the wagon.

"No!" I abandoned the trail of lost objects. "Stay in the wagon! Get back in!"

My excitement egged them on. Johnny ran one way. Noemi went another. I wished for a reset button. Johnny fell into the grass along the road. He popped up a few feet into the field. Noemi stayed on course, scuttling toward home.

Both giggled and cast glances my way, probably wondering who I'd tackle first. Johnny was closer, but Noemi was headed for trouble. Zigging and zagging from one side of the road to the other, she quickly approached a bend.

"Stop!" I screamed. "Noemi, come back!"

Johnny, fifteen feet into the field now, stopped stock-still the instant I breezed past him. Advancing tires rumbled beyond the bend in the road ahead. My heart sank. I'd never reach Noemi before the car made the turn. I could only watch as it came upon her.

Noemi zigged. The car zagged. "Noemi!" She dropped like a tree after the final swing of an ax. Tears stung my eyes. She'd almost been flattened. It would have been my fault.

The brown Ford Fairmont slowed, but it never stopped. Eaton Ballard, tribal council member and responsible big brother to Beaux, sneered at me from behind the wheel. He pointed from one child to the other and shrugged with his hands in the air as if to ask, *What the fuck?* Still, he didn't stop. He only glared for a moment more, then punched the gas. I sprinted to Noemi. She felt like a board in my arms. I hugged her and kissed her and carried her back to the wagon, relieved both for her and myself. Lula would've strangled me with her bare hands if anything had happened to the kid. The way Noemi wrapped her arms around my neck, like a cat clinging to a tree for fear of falling into a dog's open jaws, told me she was equally unnerved. Even Johnny felt the effect. He came back to the wagon without being told. He climbed in on his own and grabbed Noemi, claws away, when I set her in front of him. Arms like rubber, I refilled Johnny's bag with what I'd collected from the road. I hadn't found the second five-dollar bill. Nor did I deserve it.

"You can't do that again," I told them once we were safely inside. They'd taken to playing with Johnny's blocks in the middle of the living room floor, the harrowing event already buried in their brains. Only I continued to shake. She'd almost been mashed into the dirt.

I washed my face with cold water and gave the box fan a thump to get it going. The couch hiccupped under my weight. J.L.'s whistle signaled me a moment later. "Hey, Louie, get your skinny ass out here."

I stuck my face in the window and saw Jean-Luc sprawled out in the wagon, shirtless, his arms and legs dangling over the sides. "Come in if you want," I said. No way was I taking the kids back out.

He clomped up the porch steps. The screen door clattered against the trailer's side. "New shitter?" He laughed at the training chair by the door.

"It's Johnny's."

J.L.'s gaze went around the room and landed on the two toddlers. "Rosie's kid?"

"Yeah."

"What's he doing here? Rosie around?" Suddenly he looked more muscular. Taller, too.

"I'm watching him."

"Why?"

"Because Miss Doris is paying me ten dollars a day."

"Shaving your pits now too?" He punched me in the stomach. "I guess you can't come out and play?"

"Not until Rosie picks him up. You can wait for her with me."

J.L. flicked his eyebrows, then threw himself at the blocks on the floor. The kids' crooked castle crumbled. Noemi whined. Johnny jumped on top of Jean-Luc. Blocks ended up in every corner and scattered across the floor.

"Someone should pay me for watching you," I said.

"Good luck squeezing a penny out of my pops." Jean-Luc socked me again and then offered a little goodwill by plucking a block from where it'd landed in the plastic basin of the potty-training chair.

"Miss Doris wants Johnny to learn how to pee standing up."

A low giggle rumbled at the back of J.L.'s throat. He took a step, wavered, then lined himself up with the tiny toilet and did something I never would have predicted. He unzipped, letting all of himself hang out. Then, right there in the living room, he took a leak in the chair that was much too small for someone his size.

"What the fu—?" I started.

"Monkey see, monkey do," J.L. said to Johnny. "It's easy."

"Monkey *dooo*," Johnny echoed.

"Jean-Luc!" I started toward him, only to retreat because there wasn't a damn thing I could do to stop him. My gaze drifted from the droplets splattering the carpet to his hands between his legs. The fact that he'd surpassed me since the days when we swam naked in the river somehow made matters worse. The kids didn't know what to make of him pissing in the living room. Johnny stared. Noemi stared. I stared too.

SIXTEEN

Noemi

Uncle Louie popped a peanut into his mouth from the overflowing bowl Miss Tilly had brought him. I could hear Mom next to him, telling Rosie what went down after Luke Fisher showed up at our door.

"Who you waitin' to hear from?" Uncle Louie asked, sucking the salt from the peanut shell.

I lifted my head from the bar, the ends of my hair damp with spilled beer. "Huh?"

"You're checking your phone every few seconds. I know you don't wanna talk about it, but you're waiting for something from someone."

I put my head down again, the phone only inches from my face. It'd been seventeen minutes since Sara texted to say she was going to look for a note. Even if she'd walked, it wouldn't have taken her more than ten minutes to get to Roddy's. They only lived a few streets apart.

"I'm getting notifications." I turned my phone so Uncle Louie could see all the little red banners that'd popped up on the screen. He seemed to buy the half lie.

Sara was giving me palpitations. I'd scream if she didn't text soon.

"College boy!" Mac Langdon grabbed Uncle Louie's shoulder from behind. Old as Miss Tilly, Mac was strong as ever, easily spinning my uncle around on his stool.

"Ever gonna stop calling me that?" Uncle Louie asked, taking Mac in.

"Thought you'd forgotten all about us," Mac said. "The one who got away."

"Not likely."

Uncle Louie left for Chicago at eighteen. I was five, and devastated. I still remember crying by the window, afraid I'd never see him again. But then he came back for pow wows and holidays, until he didn't.

"My grandson's taking a trip up north soon. He's into ghosts. Says Chicago's got a lot of 'em."

"Tell him to take the Haunted Highway Tour," Uncle Louie told him. "Best ghost lore in town."

"Let me write that down." Mac dug in his pocket for a pen.

"The old place is just the way I remember it." Uncle Louie looked about the joint. "You are too."

Mac had definitely aged. The Blue Gator, though, had always seemed old—cracked vinyl covering the stools, worn veneer on the tabletops and bar, smoke-stained paneling, scuffed-up floors, haggard faces at every turn. Uncle Louie's worn façade fit right in with the others. Mac was right that he'd gotten away, though I wasn't sure he'd gotten far. But who was I to judge? I glanced at my phone again.

The thought of a suicide note hadn't entered my mind until Sara implanted it via text. I hadn't thought about it because I was so sure Roddy hadn't killed himself. He wouldn't have left me.

But what if she finds a note? I wondered. *Would it mean that he didn't love me as much as I loved him?* Pondering it was torturous. I wanted to melt out of my skin, away from my brain. Nothing felt real. Of course I knew Roddy was gone and never coming back, but something kept it from sinking in, as if aluminum foil had been wrapped around my mind. I kept thinking—feeling, really—that Roddy and I would talk about this, that we'd figure things out, that he'd be back to normal tomorrow, that he really would return the call. He couldn't be gone. We'd exchanged texts only hours ago. Young and healthy, we'd be able to fix this. Somehow, I believed we would.

It was easier to think that than to endorse the truth. With Roddy, I felt ten years younger and as motivated to make something of myself as he was to claim the morning news anchor spot. Roddy made me feel stable and secure. He boosted my confidence in a way that made me think I could undo the mistakes of my past. He made me hopeful, too. So much so that I'd met with an adviser at Central Louisiana Community College who helped me pick out classes for the fall. Graphic arts. It sounded good. I was the happiest I'd ever been. Roddy was too. We'd told each other that.

Without him, I would go back to being the old Noemi. Still broken from the failure of my six-year stint with Ben. We'd been great friends through our twenties until we hooked up and initiated a relationship laden with endless drama—both good and bad—routine shouting matches followed by day-long cuddling sessions on the couch, and unpredictability that was sometimes exhilarating, sometimes alarming. I'd have married him if he'd asked, but he was more interested in sex and money than a wife and responsibility. That's not to say Ben didn't love me. I think he did. Our energies were just wrong. I was a bird in need of a nest. He was a hound on a scent trail, always chasing something: status, a fad, the world's next billion-dollar idea. Dream after unattainable dream.

Drained from the life we'd created, I left Ben in 2018, looking over my shoulder as I went, knowing I'd have to move back in with Mom because my savings were shot and my part-time shifts at the Daq Shack wouldn't cut it, even when combined with my monthly per capita checks. Post-Ben, I was the lone inhabitant on an island of regrets with no one there to help stop new ones from forming. Now, without Roddy, I could already feel the tectonic plates moving, bringing those regrets back to the surface.

Thinking about my future produced panic within me. How was I to start over? How could I get lightning to strike the same place twice?

Van Morrison's "Brown Eyed Girl" spilled through the Blue Gator's speakers just then. Our song. I could still see Roddy smiling and grooving on the dance floor at Andrew and Olivia's wedding, one hand waving me over as that opening riff of delicious double-stops rang out. It was pure chance that Roddy and I connected that night, and it was pure luck that he didn't care about college degrees, job titles, or incoming crow's feet.

Tears rimmed my eyes again. I pressed my hands to my ears, hard. I didn't notice that Sara had texted back until the song was over.

There's no note

SEVENTEEN

Louie

I wore an old sock on my hand to scrub the sunbaked armadillo blood from the Ford's front bumper. A small dent marred the metal where the luckless thing must have taken a hard hit.

"Ouchie." Noemi pointed at the gruesome mess. "You got hurt?"

"I'm not hurt. It's just dirt." She'd been playing with her dolls on the porch, feeding them imaginary cookies from an oatmeal container lid. "Finish your tea party."

I dipped my sock-covered hand into soapy water, then scrubbed hard enough to make my elbow ache. Reddish bubbles dripped from the bumper into the dirt. Noemi squatted next to me. Her diaper grazed the ground, her eyes bouncing from me to the blood and back. She knew I'd lied.

"Gimme cookies!" The soggy sock became a puppet intent on making her smile. "Gimme all your cookies or I'll eat you up!"

Giggling at the squeaky voice I made, Noemi scrambled to escape the sock. She started toward the porch, took a quick turn, ran around the truck, then streaked across the yard.

"Gammpa!" she yipped. "Gammpa!"

I peered around the bumper to find Grandpa Joe, a large bundle in his arms, coming down the road. "Noemi!" I hopped to my feet, but the incident from the day before had stuck with her. She came to a dead stop a few yards from the road and waited for Grandpa to meet her there.

"My lark!" He shifted the bundle so that he could kiss her cheek on his way to the trailer. "What happened?" he asked upon spying the dirty water in the bucket beside the truck.

"Ma had a little accident." With one last wipe, I let the sock slip off my hand. "It's done?"

"Done," he said. I dried my hand on my shorts and carried Noemi inside. Grandpa stepped carefully behind us. The bundle he carried was large and round, and it made a hollow thud when he set it on the floor. "Go ahead. Open it."

I tore through the paper wrapped around the gift. Noemi joined in, finding the wrapping more interesting than what it revealed. The large drum was rustic yet refined, made of rawhide and wood. Grandpa crafted the instruments and sold them to support himself, and though he'd made me smaller ones before, none could compare to a grand pow wow drum.

Not just an instrument, the drum is a significant symbol. Its round frame represents the earth. Its beat mimics that of our hearts. Its rhythm keeps us steady in celebration and war.

"It's perfect," I said, fingertips trembling atop the rawhide—soft yet firm—stretched across the frame. I tapped the skin and smiled. The resultant *thwump* seemed to grow stronger as it echoed off the trailer's paneled walls.

"Look." Grandpa pointed to the frame where he'd carved six alligators in the wood. They, too, were symbolic, because gators represent life in all its forms, on earth and in water, good and evil. Revered by our tribe, they're honored as much as they're feared. The fact that they've inhabited the earth for millions of years speaks of their resiliency. The way their wounds mend fast and without infection, despite

the swampy waters in which they swim, illustrates an incredible ability to heal. Their crafty nature—floating sticks on their snouts to attract and snatch nest-building birds—shines light on their frightening
intelligence, while their cannibalistic tendencies in times of scarcity
give weight to their coldblooded will to survive. Their bite, the stron-
gest of any North American animal, combines eighty conical teeth
with jaw muscles that can close with such force that attempting to pry
them apart would be like trying to lift a truck. That strength, coupled
with the way they rotate their bodies—the death roll!—once they've
locked onto prey, makes them masters of dismemberment and murder.
The sizes of the alligators Grandpa had carved into the wood indicated that there was one for each of us: me, Ma, Lula, Noemi, Gram,
and him.

He withdrew a beater from his waistband. The superbly sanded
handle felt like velvet in my hands. I recognized the wavy grain of the
wood. Bald cypress, the Louisiana state tree.

"Go ahead," he said.

I brought the beater down hard against the drum. The resultant
boom reverberated in my chest and birthed goose bumps all over my
arms. Noemi's eyes widened. Her mouth fell open in an astounded O.
I hit the drum again and again, forgetting that Ma was asleep in the
room at the end of the hall. Noemi's head bobbed in time with the
rhythm I made.

"It's in your blood," Grandpa said. "It's in Noemi's, too." He smiled.
"There's more." He handed me a smaller bundle from his pocket. A
slew of hand-carved dowels was inside, along with dozens of feathers
that fluffed to twice their size once unwrapped. "You'll need those."

I grasped Grandpa's shoulder and gave him a hug. He took my face
in his hands.

"You look tired, Louie. Troubled."

"Just tired." I chose to keep my concerns about Aubrey, Miss

Shelby, and the three graves to myself. "I'm watching Noemi and Johnny Deshautelle during the day now."

"Exhaustion puts bags under your eyes. Worry puts wrinkles in your brow." He ran a hand over my forehead to smooth it. "What's troubling you?"

I should have known I couldn't fool him. "It's everything. . . . *This*." My eyes passed over Noemi on the rundown shag and settled on the closed bedroom door down the hall. "I have two more years of high school and then it's all up in the air. Who's gonna take care of this? And them? What are my chances of ever getting away?"

"The past has put fear into you," Grandpa said. "You think you'll get stuck here like everyone else."

"Did you always wanna stay?"

"It's home."

"I'm not saying I wanna leave." I backpedaled for fear of hurting him. "It's just that there's not much here."

"You haven't seen all this land has to offer," he argued. "Most haven't."

"Are you talking about building the bingo hall?"

His pupils narrowed. "I'll tell you something that my grandfather told me: the hungry fish swims faster than the one that has fed." He paused. "You, Louie, are the hungry fish. You don't know what will satisfy you yet, but you'll keep swimming until you find it. I know you will. You're not like the others. Your mother and Lula, they're fish that fed early. You don't have to be one of them."

I let his point sink in and then asked about what I'd seen in his eyes. "You don't like the idea of the bingo hall, do you?"

"It comes with risk."

"It does?"

"The fish, Louie. Most in our tribe want a bingo hall because they've seen the Seminoles make big money with theirs. Money might make our lives easier, but it might also overfeed the already full fish. They just might stop swimming altogether."

I understood him then. I couldn't blame him for his concern. "Everyone's counting on you to find a way to finance it. They think it's what's best for the tribe."

"I know. I'll do what's right." He put a hand on my shoulder and smiled. He looked like the most genuine man in the world when his face cracked like that. "Enjoy your drum." He kissed Noemi again, then reached for the door.

"Can we talk about the cemetery?" My question stopped him in his tracks. "It's something else that's been on my mind."

Grandpa turned, face stony once more. "Luke and Sam will find who did it."

"It's not that. There's just something I need to know." I swallowed the lump in my throat, dense as raw dough. "Why haven't the graves been reburied?" That wasn't the question I'd meant to ask. It just came out.

"You've been to the cemetery?"

"Jean-Luc and I . . . we wanted to see what was going on. We didn't go inside. We only looked."

"They'll be reburied when Luke and Sam say it's time."

"Will you tell me which bones were taken?" That's what I'd meant to ask. "It . . . it wasn't her whole skeleton, was it?"

He retreated from the door and sat. "Whether her bones are in the ground or not, your grandmother's spirit is at ease. It's one with the world around us."

"I know."

"What happened in the cemetery causes *us* pain, not her. You understand that, don't you?"

I nodded. And persisted. "I *deserve* to know. I'm a man in this tribe now. You said so when you told me I could perform the warrior dance."

"You are a man. A good one too. But you're also my grandson, and

I must do what's best for you." His impenetrable eyes indicated that his mind was made up. "You'd do the same for Noemi. I know you would."

He had me there. Still, I couldn't curb my curiosity. "What about George Saucier? Why'd he want to see his son in the cemetery?"

"Because he loves Horace as much as you love your grandmother."

"Did you let him look?"

"Let it be, Louie." Grandpa shook his head and stood. Opening the door, he asked, "What did she hit?"

"Huh?" I hardly heard him, the cemetery on my mind.

"Your mother. What'd she hit with the truck?"

"Oh. An armadillo."

His lips turned down. He hummed. "On her way to work or on her way back home?"

"She didn't say." Grandpa took a step back. The screen door fell shut. "Does it make a difference?"

"They carry disease, you know." His faraway stare shifted from the truck outside to the coffee table. At the time, I thought he'd been talking about armadillos and leprosy. Looking back, I think he meant the cans Ma left strewn about.

"So many," he muttered. His eyes narrowed the way they had when he told me and Ma about the unearthed graves. He proceeded to do something he'd never done in the trailer before. He cleaned up.

"I'll do that."

"A bag," he said.

I pulled the biggest one I could find from the gap between the refrigerator and the wall where we kept them. Grandpa collected an armful of cans and deposited them inside. And then he collected another.

"I would have gotten rid of them this morning, but—"

"I know, Louie. There are more than before."

I hadn't noticed the change in number. The increase had been gradual. I guess Grandpa could see it because he wasn't there every day. I tied the full bag up and set it by the door.

"I'd better check on Ernest now." He took a last look at Ma's bedroom door on his way out.

Though Noemi was quietly coloring in the corner, I felt utterly alone after Grandpa left. I wondered why Ma hadn't made a peep when I pounded on the drum. It was one thing for her to sleep through the arguments Lula and I had from time to time, but the drum? How could she ignore it?

I rushed to her room, turned the doorknob, and opened the door. Something crept out when I did. It wasn't something I could see or feel with my fingers, yet it possessed power so strong it made my head swim.

I saw for the first time that Ma wasn't just tired. She wasn't beautiful either. Not anymore. Not like when I was little, back when she'd sing songs while plucking wildflowers that grew tall along the road. She'd gotten herself into the grip of something awful, something that made her so sick—so spiritless, so wasted—that she could barely see me when she staggered in and out of the house. Her condition made me fear that if Noemi, Lula, and I stayed around we wouldn't just continue to be ignored, we might get sick ourselves.

"Stay put," I said to Noemi. Grandpa had just left Ern's. He looked depleted, like Ern had sucked everything out of him the same way he'd suck the head of a boiled crawdad clean. I ran to Grandpa on the road. "Let us stay with you," I said. "I don't think Noemi should be around Ma anymore. It's not good for her. It can't be good for me either."

Grandpa's shoulders slumped a bit more. "You can't leave her." He didn't even stop to consider my request. "She needs you."

"She doesn't. She barely talks to me. I've tried. She doesn't want me. She doesn't want Lula or Noemi either. She looks right through us."

"That might be a sign of just how much she needs you. Trust me, Louie. She does need you."

"For what?"

Grandpa, with all his wisdom, shrugged. "We all need something. Some people—the lucky ones—can fulfill their needs themselves. Others require a little help."

"What should I do?"

"Let her know you're there. Don't let her forget."

"But what about me? You wouldn't tell me about the bones because you said you had to do what's best for me. Well, what about now?"

"Would things get better if you came to live with me? Would *she* get better? You wouldn't stop worrying about her. You'd only worry more. Trust me, Louie."

I pulled my fingers through my hair. "Think about it?" I begged.

"Think about her. She's been left before, and I'm afraid that's why she is the way she is. If you leave her too . . . well . . . who knows what might happen to her then."

"Who left her? My father?" I'd never met the man who abandoned Ma before I was born.

"Him too," Grandpa said. Eyes to the earth, he went on his way.

EIGHTEEN

Louie

I hauled the bag of Ma's empty cans, along with our household trash, outside after Ma left for work. I set the bag of cans next to the porch steps. It'd go into the bed of the pickup when Ma got home in the morning. Bernie Mayfield over in Effie paid eight dollars for every forty pounds of aluminum I brought him. He told me thirty-four empty cans weighed one pound, which meant I had to bring him thirteen hundred and sixty cans to get the full eight dollars. It seemed like an astronomical amount, but I always ended up with eight bucks in my pocket whenever I went to see him.

I dragged the rest of the trash to the firepit behind the trailer, full of ash from last week's garbage. The sky was inky black, spotted with starry spirits. The encompassing wind felt like cool water rushing over my skin. Bending to strike a match that would ignite the trash and overpower the chill, a sudden scream made me quake. The match fell from my fingers.

Slicing the night like a razor blade through paper, the scream was high-pitched and piercing, and it sounded within reach rather than riding on the wind. Surrounded by cicadas, chest heaving, neck prickling, I scanned the darkness, fearing I wouldn't make it back to the trailer if something were on the prowl. And then another scream, so shrill it made me shiver, slapped me upside the head. It came from the direction of the river, maybe half a mile down the road.

I ran from the firepit to the front yard. Ern must have torn the screen from his window because his head and hulking shoulders, living shadows in the darkness, jutted far beyond the frame. He looked stuck.

"Louie!" he hollered.

"What's happening?" I foolishly believed that he, the ever-present watcher, could see through the blackness better than I.

Another scream exploded in my ears. I wavered between home and the unknown, eventually running for the road because someone was suffering out there.

"Louie!" Ern's volume matched that of the scream. He clung to the flimsy windowsill with one hand while ferociously pounding against it with the other. "Louie, come back! *Louie!*"

His fury frightened me. It drove me toward the scream faster than before, my arms and legs revolving like wheel rods on an accelerating train. I didn't think about the *what-ifs* of what I might be getting myself into. I only wanted to help whoever was in need.

It wasn't until the safety of my trailer was well behind me that my daring wore off. It was night. It was dark. I was on a stretch of road without a house or a human in sight. My legs slowed, then stopped. My breath came fast. I tasted dirt on my tongue. The thought that entered my brain had nothing to do with whoever might be out there suffering. It had to do with suffering I hoped to avoid.

"*The Takoda Vampire,*" I whispered. Encircled by blackness, I admonished myself for saying those words out loud. Skin crawling from head to toe, my balls pulled tight to my body. I leaped straight into the air when another scream slashed the silence. It was worse than those before it—long, grating, swollen with despair.

I proceeded with my gaze glued to the ground as I came upon the

Saucier place. About to pass it, something pulled my eyes its way. I didn't look by choice, I'm certain of that. I only saw the house in a split-second blur, but the slanted shed next to it held my eyes hostage long enough for me to see its door slowly inching open.

"*No*," I uttered, racing away. The word came out like the warning one gets when driving over a rumble strip, automatic and absolute. My six-year-old self would have seen the ghost of Horace Saucier emerging from the shed, but I couldn't allow that at sixteen. Not when the screams of someone suffering were hanging on the air.

My heart verged on detonating in my chest by the time I saw signs of life ahead. Blinding headlights, intermittently obscured by black blurs, spanned the road's width, indicating that the road was blocked. Sharp and severe voices met my ears.

I slowed. The dread that had already taken root within me yielded a leafless tree with knotted branches. Not since the heart attack that steered Jim Deshautelle into a ditch a year and a half earlier had a road been blocked on the rez. My gaze inched from one side of the street to the other. Darkened figures loomed within the light. Escaping the rays of harsh high beams, I staggered past a row of trucks, ultimately recognizing where I was. The Lavergnes' tiny house stood fifty feet down the dirt drive. It was there that I'd seen Thomas in the grass the day before.

Miss Shelby was my first thought. Autumn Lavergne, Thomas's wife, must have stumbled upon her in the darkness. Autumn must have been the one who'd screamed.

The night grew colder the closer I got to the huddled mass standing in the dirt driveway. A stew of voices challenged my ears. I couldn't tell what anyone was saying. Nor could I make out faces. I nearly pissed my pants at the sound of my name.

"Louie?"

I held a hand over my eyes to cut through the glare of more headlights. "Who's there?"

"Oh, Louie," the voice cried. Arms wrapped around me. I pulled the body close just to feel its heat, soon realizing that I had Miss Tilly in my grasp, the greasy scent of french fries and spilled beer clinging to her clothes.

Before I could ask what had happened, the screaming, which would eventually morph into sobbing, began again.

"Is that Miss Autumn?" I asked.

"That's her," Miss Tilly whispered.

"She found Miss Shelby?"

Miss Tilly's body stiffened. She held me a moment longer, then pressed a hand against my chest to put a few inches between us. "What are you talking about?"

I shook my head and swallowed to lubricate my gritty throat. "Did she find Miss Shelby?"

"No, sugar . . . it's not that."

I pulled away from her and focused until I made out Mac Langdon, Miss Vicky, Eaton Ballard, Sawyer Picote, Miss Paula, Mark Bishop, and Ray Horn facing the lawn in front of the house, their fretful fingers ushering cigarettes to and from their quivering lips. Swirling smoke drifted into the night like ghosts around them. Turning even more, I saw Sam Peltier in the front yard. Luke Fisher was there too, doing his best to keep Miss Autumn from falling to the ground, right about where I'd seen Thomas with his mower. Thomas himself stood motionless by Luke. Everything from his face to his limbs looked limp.

"What's wrong with them?" Numb from the screams and the eventual horror the scene promised to unveil, the words fell from my mouth like chunks of ice.

No one answered my question. No one needed to. An awful stench assaulted my nose precisely as the beam from Sam's flashlight swept over the grass. There, just a few feet from Autumn and Luke, was something unrecognizable at first, something smeared with sludge yet sickly yellow in spots from the beam of Sam's light. I stared at it, creeping closer, not realizing what I was seeing.

"Louie . . ." Miss Tilly tried pulling me back. The touch of her frigid fingertips against my skin made everything sink in. It was the soiled and glistening body of Miss Autumn's mother, Fay, crumpled in the grass.

I gaped at the horror, unable to look away.

"Let's go inside," Luke said to Miss Autumn. "You don't need to see this."

Miss Autumn refused. I realized then that she wasn't having trouble standing. She just wanted to get to her mother. To hold her. To soothe her. To make her better somehow.

"What happened?" I whispered to Miss Tilly.

"Fay fell into the septic tank," she whispered back. "It's awful. Just awful."

Sam turned, his light momentarily flashing over Thomas's limp limbs again. I saw now that they were coated with the same vile sludge all over Fay.

"Louie? That you?"

I squinted against the darkness. Someone approached from the other side of the yard.

"This some crazy shit, man, or what?" I recognized the voice then, distorted, probably by a wad of chewing tobacco. "Have you been here the entire time?"

"I came after I heard the screams," I said to J.L.

"I guess we all heard 'em." I thought his teeth were chattering like mine, but then I realized he was chewing, grinding. "Think she thought it was a swimming hole?" he asked. "She was losing her marbles, wasn't she?"

Thomas's body suddenly shook, as if he'd been jolted awake. He held his arms out in front of him, making it look like he was about to embrace Miss Autumn, then said, "The hose." He lurched to the side of the house and turned the spigot to rinse himself clean.

"Let us through." Luke proceeded to lead Miss Autumn through the yard. They didn't go inside the house. Miss Autumn wouldn't. They sat on the steps instead, helplessly staring toward the mound on the ground just in case Miss Fay suddenly started breathing.

"What are they gonna do?" I muttered.

"Huh?" J.L. hadn't followed Miss Autumn with his eyes. He was still staring at the dead woman.

"How're they gonna get through this?"

"They should talk with the Forstalls." The words sounded insensitive, but I don't think J.L. meant for them to sound that way. He probably thought his suggestion was the logical thing to do.

Sam covered Miss Fay's body with a sheet. Though grown, she looked small—skinny and withered. I breathed easier once she was out of sight. Grandpa Joe showed up shortly after that. So did Chris Horn, who handled the dead on the reservation. With Sam's help, Chris zipped Fay into a black bag and gently slid the woman into the back of his station wagon. He'd clean her up and prepare her body for the wake.

"I don't understand how this happened."

"What's to understand? She tried to take a swim," J.L. said.

"At this time? With no one around to stop her?" The Lavergnes had always kept a close eye on Miss Fay.

"Well"—J.L. shrugged—"let's get the lowdown." He started for the field closest to the house. "Come on."

I made sure no one was watching, especially Grandpa Joe, then crept behind him. Staying low, we cut through the tall grass that pricked our skin, ultimately crouching in the shadows on the far left side of the house, away from the front steps.

"We're gonna get busted," I whispered.

J.L. held a finger to his lips. My bladder throbbed, threatening me and my pants. Miss Autumn continued to cry. Even though we weren't face-to-face with her, we could make out what she, Luke, and Thomas—who'd joined them on the steps—said.

"You thought she was getting sick?" Luke asked.

"She'd . . . she'd been . . ." Miss Autumn said.

"She'd been quiet all day," Thomas stepped in. "Not quite herself. She went to bed early, then woke up around nine."

"Was it unusual for her to wake up like that?"

"No," Thomas said. "Dementia can make it hard to stay asleep."

"She was confused. . . ." Miss Autumn went on. "Standing in her closet thinking it was her old shed back home, looking for fertilizer. She said she had to feed her lilies. I should have left her there. . . . If only I'd left her . . ."

"Don't do that to yourself," Luke said. "There's no way you could have known what would happen." He paused. "What did you do after you helped her from the closet?"

"I . . . I . . ." Miss Autumn stammered. Jean-Luc inched closer to the trailer's corner and peeked around the side for a better look. "I . . . I just rubbed her back. I reminded her that she was at my house and that everything was all right."

I dug a pebble out of the dirt and fired it at J.L.'s head. He kicked a spray of dust back at me.

"She was restless," Miss Autumn said. "Pulling me toward the door. Talking about lilies."

"Autumn could barely hold on to her," Thomas muttered. "Doesn't make sense. . . . She was so frail."

"Did you try to stop her?" Luke asked Tom.

"I was going over bills," he said. "I was going over bills when I should have—"

Miss Autumn whimpered. "She felt warm. I thought she might be coming down with something. That's what I told Tom."

"It was my idea to take her onto the steps." His voice cracked upon making the admission. "I'd forgotten all about the septic tank's broken lid. I never would have suggested taking Fay out if—"

"The air's so cool tonight," Miss Autumn mercifully cut him off. "That's why he said to take her out."

"I thought the weather would do her good. And that she'd realize her lilies weren't out here. I told Autumn to sit with her on the steps. It's not like we'd never done that before."

"We all like to sit out on cool nights," Luke said.

"She got quiet as soon as we sat down," Miss Autumn sobbed, putting my heart in a vise. "This is the last place I hugged my mom."

The rustling of Miss Autumn and Thomas wordlessly trying to console each other lasted longer than a minute. I wondered what Luke was doing during that time. Never in a million years would I have wanted to be in his boots.

"My mama . . ." Miss Autumn cried like a child. "I want her back. I want her the way she was. . . ."

Luke let another minute pass. "Tell me what happened."

"She stopped talking about the lilies. I thought she was getting tired, so I rubbed her back . . . and then . . . then . . ."

I could barely take it. Listening to Miss Autumn recount the final moments of her mother's life was like yanking a fishhook from my eye.

"What, Autumn? What happened?" Thomas's voice was more watery than before. It hadn't dawned on me that he still didn't know exactly what had happened to his mother-in-law.

"I started to doze," Miss Autumn gasped. "I was tired. . . . I fell asleep. I didn't feel her sneak away . . . didn't know she was gone until my chin hit my chest and I startled awake. You know how that happens when you're fighting off sleep?"

"Of course," Luke said. "So you didn't see it happen?"

The question elicited a low moan. "I saw it," she cried. "At first I thought she was gone . . . lost in the field. If it wasn't for the white of her diaper, I might not have noticed her at all. She'd stripped off her clothes. We had her in a diaper because . . . well, sometimes she had accidents. She was standing over there in the dark by Tom's truck, just staring at me. I called to her. I told her to come back. When I got up to get her, she started to run. Backward. I couldn't believe it. She'd been so unstable the last few months . . . all wobbly and crooked without a walker. But she wasn't like that tonight. I thought I'd catch her at first, but . . . she ran so fast."

"I should have been out here with you," Thomas muttered.

"The worst thing about it was the look on her face," Miss Autumn said. "She was smiling at me. Like it was fun. Like we were playing a game. Naked. Running backward. The closer she got to the septic tank, the faster she ran. And then she just stopped, only a foot from it, like she'd hit an invisible wall. I ran to her and reached for her hands. She grabbed me around the wrists. 'Come inside,' I'd said, and I'd barely been able to say it because her smile was widening and her eyes weren't blinking and I'd never seen her look so strange before. She took a step backward and then she was gone, plummeting, dragging me down. And I hate to say it, but . . ."

"What is it, Autumn?" Thomas asked.

"I think she wanted to take me into the tank with her."

"That can't be! She was confused. Like when you found her in the closet. She probably didn't even know the tank was beneath her. She didn't know she was in danger."

"Maybe . . . but I swear, Tom, she was smiling when she took that plunge, yanking me to my knees. She wouldn't let go of my wrists."

NINETEEN

Noemi

My sight had gone so blurry that I couldn't reread the words in Sara's last text. Did it say what I thought it said? Were those tears of joy muddying my vision, or were they in response to a truth I wanted to deny?

I grabbed a square napkin from the caddy holding straws and the little paper umbrellas Miss Tilly liked to stick in her homemade Hurricanes. I dabbed my eyes and read the message again.

There's no note

Fingers trembling, I had to fix four typos before sending my response.

I knew it!

So relieved I could whoop, I hugged the phone to my chest, nearly toppling off the stool.

Uncle Louie jolted in my direction, probably thinking I was going to fall. "Are you . . . ?" he started.

I spun around without answering, waiting for whatever Sara would send next. I'd known I was right from the start because when you know, you know, like when Andrew and Olivia announced they were pregnant and I instantly knew she was carrying a girl, or when Roddy bet that they'd ask us to be godparents and I told him there wasn't a chance in hell because Olivia thought I smoked too much weed. I was right on both accounts. Roddy hated when I'd rub it in.

Still no response from Sara. My anxious fingers tapped at the screen, composing a message I immediately knew I shouldn't have sent.

I told YOU!

I couldn't remember if I'd told Sara she wouldn't find a suicide note or not, but I'd told everyone else that Roddy wouldn't have done *it*, so I didn't bother walking the text back. In the moment, the relief of knowing that he hadn't chosen to leave me felt like a win, like everything would somehow be okay. I wanted to call him again to talk it through. But then the next text dropped, and my heart broke into smaller pieces than before.

Are you gloating!? No note doesn't change things. My brother is still dead!

Dead. I don't know much about how the brain works, but it does an incredible job of putting up walls right where and when you need them. Sara's text took a wrecking ball to the wall protecting me from crippling pain, leaving me vulnerable, unsheltered, and cold. Roddy must have been cold too. I'd never feel his warmth again.

Short of breath, I was sliding from the stool. My feet touched ground. Another text lit up my screen.

When's the last time you were
here?

Rewinding to three days earlier, my brain poured the foundation for a stronger fortification. I had to defend Roddy against the accusation made against him.

Tuesday

I'd gotten to Roddy's a little after four. We stretched out on the couch, Roddy's strong hands kneading knots out of my back, before going to dinner at the new Cajun barbecue in Ruby, recommended by the food hound who reviews restaurants on the morning news. We were back on the couch before seven, digesting until cuddling turned into . . .

A gut punch that would wreck any wall knocked the breath out of me. I'd never have him again.

Was the mirror like this?

A photo came attached to Sara's text, showing the mirror that hung in Roddy's living room. It was cracked with the worst of the damage smack-dab in the middle, a spiderweb of fractured glass, as if a fist had punched it, as if whoever had been looking into the mirror had tried to knock himself out.

Did u need a key to get in?

What's it matter?

It just does

The door was locked

I bit the inside of my cheek, accepting that Roddy must have smashed the mirror himself. I couldn't remember looking at it on Tuesday, but I probably would have noticed if it was broken.

Don't think it was cracked

Could someone have been with him?

Toad saw Roddy leave alone

Toad was the kid next door. So Roddy must have left his place and locked the door behind him. But why break the mirror?

It could have been an accident, I thought. Accidents do happen. Or maybe something had gotten him a little too upset. Maybe he had a rough day at work.

Has anyone talked to his boss?

Yeah. That explained it. He probably hit the mirror in frustration, then hit the pavement to blow off some steam, his preoccupation distracting him from where he was going . . . and from that fucking Jeep.

I could accept that Roddy had broken the mirror accidentally or that he'd done it out of irritation, but I couldn't entertain the third option. There was no way he would have wanted to smash his news anchor–worthy face.

TWENTY

Louie

Thomas Lavergne's words echoed in my ears the morning after the accident.

She must have slipped, he'd said about his mother-in-law. *She never saw it coming.*

Considering Miss Autumn's version of things, I wasn't so sure that Thomas was right. My unease about Miss Shelby, Aubrey, the unearthed graves, Horace, and the Takoda Vampire—always the vampire—may have tainted my interpretation of what Miss Autumn had said, but it didn't sound like Fay had simply taken a misstep into the septic tank. It sounded like Fay knew what she was doing, and like she'd wanted Miss Autumn to join her in that god-awful pool of sludge. It sounded like Miss Autumn believed that too.

I resolved not to look at the yard when I, Noemi in the wagon behind me, came upon the Lavergne house on my way to Miss Doris's, but horrible things have a way of demanding attention, and I couldn't ignore it. My eyes went straight to the scene of the supposed accident, yellow tape warning me to stay away.

My rib cage tightened around my lungs. The squeak of the wagon's wheels competed with the echo in my head.

She wouldn't let go of my wrists.

I ran the rest of the way to Miss Doris's trailer. Miss Paula Bishop was driving away when I reached the door.

"That poor, sweet woman," Miss Doris said the instant Noemi and I stepped inside. "Poor, poor Fay."

"Miss Paula was here?" I knew she must have given Miss Doris an earful.

"Can you imagine?" Miss Doris shook her head. "What an awful way to die."

A monkey-man howl punctuated Miss Doris's declaration. Johnny leaped from behind her chair and collided with my legs, sending a stab of pain deep into my left knee. Better than my balls, I thought.

"Easy, big guy." I set Noemi down.

"I'm a gorilla!" Johnny darted behind the chair again.

"Were you at the Lavergnes' last night?" Miss Doris asked.

I reluctantly nodded, rubbing my knee.

"You must have heard the screams. I heard them from here. I would've gone down the road to help, but my back . . . well, you know how it is. I just wonder what Fay was doing out alone at that hour. I mean, she must have been alone, right? She wouldn't have fallen in if they'd been watching her."

I kept Jean-Luc's and my secret to myself. "It's so sad," I said, hoping she'd let that be the end of it. I picked up Johnny's bag to let her know I was ready to go.

"How in the world . . ." She pressed her palms to her temples. "Thomas and Autumn . . . God's grace be with them." She made the sign of the cross over her body. "They're so young and capable. You'd think they'd be able to keep a declining senior safe. They're not encumbered like me. If Little John got loose . . . well, I don't even want to think about that. . . . I'd never be able to catch him."

"Does he have his shoes on?" Listening to her speculate was worse than having a screw twisted beneath my thumbnail.

Miss Doris sighed. "Little John!" She smacked her flyswatter against her tray table. He burst from behind the recliner on his hands and knees, his shoes already laced up. "You'll pass the Lavergnes' house on your way home, won't you?"

"Yes," I confessed.

"Then do me a favor." Pushing down hard against her cane, she stood. "I have this nice pie here that I'd like you to bring them. It should be just about ready." She lumbered to the kitchen and pulled the oven door open.

I wasn't aware of the pie until she mentioned it. Its warm aroma suddenly encircled me. "You baked?"

"It was already baked, I just had to warm it from the freezer. Blueberry. It's right for mourning." She slipped her hand inside a mitt and took the pie from the oven. "It's hot, so I'll just put it in this box here, and you can drop it off for me. Make sure you tell them how sorry I am."

"Wouldn't you rather tell them yourself?" My mind spun in search of ways to get out of the task. The thought of knocking on the Lavergnes' door the morning after they'd fished their mother from their own waste made my stomach lurch.

"My back's extra stiff today." She hobbled toward me while struggling to balance the pie box with one hand. "You tell them that. They'll understand why I couldn't come."

I ended up with the pie in my hands and a lump in my throat that prevented me from saying no.

"Tell them I'll see them at the wake."

No way in hell was I going to tell them that.

Miss Doris dropped onto the edge of her chair and snagged Johnny with one hand. "You listen to Louie." She pulled him close and gave him a kiss on the head.

"I'm a gorilla," he said again on our way out the door.

Babbling in the language only toddlers understand, Noemi and

131

Johnny rode happily behind me while I fretted over the pie, ever-so-appetizingly riding atop the potty-training chair. I considered giving it to Ern, knowing he'd get rid of the evidence for me. And fast. But there was always the chance that Miss Doris would ask the Lavergnes about it later. I never could tell what would come out of her mouth.

I stopped the wagon where the Lavergnes' dirt drive met the dirt road. The curtains over the house's windows were closed. Miss Fay would never wave to me again.

"I guess I gotta do it." I turned to the kids as if they might offer me a way out. Johnny hoisted a foot over the side of the wagon. I prevented him from planting it on the ground by turning down the drive.

Nowhere to turn, I felt like I was in a tunnel on my way to the door, trapped by my conscience because Miss Doris had asked for a favor and I hadn't had the stones to tell her no.

I dropped the wagon's handle at the base of the stairs and slowly picked up the pie. It warmed my hand through the box. My mind's eye could see what I needed to do—climb the steps and knock on the door. Problem was, my body wouldn't do it. It just left me standing there, stupidly staring. Sweat trickling down my temples, dread began to rise. The door was going to open. I could feel it. I could feel something else there too. Something cold, as if the chill from the night before was still swirling in that spot. Desperate to get gone, I dropped the pie onto the step where Miss Autumn had last embraced her mom.

"*Shhh.*" Shushing the kids, I ran for the road, the wagon wheels' high-pitched squeals ratting me out. Stealing a glance over my shoulder, I saw a curtain move.

"Louie," the ominous speck called the instant home came into sight. Flat, Ern's voice was nothing like the angry howl it'd been in the night. Too distraught to talk about Miss Fay after J.L. and I had eavesdropped on the Lavergnes, I'd yet to tell Ern what the screaming had been about. I motioned toward the kids and shrugged, hustling them inside.

They found my drum in no time, and I didn't feel bad letting them beat it. Ma had already proved that she could sleep through anything. I worked on the adornments that would add intensity to my pow wow outfit while they played. Lula had given me beads she'd gotten from Grandpa a few years back. She'd been instructed to use them on an outfit of her own, but she never had. Maybe, I thought, amid cursing at the needle I couldn't thread, Lula would have done things differently if Ma had done them with her.

"Your turn, Douie." Noemi tried to put the beater in my hand. "Make it go *boom boom!*"

Having finally gotten the thread through the eye, I pinched the needle tight. "Sing me a song," I told her.

Making up a melody of meaningless sounds, she sang, Johnny drummed, and I stitched beads onto my buckskin vest, doing my meager best to make my pow wow outfit look a little less crude. With as many pricks in my fingers as in the buckskin, I ultimately settled on a simple design that almost resembled the ridges on an alligator's back.

In addition to fine beadwork, most dancers wore bells around their knees or ankles. Too poor to afford good janglers, I used what I had at hand: tabs from the tops of Ma's cans. Strung up right, they jingled just like bells.

TWENTY-ONE

Louie

I brushed my hair with my fingers and wiped sweat from my forehead knowing I'd be dripping by the time I arrived at the Lavergnes' house. There was nothing I could do about that. Ma rustled in her room. A snap and fizz echoed between her walls. I asked if she wanted to come, my mouth inches from her closed bedroom door. Several long seconds ticked by. She said no. There was nothing I could do about that either.

I passed the Saucier place on my way to the wake. I didn't think about Horace or what the vampire took from him, aside from his life. I just thought about Miss Fay, sludgy and sickly yellow, illuminated by the glow of Sam Peltier's flashlight. I knew Fay couldn't possibly look worse than she had atop the freshly mown grass, but I still dreaded setting eyes on her in her casket.

Four cars sat parked in the Lavergnes' drive. A bouquet of wild-flowers hung by a string from a hook on the door, and an unattended fire burned in the pit where the Lavergnes usually burned their trash. I willed myself to go inside the house, a feat as arduous as pulling one of my own teeth. Oppressive air washed over me inside. Hot. Humid. Swollen with sadness. My chest tightened like a snake constricting around its prey. The Lavergnes' place was bigger than ours, sprawling with a designated dining room and an extra bath. The biggest difference between our homes that day, though, was the slew of folding chairs stationed in front of Chris Horn's casket stand in the living room.

Woeful eyes cast solemn stares in my direction as soon as the door clicked shut behind me. I wished I were like the painted turtles I saw swimming in the river. I longed to pull my head inside a shell, to block out the mourners and the casket on the stand.

I lowered my gaze while dropping onto the seat of the nearest empty chair. The almost-cool breeze of an oscillating fan offered split-second relief, and then it was gone, leaving me more uncomfortable than before. I knew the proper course of action was to offer Miss Autumn and Thomas my sympathy, but I couldn't do it. Both were on the couch, two sorrowful spirits among throw pillows, Miss Autumn clutching a stuffed bear in a bloodless fist.

"Louie," someone whispered.

My eyes shot up and my gaze collided with the casket. Open. Horrific. The graceless form of Miss Doris approaching through the folding chairs mercifully obstructed my view. I noticed J.L. a few feet to her right, sitting beside his dad in a collared shirt that looked out of place on him.

Miss Doris fell onto the seat next to mine. "There's food on the kitchen counter," she said, in what should have been a whisper but was just an airier version of her regular voice.

I glanced into the kitchen, spotted the blueberry pie.

"Miss Paula gave me a ride. I wouldn't have made it otherwise." Miss Doris grabbed her back and sucked air through her teeth.

"That's good," I rasped.

"Go on." She motioned with her cane. "Pay your respects, then get a nice bite to eat."

My jaw clenched, my stomach gurgled, my masochistic eyes

looked straight at Fay. Photos, knickknacks, and small gifts sat on display around her casket, alongside prayer feathers—representing the belief that eagles carry prayers up to the Great Spirit in the sky—and carved sticks meant to reinforce even more prayers for Fay. A crucifix hung tacked to the interior of the casket's lid. The offerings were there in accordance with traditional tribal beliefs. The crucifix was there in accordance with our adopted Catholic faith.

I stood to get the inevitable over with. Miss Doris's cane would have made my journey a hell of a lot easier. I didn't look at Miss Fay's face when I sidled next to the box. Her wilted body, wrapped in a mulberry bark blanket, was bad enough.

Hand shaking, I spilled some candies next to the other offerings just as the trailer door creaked open. Turning with the rest of the mourners, I saw Grandpa Joe step in, followed by Ma, wearing the shapeless T-shirt she'd worn to bed.

"How'd you get her to come?" I whispered to Grandpa upon fleeing from Miss Fay.

"Fathers have power sons don't possess." He proceeded to do what I hadn't. He faced the Lavergnes. Thomas stood to shake his hand. Miss Autumn reached up and wrapped him in a feeble hug.

"Ma," I said. Unable to remember the last time we'd embraced, I wanted to hug her like Grandpa hugged Miss Autumn. I reached for her, but she didn't see me, only the bottle of whiskey on the counter with the food. She resisted rushing to it, staggering instead to the chair in the corner where she plopped onto her ass, her chin burrowing between her breasts.

"Hardly recognized her," Miss Doris said, her voice still a little too loud.

"Huh?" I grunted, reclaiming my seat.

"Your mother?" Miss Doris's face was puzzled.

"She works nights." The excuse fell out of me. Miss Doris smiled for my sake, staring at the corner where Ma, eyes closed, sat like a stuffed toy, formerly loved but tossed aside for one that hasn't lost its filling yet.

My stomach grew heavy. I wondered how long I'd have to stay and how long the rest of them would sit staring at the old lady in the box. While the others grieved, I reacquainted myself with a six-year-old scar on the back of my hand, a reminder of the rock that bit into my flesh after I took a hard fall from one of the trees hanging over the river. I remembered how the blood burst into the water, like a cloud blowing away on the wind.

"Louie?" Miss Doris's breath tickled my ear. "Would you bring me a nice piece of pie?"

The question drained me. How could she eat in front of Fay?

"Louie?" She nudged my side hard enough to make me sway. "Did you hear what I said?"

My chin dipped. Somehow, I stood and tottered to the counter. The blueberry pie, lumpy filling oozing out like a reminder of what I'd seen smeared all over Fay, made my upset stomach judder. A whimper slithered from my throat. If Miss Doris noticed my trembling hands when I handed her the paper plate with her piece of pie on it, she kept her mouth shut for once.

I listened to her chew. "Blueberry is good for mourning," she remarked, mouth full. The trailer door creaked again. I choked on air when George Saucier stepped inside.

A rosary clutched in his hand, he looked lost until his eyes landed on Thomas and Miss Autumn, still in the company of Grandpa Joe. George quickly crossed the room to the Lavergnes. My gaze followed. George, Thomas, and Miss Autumn whispered for a while. Grandpa whispered with them. My ears strained to hear what they were saying, especially when Grandpa and George started whispering to each other.

Ma continued to doze in the corner. Miss Doris continued to chew. I noticed that George's veiny hands shook like mine when he gave Miss Autumn his rosary. I also noticed that his skin looked gray. Like it never saw the sun. Like that of a vampire.

George's wobbly arms wrapped around Miss Autumn. I figured he'd go as quickly as he'd come, but a shriek that rang out from the first row of folding chairs impeded his exit.

More shrieks and countless gasps followed. Chairs toppled as frantic witnesses to the abnormal occurrence taking place raced to put distance between themselves and the horror in front of them. Miss Autumn unleashed the same scream that'd woken the reservation two evenings earlier, only quieting after Thomas wrapped his arms around her so tight that she couldn't fill her lungs with any more air.

I jumped to my feet because it was no longer possible to sit. Even Miss Doris stood without the assistance of her cane. The only one who may have remained in her seat was Ma, but I didn't look at her to check. My eyes belonged to the woman sitting straight up in her casket.

The mulberry bark blanket fell away from Fay's body. Stiff and still at first, she mimicked a post or a tree on a windless day. Then, lower jaw falling open, eyes wide and white, her head jerked to the left, making a click like that of an old TV dial being snapped into place. Chin toward her chest, her eyelids dropped, then sprang up and down, up and down, mimicking those of a baby doll that blinks when rocked just right.

Staggering backward, a scream rose in my throat, only to be stifled by my inability to breathe. She was the most hideous thing I'd ever seen, far more frightening than anything my imagination had ever cooked up about George Saucier.

Fay's head moved in irregular motions until her unseeing eyes lined up with Miss Autumn's.

"God help us." Miss Doris looked like she might spill her pie back onto her plate. She made the sign of the cross over her body, again and again, like she couldn't stop. "Lord, lead her to her rest."

"Everyone out." Grandpa spread his arms out at his sides to usher us toward the door. His order went ignored. Fay, if it really was her, had us firmly under her spell. We whimpered when her jaw clicked open. We screamed when sound came out.

Footsteps hammered the floor. The screen door slammed.

"Tom!" Miss Autumn shrieked, sinking, sinking, sinking.

"Go!" Grandpa Joe commanded, a finger pointing toward the door. Ma, unmoving in the corner, mirrored Fay in the casket, her head cocked at the very same angle. Even her eyes looked just as dead. She was as unaware of Fay as she was of me. I staggered backward and saw Thomas, who looked like he didn't know whether to comfort or condemn his mother-in-law, scoop Fay into his arms. She fell limp the instant he touched her, definitely dead.

TWENTY-TWO

Noemi

Two texts that weren't from Sara came through. I left them unread, my fingers thrumming against the phone screen to keep it from slipping into sleep mode. Uncle Louie's apprehensive expression matched mine. A can tab pinched between his forefinger and thumb, he tapped it against the bar as Mom signaled for another round. I wondered where he'd found the tab. Miss Tilly only served straight from the tap. He pulled his fingers apart when he caught me looking, revealing the perfect impressions the little piece of metal had made deep in the flesh of his fingertips.

"Brought you some hot ones, sugar," Miss Tilly said, setting a steaming basket of beignets, fresh from the fryer and dusted with powdered sugar, in front of Uncle Louie.

He shoved the can tab deep into his pocket. "Shoulda ordered a Diet Coke," he said. I couldn't tell if he was joking.

"I'll get you one." Miss Tilly didn't look so certain either.

"I'm sorry," he said before she had a chance to grab a glass. "These look really good."

Finally, another text from Sara.

> Dad just talked to Roddy's news
> director.

Miss Tilly patted Uncle Louie's hand, proceeding to get someone else another something. Uncle Louie took a big bite of beignet, shedding sugar on his shirt.

> And?

Mom's phone rang.

"Where are you?" she answered, followed by, "What? Hang on." Phone to her ear, she turned to me and Uncle Louie and mouthed *I'm going outside.* Uncle Louie nodded, gesturing with the beignet, dropping white dots all over the place. Mom didn't look amused. She stepped away from her stool, escaping the clinking glasses, the elevated voices, the jukebox's song, leaving Uncle Louie looking straight at Rosie Deshautelle. She was picking at peanuts until she glanced in his direction.

Risking whiplash, Uncle Louie jerked his head up and fixed his gaze to the TV above the bar. News 11's Friday night broadcast was beginning. I wondered if the anchors would report about Roddy. Unable to hear the broadcast above the jukebox, I detected the low rumble of Rosie and Jean-Luc talking in offended tones. About Uncle Louie, I supposed. Chewing fast as a rabbit, he downed the last bite of his beignet.

"We see you, Louie," Rosie said.

His eyes dipped from the TV to the basket of fried dough. Somehow he'd gotten powdered sugar on his nose. It accentuated the scar on his left nostril.

My phone buzzed.

> She said Roddy seemed like his
> usual self at work today.

Uncle Louie slid the beignet basket to Rosie. It collided with her bowl of nuts.

"They're good," he said, taking slow and steady breaths.

I texted Sara back.

> He wasn't given any bad news
> or anything like that?

Rosie swatted the basket of beignets toward Jean-Luc. He grabbed one with each hand. "You shouldn't have come back," she said to Uncle Louie.

His Adam's apple bobbed. Lips still dusty, they pulled apart, but no words came out. Rosie didn't bite her tongue.

"It follows you, doesn't it?" She examined him with incensed eyes. "You look like a dried-out dead toad."

"*It?*" Uncle Louie gasped, making me think they were referring to different things.

> No

"Don't you fucking mess with me!" For a moment—while processing Sara's one word text, trying to think of something else that might have gotten Roddy worked up enough to punch his mirror—I thought Rosie was going to lunge over Mom's stool to rake Uncle Louie with her nails. She flung a fistful of peanuts instead.

"Easy, babe." Jean-Luc flicked his eyes at my uncle. He finished his beignets before putting an arm around Rosie, leaving a streak of sugar on her shoulder. "What's happenin', Louie?"

He must have taken Uncle Louie's silent stare as an insult.

"You're not better than us," he said.

Uncle Louie shook his head, clearing his throat. "Never said I was."

"I guess you didn't hear me, then." Jean-Luc's hand slid down Rosie's side, cupping her rear.

"Pow wow starts tomorrow," Uncle Louie said.

"Don't have to tell me that." Jean-Luc's free hand reached into the basket for another beignet.

Uncle Louie shrugged, looking back at the TV. "That's what's happening."

Seconds ticked by. Not a word was spoken.

> Was he fighting with ur
> parents?

I didn't think Roddy was having trouble with his mom or dad, but I couldn't think of anyone or anything else that could have gotten him so steamed up.

"Just pissed out a kidney stone. Feelin' fucking great," Jean-Luc announced. "Thanks for asking."

Uncle Louie glanced back at him. "Should I care?"

> They're asking the same
> about you

A bewildering smile crossed Jean-Luc's lips. "Still mad at me, huh?"

Uncle Louie didn't answer.

> No!

Roddy and I never fought. Small disagreements, sure, but no raised voices. I'd learned a lot from the mistakes I'd made while dating Ben, including how to talk to someone you love.

"Mad at you for what?" Rosie asked Jean-Luc.

"It's between me and Jean-Luc," Uncle Louie answered for him.

"Fuck him." Rosie angled her body even more toward Jean-Luc, shutting Uncle Louie out.

"Rosie, I—" Uncle Louie started.

"Fuck you, Louie!" She reeled right around, leaning halfway over Mom's stool this time, Jean-Luc barely holding her back. "You think you're so great. Who the fuck are you to be mad at him"—she flung a hand backward, hitting Jean-Luc in the face—"when I still haven't forgiven you for what you did?"

"Whoa, Rosie!" Abandoning my phone on the bar, I jumped up to temper her, my arms around her the way Mom's had been around me on the couch at home. The tears glistening in her eyes were as swollen with grief as the ones I'd wiped from my own eyes earlier.

"I'll never forgive you, Louie," she seethed. "*Never!*"

As if someone brought the hammer down a second time, my heart took another hit seeing her—the woman I'd called Auntie Rosie as a kid and sometimes still did—like that. Considering that Uncle Louie hadn't been around in twelve years, I wondered if she'd been suffering all that time. Longer, even? Longer than any of us?

Motioning with my eyes, I told Uncle Louie to take a hike. He slumped to the restroom, where he'd swab the sweat from his forehead and wash the powdered sugar from his lips. Jean-Luc followed him from the bar—"Babe!" Rosie called after him—but the intimidation tactic fizzled when Jean-Luc took a left outside the restroom door, where he stood hunched over the jukebox, flipping records.

"I'm fine," Rosie said, shaking me off. "Don't ask."

Plenty curious, I was eager to return to my phone, to reply to Sara so that she wouldn't think I was cooking up a lie.

144

Everything was great between

me and Roddy. I swear!

Sending such an insistent text made me feel whiny and adolescent. I just needed Sara and her folks, people who'd never given me much of a chance, to know I hadn't fucked up this time.

TWENTY-THREE

Louie

I lingered in the house just long enough to see Miss Autumn make a desperate grab for her mother as Thomas set Fay back into the casket.

"Come on." I snared Miss Doris's arm to help her out the door and down the steps. The Lord's Prayer tumbled from her lips. A weepy mass had gathered around the fire outside. I ushered Miss Doris to the others, then joined J.L. on the sunbaked lawn, alone with a twisted expression on his face. Chris Horn rushed Fay from the house to his station wagon a few seconds later, the mulberry bark blanket around her. I only saw Fay in a split-second blur as Chris dashed by, but I could tell that she was silent and still.

We all watched Chris, Autumn, and Thomas speed toward the hospital where I knew they'd be given the same explanation the Forstalls had been given about Aubrey. I also knew that what I'd seen and heard was neither the result of muscle contractions nor gas. That was no belch that'd passed over Fay's lips.

We collectively shivered once Chris Horn's station wagon was out of sight, the sun momentarily stripped of its power to make us sweat. No one spoke. No one knew what to say. It was Ma who broke the silence when she finally lumbered out of the house.

"Told you they wouldn't want us here." Her tone was neither petulant nor annoyed, just tired. Grandpa followed her out. George exited after him. Ma, a hand on her forehead to block the sun from her eyes, brushed by me. She got into the passenger side of the truck and put her head against the window.

"Hop in back," Grandpa said to me.

"I'll walk."

"I'll be with him," J.L. said.

"George?" Grandpa called to Mr. Saucier, still standing in the shadows at the top of the steps. "Get in the cab. You're on the way."

George turned the offer down with a shake of his head. He strolled past us without saying goodbye.

"The river," J.L. whispered.

We walked close to each other, neither saying much at first.

"This is exactly what happened at Aubrey's wake," I muttered, troubled.

"It was black," he replied.

"What was?"

"Her bra."

"Whose?"

"Autumn's. Didn't you see it?"

"What are you talking about?"

"Don't tell me you missed it! Autumn. She gave a good glimpse of what she's got goin' on when she was fightin' with Tom."

"You mean when she was struggling to see if her dead mother had begun to breathe?"

"It was right after Tom grabbed her. She swung her arm, and her top went up." He whistled. "Man, you missed out." His sincerity staggered me. "Boobs!" He socked me in the arm.

"Something that doesn't make any sense just happened in that house."

"So why try to explain it? We both know I'm too stupid for that."

"Can we just talk about it for a minute?"

"Yeah, they were big and round and—"

"Just tell me what you heard."

"Screams. Lots of screams."

"That's not what I mean. Tell me what you heard Fay say."

"Say?" he echoed.

I felt the blood drain from my face. "Did you hear anything other than screams? Any noise from Fay?"

J.L. sighed and swiped his hair from his eyes. "I don't know, man. Just . . . like a burp or somethin'. Don't tell me you turned it into words?"

I shrugged. "Maybe I did."

"What do you think you heard?"

"Forget it." I shook my head. "I can't make sense of it either."

"Aww, come on, man. That ain't fair. What'd you hear?"

I wished I hadn't opened my mouth. A rock skipped into the brush from the toe of my shoe. I wished I could disappear too. "Did you happen to hear what George and my grandpa were whispering about?"

"Just old fart talk. What'd Fay say?"

"Probably nothing," I murmured. "Hey, look at that." Coming down the road was the sheriff's white Plymouth Gran Fury, gold lettering on the side and spinners on top.

"What's he doin' here?" J.L. wondered.

The car rolled to an unexpected stop twenty feet ahead.

"No clue," I whispered.

The driver side door swung open. A pair of boots settled on the hard dirt. The passenger door opened next. Another pair of boots appeared.

"Should we run?" J.L. whispered through his teeth.

"No. You'd outrun me, and I'd get caught."

"Caught for what?"

"Just be cool. They can't do anything to us." For the most part, that was true. The sheriff from town had no authority on our land.

Two men got out of the car. White and tall, they wore thick mustaches as proudly as they wore their badges. Each walked around his respective door, coming to a stop on either side of the hood. They stared at us.

"I'm gonna bolt," J.L. whispered.

I grabbed the back of his shirt. Though the sheriff and his deputy, distinguishable by the size of their hats and the color of their 'staches— one brown, one gray—didn't speak, they obviously wanted something. J.L. broke the silence when he raised his right hand and said, "How!"

I cringed. The men remained blank-faced for a moment, then the deputy laughed.

"Something wrong?" I asked.

The sheriff took a few steps forward and said, "Joseph Broussard?"

"What about him?"

"Know where I can find him?"

"What for?" Had I ever been so daring?

"Do you know where he is or not?"

I hesitated, knowing how Grandpa felt about the chiefs of white men.

"Listen, kid . . ." The deputy stepped forward. J.L. elbowed me in the side.

"Keep going straight." I told them where to turn because the roads on the reservation were unmarked. Without a thank-you or a goodbye, they got in their car and peeled away, leaving us in a cloud of dust.

"What do they want with your gramps?"

"Must have something to do with George." I was still thinking about the whispers between Grandpa and Horace's dad.

"You're kidding, right?"

"Yeah." I realized how foolish I sounded. Every suspect thing couldn't revolve around my childhood fears. "Come on." Tempted to run to Grandpa's place, I pressed forth to the river, where I wasn't without apprehension.

"Maybe it has to do with Miss Shelby." J.L. practically voiced my unease about the water.

"Yeah . . . that must be it." Grandpa had said something about contacting the sheriff in town for help.

"Do you think they found her?"

"I don't know. . . . Luke thought she might have fallen from the bridge."

"No shit?" J.L. whooped and ran down the riverbank, nearly sliding on the mud into the water himself. "I don't see her. Hey, Shelby, you in there?"

"Knock it off." I perched atop a fallen branch ensnared by Spanish moss.

"Oh, come on, let's see if Luke's right." J.L. picked up a long stick with branches at the end and dipped it in the water. He dragged it up and down a small section of the riverbank, combing the mud. "Nothin'." He tossed the stick aside and sat next to me. "I guess it's good I'm dumber than you. We balance each other out."

"Yeah," I agreed, surprised that he was still thinking about that. We sat there for a while, letting the afternoon pass like the water in the river. When he got restless, he thrust his hand at me, and I slapped my sweaty palm against his. He got to his feet, pulling me up.

"I don't wanna swim," he said over the rhythm of a woodpecker hammering a hole overhead.

I didn't want to swim either. Not until we were sure Miss Shelby wasn't in the river. J.L. took a running leap and grabbed on to some low-hanging branches, which swung him and long strands of Spanish moss out over the glittering water. The woodpecker picked up its pace as J.L.'s feet returned to shore.

"Fay's dead, right?" He launched himself over the river once more. I wished he hadn't brought her up again.

"She looked dead in Chris's arms."

"Think they'll bury her?"

"I guess. . . . They buried Aubrey."

"Be honest, Louie. Were you scared when she sat up?"

Shocked. Surprised. Fear was at the root of those things. "Sure. Weren't you?"

"Are you kidding? It was the freakiest fucking thing I ever saw."

I wasn't sure if that meant he was scared or not.

"Ready to tell me what you heard?"

"It was nothing." I was starting to believe that. Fay couldn't have said anything. It wasn't possible.

"Fine. Don't tell me if you don't wanna." He kicked a rock at me. It bounced off my shin. "I shoulda touched her."

"Why?"

"To see if she was warm."

J.L. landed again and let go of the branches. His deep-set smile reminded me of the devious devil on the side of the cinnamon candy boxes Gram used to give me. "I'm gonna go to the burial," he said.

"I'll be with Noemi and Johnny." I supposed that was true. I didn't want to go. Didn't want to be anywhere near the cemetery.

"I'll tell you all about it."

I nodded. The woodpecker's rapping reverberated off the water, fast as a drumroll.

"Maybe I can get a look at those other graves." J.L. reminded me of the question I'd asked Grandpa, about the bones and which ones had been taken. "Maybe they're still uncovered."

"If you do get a look . . ." I paused, thinking. "Don't tell me what you see. I don't wanna know anymore."

"Whatever you say." J.L. wiped his dirty hands on his collared shirt, then pulled a wad that looked like a walnut from his pocket. I recognized what it was the second he unraveled it, a small slingshot made of old leather straps and braided rubber bands, dating back to our first year of middle school. J.L. had made it himself, small so that he could carry it without anyone knowing. How he'd managed to launch so many pushpins across our classrooms without getting caught was a mystery to me.

He picked up some stones and sent them sailing over the river. In the amber light of the setting sun, he looked like a painting come to life, focused, mysterious, and strong as he took aim along the water. I admired him, not paying attention to what he was aiming at until the woodpecker's drumming ceased. The abrupt cessation of sound sent my gaze into the trees. A split-second blur of a redheaded bird with a white belly fell through the leaves.

"Did you just—?" I said.

"Got him!" The impish smile was back.

"Why?"

"Why not?" He fired another shot at something I couldn't see. And then another.

"You know the rule!" I was referring to the tenet that's always been part of our traditional beliefs. It revolves around respecting every spirit in, on, outside of, and above the water. Taking life enacts power that must never be abused. The warning from the story we both knew well rang in my ears, then passed over my lips: "Should the Takoda people become sneaky like the snake when it silently slithers behind its prey, or callous like the bobcat when it kills for its own amusement, then the red and blue gators would swallow the Takoda whole, for alligators only use their teeth to shred and to tear. Tamahka do not chew."

J.L. sighed. Then he did something I'd never known him to do. He lied.

"I didn't mean to hit it." He balled the slingshot up and shoved it deep into his pocket. "It's gettin' dark. You should probably head home."

I nodded, expecting him to go his way as I went mine. He didn't. He stayed there by the river. I felt him watching me as I walked away, watching me like Ern. Heavy as his eyes were upon me, I didn't look back. I held steady until the river was far in the distance and then started to run.

I sprinted past the yard where Fay had died an undignified death. The Saucier place, too, went by in a blur. The sun disappeared beneath the horizon just as home came into sight. Having safely made it past the two places that could haunt my dreams, I never expected that something on my own front porch would keep me up through the night, fearfully hearing the phantom sounds of rocks ricocheting off my window.

I came to a grinding halt at the bottom of the porch steps. Despite how hard I'd run, I felt cold inside, as if liquid nitrogen were flowing through my veins, and that was before I got a glimpse of the chilling creature sitting outside my door. I didn't see the loathsome thing until I lumbered up the steps. It was in the corner of the porch, quiet and almost unnoticeable. Almost.

Small, grisly, and gray, the armadillo sat on its hind legs. One of its front feet was missing—torn away—and intense tears separated its armored bands. The animal embodied Fay, peering out of her casket through sightless eyes. I glanced behind me at the patch of dirt where the truck would have been if Ma hadn't already left for work and remembered the bloody bumper I'd scrubbed clean. It couldn't be. No way, no how. Looking back at the armadillo—zeroing in on its pointed, broken face—I shivered in response to how it stared, senselessly blinking.

TWENTY-FOUR

Noemi

Surrounded by back slapping, line dancing, and off-key country crooners, I wondered what I was doing there, how many glasses I'd drained—Miss Tilly collected them too fast for me to keep count—and how many more it'd take to make the pain go away.

"An old-fashioned," I said the next time Miss Tilly made her rounds. Roddy's drink. A gentleman's drink. Sara hadn't replied after receiving my last text, marked read. I assumed she was done with me, forever.

Mom slipped back in just then.

"I swear, Lula, if he wasn't your brother," Rosie said to her. The two huddled close as Rosie filled Mom in on what she'd missed, both secretly loving the drama I'm sure. They'd start whispering about me next, or about Mom's boyfriend, who still hadn't arrived. I told her he wouldn't. When you know, you know.

A glass broke near the stage where Uncle Louie, having emerged from the restroom, was watching Mac tune his guitar. People shouted. Miss Tilly grabbed a broom and cleaned up the mess as the Brooks & Dunn song blasting through the Blue Gator's sound system faded, quickly replaced by Mac Langdon's steadfast voice—smooth and low—delivering a faithful rendition of Conway Twitty's "Hello Darlin'".

How many years had Mac stood on that stage to entertain us? How many years did he have left in him? My eyes welled with tears when he started the last verse, about saying goodbye.

Mom, frowning now, checked her phone almost as often as I'd checked mine when texting Sara. Her cheeks sagged a little more each time her eyes hit the screen. I wished she'd leave him already. The next one might not be any better, but he couldn't be much worse.

Miss Tilly set the old-fashioned on the bar. A face seemed to be smiling up at me from atop the whiskey, but then a bubble burst, and the face's features shifted, turning it into something messy and wounded, like me.

"Noemi," Mom called. I raised my watery eyes. She patted Uncle Louie's empty stool next to her.

"I'm all right," I said.

A chorus of hoots rang out in response to Mac strumming the familiar chords of a song I couldn't name, another tearjerker. I gazed at the crowd around the stage. Uncle Louie was lost somewhere inside it now, nowhere in sight. I didn't see Jean-Luc anywhere either.

"Noemi?" Mom said again. And since I hadn't slid onto Uncle Louie's stool, she made the move, shifting the stool even closer to mine. Her hand went up my back, pulling me in. Before I knew it, my eyes were pressed against her bare shoulder, making it slick.

A dozen *sorry*s tumbled from Mom's mouth, her arms wrapping tighter around me. The embrace felt as loving as Roddy's hugs always had. Maybe more.

"Let's go home," she said. I shook my head against her shoulder. I'd just be restless at home. I needed the booze and the noise to distract me. She moved one hand from my back. A second later, she was shoving napkins into my grasp, though she did all the wiping when I lifted my head. It'd been a long time since I'd let her get so close.

"What do you wanna do?"

I shrugged, my gaze shifting to Uncle Louie, who'd appeared beside her, looking awkward and out of place, one hand up around his mouth.

"I'm gonna get some air." He pointed toward the door.

I wiped the places on my face that Mom had already wiped. "Mind if I . . . ?" I said to him.

He waved me over. Mom pecked my cheek. I followed Uncle Louie toward the door, both of us distracted by the writhing pillar of flesh and hair to the right of it. I didn't need to see faces to know that it was Henry Hotard—Miss Tilly's and Mac's grandson—and Jade Peltier locked at the lips. Their PDAs were nothing new on the rez. Cain Fisher had caught them screwing in the center of the pow wow circle the previous summer.

"Don't get sucked in," Uncle Louie said, attempting to lighten the mood.

Angry, envious, and sad, I ached at the sight of the young lovers as Uncle Louie led me through the gray pall billowing from the smokers talking shit outside the door.

He draped an arm around my shoulders. My instinct was to shrug it away, sure that it was awkward for him as well. I wondered how long it'd been since he'd comforted somebody, especially somebody in shoes like mine, fit for a funeral. His hands soon sought the safety of his pockets.

A million cigarette butts at our feet, we leaned against the side of the Blue Gator Grill, right at the corner where a defunct pay phone stood testament to days gone by.

"How long you gonna stay?" I asked. I didn't really care. I just didn't know what to say.

He scratched his temple. "Was just thinking about heading back." He looked in the direction of the resort, imperceptible from where we stood.

"I meant on the reservation."

"The weekend," he said. "Unless . . ."

I waited, then prompted. "Unless what?"

"Unless there's a reason for me to stay."

"What about work?"

"Summer break until late August. I can go remote after that. Or take the semester off. It'd be a relief, really. Same soul-sucking shit every semester for the last twenty-seven years."

I thought about the graphic design classes at Central Louisiana Community College I'd signed up for, starting in the fall. I'd probably drop them now, not that it mattered. I was only fooling myself thinking that I stood a chance of passing and putting a title I could be proud of next to my name.

Noemi Broussard, Graphic Designer

I'd never done good in school anyway.

Uncle Louie took a deep breath and blew it out, making his lips inflate. I did the same, suddenly wondering about him, the one who'd gotten away, gone to college, built a family and a career. I couldn't ask the question out loud, but in my mind I wondered if it was worth it. And if he'd do it again, especially after what he'd just said. From the outside looking in, he didn't appear to be much better off than I was now.

"What do you think the point of all this is?" I asked, a quaver in my voice.

"*This?*"

I didn't want to say *life* because it sounded so dramatic, but that's exactly what I meant. "Being," I said instead.

He thought for a while, and for a while I thought he wasn't going to answer. "I don't know if there is a point," he eventually said, confirming what I'd suspected, that we were both in the same boat, or at least in similar vessels navigating the same stormy waves. Looking out at the darkness above the trees across the street, it was easy to imagine that everything was nothing, here for a while then gone, forgotten, never to return.

I kicked at the cigarette butts and looked to see if Germy was still around. I could've used another smoke. "Do you think life is pain broken up by moments of happiness, or happiness interspersed with moments of pain?"

Uncle Louie grimaced, and I knew what his answer would be without him having to say it. Pain was the capital letter at the beginning of every sentence, it was the punctuation in between, and the period at the end. We come into this world crying, and though the tears dry up from time to time, there's no such thing as a forever drought.

"Either way," he said, "there's always something to make it worthwhile."

I clenched my jaw to keep from crying. There was truth in what he said. I just didn't know what my *something* was anymore.

"Tell me about Roddy."

I swallowed. Cleared my throat. "What do you wanna know?"

He shrugged. "Anything. Tell me what you loved most about him."

Memories spooled through my mind, most of them mundane but perfect. Roddy singing in the shower. Roddy getting excited every time he saw a dog. Roddy making chocolate chip pancakes in his boxer briefs. Roddy whooping while reeling in a fish. Roddy leaving his laundry in the basket because he was too lazy to fold it. Roddy kissing my forehead when he thought I was asleep.

"He had a secret wink," I said, not sure why I was revealing something that had only ever been between me and him. "Whenever he was reporting live on TV, he'd wink with one eye, just for me. His way of saying I love you." I felt myself crumbling, sliding down the side of the Blue Gator.

"That's special," Uncle Louie said. I appreciated that he didn't try to pick me up or dry my tears. "The nice thing about memories is that you can replay them whenever you want." He pulled his hands from his pockets. "You staying?"

I nodded. I wasn't ready to go home alone yet.

"Okay. Tell your mom I called it a night. And give this to Miss Tilly." He handed me a twenty that I shoved into my pocket. "I'll come by in the morning."

With a wave and a hopeful smile, he was off, crossing the lot and starting down the street.

"You're walking?" I called out to him, alarmed because of what had happened to Roddy in daylight, yet simultaneously thinking about the joint I'd pocketed when Uncle Louie showed up unannounced at the trailer. I'd forgotten about it until I'd shoved the twenty beside it. I'd light it as soon as he was gone.

"Left the rental at the hotel." He turned back to look at me. "Thought I'd hitch a ride back with your mom."

We both screamed a split second later when a gunshot rang out. Uncle Louie dropped in the street, his hands reaching for his head. I sprang to my feet, sure that he'd been hit.

"Louie!" I ran to his side, thinking only of him and not about what I'd do—or if I'd even be spared—should another shot ring out.

Uncle Louie popped up right as I reached him, his face craggy with fury. I didn't see what he saw at first, looming in the shadows.

"You son of a bitch!" He barreled past me, only to stop a few feet off the street.

I couldn't make out the face of the figure Uncle Louie was glaring at, but the stringy body leaning against the side of the Blue Gator, right around the corner from where Uncle Louie and I had been standing, was Jean-Luc. A cigarette glowed between his lips and moonlight glinted off the revolver hanging in his hand.

"Saved your life," he said.

"You almost killed me! The bullet whizzed right passed my head!"

"I didn't miss," Jean-Luc said. He raised the revolver again, and though he was just using it to point, Uncle Louie and I both ducked.

Straining to keep one eye on the gun, I gave in and looked behind me at where Jean-Luc was pointing. Just off the shoulder on the opposite side of the street, only feet from where Uncle Louie had been walking, was a heap of fur.

"What is it?" Uncle Louie said.

I inched closer. I thought it was a dog like Good Boy at first. Pointed ears, a bushy tail, a narrow muzzle streaked with red. My stomach churned. "The coyote," I said. It was a sizable female. An alpha. She was on her side, legs limp, her neck dark and glistening. A single unseeing eye was aimed up at me.

"Put it away!" Uncle Louie charged toward Jean-Luc again. "What the hell's wrong with you? Drinking and waving a gun around . . . They don't even attack humans!"

Jean-Luc stepped out of the shadows. Sneering, he said, "Sometimes they do. . . . You owe me one." He flicked his cigarette to the ground and tucked the revolver into his waistband on his way back into the Blue Gator.

Uncle Louie rushed toward me. "You all right?"

Aside from the ringing in my ears and my heart on the verge of bursting in a bloody disaster against my ribs, I was fine.

"Is it—" Uncle Louie turned toward the coyote and froze. I turned too.

The heap of fur was gone.

TWENTY-FIVE

Louie

Brandishing the broom the next morning, I pretended to sweep the steps when really I was making sure the armadillo was gone. It hadn't left a trail of dusty footprints or even a drop of blood on the porch planks to prove that it'd been there. All was clear, as well, when I returned from Miss Doris's trailer with the kids an hour later.

Having Noemi and Johnny around kept me from plummeting into the depths of dread that had begun to overtake my mind. Their unknowing smiles and endless laughter lifted the fog of fear blanketing the reservation. They prevented me from thinking about the unsettling things that kept me awake at night.

Johnny ran straight to my room. I ran after him. He grabbed the drum beater, and I grabbed the bustle I'd busied myself with through the dark hours.

"What's that?" Johnny asked. I held the bustle high because I knew it would be in pieces if he or Noemi got ahold of it, not because they were rough, but because I'd slapped it together without any skill. It'd never stand up to the beautiful bustles the more experienced dancers wore.

"It's a headdress," I explained.

I'd used the black, brown, red, orange, and yellow feathers from the bundle Grandpa had given me. The fierce colors commanded Johnny's attention. He dropped the beater and hitched up onto his tiptoes, arms stretched over his head, fingers wiggling like puppies' tails.

"Lemme see!" he whined.

I placed the headdress on my head. It may have been far from the best-looking bustle ever created, but it fit perfectly. I'd used leftover buckskin for the base. The wooden dowels Grandpa had carved held the feathers straight toward the sky. I'd stuck some bobby pins in there, too, to clamp the pieces together. For once, I couldn't complain about the mess of hair supplies Lula left in the bathroom. Unorthodox as it was, the bustle's base was nicely round, representing life cycles and unity, and the feathers stood up straight, creating a proper channel between the spirits in the sky and the ones here on earth.

"Lemme see!" Johnny's demand lured Noemi closer. She cocked a curious stare at the top of my head before reaching for it as well. I laughed and ran from the room, the two of them on my tail.

The little Indians clawed at my waist while I endeavored to dance in the middle of the living room. I'm sure I looked like a wounded duck, jerking and flailing in semicircles, but I didn't care.

"I have an idea," I panted.

"No, Douie!" Noemi stomped a foot. "You share."

"No fair!" Johnny's index finger jabbed the air, pointing at my bustle. "Lemme see!"

"Hold your horses." I ran to my room and gathered the leftover feathers. Red, blue, green, black, white, and pink, they looked like bouquets when I offered them to the kids.

Noemi's face lit up like a quick-strike match. She plucked the feathers she liked best from my fists while Johnny reached for the ones on my head. I stood up straight before he could do any damage, then showered the remaining feathers over him. The colorful storm made him growl. Noemi painted an invisible portrait with the feathers in her hands.

"Now you can make your own headdress," I said.

Johnny eyed the feathers at his feet, entertaining the proposal, then kicked two of them into the air. Noemi carefully positioned pink and white feathers behind her ears. I stuck a few more in her hair.

"You're so pretty," I said.

"*So* pretty!" she echoed, commencing a dance of her own. Her movements, a lot like mine, chipped away at my already-cracked confidence. Johnny watched for a while, then scooped two handfuls of feathers from the floor. I thought he'd join in on the dance, but he climbed onto the couch and flapped his arms instead.

"I'm a bird!" he proclaimed, jumping from the cushion.

"Whoa! You flew high!" I shouldn't have encouraged him. He climbed onto the couch again, flapped some more, then jumped farther than before. He may have been small, but he sent a jolt through the trailer that rattled the dishes in the kitchen cabinet upon touchdown.

"Grammy's pretty too." One hand on Johnny to slow him down, I turned to find Noemi at the end of the hall. Bent outside Ma's bedroom door, she was stuffing pink feathers beneath it. "Grammy's *so* pretty!"

"Yeah, she is," I halfheartedly agreed.

Johnny broke from me and scrambled onto the couch again. I caught him when he jumped. Another mistake because it only egged him on some more. Each time I nabbed him, he flailed to get away, laughing as if I were tickling him with all those feathers at once.

In search of more height, the boy climbed onto one of the couch's arms. Following a few bold jumps from there, he turned the end table into a diving board before scrambling up the back of the couch.

"That's it. No more." Voice firm, actions lax, I didn't stop him from scaling his Everest because it made him so happy. His bubbling laughter. His deep-set smile. The little glance he shot my way to make sure

I was watching. All those things helped me forget what I'd seen in the Lavergnes' living room.

"I'm going to call you Flying Frog," I told Johnny. "Or Bounding Gator."

"My turn, Douie," Noemi said.

"You want a name too?"

She nodded and sprinkled a few feathers in front of the box fan. The way they burst across the room elicited bubbly giggles.

"Okay, Pink Feather, get ready." Having snagged some feathers from the carpet, I sprinkled them over her head. She twirled in the fluffy downpour as Johnny sprang from the couch, straight into the deluge. The happy children and the rainbow of colors swirling around them created a cartoon in the middle of the living room, one in which we were free of fear and impervious to harm. In that moment, all was well.

"Grammy's turn," Noemi said, feathers ready in her hands.

My smile faded. I couldn't recall a single instance during the last three years in which Ma had played with Noemi. I barely remembered her playing with me as a kid. My best memory revolved around a bag of balloons, colorful as the feathers, that she'd brought home from work. We'd filled them with cold water from the tap. Ma had knotted them for me because water squirted all over the kitchen whenever I tried to do it myself. I remembered how she, Lula, and I, laughing and screaming, had run around the yard, busting the balloons against one another's bare skin, dreading the sting but enjoying the cold trickle that ran down our flesh. That was long before Ma stopped picking wildflowers along the road.

"Let's go, Flying Frog." I tried to keep the happiness from withering. "To the sky spirit!" I grabbed Johnny by the waist and thrust him in the air, proceeding to fly him around the room.

"Me, Douie! Me!" Noemi chased after us, yanking at my waistband the entire time.

Johnny roared with delight. I flew him past the window and into the kitchen, allowing him to snag a cookie from the box on the counter. Seeing the treat in his hand made Noemi even more envious.

"Douie!" She stomped both feet this time, one after the other. "My turn!"

"All right, all right." I brought Johnny in for his landing, and, despite the wildfire spreading from my arms to my back, I gave Noemi one hell of a ride. She endured seven extreme dips that turned her hair into windshield wipers in front of her eyes. Zooming through the kitchen, she snatched two cookies in her greedy fists.

"Prepare for landing!" I took a bite of the cookie in her left hand upon setting her down. She squealed and ran to the corner like a rat protecting its food, her square teeth gnawing the cookie to crumbs. Johnny finished the last bit of his, and, instead of demanding another, picked up one of the red feathers from the floor. He climbed onto the couch as I stood back, watching through the corner of my eye.

Pressing the red feather against his forehead, he flapped an imaginary wing with his opposite arm. At first, I thought he'd picked up the feather to be like me with my bustle, but his eyes weren't on my headdress anymore. He was looking at something outside the window, mimicking it.

"Is that . . . ?"

I only saw what had his attention for a split second before it flew away. I'd testify in any court and swear on any Bible, though, that a redheaded woodpecker had been perched in the brush beside the trailer, its white underbelly streaked with red.

TWENTY-SIX

Noemi

Uncle Louie gasped and started to sink. Knees against the ground, he dug his phone from his pocket and turned the flashlight on. The bright light illuminated a pool of blood, making what happened to Roddy even more real, and making me whimper, wondering how the coyote could still be alive.

"Where'd it go?"

Uncle Louie redirected the light, shining it into the growth beside the street, then along the asphalt. A glistening blood trail led into the darkness.

Uncle Louie deflated even more, shoulders sagging, spine curling, his head shaking from side to side.

"What?" I demanded.

"You said it was *the* coyote?" His words were stilted. He sounded spooked.

"There was blood around its mouth."

"But that's not where it was hit, was it?"

"Neck shot," I said.

"Think the bullet hit the spine?"

I pressed on my neck, thinking about where the coyote had been hit. "Maybe."

He muttered something I couldn't make out, then sprang to his feet. "Come on!" he said, as if he'd just made the most important realization of his life. He hurried down the street, following the trail, one hand wind-socking above his shoulder for me to follow.

"What are you doing?" My gaze bounced from him to the Blue Gator Grill and back. "Wait!" Despite the pit in my stomach, I went after him, knowing I'd only be tormented by more unanswered questions if I went back to hang my head over another beer in the bar.

Moving fast without running, he kept his light aimed low, illuminating drop after gleaming drop, like chocolate opals on the asphalt. I caught up to him quickly.

"Why are you *following* it?"

"It's sticking to the street. Don't you find that strange?"

"I don't understand." He was right, though. The droplets didn't dwindle on the asphalt, and a carcass didn't appear. Why hadn't the coyote run off into the woods?

"Look at the drops," he said. "What are they? Six feet apart? And consistent. The coyote's moving at a steady pace. Could you do that after taking a shot to the neck?"

I'm not a hunter, but I know well enough that not every shot is fatal. Some animals need to be tracked. Still, the hairs on the back of my neck prickled. I'd seen the coyote on the street after it'd been hit.

"That doesn't explain why we're—"

"There's a story I share in my classes when I get to the section about Native mythology," he said, revved up, talking fast. "It's about Coyote from the Caddo Nation. It starts with Coyote looking for something to eat. He enters Rattlesnake's territory, but Rattlesnake isn't there to defend it, which makes Coyote think that Rattlesnake isn't as powerful or poisonous as people believe. He says to himself, 'If I ever find him, I'm going to show him how powerful I am.'

"Later, he crosses paths with Rattlesnake and says, 'I've heard that you have great poison. People say you are more dangerous than me. Now that we've met, I want you to show me how you are more powerful and dangerous than I am.'

"'I look small to you,' Rattlesnake says in return, 'but I am given power by our Creator. I have killed many animals, big and small. Whatever you want me to do, I will do it.'

"'I want to see which of us has the most power,' Coyote says.

"Rattlesnake thinks for a moment. 'You may bite me once wherever you want,' he says, 'and I will bite you in return. In that way, we will see who has more power.'

"'All right, but you have to bite me first,' says Coyote.

"Rattlesnake agrees and bites Coyote on the tip of his nose, saying, 'That is all I can do.'

"Coyote stands as if he isn't hurt at all. 'Then it is my turn to show you my power,' he says, and nearly bites Rattlesnake in two.

"Rattlesnake cries in pain. Coyote says, 'Now you go lie over there, and I will lie here. We will call to each other from time to time and in this way we will see who lives the longest.'

"Coyote thinks Rattlesnake will die fast, and so he calls out to him. Rattlesnake responds in a weak voice, sounding almost dead. After a while, Rattlesnake calls to Coyote. Coyote answers in a loud voice. They do this throughout the night. When Rattlesnake calls Coyote in the morning, Coyote doesn't answer. It's then that Rattlesnake slithers over to see what's wrong. Victorious, he finds Coyote swollen and dead."

Uncle Louie let the story sink in, then said, "I need to see how powerful this coyote is."

I still didn't understand why, but I remembered the way he'd reacted when Luke Fisher told us about the coyote that might have made a meal of my boyfriend. "There's something you're not telling me."

He didn't deny it; he didn't explain either. Not fully, anyway.

"If the coyote we're following is more powerful—more *invulnerable*—than the one in the tale, well, then, it might just mean that Roddy's death wasn't an accident." He swallowed hard. "Or a suicide either."

His words winded me. I could barely keep up.

TWENTY-SEVEN

Louie

The bags under my eyes felt as heavy as the one loaded with Ma's empty cans that I hauled from the trailer after she left for work. I didn't let the screen door slam behind me when I stepped onto the porch. I didn't pound down the steps either. I didn't even shift my gaze upon hearing the ruffle of blinds from Ern's side of the field.

I set the bag at the bottom of the steps so that I'd remember to toss it into the bed of the pickup after Ma returned in the morning, then turned to go inside.

"Bring the full ones out next time." Ern must have heard me the instant I opened the door. He may have been caged, but I couldn't ignore him. He was hard to escape.

"Huh?" I hollered across the field.

"The full ones," he said. "Bringin' out the empty ones doesn't do anyone any good."

I looked at Ern, light glowing around his head, his silhouette blackened by the night, then at the bag by the steps. I supposed he could have heard some rattling, but I wondered how he knew exactly what was inside. I'd been careful. The cans hadn't been that loud.

"Come over."

I opened the door. "I'm tired. Didn't sleep last night."

"Me neither."

I couldn't escape him.

"Come over."

I dragged my feet across the field to join the specter who appeared as little more than a shadowy mouth to me, his blinds having fallen into place when I got close. "I can't stay long." I sat on the bottom step and sighed. We kept quiet for the first few minutes. Drowsy, the silence didn't bother me. Ern didn't say anything to keep me there, but he had the same pull on me as Fay's body in the grass; even if I didn't want to look, I couldn't just walk away.

"After all these years . . ." he finally said, his voice like a soft wind picking up over the field. "After all these years I think I know how you feel."

It took me a moment to sift through the statement, my head like a bucket of sand. "What are you talking about, Ern?"

"Your ma."

"What about her?" I didn't want to acknowledge it, but I knew what he was talking about. Deep down I did.

"Your ma—"

"Has my grandpa been by?" I cut him off because I wasn't ready to hear him put the things I'd slowly been starting to realize into words.

"When?"

"Today. Or last night."

"Haven't seen him since the day he brought you your drum. Did he tell you he was comin' here?"

"Huh?"

"Today or last night. Why'd you ask if he'd been by?"

I'd asked because I'd been thinking about the sheriff and the deputy J.L. and I had crossed paths with on our way to the river. I'd assumed they'd wanted to speak with Grandpa Joe about Miss Shelby.

"Just thought he might've checked on you," I said, then changed the subject again. "I heard rocks against my window last night." Voicing those words heightened my vulnerability. They reminded me that I was outside, unarmed, and under the moon. "That's what kept me awake . . . the rocks."

"You don't really believe he—"

"I saw him by the river once with rocks in his hands. Jean-Luc saw him too."

"So you saw him with rocks." Ern's hefty jowls sagged. "Doesn't mean the story's true."

"None of it?" I asked. "You're sure?"

Ern didn't reply quick enough to make me believe the story was a bunch of bull. All he said when he responded was, "I don't believe it."

Thinking about the story gave me goose bumps bigger than my mosquito bites. I turned on the step and pulled my legs close to my chest for warmth. I didn't want to spend another night haunted by Horace, but he, like Ern, was hard to escape.

The incident that had inspired the legend about what would happen if a rock hit your window occurred sometime between the afternoon when J.L. and I saw Horace by the river and the night the vampire killed him. J.L. and I didn't fear Horace when we saw him. We were only five, brand-new best friends. Horace had been just another face we passed along the shore on our way to what would become our favorite spot upriver. I'll never forget the rocks in his hands. He'd been skipping them over the water.

It wasn't long after J.L. and I saw him that Horace, according to legend, single-handedly put an end to the Hensley name on the reservation.

There were three things we knew for sure about the legend. The first was that the Sauciers and the Hensleys hated each other. The second was that Gus Hensley; his wife, Sheila; their boys Gus Jr., Vincent, and Blake; and their daughter, Emmy; were the last in the Hensley line. The third was that all six Hensleys ended up dead.

The Sauciers and the Hensleys had been the Hatfields and Mc-
Coys of the Takoda reservation, only it wasn't a murder or a stolen hog
that put them at odds. Their feud started over a lawnmower and ultimately ended with the Hensleys filling six graves in the tribal cemetery. The story went like this:

George Saucier bought a Craftsman walk-behind lawnmower from
Gus Hensley. Gus guaranteed that the lawnmower worked, and since
the men had known each other their entire lives, George had no reason to doubt him. He paid Gus eleven bucks and pushed the old thing
from Gus's place to his, where he parked it in the shed. It wasn't until
two days later that George tried to start the mower up, but no matter
how many times he pulled the starter or primed the engine, the damn
thing wouldn't start.

Frustrated, George marched straight to Gus's and demanded his
money back. Gus refused, swearing up and down that the mower
worked. Even if it didn't, he said, George had gotten a steal because
he'd talked Gus down from fifteen dollars to eleven.

You've had it for two days and now you're gonna say it doesn't work?
Nice try, old man, Gus had said. *As is. No returns.*

The two men never got along after that. Neither did their families.
No more lazy days fishing with the boys. No more sweet tea together
on hot afternoons. Instead, the Hensleys amused themselves by pro-
voking the Sauciers. Sheila danced across June's flowerbed. The Hensley boys splattered the house with eggs. Gus spat chaw at George for
being called a liar. Someone left a trail of loose trash—mixed with
shit, according to some accounts—all the way from the road to
George's front door.

The feud went on for years. The Hensleys always the aggressors.
The Sauciers always the silent victims. That is, until Horace got the
greatest revenge of all.

It was spring. The Hensleys, having bought a "new" used lime
green 1973 Chevy Cheyenne, were showing the pickup truck off to

anyone who would look. The three boys were in the back, their sun-baked arms hanging over the edge of the bed, wind blowing through their hair. Gus and Sheila were in the cab with two-year-old Emmy on the seat between them.

They cruised the dirt roads, doing laps around the reservation. Gus eased down on the brake each time he passed the Saucier place, their broken-down beater on blocks in front. Neither George nor June paid the passing pickup any mind. Horace, however, couldn't ignore it. Watching from his bedroom window, he grew angrier by the minute. The Hensley boys laughed at him each time they drove by, pointing and sticking out their tongues, becoming cruder with each pass. That is, until the seventh circuit, upon which they spied nothing more than Horace's curtains hanging in the window.

Horace hadn't ducked behind the curtains to hide from the Hensleys. He'd sneaked out the back of the trailer in pursuit of the river. There, he gathered rocks from the shore, then waited for the Hensleys in the brush just beyond the eastern end of the bridge. When the Hensleys arrived at the river on their next lap around the reservation, Horace chucked one of the river rocks at the Chevy Cheyenne's windshield just as Gus was coasting down the eastern side of the bridge.

The windshield burst into a web of broken glass. Gus, given the fright of his life, swerved to the left, causing the truck to careen into the low wing wall extending from the bridge. The wall, too short and too old to support the truck's weight, crumbled. The truck slid down the steep embankment, picking up speed. When its tires hit mud, the Cheyenne flipped, landing upside down on the shore, its tailgate touching the water.

All three boys were tossed from the bed in back. Vincent landed clear across the road, his neck bent at a ghastly angle against the base of a tree. Blake had tried to hold on to the edge of the bed, but he got tangled in one of the rear wheel wells when the truck turned, tires spinning, which rubbed his flesh raw, leaving him looking like bacon. Gus Jr. got it the worst. No one found him until they hauled the Cheyenne away. His body, crushed beneath the truck's cab, had to be dug out of the mud.

Gus and Sheila didn't go far from where they'd been seated. Like the conclusion of a Shakespearean tragedy, they ended up entwined together between the hood and the ground, their legs wedged in the space where the windshield once was. Little Emmy was ejected completely. A fisherman found her floating face down a quarter mile downriver. It wasn't the impact but water in her lungs that killed her.

Screams rang out before the truck flipped, but only Horace heard them. When questioned about what he saw, all he said between nonsensical stammering was, *Mr. Hensley tried to hit me.*

"If not Horace, who do you think threw the rock?" I questioned Ern about his doubt.

"No one. No rock was ever thrown."

"What about the windshield?"

"Broke when the truck flipped. The windshield didn't start the accident. Gus did when he swerved off the road. Who knows why he swerved. Maybe he really was tryin' to hit Horace. Or maybe he was just tryin' to give Horace a good scare. For all we know, Emmy coulda grabbed the wheel. Any number of things coulda caused that accident, Louie. Horace and a rock just make the spookiest story."

"How can you be so sure?"

"Because Horace was always misunderstood. What happened with the Hensleys is no different from when Horace got caught diggin' in the cemetery. It looked like he did somethin' wrong both times, but he never did. Besides, don't you think he'd have been in big trouble if anyone coulda proved it?"

Ern could have been right. The bits of broken glass from the Hensleys' windshield had been too small and scattered to tell what had made them that way. No one found a rock in the truck, but that didn't mean much, considering countless rocks lined the shore all around the river. Any one of them could have been the one Horace threw. Hell, it could have been the one he had in his hand when Albert Picote, J.L.'s grandfather, drove up on the accident and found Horace sitting atop the remains of the bridge's battered wing wall, staring at the carnage.

"If Horace didn't run to the river with the sole purpose of getting his hands on some rocks, why do you think he went there?"

The blinds bobbled. "Already told you. Horace liked lookin' at the river rocks. Lookin', not throwin'. Sometimes he'd find stuff like that trade bead mixed in with 'em. The river was a safe place for him. Made him feel okay. He didn't hurt anyone. Never did."

"He didn't help anyone either."

Ern didn't argue. One thing we all knew about the Hensley tragedy was that when Albert Picote told Horace to get help, Horace didn't run to notify Charlie Fisher, chief of the tribal police back then. He didn't even tell his parents about the accident when he got home, which is where he went. He kept the story to himself as if he wanted to own it.

Horace's actions gave birth to the legend about windows and rocks after he fell into the vampire's deadly grip. If Horace wanted you dead—because you'd ignored him, or because your dads didn't get along, or because you whispered rumors about him and his family— all he'd have to do is hit your window with a rock and then the vampire would take your life the way it took his.

"You didn't really hear rocks against your window last night," Ern said.

I shrugged.

"Why do you believe that legend, Louie? It doesn't even make sense."

"We believe a lot of things when we're young."

"You still believe it now. You believe in the Takoda Vampire as much as you believe in your mother. Both have you fooled." He brought us back to where we'd started. "After all these years," he said again, "I think I know how you feel."

"How's that?"

"To live without a ma."

"I have a ma."

"No, Louie." Ern waggled his jowls. "You haven't had a ma since God knows when. Maybe you never did."

"You're not making sense."

"You just don't understand. Tell me, Louie, what is a mother?"

"This is stupid." I lowered my feet from the step, about to head home.

"Is a ma someone who puts money on the table for groceries when the cupboards are bare? Is she someone who walks past you when you ask how she's doin'? Someone who never asks the question in return? Someone whose door is always closed?"

"She works nights." It was the best defense I could conjure against his flood of truth, a flood that gave me chills because—watchful as he was—he shouldn't have known so much.

"Not sayin' she's a bad ma, Louie. Just sayin' mine's gone now and I think I know how you feel. I had a mother. She loved me. Now that she's gone, I know what it's like to live without her." He wheezed. "Been over a week. . . . She ain't comin' back."

"How do you know?" I forced him to face his own uncomfortable truth.

"She's never left me alone this long. Never would."

"Maybe . . ." I said, hesitant to finish the thought. "Maybe she went to see what else is out there." I recalled our conversation from a few nights earlier. "Maybe she wanted something more."

"Wouldn't have left the rez," he said. "Not with responsibilities as big as me."

177

"Maybe she left *for* you. So that you won't be so dependent on her anymore."

"Yeah right, Louie. She wouldn't have just walked away."

"Don't give up hope, is all I'm saying."

"Goes for you, too. Both our moms are gone, but you might be able to bring yours back."

"Mine's not gone," I insisted.

Ern bobbled the blinds again. "Bring the full cans out next time."

TWENTY-EIGHT

Louie

An anole, its flesh perfectly matched to the weathered wood beneath its feet, scurried away from my hand as I reached for the Blue Gator Grill's door. Even with the ceiling fans spinning overhead, the air was stickier and more stifling inside than it was out beneath the sun. The comingled scent of cigarette smoke, french fries, and spilled beer swirled around me. The voices of my people, some sober, some slurred, filled my ears. It looked like everyone on the rez had squeezed inside. Ern, of course, was missing. So was Ma. So was Miss Shelby.

A sharp whistle pulled my gaze to the end of the bar where J.L. sat atop a stool, his right hand deep in a bowl of peanuts.

"Did you see the VCR?" I asked him.

"I woulda saved you a seat if I knew you were comin'," he replied, nodding.

"I always come."

"Hey, sugar," Miss Tilly said from behind the tap, preventing J.L. from unleashing the dirty joke on his lips. Her hands worked in different directions, slinging drinks and fried food onto the bar. I smiled at her.

"You're the one who never shows," I said to J.L. He sat wedged between his uncle Sawyer, chatting with Chris Horn next to him, and Mark Bishop, Miss Paula's husband from Tallulah. Mark didn't share our blood, but he fit right in at the bar.

"Any idea what your gramps is gonna say?" J.L. asked.

Something to do with the sheriff we saw would have been my best guess. "No clue," I said.

"I already told you it's about Miss Shelby," Sawyer interjected, turning from Chris Horn to take a swig of beer.

"What about her?"

"Wait and see." Sawyer flicked a peanut shell at his nephew, then leaned close to Chris again.

"I'm gonna find somewhere to sit," I said.

J.L. snuck a sip from his uncle's unguarded glass. "There's a spot over there." He pointed to the back of the bar where Grandpa always stationed himself atop the shallow platform Mac used as a stage to strum Cash and Haggard tunes for the weekend regulars.

I sat between Miss Doris and Edgar Forstall. Edgar was alone. I figured it was the first time he'd ventured out of the house since his son's death. His faraway gaze suggested he was observing something much more important than the happenings around him, as though he were looking into the future, or perhaps the past.

"He didn't say hello to me either," Miss Doris whispered in that too loud way of hers. "Haven't seen your granddad yet. Don't suppose you know what this is all about? After what happened to Fay, I don't know how much more I can take."

"Speaking of Miss Fay . . ." There was something I hadn't been brave enough to ask Miss Doris the last two times I picked up Johnny. "What'd you hear when she sat up in her casket?"

Miss Doris's eyes softened. She put a hand over mine. "It was only a belch, Louie. That's what the medical examiner told the Lavergnes . . . just a bit of gas seeping out."

"I know what the Lavergnes were told, but what did you hear?"

"Just a belch. Nothing to be afraid of."

"Oh." Why hadn't she and J.L. heard what I had?

"Did you think—?"

"Sawyer says my grandpa has something to say about Miss Shelby," I quickly said.

"Dear lord, they found her body?" Miss Doris's eyes widened. Her mouth pulled tight.

"Sawyer didn't say anything about that."

"Well, we would've heard if she was alive and well, don't you think?"

"Maybe . . . Your back feeling better?" She hadn't been able to tie Johnny's shoes that morning.

Miss Doris's face turned graver than before. Reaching for the small of her back, which she couldn't quite caress, she shook her head. "Feels like I've been rolled over. If Paula hadn't picked me up, I'd still be stuck in my chair."

My eyes drifted through the smoke to J.L. Curled fingers reached for his uncle's glass. I felt like I was supposed to be mad at him after the way we'd left things by the river, but I wasn't mad, just uncertain about where we stood.

"Those feathers!" Miss Doris clutched her chest and leaned backward, her nose in the air. Forced laughter boomed from her throat. She slapped a hand against the table as if she'd told a joke she wanted everyone to find funny. I'd missed something while lost in thought. "My goodness, those feathers," she carried on. "The way Little John flaps around the house, I tell you, he thinks he's a sparrow. Actually, he's more like a Louisiana waterthrush the way he warbles."

"The feathers, right. . . . I hope you don't mind. He's not making a mess, is he?"

J.L. took a sneaky sip, then caught me catching him peeking past the V of Miss Tilly's top. He wiped the foam mustache from his upper lip and made a gesture with his hands to exaggerate her size.

"Not making a mess?" Miss Doris hooted. "Of course he's making a mess, but boys will be boys, and he absolutely adores you, Louie."

"What's that?"

"Little John. He can't get enough of you. Can't you tell? Every afternoon after Rosie brings him home, he hops around blabbering about Louie, Louie, Louie."

"He's a good kid."

Jean-Luc downed the rest of his uncle's beer, then upped his game by leaning over the bar to refill the glass straight from the tap. I pretended like I hadn't seen when he turned to share his conquest with me.

"I've been thinking that we oughta extend our agreement beyond the summer," Miss Doris blathered. "Would watching him after school be too much for you?"

"Huh?"

"Come fall when you're back in school, would you still be able to spend time with Johnny? Just a couple hours in the afternoon?"

"Oh, I don't know . . . I guess I'd have to see what—"

Grandpa Joe walked in just then. He brought a hush with him that fell over us like a cast net thrown by one of the shrimpers off the coast. Luke Fisher followed closely at Grandpa's heels.

"Thank you for coming on such short notice." Grandpa stepped up on the platform. His surveying gaze swept from one side of the Blue Gator to the other. "As you're aware, tragedy has fallen upon us once more."

I didn't want to look for fear of locking eyes, but I couldn't stop myself from scanning the crowd in search of Miss Autumn and Thomas Lavergne. They were at a table by the door, each holding tight to the other.

"In light of these tragedies, I'd like to appeal to the spirits that sustain us," Grandpa said. "Put down your drinks and leave them down until we're done. Even after that, if you can. Treat this as you would a sacred place. All of you."

Heavy pint glasses clunked against tables. From the corner of my eye, I watched J.L. drain what was left in his uncle's glass before setting it aside. The poor focus of my peripheral vision made him look a little too comfortable on that barstool. Older, too.

Satisfied, Grandpa turned his palms toward the smoke-stained beams that crossed the Blue Gator's ceiling. "We affirm the earth spirit who feeds us with the harvest of her fertile dirt, and who shelters us with the trees of her abundant land," he said. "We affirm the sky spirit who gives us wind to spread our voices, water to quench our thirst, and light to illuminate our way. We affirm the spirit of the mighty fire that gives us warmth, and the mighty spirits of the creatures that lie down for us so that we may be mighty ourselves. We affirm the spirits of good and the spirits of bad. We ask that balance between the two, like the ever-present balance between light and dark, when night turns to day and day turns to night, be restored upon our reservation so that no one else feels the pain of a life lost before youth can find its balance in old age, or before life has run its natural course."

Only the whir of the ceiling fans and Miss Autumn's gentle cries broke the silence following Grandpa's appeal. Miss Doris wiped a tear from each eye. Mr. Forstall held as still as an old oak, one whose trunk has already been irreparably damaged by the swing of an ax.

"We must be strong," Grandpa Joe said. "We must support one another always and in all ways. That's the reason I called you here. Chief Fisher." He motioned to Luke standing to the left of the small stage.

"I'm asking for volunteers." Luke stepped onto the platform. "I appreciate everyone's help over the last few days, but Miss Shelby's still missing. We're going to have to drag the river."

Luke birthed a ghastly image in my mind, of Miss Shelby all bloated and pale, like the dead fish that sometimes floated to shore, where they bobbed in the shallows of the riverbank, becoming grotesque and odorous as they baked beneath the sun. I hated how they smelled.

"We'll start at the bridge and work our way to the bend downriver," Luke said. "If Miss Shelby lost her footing and fell into the water"—he paused—"the current wouldn't have swept her past the boulders in the riverbend."

. "When?" Mr. Forstall quietly asked.

"We'll begin in the morning. Bring your boats, your canoes, and your nets. Waders, too, if you've got 'em."

"What if we don't find her in the river?" Miss Doris asked as if she'd be taking part in the search. "What'll we do then?"

"I'm still talking with the sheriff in town," Grandpa said. "I'm hoping he'll decide to help. In the meantime, I want you to think back to the day Miss Shelby went missing. Try to remember if you saw anything out of the ordinary on the reservation. A person. A car. Anything."

My mind jumped to Aubrey Forstall and the memory of what had happened to him at his wake that day. Things don't get much stranger than that. I pegged Mr. Forstall with my gaze.

"Do you really think she was taken from us?" Miss Paula asked. "Who would do that? Why?"

"We're not jumping to conclusions," Luke said, allowing a few silent seconds to tick by. "We'll start with the river and take it from there. Tomorrow, eight a.m. The more help we have the bet—"

The Blue Gator's door swung open hard and fast. A frightening bang rang out when it slammed into the siding. Miss Doris gasped next to me. Mac Langdon nearly jumped over the bar. J.L. toppled the bowl of peanuts he'd been picking at.

Sam Peltier raced through the door. His hair slick with sweat and the flesh from the base of his neck up to his eyes as red as a welt, he looked confused and like he might hurl. Paying no mind to the eyes upon him, he ran to the back of the bar, peanut shells crunching underfoot, where he stumbled on the platform. The sound of his knee-cap cracking against a board suggested that he'd need a minute to shake off the pain, but he sprang right up and threw himself at Grandpa and Luke.

"What in the world?" Miss Doris's left hand groped for me again. She stared, mouth agape, in wonder at what had driven Sam to the stage.

I could see a sliver of Sam's chin from my vantage point. It moved up and down with the speed of a sewing machine's needle. Miss Doris and I leaned as close to the stage as we could. Ears straining, I didn't hear much more than the hiss of Sam's whispers, but I did pick out two words before he staggered backward, nearly falling from the stage.

. . . *from underground* . . . he'd said.

Sam lurched back to the Blue Gator's door and took two steps outside. He stalled, then whipped around and shouted, "Did you hear me?"

Our collective gaze ricocheted from Sam to my grandfather and Luke. They looked almost as puzzled as the rest of us.

"What the hell's going on here?" Mac hollered from behind the bar.

Grandpa Joe stiffened like a mouse cornered by a canebrake rattle-snake. "Head home." His mouth barely moved. "Get some rest. Morning will be here soon." He stepped down from the stage and barreled through the crowd, ignoring the barrage of questions that rolled toward him like the rumble of thunder from an approaching storm. Luke followed close behind, dodging frantic hands, trying to get them to stop and explain. The men stalled for a second near the door, giving their attention to the two people who wanted it least. Miss Autumn moaned in response to whatever Grandpa whispered in her ear. Thomas and Luke helped her up and then the four of them, led by Sam, left the Blue Gator.

"What in the world?" Miss Doris muttered. Though she hadn't budged from her chair, she was short of breath. "Louie, do you have any idea what that was about?" I could barely hear her over the speculation spilling into the air. "Louie? *Louie?*"

I slowly stood, my mind racing to piece together the puzzle of our lives.

"They drove away in their trucks!" Chris Horn, who'd followed them outside, exclaimed from the doorway.

"The cemetery," I muttered. It was the only thing that made sense.

"What, Louie? What'd you say?" Miss Doris yanked my arm to bring me back to her, but I couldn't tell her what I'd concluded because I didn't want her to tell everyone else. Sam had been surveilling the unearthed graves. He'd come from the cemetery. Odds were he was going back to it.

I broke from Miss Doris's grasp and ran for the door. J.L. caught me on my way out. "What the hell?" he said, beer on his breath.

"Come on!" Brothers again, we stormed out of the Blue Gator Grill. The distant taillights cut through the dim early evening light, glowing like the fiery red tips of lit cigarettes in a smoky cloud of gray dust. We chased the trucks until their lights were gone, leaving us to follow my instinct after that. The cemetery wasn't far from the Blue Gator. Nothing on the reservation really was.

We found the trucks parked beside the path leading into the cemetery. Four shadowy figures stood huddled around what I assumed to be Fay's grave not far in the distance. A fifth silhouette, something in its grasp, emerged from Ray Horn's supply shed and sprinted toward the huddled mass.

"What are we waiting for?" J.L. asked.

Distressing screams had stopped me in my tracks, my arm out as a barrier across Jean-Luc's chest. "Where're they coming from?" I said.

Looking confused, J.L. pointed. "They're right over there." He barreled past me, running straight for the grave and the group gathered around it, not slowing until he was within feet of the burial plot. I expected Grandpa or Luke to run him off, but neither took notice.

"Good for nothing son of a bitch," Tom growled as I crept up behind J.L., the screams growing louder. "Why didn't you dig? You stupid bastard. You goddamned—"

"Tom, stop!" Miss Autumn pled. "Don't say those things." She tried to put hands on him, to calm him, but he twisted each time she got close, effectively deflecting her with his elbows. He'd heaved a foot of dirt from the grave by the time I got there, which seemed to spur the screams on. I suddenly realized where they were coming from.

"Make it stop . . . oh god, make it stop . . ." Bent at the waist, his back to the grave, Sam's index fingers plugged his ears, the grimace on his face illustrating his agony. "Do you hear it?" he brayed.

"You stupid son of a bitch," Tom seethed, casting another shovelful of earth from the hole. The screams surged higher. "How could you just leave her here?"

The shrill cries coming from beneath the ground were too much to bear. They had the pitch of fear. The pitch of pain. Could Miss Fay really be alive beneath all that dirt?

"I thought it was in my head," Sam cried. "I didn't know what to do."

Miss Autumn fell next to the grave, head in her hands, anxiously waiting for her husband to fling the final shovelful of dirt. I staggered backward, my knees like lumps of wax beneath a hot sun.

"You bastard. You stupid—"

"Stop, Tom." Luke finally stepped in. The way he reached for the shovel indicated that he wasn't just referring to Tom's verbal assault.

"To hell with you, Luke!"

"We need a moment to sort this out," Luke said. "Sam, get back to your truck. Tom, I want you to come with me."

"What the fuck's goin' on?" J.L. whispered in my ear.

The cries soared higher as the wind gusted across the cemetery.

"Can't you . . . can't you hear?" I stammered, pointing at the nearly open grave.

"Hear what?" His obliviousness gave me shivers all over again.

"Just make it stop." Taking Luke's orders, Sam retreated to his truck. "Please, God, just make it stop. . . ."

"Tom!" Luke snapped.

"Please!" Miss Autumn crawled to Luke's side and wrapped her arms around his legs. "My mom . . . I have to see my mom!"

I grabbed Grandpa by the shoulder. "Do you hear it?"

His worried eyes flicked over me, briefly meeting with mine. His face both uncertain and sad, he pulled at his chin. I couldn't tell what, if anything, he heard. "Let Tom dig," he said.

Luke stepped back, his hands on his hips. "You shouldn't be here," he grumbled to me and J.L., though he didn't order us to leave. I wouldn't have been able to if he had. Not with Miss Fay wailing beneath us.

Tom dug faster as I inched backward, not wanting to see yet unable to look away. J.L. crept closer to the hole. The cries kept coming. Louder. Higher. As terrifying as the one who produced them was terrified.

Finally tossing the shovel aside, Tom vanished into the pit, then popped up with a growl-like grunt. Straining, he managed to prop the casket, a cheap pine box, up in the hole, its tip protruding out of the earth. The cries coming from within bore into my brain like wailing worms wriggling through my ears. Tom climbed out of the grave, then he, Miss Autumn, and J.L., who couldn't resist getting in on the action, hauled the casket up onto the grass.

"I really don't think—" Luke shook his head, but it was too late to stop them. Thomas used the shovel to pry the casket's lid open. Four screams exploded on the air when he did. One leaped past his lips. Another tore from Miss Autumn. The third streamed out of me. And the fourth came from whatever had fooled us into thinking that Fay had been buried alive.

There was no life in that awful box, nothing that could have stung our ears the way those screams had.

Miss Autumn turned away. Body quaking, her forehead hit the ground while J.L. inched closer to the casket.

"Go home, Louie." Grandpa Joe turned away, pulling at his chin again.

"What just happened?" I asked.

"You heard what Sam heard?"

"Didn't you? I still hear it now." Though the screaming had stopped, the cemetery wasn't silent. Cries carried on the air, from Miss Autumn and from something I couldn't see.

Grandpa shook his head.

"What's causing all this?"

"I don't know."

I thought back to what he'd said at the Blue Gator Grill. "Spirits?"

"I've never . . ." He paused, then gave a quick shrug. His face, weathered and grim like the old stones sticking out of the ground around us, creased with confusion. "I've never known the spirits to do something like this."

I wanted to argue, but I kept my mouth shut. All I could think of was Fay's wake.

She'd sat up, and I'd heard her cry for help.

TWENTY-NINE

Noemi

"Louie, wait!" I screeched. He'd taken off in pursuit of the bloody trail. Made numb by what he'd said, I thought I'd fall on my face with each unstable step I took. What did he mean that Roddy's death might not have been an accident or suicide? What else could have caused it? And what the hell did that have to do with the coyote?

Somehow, my feet found their rhythm, though I felt like a two-year-old running all wobbly and wild, my arms out in front of me in case I took a tumble. I could barely see Uncle Louie ahead of me, just the light of his phone steadily bobbing up and down, up and down as we left the Blue Gator Grill's parking lot behind, only darkness ahead of us for now.

"Stop!" I cried a minute later, once we were surrounded by trees whose bark looked black. Already winded by his words, I couldn't keep up with his pace. I stopped to suck cool air into my lungs. Uncle Louie put on the skids and shined his light toward me.

A text arrived before I got my breath back. Sara again.

He was off his meds.

Meds? Just like that, I was plummeting. And soaring. Both at once, my heart racing, blood pressure rising.

What meds?

Roddy wasn't on meds. He took a multivitamin before work and extra vitamin C if he was feeling rundown. Throughout our "three" years together, I'd only seen him stuffy once. Nothing a little VapoRub couldn't fix. He was healthy as a horse. A stallion.

Uncle Louie jogged back to me. His eyes passed over my phone in my hands. I turned it away from him because I didn't want him to see, didn't want him to give up on the mysterious, crazy notion compelling him to follow the blood trail.

What the fuck are you talking about!?!

I should have reworded that, but the tornado in my brain had cast my manners aside. Sara would probably make me wait longer as punishment.

"What'd you find out?" Uncle Louie panted.

I didn't answer. I couldn't. I was trying to think of things for which Roddy might have needed medication. Given the situation, one dreaded illness rushed to the top of the list.

But Roddy wasn't.

A single word from Sara contradicted what I knew to be true.

Antidepressants

My hair swung. My head shook. My hand squeezed the phone with all its might, as if to see whether my bones or the metal and glass would crumble first.

"What's wrong?" Uncle Louie pressed closer, trying to steal another peek at my screen. I put my back to him.

There's no way

Roddy? Depressed? No fucking chance! Suddenly, I had an ugly thought about Sara. That she was making this up, leading me on. But even though I knew she didn't like me, I didn't think she'd stoop that low.

How do u know?

I knew Roddy better than anyone. The same could be said of him about me. If anyone had known about Roddy's depression, it would have been me.

But Roddy wasn't depressed! He was the direct opposite of sad—the happiest man in every room he entered. So happy that it rubbed off on others. How many smiles had I seen him spread? How many giggles had I heard validating his corny jokes? Roddy was quick in conversation and charismatic. He was like a dog in the very best way, everyone's friend.

"Noemi!" Uncle Louie's voice boomed in my ears. I raised my gaze from the phone and turned back to him. "What is it?"

"Nothing," I said, and, lacking an explanation from Sara, that's what I willed myself to believe: the meds meant nothing. "Let's just . . ." I motioned ahead. We went forth at a slower pace, the darkness keeping me from seeing whatever worried expression Uncle Louie might have worn, and him from seeing the grimace on my face.

The blood trail passed three broadly spaced houses. Uncle Louie stalled outside the fourth. "Miss Doris," he said.

I was still focused on my phone, waiting for whatever Sara would send next.

"Used to be a trailer on this lot," Uncle Louie went on. "We used to come here. You and I."

I looked up at the house, set back beyond a sizable front yard. Still, I could see in through the wide front window. The TV was on, tuned to News 11.

"She's dead now," Uncle Louie said.

Dead got my attention. "Who?"

"Miss Doris." He made the sign of the cross over his body, something I'd never seen him do before. It seemed strange, but then again, who knew how he'd changed while he'd been away. "Strong woman," he said. "Forgiving."

I might have questioned him about his relationship with the dead lady—Rosie's mom, I remembered—if I wasn't so distracted by the nightly news. The anchor was smiling like Roddy always had, birthing another ugly thought, one that wrenched my stomach, making me want to gag.

Was the man I knew and loved the real Roddy, or was he Roddy from the news, always well-tempered, always *on*? I tried to list things that separated the Roddy I could hold and kiss from the Roddy I could only see on TV.

Panic blossomed when I couldn't immediately come up with anything.

Of course I knew things about Roddy that the average television viewer didn't, but did that mean I truly knew him? Was there a side to him I'd missed? A side he'd never let me see, complete with feelings I'd never known he was feeling?

A memory came to me then, from when Roddy and I drove to the flea market in Deville. He'd been quiet and glum, not once asking any of the sellers *How much for your fleas?* as he normally would, and completely uninterested when—as I was checking out a chest someone was selling—I discovered a hidden drawer full of old Pokémon cards, which he would have excitedly called a *Good find!* on any other occasion. I'd chalked his sullen demeanor up to a bad day. We all have them. But what if it wasn't just a bad day? What if it was Real Roddy leaking through, too glum to keep up Reporter Roddy's façade?

I tapped again on my phone screen.

Please tell me how u know

He wouldn't have done it

My faith was slipping.

THIRTY

Louie

The cries began again on my way home from the cemetery. Whether they were produced by spirits or awful dead things in the ground, I couldn't say, and given the fact I was alone, I didn't want to think about the possibilities. I passed the pow wow grounds; vast and vacant, the site bolstered my unease. Had there been a group of singers practicing around a reassuring drum, the music might have steadied the reckless beat of my heart.

Instead of music, the cries swirled around me. And while they may not have been real, I didn't doubt that whatever had caused them was. I could sense it. Feel it. Humid and thick, like blasts of warm breath against the back of my neck. I bristled each time I felt its sultry touch. My legs picked up speed until they broke into a run. I told myself that the presence I perceived was a product of my frightened mind, just like the lingering cries, but I couldn't believe it. The feeling was too real.

Something rustled in the brush to my left, the patter of invisible feet sounded on the road behind me, and unintelligible whispers floated on the wind. The unsettling sounds created a cacophony that competed with the cries. Each fought for dominance, demanding to be heard. But why? To scare me? Or was I scaring myself?

The road moved slowly beneath my frantic feet, the footsteps keeping pace behind me as the rustle in the brush moved from my left to my right.

"*Louie!*" the wind whispered. It sounded like a threat.

I winced, wondering if Sam, Tom, and Miss Autumn were hearing similar things wherever they were. I thought about the tribe's old beliefs. The spirits. Some good, some bad, each essential for keeping the other in balance. Could the balance have been broken as Grandpa had surmised, or was there another explanation altogether?

Like a dog on a leash that's run out of slack, I came to a sudden stop before home was in sight. I didn't realize where I was until the wind gusted a belly laugh in my face. It forced me to turn away from the field on one side of the road in exchange for the old trailer and its lopsided shed on the other.

My eyes squeezed shut upon beholding the haunted place—haunted by legend, haunted by history, potentially haunted by Horace and the Takoda Vampire. The sight remained when I lifted my eyelids, and while I wanted nothing more than to resume running, something held me hostage there. The grip of chains around my ankles felt as real as the humid breath tickling the nape of my neck.

"The vampire," I gasped. The stories we'd told as kids maintained that the Takoda Vampire would kill you if Horace showed up outside your window with one of his rocks. *What if,* I wondered, *it could do more than that?* What if it could lure old ladies to their deaths, dig up graves, make next-door neighbors go missing, and compel corpses to cry?

"No!" I said, reminding myself that I'd be seventeen soon, and that the stories I'd grown up with were made up by kids like me. Time, however, can do bizarre things to our brains. With time, things that are made up sometimes become beliefs. And people who question those beliefs are sometimes called crazy.

I wouldn't have called myself crazy for denying the vampire, but I didn't feel crazy for believing in it either.

The trailer appeared to list like a ghost ship riding rocky waves beneath its hull. The curtains in Horace's window swayed. I knew the movement wasn't possible, but still I felt seasick watching the trailer bobble. Maybe it was because I knew what had happened behind those curtains.

Not a single light shined in any of the trailer's windows. The over-grown grass rustled in the wind around it, each brown blade a resur-rected corpse. Looking like it'd succumb to zealous wind itself, the shed stubbornly held its ground each time a gust laughed in my face. The unloved old shed laughed at me too. The rattle of its rusted door intoned a heartless cackle.

"*I dare you. . . .*" the wind whispered.

"No," I said.

"*Do it. I dare you. . . .*"

A chill from the invisible chains crawled up my legs and settled deep within my chest. The challenge whispered by the wind sounded a lot like the taunt we'd goad each other with as kids. Always from the roadside. Always ready to run. Always when there was plenty of day-light left.

None of us had wanted to be the one to run across George Sauci-er's overgrown grass and look through the window of the room where his son once slept, but we all wondered what we'd see if we did. It was one of the greatest challenges we could issue each other back then. The only thing more daring would've been to open the shed's door.

"*I dare you. . . .*"

Only one person had ever accepted the dare to peek past Horace's curtains. Jacob Bloom. Four years older than me, Jacob was in Lula's class at school because he'd been held back a year. I wasn't there when Jacob's stoned buddies dared him to press his face against the glass.

Neither was Lula, but she'd gotten it on good account from Rosie Deshautelle, who'd shared her first kiss with Jacob at the age of twelve, that he did it.

What Jacob saw gave us reason to believe the legend. It helped the legend grow. When he grabbed the windowsill and hoisted himself up to see inside, he let out a scream that brought George Saucier out of the trailer gripping a steak knife in his hand. It wasn't anything in the trailer that'd made Jacob scream. He hadn't been able to see past the curtains. What he saw was his face reflected in the glass. And something far less familiar standing behind him.

"I dare you. Do it."

My teeth chattered at the thought of what Jacob had seen. Fiery eyes. Dark green skin covered with growths like teeth. An alligator's smile.

"I dare you."

"No."

"Do it!"

"No!"

Jacob never made it to the shed. He fell from the windowsill after screaming, whereupon he struggled to find his feet as his eyes darted this way and that in search of what he'd seen reflected in the glass. George, according to some reports, brandished the knife. Jacob's brainless buddies fled, hooting and hollering down the road, while Jake—some said—ran straight home into his mother's arms. Rosie never confirmed that part of the story.

The wind blew stronger. The shed's door rattled louder, like phlegm in an old man's chest, wheezing laughter. The shed wasn't just cackling at me anymore, it was daring me too, gloating because it hadn't been torn down after Horace was laid to rest. I tried to flee, but my feet remained glued to the ground, just like my eyes remained glued to the god-awful shed.

"Open me up," it grumbled. *"Come see what you find."*

"No!" I screamed. "You shouldn't still be standing. You should've been knocked down years ago!" The same could have been said about the trailer. George Saucier's discovery of Horace's body in Horace's bedroom had sent a paralyzing jolt through the reservation. What George found in the shed, on the other hand, nearly robbed us of our faith in anything good.

"Open me up. . . . Come, Louie . . . see what you find."

I refrained from hollering at the rusted heap again for fear of luring George out of the trailer. And because I was yelling at voices in my head. They had to be. Believing in the vampire may not have meant I was crazy but hollering at a damned shed just might.

Eyes clenched, I took a deep breath and let it out slowly. My body fell from whatever had been holding it prisoner, though the chill from the invisible chains remained. So did the whisper floating on the wind. It followed me when I resumed running. As did the footfalls behind my back, picking up speed.

With the brush still rustling on either side of the road, it occurred to me that I might be escorting the unidentified evil home, leading it from the shed or wherever it resided. Terrifying as that thought was, I had no way to shake the dreadful presence I felt. How do you get rid of something that appears as nothing? I reeled, squinting through the darkness, then plowed forth again. I couldn't just linger in the road all night, hoping everything would be all right.

I expected the battered armadillo to be waiting on the porch at home, but it wasn't on the steps or outside the door. I leaped onto the porch and surveyed the land around me, striving to see into the shadows. I didn't want to go inside until I was sure nothing would follow me in. To my relief, the wind had reverted to singing its nightly song, accompanied by a band of crickets, cicadas, and frogs. Turning to open the door, a voice boomed through the darkness.

"What'd he say?"

My heart kicked so hard it nearly knocked me off the porch. What did who say? The thing that wanted us to believe Fay was screaming in the cemetery? The wind? The damned shed?

I spun to face the darkness. "Who's there?" I barked. A lightning bug, ass aglow, landed on the bridge of my nose. My eyes crossed. My vision blurred.

"Me."

I should have recognized the flat tone, but I saw something move beyond the glowing bug on my nose, something inky as the darkness. It prevented my mind from distinguishing between the familiar and the unknown.

I swatted the bug away, wishing it could light up the night, and ducked beneath the porch railing for protection. Again, I saw nothing in the field other than shadows. Shadows that could easily conceal something fiercer than the monster in Horace's myth.

"Come here, Louie." It was Ern, of course. Who else would it be?

"Do you see something?" I hissed across the expanse.

"See what?"

"Anything."

"You," he said. "Come over. Bring me somethin' to eat."

I wavered on the porch, then slipped inside the trailer. My hand intuitively locked the door behind me. Safe inside, I knew I ought to stay that way, but with Ma at work and Lula snuggled beside Noemi behind their closed bedroom door, I wanted more than security and silence that could be filled by fear. I wanted noise I knew was real, even if that noise came from someone who'd spooked me as much as Ern.

I took the carton of milk from the fridge and snagged the generic box of honey-flavored cornflakes—I'd never had the thrill of shaking a prize from a brand name box of cereal into my breakfast bowl—from atop it. Having collected a bowl, a spoon, and a serrated knife from the sink, I went out again. My legs needed extra coaxing to venture down the steps, but with the milk, cereal, and bowl clenched against my chest with one arm like a shield, the spoon in my pocket, and the knife brandished by my free hand in front of me, I conjured enough courage to trek across the field.

"Haven't had milk in days," Ern said. He kept the blinds in place as he raised the window screen and reached out for the food. The noise I craved came in the form of Ern's aggressive crunching. I sat on the bottom step outside his door, the butt of the knife against my knee, the blade sticking straight up in the air.

"What'd he say?" Ern asked again, having inhaled two and a half bowls of cereal, all he'd been able to shake from the box.

"What did who say?" I still couldn't make sense of the question. I didn't see how Ern could have known about the voices I'd heard.

"Your grandpa. What'd he say at the Blue Gator?"

"Oh." I let out the breath I'd been holding. "How'd you know about that?"

"Came by earlier today. Said he'd fill me in after the meeting, but he ain't been back."

"He . . ." I decided not to say anything about the cemetery. I didn't want to talk about it. "He must be busy."

"What'd he say?"

I sighed and gave him the news. "We're gonna search the river . . . from the bridge to the bend. Luke and Sam are starting in the morning. They've asked for everyone's help."

Ern dropped the blinds to just a few inches above the windowsill. "Do me a favor, Louie. Be the first to tell me what they find."

"Why?"

"Because you always tell me things in the dark." The blinds fell. He didn't say anything else.

THIRTY-ONE

Louie

I thought the screams were in my head. I stayed still, listening, my face flat against the pillow, wet beneath my mouth. The screams came faster, climbing higher. I rolled over, squinting. The single ray of sunlight sneaking through the sliver between the curtains stung my eyes. It was just after seven in the morning. I'd been asleep for a few short hours.

"Louie!" The shriek hit like a blow to the belly. "Louie, get out here!"

The screams were Lula's. Noemi was my first thought. Then Fay in the grass. And Aubrey in the kitchen. I scrambled out of bed so fast I nearly fell atop my drum, the top sheet roped around my ankles.

"Lula!" I threw open my bedroom door. She stood there trembling, tears streaming down her cheeks, Noemi limp in her arms.

"No!" I reached for my niece. "What happened?"

Lula retreated until her back was against the wall. "I think she's dead." The four words fell from my sister's mouth like bombs from a fighter jet. The sob that escaped her exploded in my ears.

I reached for Noemi again, my hand landing on her back. She was warm. Breathing. The pissy scent of her dirty diaper snaked up my nose.

"She's all right," I said, feeling both a warm rush of relief and a cold stab of confusion upon beholding the dismay still making Lula's eyes water. Noemi lifted her head from her mother's shoulder and looked at me. Her eyes were worried as well.

"Not Noemi." Lula pointed to the living room. The front door was open. Filling the lowest part of the doorway was something I couldn't comprehend. I stood stock-still. Staring. Blinking. Trying to make sense of what I was seeing.

"It's Ma!" Lula screamed.

Then I saw it. I saw *her*. Bloody. On her back. Jet-black hair matted across her face.

"Ma?" I said, buried in disbelief.

"She's dead," Lula sobbed.

Ma was flat on the floor, half in and half out of the trailer, which is why she'd looked so strange to me. I could only see her upper body and head, tufts of hair all over the place. Her legs were out the door, resting on the porch. My heart constricted like a party balloon twisted into a dog or a rose. I took cautious steps closer.

"What happened?" My voice barely carried the words. Bile burned at the back of my throat.

"I don't know. I just found her like this."

The shame of guilt brought tears to my eyes. The Takoda Vampire. It must have followed me the night before. More accurately, I must have led it here from the damned shed or wherever it'd been hiding. I'd brought it home, and it'd made my mother suffer because of me.

Tears flowed to the bottom of my chin. I moved closer to the body and roared. Short of putting a hole in the trailer's ugly brown paneling, it was all I could do to vent my pain, my anger. Clenched in Ma's bloody fist was a paper bag. A bloated brown bag just like all the others she'd brought home from work.

My legs gave out, forcing me to kneel next to her. My head hung over hers. My hair swept her wounds. The tears dripped from my chin onto her mottled skin. Blood streaked her face, her neck, her hands. The vampire must have gotten her on her way home from work. Horace must have thrown one of his rocks at her windshield like he'd done to the Hensleys.

"Do something, Louie," Lula said, as if I could wave a wand and make Ma better. She came closer, one hand on the back of Noemi's head to keep her from looking.

I brushed the matted hair from Ma's face. Her swollen eyes were closed. Blood brimmed between split flesh on her forehead. Another wound yawned at me from her right cheek, gaping like a toothless grin about to utter something ugly. A small flap of skin hung open on her chin. The beauty I'd once seen in her was gone, stained red.

Tiny cuts glistened all over Ma's hands, forearms, and wrists. Blood stained the bloated brown bag clenched in her fist. I bowed my head and cried, letting my sadness, guilt, and regret compel me. My body shook. My heart ached. I thought I was to blame.

When George Saucier found Horace the morning after the attack, Horace was bloody, but his body had been drained of blood. No one would know that until after the medical examiner inspected Horace's corpse. There were wounds on Horace's wrists. Wounds on his neck. And one great wound in the middle of his chest.

Teeth, according to the coroner, were the primary weapon used in the attack. Teeth like those in an alligator's smile. Teeth used only to shred and to tear. Tamahka don't chew.

My eyes slowly wandered from my mother's torn-up hands to her chest. Her embroidered work shirt was bloody, but it wasn't ripped. Short of peeling back the fabric, I had no way of knowing if she still had her heart.

No one had realized it at first. They'd seen the horrific wounds on Horace's body and the blood that had dried on his flesh, but they couldn't see what he internally lacked. Horace's heart had been taken from him. Taken by the vampire. The medical examiner, some said, discovered the organ missing precisely as George Saucier stumbled upon it in the shed.

That damned shed.

George had gone out to get the gardening shears so that he could tame the greenery growing wild along the edge of his property. Physical labor, I suppose, was his way of coping with the pain. He found more than just the shears in the shed. Sitting on a shelf with dirt and a little sawdust sticking to it, wedged between a can of WD-40 and wasp repellent, was his son's mangled heart.

My fingertips swept over the red stain on my mother's shirt, only to withdraw before applying real pressure. If there was a hole in her chest, it was a discovery I didn't want to make.

"Do something, Louie." Lula had taken to pacing in the hall, eyes averted, each inhalation more labored than the last.

"Ma!" My mind blanketed itself with denial, searching for ways to save her rather than accepting that she was gone. "I'm sorry," I sobbed. "What can I do?"

The bloated brown bag. Didn't it bear some responsibility? It wasn't only I who'd done my mother harm by bringing the vampire home. It was that bag and what it concealed. I tore the sack from her grasp and threw it aside. Still sobbing, I crawled over her body out onto the porch. The morning dew clinging to the cool air dissolved like sugar on my tongue each time I gasped. Grasping for something stable, I reached for a baluster. Droplets of blood that led down the steps and into the dirt drew my eye as I pulled myself to the edge of the porch. An anole carrying a desperately twitching cricket in its mouth scurried past the droplets. My stomach sank. I knew I'd find Ma's heart if I followed the bloody trail.

Staggering to my feet, I screamed, "Ern!"

His blinds were down, and he didn't reply. I screamed his name three more times before the blinds finally inched up.

"Did you see it, Ern?"

"See what?" He sounded groggy, unalarmed by the fear in my voice.

"The vampire! The attack! Did you see what it did to my ma?"

"Didn't see a thing."

Flames erupted within my rib cage. How could Ern see so much— Ma putting money on the table for groceries, her closed bedroom door, the concealed cans in the garbage bag—but not see a murder outside his window? "It was the vampire!" I screamed. "It was here. It got her."

"Didn't see a thing," he said again. As my astonishment waned, I made sense of his claim. George and June Saucier, asleep in their bedroom down the hall from Horace's, hadn't heard a thing the night Horace lost his life. Hell, I'd only been a few feet away inside our small trailer and I hadn't heard so much as a sniffle.

"Louie!" Lula cried. "Louie, get back here."

I reeled around and leaned in over Ma's legs, using the doorframe for support.

"Look!" Lula pointed. Ma's right eye had popped open, a black olive in brine. The left one remained swollen shut.

"Is she . . . ?" I knew by then that movements made by the dead didn't mean a damn thing. Ma moaned. That, too, didn't mean she was alive. *It was only a belch, Louie,* I heard Miss Doris inside my head. Despite how lifeless Ma looked, the moan sparked hope. I lunged through the door and down to her side.

"Ma . . . Ma?" I panted.

"She's not dead," Lula said. "Oh, thank God, she's not dead."

I leaned close to Ma's face. Even with one eye open, she didn't seem to be seeing. Her pupil didn't move when I waved my hand in front of it. She moaned some more, the low noise like a purr.

"Do something," Lula said.

"Get Grandpa!"

Lula could have called him on the phone, but her adrenaline led her to leap over Ma and out the door with Noemi in her arms. Ern called her name as her bare feet hammered the hard earth.

"Ma? Can you hear me?" I brushed more hair away from her face, being careful not to upset her wounds. I could see her chest heaving now, inhaling deeper, faster breaths that rattled in her lungs.

"Starry," she wheezed. Her open eyelid sagged.

"What happened?"

A jumbled mess of sound came in response. She pushed her hands against the floor, intending to sit up.

"Don't." I held her down. "Not yet." I ran into the kitchen to soak a dish towel in cold water and to get some ice. "Who did this to you?" I wrapped the ice in the towel and pressed it against her left eye. She moved her head to escape my hand, her moans growing louder. "Who did this?" I demanded, knowing I should be asking *What did this?* "Who?"

She groaned and closed her working eye. Her breaths became shallow again, nearly impossible to perceive. I saw her mortality for the second time that morning. It filled me with fright equal to that inspired by Horace and the vampire. It scared me because I thought I might lose her before ever really having her.

"Can you tell me who did this?"

Her head rocked from side to side, confirming what I feared. I suddenly felt like we weren't alone in the trailer, as though whatever had followed me the night before was sitting in wait, as though it had wanted me and not my mother all along.

I considered dragging Ma all the way inside so I could lock the door, but what if we needed to make a quick escape? I couldn't determine if we'd be safer inside the trailer or out of it. I sprang into the kitchen and grabbed the knife I'd taken to Ern's. Wielding it—hand trembling like a leaf in the wind—I went from room to room, searching every closet and beneath each bed, expecting something to grab me, something that would shred and tear me. I encountered nothing with teeth.

"Louie!"

I nearly pissed my pants.

"Louie, where are you?"

"Grandpa!" I popped back into the living room. He was standing outside the door, Lula and Noemi behind him. His eyes darted up from his daughter to me with the knife in my hand.

"He was already on his way over," Lula said. "Is she gonna be all right?"

"You were coming here?" I asked Grandpa Joe. He stepped over Ma to get inside and knelt beside her.

"Mark Bishop found the truck on the side of Old River Road." He picked up the bloody towel and wiped it over Ma's wounds. "She crashed it."

But how did she crash it? And why? Was it like what happened to the Hensleys?

"Because of this," Grandpa said, reading my thoughts. He picked up an empty can by the door and hurled it out onto the grass. I thought about the droplets of blood on the porch and in the dirt. They weren't leading away from the trailer as I'd originally thought. They were leading to it. I realized that in my state of fear I hadn't noticed that the truck wasn't parked in its usual spot. Ma must have made her way home on foot, bleeding all the way from Old River Road to our front door with that bloated brown bag in her hand.

"They're not deep." Grandpa wiped most of the blood away. I could see then that the wounds were more likely made by broken glass than teeth. "You got lucky, Mae," he said. "This has to stop."

A moan met our ears. Grandpa sighed and stood. "I'll bring you some bandages. Take her to her room."

Grandpa didn't ask why I had the knife in my hand, but I think he knew. I put it back in the sink, then eased Ma up until she was sitting on her own.

"Careful, Louie," Lula muttered.

"Can you stand?" Ma's one working eye reeled in my direction. She smiled, her uncanny expression filling me with repulsion and dread, triggering my instinct to flee. A pink film of blood coated her teeth. Obliviousness swirled in her cycloptic gaze. For all I knew, she didn't recognize me at all. I snaked my trembling arms under hers and said, "On the count of three. One . . . two . . . three . . ." I heaved her up. She found her feet and then started to sag. I slung her left arm over my shoulders and wrapped one of mine around her waist. It was the closest we'd come to hugging in years. "It's only a few steps. You can make it."

Her coordination was inferior to Noemi's, her way of communicating was even worse. Finding some strength, she grunted and ground her feet against the floor.

"What?" I wondered. She grunted some more, pulling me back toward the door. "You've gotta get to bed. You need to rest." She shook her head, continuing to drift. I relented and went with her, but it wasn't the door she desired. It was the bloated brown bag with bloodstains on its sides. She nabbed it, then redirected us toward her room, clinging to the bag tighter than she clung to me.

"You're ugly like this." My voice quavered as I set her at the foot of her bed. My eyes couldn't see past the blood, the wounds, or the swollen flesh obstructing her sight. I couldn't see the woman I'd once thought was beautiful when she sang and picked wildflowers along the road. Still, I didn't want to let her go. "You have to stop. You don't need this." I tried to take the brown bag from her. She slapped me across the face.

The slap lacked strength, yet it stung in so many ways. I squinted to keep more tears from spilling over my eyelids. "What's it going to take for you to stop?" I seethed, bitterly aware that the tables should have been turned. I should have been the teenager learning life's lessons.

She grabbed the bag with both hands and tottered. It looked like she might fall limp atop the mattress. "The bingo hall will make things better," she said after some time. "You'll see. . . . The bingo hall will fix everything."

I left her with her bag and closed her door behind me. My fingertips trembled against the doorknob as realization sank in. I'd been wrong. I'd convinced myself that Ma was okay because she could still get to work and back. At least she could do that, I'd thought. What motivated her is what I'd overlooked. It wasn't responsibility or obligation that got her to work each night and back home each morning. She wasn't doing it for me, Lula, or Noemi, or to put money on the table when the cupboards were bare. It was an addiction she chose to feed. An addiction she likely mistook for the need Grandpa had told me about. She only took up her nightly shift at Roscoe's Get 'n' Go because it was there that she could easily fill the brown paper bags. The gas station mini-mart sold more than just Swiss Rolls.

The realization hurt so bad all I could do was shake. Grandpa's words from days earlier came back to me.

Let her know you're there.

I burst back into the room. On her side with her back to me, Ma had pulled her feet up onto the mattress, the brown paper bag nestled within the L of her torso and thighs. One hand rummaged deep inside.

"Ma. I'm here," I said.

The paper bag's rustling ceased. Ma's hand reappeared, empty.

"I'm tired, Louie."

"Did you hear me?"

She didn't reply. I didn't feel my feet bring me to the bed, but I did feel the mattress yield to my weight. I stalled, questioning what I was about to do, then I did it. I wound one arm over her and the other beneath her.

"I'm here," I said.

Silence. An arduous inhalation. Heartbeats that seemed much too slow. A gurgling exhalation.

"I know," she said.

I didn't fight my tears. They leaked into her bloody hair.

"I thought it was the vampire. . . ." I cried and hugged her tight, loving her even if she couldn't love me. "I thought it was the vampire."

THIRTY-TWO

Noemi

I was starting to think that Sara might be a sadist or that there might be an even darker reason behind why she was taking so long to justify her claim that Roddy was off meds I'd never known him to take.

My phone rang. Scrambling, I nearly dropped it, only for disappointment to set in when I saw Mom's face on the screen. I quickly rejected her call, almost angry that she'd dare to come between me and the text that still hadn't come. Uncle Louie's phone rang a few seconds later.

"She's with me," he said. His phone's flashlight now up around his head, we proceeded without seeing any glistening droplets on the pavement. "Don't worry. I'll bring her home."

"I hate when she does that," I said after he hung up.

"Does what?"

"Checks on me like I'm a little kid."

Uncle Louie shined the light on the trail again. I had to let him lead because I couldn't keep my eyes on the crimson drops for long. My feelings about the coyote and what it might have done to Roddy aside, its life was leaking out of it, and I couldn't help feeling sad.

"She won't always check on you," he said, and I instantly understood the underlying message. Now I felt sad and bad, especially after what he said next. "No one ever annoyed me like that."

Was it wrong of me for never thinking about how he and Mom were raised, so often on their own?

"Guess I should be thankful," I said.

"Just pick up her call next time."

How many calls had I rejected over the years, never thinking about what my silence was doing to her? Waiting to hear from Sara now helped put things into perspective. It made me understand why Mom would drop in on me unannounced before I'd moved back in with her. She'd bring groceries or premade dinners that spoke of the worry she kept quiet inside.

"Hold up," I said, the peripheral light of the flashlight's beam having illuminated a sign on the corner of the cross street we'd just passed.

"What's wrong?" He kept his eyes aimed in the direction of the trail while mine wrestled with the darkness as I backtracked to the corner. The sign was an old piece of plywood painted white. The words **FREE FIREWOOD** in sloppy black strokes hovered atop an arrow pointing to the left. I'd passed the sign a million times before, always in my Jeep, on my way to Roddy's.

"Come on!" I said, starting to run again, just not in the direction of the trail. Indifferent to what the night might be hiding ahead of me, I plowed forth, too impatient to turn my own flashlight on.

"Noemi, come back!" Uncle Louie called. I could tell by how long it took for his footfalls to sound behind me that he'd considered carrying on without me. If he'd taken any longer to make up his mind, he wouldn't have seen me swing a right at the next cross street.

We didn't meet again until after I stopped where the asphalt met the lawn of the house that still belonged to Roddy until his family settled his affairs.

"Is this . . . ?" he panted, not needing to finish the question. He knew where we were.

Every light in the house must have been on. A Ford Taurus that wasn't Roddy's sat parked in the driveway.

"We'll lose it," Uncle Louie said, a hand on my upper arm, trying to pull me back to the trail.

"Just . . ." I shrugged him off and proceeded up the walk, leaving him on the street. It felt weird to knock. I never had before. Roddy always left the door unlocked when he knew I was coming over. Voices sounded inside, low murmuring. A curtain flapped in the window to the left of the door. More murmuring leaked through. They kept me waiting for more than a minute, then the lock snapped and the door opened a few inches. An eroded face peered out at me, one far too young to look so old.

"Sara," I gasped, winded, my emotions mounting. I moved toward her, expecting to be united by shared grief, but she didn't open the door any wider or even offer a hug. She just slipped through those few inches and pulled the door shut behind her.

"I told you not to come." She didn't sound mad, just dispirited, exhausted, and sad. Her arms, clothed in the blue button-up shirt Roddy had worn on air that morning, crossed over her chest.

"I bought him that shirt," I said. It hung low on her tiny frame.

"What are you doing here?"

"Can we . . . ?" I motioned to the door.

She turned to look as if she didn't know what was behind her.

"My parents," she said, shaking her head. "Now's not a good—"

"You didn't answer my text."

"Noemi . . ." She sighed, and I thought she might collapse, as if she'd just emitted what was left of her strength into the air.

"The meds," I said. "How do you know?"

Her eyes, rimmed with tears, looked up at the light above us, moths flitting about. "I found two prescription bottles of Zoloft."

The last word—the name—didn't register. And then it did. Denial ensued.

"Where'd you find them?" I used Roddy's medicine cabinet regularly. I had a toothbrush in there, next to his vitamins. I'd never seen any prescription pills.

"Sock drawer," she said.

Had I ever gone in there? Before I could create a counterargument, she reached into her pocket and pulled one of the pill bottles out. She passed it to me.

Eyes blurry again, I struggled to read the label.

TAKE ONE TABLET BY MOUTH ONCE PER DAY.
QTY: 30

Roddy's full name was printed above the instructions.

"One bottle was filled a few weeks ago," Sara said. "The other was filled a month before that. Both are still full."

My mind frantically strung the details together. The fact that the bottles were full unraveled a line of reasoning that went like this: the bottles are full, which means he wasn't taking the pills, and if he wasn't taking the pills, he clearly didn't need them, and if he didn't need them, he must not have been depressed, and if he wasn't depressed, he wouldn't have . . .

My head spun, dizzy because I had to believe the long line of *ifs* if I wanted Roddy's death to be an accident. The memory of Roddy at the flea market, though, had brought another memory with it, of the time he'd canceled our plans to visit the waterpark in Baton Rouge only an hour before we were supposed to go, no word of warning. And then that memory spawned another, of Roddy skipping Mom's birthday dinner, saying he just needed some time *off*. I didn't want to admit it, but Roddy hadn't just had one bad day, he'd had a string of them.

"Please," I motioned toward the door again.

"Noemi." She sounded more exhausted than before. "Go home. It's the best place for you right now."

I didn't bother telling her that I'd always felt every bit as at home walking through Roddy's door as I did walking up my own porch steps. Needing to sit, I leaned against the rim of the large planter beside me.

"Maybe he didn't need the pills." I had to push my side of the argument, hoping it'd find its footing.

"He's needed them since he was seventeen."

She'd knocked the wind out of me again, right as the icy fingers of resentment wrapped around my spine. I should have known more about Roddy than her.

My mind teetered, trying to manufacture something stable I could cling to. If Roddy had been on antidepressants since he was seventeen, then it must have been a big decision for him to alter his routine. He must have had a significant reason to stop taking the pills.

"We need to talk to his doctor." As if I knew who his doctor was. I sank lower on the edge of the planter. It didn't make any sense. None of it. Assuming the meds had helped Roddy throughout his teens and twenties, he must have known that they could continue helping him. Wouldn't he have started taking them again if his old symptoms had returned?

Happiness, I reasoned, must have been at the root of why he'd decided to stay off the meds. He must have been content, I thought, with his family, his friends, his career, the promise of a fruitful future, and me. A mix of emotions—hope, reassurance, relief—that refuted what I'd been feeling flooded my chest. Gloom quickly followed.

Had his happiness worn away? Had his despair reappeared with brute strength, like a villain in a slasher film who cheats death time and again to claim a higher body count in the subsequent sequels? Had he been so overcome that he couldn't save himself?

"You don't really think . . . ?" I asked.

Sara's eyes shot up to the light again. She used the sleeve of Roddy's shirt to dry her eyes. "I wouldn't have thought *this*," she said.

"He never said any—?"

She was shaking her head before I could finish the question. "None of us had any reason to think he'd want to harm himself."

I thought about the busted mirror. I wanted to see it for myself but knew better than to ask. I turned the pill bottle over in my hand to cover its label.

"Your parents. What do they think happened?"

She shot a glance over her shoulder, again seeming to forget that the door was closed behind her. Her voice was lower when she spoke. "I haven't told them about the pills yet. I don't know how."

"We could do it together."

She took the bottle from me. Finally noticing Uncle Louie by the street, she said, "I'm glad you're not alone." Reaching behind her, she opened the door and took a step back through the threshold. "I'll text you, all right? If I find anything else." She began to shut the door, slowly, as if it would hurt less than if she were to slam it.

"Sara," I pleaded.

"Go home, Noemi. Get some rest."

The dead bolt slid into place almost as slowly as she'd closed the door. I sat there staring up at the moths, each futilely trying to feed by bashing against the glass globe surrounding the misleading light, each wanting but not receiving, a lot like me.

Still stubbornly refusing to believe that Roddy jumped in front of the Jeep, I had to accept the verifiable facts. Maybe I hadn't known him as well as I thought I had.

THIRTY-THREE

Louie

I told Miss Doris I wouldn't be able to watch Johnny that day. Lula called her boss at the hair boutique to get some time off work. Grandpa set off to meet Sam and Luke at the river, while I walked to Old River Road to assess the damage done to the truck, leaving Lula at home to watch over Ma.

Keeping my distance, perhaps fearing it would wake if I got too close, I circled the truck upon finding it at the far end of the Bishops' land. The front bumper had hold of a massive oak fifteen feet from the road. The windshield was all but gone. Jagged spikes of glass hung from the passenger side window frame. Fragmented shards littered the dash, making it hard to believe that only Ma's head and hands had shattered the windshield. My eyes swept over the rocks on the ground. They didn't look so innocent to me.

"She's a hundred and twenty years old," a voice came from behind. I reeled around, startled.

"The oak," Mark Bishop said, blowing a puff of smoke from his lungs. "She's been standing longer than any of us ever will."

"I'm sorry," I said in a quick burst. "I'll get the truck outta here as soon as I can." I ran to it. The driver side door was open. Spots of blood speckled the grass beneath it. Half of the steering wheel was red. Handprints marked the dash, the seat, the door. Despite the blood, I hopped in and turned the sticky key still stuck in the ignition. The engine coughed, then turned over.

"Come on out," Mark said from the passenger side, stopping me from throwing the truck in reverse.

I reluctantly slid off the seat and faced Mark from across the pickup's bed. "I can give you some money for the damage," I said, thinking of the few bucks I'd saved from watching Johnny.

Mark dragged on his cigarette. "No need for that." He rounded the truck and pointed down with his smoke at the rut beneath the rear tire. "She already tried to back out. I've got some bricks behind the house. Come get 'em."

I followed Mark around the house. Miss Paula watched from one of the windows. She waved. I attempted an unsuccessful smile, then quickly looked away.

"Got some old rags in the shed. If you go grab 'em, you can use 'em for the blood."

I told Mark thanks, but I just wanted to get the bricks and get out of there. It was bad enough that Miss Paula would tell everyone on the rez what had happened. There was no sense in prolonging my misery. He helped me haul the bricks to the truck and, between flicking away his old cigarette and lighting a new one, he even placed them beneath the tires so that I'd have enough traction to get on the road. The bumper practically sighed when it separated from the oak, which bore a wound in its bark as telling as the one on Ma's forehead.

I eased the truck onto the road, where I put it into park. Mark pushed against the door when I tried to swing it open.

"I'll bring the bricks back to the house," I said.

He shook his head again. "She could have killed herself."

That had already occurred to me. Hearing him say it, however, put another lump in my throat.

"Never mind her, it could have been a person instead of the tree."
That had occurred to me as well.

Mark reached into the bed of the pickup and retrieved one of the
plastic bags filled with cans. He held it up next to the window.

"I bag them up and take them to Effie. Bernie Mayfield pays me
for them."

"You didn't bag these," he said. "I did. Found them all over the cab."

My face burned, embarrassed as hell.

"I don't care if she drinks till she drowns. Shit, I can throw 'em
back with the best of 'em. But when I do, I walk. If I ever see her sitting where you're sitting now . . ." He looked me dead in the eyes and
stamped his cigarette out against the side mirror. "I'll shoot out all four
tires."

I inhaled deeply, taking in the last of what the smoldering cigarette
had to offer.

"Fair?" he asked.

I nodded. "Fair."

I drove away slowly, my sweaty palms revitalizing Ma's dried blood
on the steering wheel. I didn't pull into the drive when I got home. I
kept going, aimlessly at first, until I came upon the river and saw
everyone there.

I parked near the bridge where dozens of onlookers were watching
the volunteers with their waders and rafts, all wondering what the
mysterious outcome would be.

Sidling next to some kids, I rested my chin atop the bridge's rail
without looking down at the gaps Miss Shelby had supposedly slipped
through. The rush of the river sounded gentle and inviting, like it
wouldn't have done Miss Shelby harm after welcoming her in.

I listened to the kids whisper—cooking up ghost stories and legends of their own—while drifting in and out of a sleepy state. For a
moment, it felt like I'd escaped myself, like the river had washed my

worries away. I welcomed the feeling, though it didn't last long. An anxious touch brought me back to the reality at hand.

"Does it still run?"

I lifted my head. Grandpa lifted his hand from my shoulder. "She'll need a new windshield, but she hasn't died on us yet."

He nodded and pointed down at the riverbank. "Sam and I are taking his boat downriver. We could use an extra pair of eyes."

"Sure," I reluctantly agreed. "Grandpa?" I stopped him before he started down the bridge. "I don't think Ma should be allowed to drive the truck anymore. She's had two accidents in a matter of days."

"Is that something you're willing to tell her yourself?"

"Yes." I refrained from telling him about the agreement I'd made with Mark.

He nodded again and held out his hand. I placed the truck's key on his palm. Red specks still colored the metal. Grandpa's sleeve was red too. "She'll be angry," he said. "But you'll be strong. You always are." He headed down the bridge. I followed him, right past the spot where the Hensleys had died.

Sam had one foot in his camouflage-patterned duck boat and one on the shore. He looked like his old self again, not the trembling mess he'd been in the cemetery the night before. The mound of a net that'd yet to be cast rested on the bottom of the boat. I didn't want to get in, but I couldn't say no. Grandpa climbed aboard first. I crouched between him and the net. Sam kicked us away from the shore, his boot bringing a light spray of water into the boat; I shivered when it touched my skin.

"It'd be a beautiful day if it weren't for . . ." Sam didn't need to finish the sentence. His eyes landed on the net next to me. I'd never been on a duck hunt before, but I knew well enough that Sam wasn't in the habit of hauling around a net.

He used the trolling motor clamped to the back of the boat to steer

221

us downriver. The current did most of the work. I helped him drop the net into the water once we were away from the others. It had a float line attached to it, which spread the net from one side of the river to the other.

"What about the fish?" I absently asked.

"We'll let the little ones go." Sam did his best to smile, but I could tell he was feeling almost as sick as I was. It was one thing to cast the net. It'd be another to haul it in with the remains of Miss Shelby tangled inside.

"We're only going to the bend, right?"

"Yeah." Sam answered quickly. "Couldn't get over the rocks even if we wanted to."

Unusually seasick, I watched the float line bobble behind us. A sharp pull would mean the net had snagged something big. I dreaded the pull. I prayed it wouldn't come.

We rode along in silent anticipation for what seemed like hours, though that couldn't have been because it didn't take that long to reach the bend. Grandpa turned his gaze away from the water rushing ahead of us to look at me and Sam as we approached the halfway point. His lips moved in waves until he figured out what to say.

"We should talk about what happened in the cemetery last night."

Sam bristled.

"You and the Lavergnes weren't the only ones to hear whatever you heard, Sam. Louie heard it too. You both had the same panic in your eyes. That's why I told Luke to let Tom dig."

Sam exhaled a heavy breath. "But why? Why couldn't you and Luke hear it?"

"Balance would be my best guess," Grandpa said.

"Balance?" Sam echoed.

"It's what I was saying at the Blue Gator before you got there. There's a balance to everything. Good, bad. Young, old. Life, death. Sometimes that balance gets thrown off."

"But how?"

"And why?" I redirected my gaze from the back of the boat to the front. "Why is any of this happening?" My eyes zeroed in on the water trying to outrun us. It had a hypnotizing effect that turned my mind into a puddle as muddy as the riverbanks.

"I can't give you a clear-cut answer," Grandpa said. "Life, however, has purpose. One day we'll know the answers to our questions. We'll understand. Balance will be restored."

At what cost? I wondered.

"It was horrible, Joe," Sam said. "And now Tom . . . he wouldn't even look at me this morning. I tried to talk to him, but he just checked me with his shoulder on his way past."

"Give him time. He and Miss Autumn need our support right now."

"Gator!" I exclaimed, startling even myself. The ridges of what must have been an eight-foot alligator bathing in the sun jutted above the water's surface just twelve feet ahead. Its snout floating on the water, it watched us through one eye aimed in our direction.

I sat higher in the boat. Grandpa stood. "Where?" he said.

I pointed at the gator gliding toward the shore. Its tail left small swirls in the water. "There! Right there!" The words were barely out of my mouth before the gator dipped beneath the water's surface. "Did you see it?"

"I haven't seen a gator in this river since 1980," Grandpa said, shaking his head. "They prefer the coastal marshes."

"If there's one there, we'll get him," Sam said.

I looked back at the net, expecting it to snag something big. The float line attached to it bobbed along, giving no indication that the net had snared anything significant. We reached the bend with all its enormous rocks. Sam turned the boat to keep from colliding with them. I examined the shoreline to see if the gator had climbed out of the water before the net could wrap around it. I didn't see the beast, but I did spot a hunched figure standing with its hands in the water and its legs straddling a boulder right where the gator had been headed.

"J.L.?"

He looked startled, like he wanted to disappear beneath the waves as well.

"Louie?" he called, thrusting his busy hands deeper into the water.

"What are you doing out here?" Grandpa asked. "It's not safe to be in this part of the river alone. Come on. We'll give you a ride back to the bridge."

"Did you find something?" Sam said.

J.L.'s eyes wavered. He stood, bringing his hands out of the water. A drenched and dripping scrap of fabric hung from his fingers, shiny with black mud.

"It was snagged on the rocks," he said.

"What is it?" Grandpa wondered.

Sam steered the boat to shore. J.L. climbed over the rocks in our direction.

"Help me with the net," Sam said to me.

I kept my eyes on my hands as they mechanically hauled the net in, bit by bit. The ease with which it came out of the water indicated that it hadn't snagged anything heavier than the handful of fish and turtles that flopped into the boat. Even so, I refused to look over the edge to see what was coming next.

"Bring it here," Grandpa said to Jean-Luc. "Hold it up."

Staying put, J.L. held up the scrap of fabric he'd pulled from the rocks. The frayed sleeve dangling from one end of the scrap, and the single mother-of-pearl button still fastened in its hole left little doubt that J.L. had found the remains of a dress or a blouse.

Grandpa reached for the scrap, being careful not to tip the boat. J.L. tossed it to him. "Nice catch, old man."

Grandpa knelt and reached over the side of the boat to rinse the sleeve in the water. When he held it high again, it looked like it was purple or a dark shade of blue.

"I think I've seen it before," Grandpa said.

"Is it Miss Shelby's?" I asked.

Sam dug into the pack he'd brought with him and pulled out a plastic bag. "It could be evidence." Grandpa dropped the scrap into the bag. Sam quickly sealed it. "I'll ask Ern if it was hers."

"If it was . . ." Grandpa looked toward the rocks. "She might still be here."

Or the gator could have gotten her, I thought.

"I didn't see nothin' other than the scrap," J.L. said.

"I still have to search." Sam pulled on a pair of waders that came up to his chest and took hold of a rope tied to the boat. "Stay put." He proceeded to trek along the shoreline to the wall of rocks. Clinging to the rope, he carefully climbed over the boulders while we sat in silent anticipation of what he might find lodged between them. I breathed easier with each big rock he passed until he got to the highest point of the barrier, where he paused, ultimately stooping for a better look.

"What is it?" Grandpa said.

"I can't be sure. . . ." Sam turned his shirtsleeve into a glove by wrapping it around his hand, then reached down between the boulders. A grimace that withered his face like a dried-out apple overtook his expression. "Looks like part of her might have made it past the bend." He pulled a bone from between the rocks, broken—bitten?—at one end.

THIRTY-FOUR

Louie

Grandpa drove the battered and bloodied truck back to his place. Sam, having to go my way, gave me a ride home from the river. I went inside, then crept out into the bushes beyond the porch after he backed out of the drive. He drove slowly to the trailer across the field, and he didn't bother climbing the steps to Ern's front door when he got there. He just stood below Ern's window, gazing up as if evaluating a piece of abstract art.

"Hanging in there, Ern?"

I strained to hear.

"Bring me somethin' to eat?"

Sam shifted his weight from one foot to the other, the blinds blocking his view of Ern's face likely making him uncomfortable. "No, Ern . . . it, well, I just came by because we dragged the river today . . . from the bridge to the bend." Sam's hands squeezed his hips. The plastic bag with the scrap of clothing inside hung from his back pocket. His eyes fell to his toes, which were digging divots in the dirt.

"Find her?" Ern's low voice carried well across the way.

"No. It ain't that," Sam said.

"Wasn't in the river?"

Sam's head bobbled. "About that, Ern. . . . We found something in the water. I was thinking maybe you could look at it."

Despite the distance between myself and Ern's trailer, I saw Sam's hand shake upon reaching for the plastic bag. He pulled it free and held it over his head. "You'll have to lift the blinds."

They didn't rise, but a couple slats parted.

"It's still a little muddy and wet," Sam said. "Maybe you could tell me if it was your ma's?"

Ern didn't say anything. He just stared through the gap in the blinds at the bag with the scrap of fabric inside.

"I can take it out if it'll help. Or I could come in and show it to you." Sam sounded as enthused as if he were offering to pull out his own hair.

"It's fine right where it is."

"So?"

The slats flapped back into place. "It's hers," Ern muttered behind his mask. "It's what she was wearin' the day she left."

Sam's hand fell to his side. He let the scrap dangle for a moment, then stuffed it away, concealing it like a secret or a lie. "I'm real sorry, Ern. This ain't easy for any of us."

"Knew it all along. . . . What am I gonna do now?"

"We'll help you through this. Everyone on the rez is worried about you. . . . We care about you, I mean."

Ern wheezed. "Haven't had lunch," he said.

"I'll see that you get some. Anything else you need?"

"Just my ma, Sam. I want my ma."

Sam kicked up a spray of dirt. "We ain't gonna stop looking for her. . . . I'm sorry, Ern." Sam slowly backed away and got into his truck. He lingered in the drive, perhaps paying his respects, but once he put the truck into gear, he got it moving like wind in an open field, leaving Ern behind without saying a single word about the bone. I thought it was good of him to keep that quiet considering no one knew who it belonged to. I cringed, though, remembering the request Ern had made of me the night before.

"She hasn't come out all day," Lula said a split second after I entered our trailer.

"Have you checked on her? Is she all right?" I headed for Ma's bedroom door.

"Wait." Lula set aside the bottle of yellow nail polish she'd been about to unscrew. "Listen."

I heard a rustle followed by the crisp hiss of a can cracking open. I grabbed the doorknob and turned it. Tried to, anyway. The knob held firm.

"It's locked." The door had been closed for years, but it'd never been locked. "Why is it locked?"

"Don't ask me, I didn't do it." Lula rolled her eyes. Her nails were calling.

"Ma?" I thumped on the door, jiggling the knob. "Ma, it's Louie. Let me in."

The door stayed shut. Ma stayed silent. The lock remained locked. I could have easily jimmied it with one of Lula's nail files, but that wouldn't have changed things. I'd still have been unwanted on the other side of the door.

I reeled around and staggered into the living room, noticing that the trailer had fallen into disarray. Dirty dishes cluttered the table. The blankets that usually covered the holes in the couch had fallen deep into the crevices around the cushions. The living room lawn chair was on its side, and toys littered the floor next to drops of blood that had yet to be cleaned from the carpet. More empty cans had sprung up like weeds all around. On the coffee table, the counter, on top of the TV.

"I thought you said she was in her room all day?" The question was an accusation against Lula.

"She was. I think."

"You were supposed to be watching her."

"Do you know how damn hot it gets in here?" Lula snapped. "Noemi and I just went out to sit in the shade for a while. Is that all right with you? It's not like I left Ma on her own. I'm the one who bandaged her wounds."

I bit my tongue because I could have told her exactly how hot the trailer got, in addition to saying a lot about her and Noemi and the fact that I'd never been asked to take care of the kid, let alone paid or even thanked for it. I stormed from one end of the living room to the other, snatched two cans from atop the TV, then retreated to my room.

"What are you doing now?"

I didn't answer. Lula didn't care enough to ask again. The scent of her nail polish filled the air.

I didn't know how hurt I was until I slumped on my bed and fought off tears that would have traced tracks down my cheeks like scars that would evaporate, robbing me of evidence that would show the world my pain. I would have hugged Ma again if she'd have let me. Instead, I silently endured the sting of her rejection. It burned bad, mostly because I believed that she wanted what she carried home with her every morning in her bloated brown bags more than she'd ever wanted me.

I took the two cans I'd snagged from the TV and set them on the dresser in front of me. Ugly twin cans, slightly dented along the sides where Ma's grip had held them tight. Them, not me. The mocking indentations told me how warm my mother's hand had been. Grunting, I slammed the dresser against the wall. The cans wobbled but they didn't fall.

"Louie?" Lula shrieked.

I stormed back to Ma's door. I had to say that I'd tried.

"Ma! Talk to me. Please. Tell me what's wrong and what you need. I'll listen. I'll do whatever I can to help."

She stayed silent. The lock stayed locked.

"Please, Ma. If you don't open the door, I . . . I'll . . ." A sigh leaked from my lungs. What threat could I make? I couldn't hurt her any more than she'd already hurt herself. And she didn't seem to give a damn about that.

"Leave her alone, Louie. She doesn't wanna be bothered."

"What about what I want?" My eyes fixed to the grain of the door, my hand held tight to the knob.

"Don't be stupid." Lula blew on her nails. "Don't you know it doesn't matter what we want? I hate to break it to you, but we've got what we were given, and this is as good as it's gonna get."

"That can't be true."

"You'll see."

My head shook. "I know how hot the trailer gets."

Lula's nail polish bottle clanked against the coffee table. "I know you do," she said after some time.

My forehead came to rest against the door. "Was it her fault?" I asked. "Is Ma the reason why you had Noemi?"

"What are you talking about?"

"The hole. The emptiness inside."

"Louie . . ."

"I feel it too."

"I was young. Dumb."

"You were my age."

She tried to laugh.

"Do you regret it?" My voice trembled.

Lula exhaled a heavy breath not meant for her nails. "No one told me it would be this hard."

I peeled my fingers from the doorknob and slunk back to my room.

Back to the twin cans atop the dresser. Ugly as they were, I knew how to use them.

Cuffs. Many men wore them around their arms or wrists while performing the warrior dance. Most of the cuffs I'd seen were beaded. Some were made of metal. I took hold of the antler-handled knife Grandpa had given me and carefully sliced through the aluminum, removing the top and bottom of each can, then used the butt of the knife to hammer the raw edges over onto themselves so that they wouldn't carve into my skin.

I knew others might laugh at my cuffs, but I didn't care about that. I had reason for wearing them. While Ma may have been cuffed to the cans behind closed doors, they'd be cuffed to me for all to see. While they cut her down, they'd be the part of my warrior outfit that kept me from getting cut.

THIRTY-FIVE

Noemi

Walking away from Roddy's house after being treated like a stranger on the stoop left me feeling stripped bare, emptier than before, and embarrassed as hell. Uncle Louie was caring enough not to remark on how I'd been treated. He just followed his light back to the bloody trail while my mind rewound to the challenge it'd issued itself earlier, to list the things that distinguished Boyfriend Roddy from Reporter Roddy. Still, I couldn't come up with much, my mind blank on the spot, like being at a party and coming up empty when asked to add songs to the playlist.

Uncle Louie's light landed back upon the trail, making the droplets gleam. A text came from Sara a second after that, sooner than expected. It wasn't the apologetic *come back and come inside* message I'd hoped for.

Did he give you a key?

Something insulting lurked within the question. I sensed where it was leading, and so I didn't rush to answer.

My mom wants to know

I gritted my teeth.

Why?

She doesn't want anyone
messing around in here

Mrs. Bishop didn't mean *anyone*. She meant me.

No key

I wasn't about to tell her that I knew the garage code.

U shouldn't be in there either.
The police will wanna look

They're on their way now

I had to lower the phone from my face, resentment rising at the thought of all of them sifting through Roddy's business, pretending like I hadn't been by his side the last three years, like we weren't finally talking about moving in together, and like it was someone else's photo framed on the shelf above the TV. I wasn't just offended, I was hurt.

"Wanna talk about it?" Uncle Louie said beside me.

I hadn't told him anything about the pills. I wondered how much had floated to his ears from across Roddy's front yard. "What'd you hear?"

"Wasn't listening."

I wasn't sure I believed him. "I'd rather talk about what you said earlier."

He stumbled on the street, caught himself before he fell. "What I said?"

"The questions you asked Luke, about the colors of the Jeeps. And Roddy's expression at the moment of . . . impact."

"I was just trying to put pieces together . . . trying to see the big picture."

"Pieces," I muttered, wondering what the completed puzzle would look like if we took the known facts about the *incident* and combined them with our secrets, his and mine. "I can't help but feel like there are things you're not telling me."

He didn't refute my suspicion. He didn't have to. Another text distracted me.

> Who else would Roddy have
> talked to today?

The question made me feel like I had one up on Sara. Maybe she didn't know Roddy as well as she thought she did.

> Probably Mike. And people
> at work

> I'm curious about his
> voicemails and texts

> His phone went with him to the
> morgue, but if his messages
> were backed up, I might be
> able to access them through
> his iCloud account

> Do you know his login info?

The fact that Sara didn't know Roddy's passcode soothed me some more. Unfortunately, I didn't know it either. I would have stolen her idea if I did.

Don't know it

I'll figure it out

Of course she thought she would. If managing my own passwords wasn't such a challenge, I would have tried to beat her to it.

Lost in my head, my eyes on my phone, I almost didn't hear the approaching tires. Uncle Louie nudged me closer to the side of the street, though the pair of oncoming cars was in the opposite lane. Tribal PD.

"Who was that back at the house?" he asked.

I hesitated before telling him that it was Roddy's sister.

"I'm sorry that she's making the situation harder on you."

"I thought you weren't listening?"

"I wasn't. I was watching. And I'd be lying if I said my heart didn't break when she left you standing outside that door. I know it's never easy losing someone you love."

"Did you ever know anyone who . . . ?" I couldn't finish the thought. I didn't have to.

"No. Not really," he said. "Are you starting to think . . . ?"

The meds on my mind again, my conviction seeped out on the breath I exhaled. Like an apparition floating above me, it hung out of reach but not yet gone for good, forcing me to accept that I could no longer say with certainty that Roddy hadn't done it.

"Don't answer that," Uncle Louie said about the quasi-question he'd asked. "Let's just see what's at the end of this trail."

"What are you—we—hoping to find?"

"I'm not sure, to be honest." I could hear how conflicted he was, which only confused me more. "But you're right . . ." he said, "there are things I haven't told you."

I looked straight at him. The muscles in his neck flexed. Eyes still on the street, searching for the next drop and the next, he said, "Something happened in the summer of 1986. Something I've never told anyone about. Something I didn't think could possibly happen again, but with the coyote . . ." The light wavered as he wiped sweat from his face. "You were three that summer. I guess you wouldn't remember any of it."

He was mostly right. There was something I remembered from that summer, though. Some*one*, really. He was a person no one ever talked about. Even I hadn't thought about him in twenty years or more.

"I remember Johnny," I said.

THIRTY-SIX

Louie

Johnny flicked a green feather at me. It billowed in front of his face as beads of sweat arced through the air. The droplets flew from the tip of my nose, my chin, the drenched ends of my matted hair each time I made an erratic turn. My movements didn't feel right. None were precise, confident, or controlled. I must have looked like a fish on land rather than the proud warrior I was supposed to be.

"Too loose!" Ern hollered from across the way. He'd been giving unsolicited advice for the last half hour, advice that lit my fuse because he wouldn't have been able to take more than ten steps without his cellulite-dimpled knees giving out. "Keep your muscles tight!"

I growled and ground my feet into the dirt. The can tabs attached to my ankles stopped jangling. "What would you know about that?" I hollered. The heat, the sweat stinging my eyes, and the second skin of my pow wow outfit had me on edge. Not to mention that my fatigued muscles felt like skewered meat roasting above a raging fire. "I bet you can't even remember the last time you saw the dance live!"

"Don't matter. I know what it's supposed to look like. You're supposed to be a warrior, not a damn worm on a hook!"

I huffed and swiped the bustle from my head. Its buckskin base thick with sweat, the feathers remained aimed at the sky, a small victory for me.

"Dance more, Douie!" Watching from the porch, Noemi and Johnny looked more amused than when they watched their favorite cartoons on TV.

Panting, I drank water from the cup I'd set on the railing, then splashed some onto my face. Johnny hopped over.

"Me too!" He clawed for the cup, and I emptied it over his head, making him laugh like it was the greatest thing in the world.

"Dance more," Noemi said again. "Dance! Dance!" She wiggled her bottom against the porch plank beneath her.

"All right, Pink Feather." I took a position in the patch of dirt where we used to park the truck. I knew that the dance, like all Native dances, was more than the word *dance* could convey. It was a ceremony and prayer put into motion. It was supposed to look paced and proud, never frenzied or slack. My movements were meant to mimic those of a warrior stalking his enemy or prey. They were supposed to incorporate smooth hops and turns without ever rotating all the way around because a warrior never takes his eyes off his enemy. I put the bustle back on and began again, can tabs jingling.

"Like an eagle, Louie!" Ern hollered. "Think of an eagle. Swoop, dive, and turn. Swoop, dive, and turn!"

My arms were swooping. My legs were diving. I was sweating my balls off.

"Too jerky. Too heavy on your feet. You'd never take anyone by surprise."

Too heavy? I scoffed and turned my back to Ern. My blazing muscles made it impossible to land lightly. My calves and quads were like bricks beneath my skin, my lungs like bombs about to explode. On the verge of calling it quits, I felt something peg me between my shoulder blades. Obnoxious braying met my ears.

"What the hell?" J.L. laughed. "You better hope no girls see you jumping around like that, man, or you'll never get any pussy."

"Don't say that in front of the kids."

"They don't know what I'm talkin' about." He popped something into his mouth—another grasshopper, I thought, snatched from the weeds. He crunched and swallowed. "And if they did know about P-U-S-S-Y," he said, "I bet they'd agree."

I glared at him. "I've gotta practice for the pow wow."

"What's there to practice? You just bop up and down, pretending like you're about to hatchet somebody." He hopped around the front yard, effortlessly looking a million times better than me.

"I'll hatchet you!" I flung myself at J.L., grabbed on to his burly shoulders, and pushed up off them as if he were a pommel horse. I landed in the dirt. He stayed standing. Johnny growled and, flapping imaginary wings as he ran, hurled himself at J.L. as well.

"See, Louie, kids love me." J.L. hoisted Johnny high above his head. "And I bet he loves pussy, too!"

I socked J.L. in the stomach, then leaped onto the porch so that he couldn't hit me back. Groaning, he set Johnny down and spat into the grass. "Just wait till I introduce my foot to your balls," he gasped.

My bustle had fallen from my head in my haste. J.L. picked it up and swung it around, insinuating that he'd soon send it flying into the field.

"Don't," I begged.

"Looks like a dead bird." He pointed to my outfit. "You're not really gonna dance in that?"

"Does it look that bad?"

He tossed the bustle to me. "How come you didn't tell me about your ma?"

I wiped sweat-soaked hair from my face. "How'd you hear?"

"Everyone knows."

"Miss Paula," I muttered.

"She all right?"

"Same as always." As far as I could tell, that was true. I'd intercepted Ma on her way to the bathroom that morning. She'd looked right through me. If she'd been in pain from the accident, she sure as hell didn't show it.

"Heard she was bleeding pretty bad."

My gaze dropped to the dried blood on the porch planks. "I guess I should clean it up."

"Yeah, and hose yourself off while you're at it." He came up the steps for a closer look at the blood. "Man, you stink." He made a motion like he was going to slug me. I doubled over. He jumped aside without his revenge.

"It's not me," I said, though I could smell the sweat on my skin. "It's the garbage baking out back." I'd been about to burn the trash the night Miss Fay met her maker, but I'd been too troubled to do it since, leaving it rotting in the sun.

J.L. inhaled through his nose. "That ain't only garbage, man. That's a whole lotta you."

"Just give me a hand or get lost. I gotta get these two inside."

J.L. wrangled Johnny while I ushered Noemi like a princess through the door. I secured my bustle in my room, grabbed the matches from the counter, and started collecting the burnable trash my family had left lying around: dirty napkins, Noemi's popsicle sticks, Lula's makeup-stained tissues, Ma's empty brown bags, fliers advertising things we'd never afford.

"Ahhh," I heard J.L. sigh. "Sweet relief."

I turned to find him standing over Johnny's training chair. "Hey! You splattered the carpet last time." I hadn't cleaned that either.

J.L. laughed and backed away, his pants zipped up. "My aim's gettin' better." He winked. "How about him?"

"Still working on it."

J.L. squatted next to Johnny. "Big boys stand, man."

"He'll figure it out when he's ready."

From the floor next to him, J.L. picked up one of Lula's catalogs, open to the intimates section, full of photos of women modeling bras.

"Is this what your sister wears?" He practically drooled onto the page.

"How would I know?"

"Look at this one." He whistled. "What I wouldn't give to see your sis in that . . . or out of it."

"Come on, man."

"Did she breastfeed?"

"Shut up."

"Think Rosie did? Lucky little bastards."

"Hey!"

"They don't know what it means."

I snatched the catalog from him. "Are you sticking around?"

He shrugged.

"Make yourself useful and watch them while I take this stuff out back." My arms were full of trash.

"What's in it for me?"

"Cookies on the counter."

He shrugged again. I took that as consent and headed for the back door. Just as I hit the latch with my elbow, J.L. grabbed Johnny's right wrist and ankle and began spinning him around the room.

"Easy!" I warned.

"No one ever got hurt from an airplane ride."

I knew the opposite to be true. Johnny tittered. Noemi threw feathers in the air.

"Don't break his neck, all right?" I hauled the trash to the pit and threw it in with the rotting rest. Having sat in the sun for so many days, the garbage emitted a sharp stench that stabbed my nose each time I inhaled.

It lit easily, though. The paper scraps especially. I squatted beside the pit and picked up the sooty poker I'd left lying in the grass. Turning the trash kept the flames at their hottest and highest. It gave them something new to devour.

Red and orange embers leaping toward the sky, the spirited flames lulled me into a state of calm that made me so fuzzy around the edges, I barely felt the dry heat on my face or the beads of sweat bubbling along my temples. I barely heard J.L. screaming my name.

Tossing the poker aside, I jumped to my feet, making myself dizzy. I wavered until the blood that'd pooled in my legs caught up with my heart, then ran to the trailer. Lunging over the back steps like an Olympic long jumper, I landed on the stoop with my face against the closed screen door.

"Did you drop him?" The fact that Johnny wasn't crying put my stomach in knots.

"I didn't drop anyone. Look." His face sweaty and red, J.L. pointed to the corner where Johnny, slightly swaying, stood over the training chair, his back to me.

"Is he . . . ?"

"Standing like a big boy!" J.L. proclaimed.

I blew out a long breath and laughed to settle my nerves. "How'd you get him to do it?"

J.L. hiked his shoulders and cocked his head. I guess I wasn't supposed to see the box of cookies poking out from behind his back. "It was easy. Watch out, Louie, or I'll steal your job."

"I've got a job for you," I muttered. "Empty the chair when he's done. Don't spill it!" I went back to poke at the flames. Something fluttered by when I knelt next to the pit. I paid it little mind until— *ta-ta-ta-ta-ta-ta-ta-ta*—I heard it drumming against the aluminum siding of our trailer. I didn't need to look at it to know what it was, but I did need to see it to believe it.

One glimpse and I was on my ass. The bird with the red head and white belly stained red had ahold of the frame around one of the living room windows. Its fractured beak didn't impede it one bit.

Gasping, I steadied myself in a squat and squinted up at the bird, wondering if it might be a figment of my imagination. I stood and took two steps toward it, watching it widen the dent it'd made.

Tsss. I hissed through my teeth. "Get!" I clapped my hands so hard they stung. The damned thing didn't care. Its head sprang back and forth like an inverted pendulum. It pecked faster than any woodpecker I'd ever seen, frantically striking the trailer as if it had serious business to tend to inside.

I took two more steps, then stopped, silence suddenly taking over. The woodpecker didn't just quit pecking, it fell from the window and landed in the grass. Apparently dead. Again.

Unnerved, I didn't move for a full minute. Maybe more. Regaining my wits, I snagged the poker from the firepit and approached the spot where the bird had landed. Slowly, carefully, I prodded the grass, expecting the damned thing to launch at me, to clamp its tiny talons around my bottom lip and peck my eyes out.

"Rawwwrrrr!"

The roar sent me reeling backward. The poker fell from my hands, and I landed on my ass again. The screen door slammed against the side of the trailer. Johnny came tearing out.

His roar was a growl and a groan rolled into one. He ran down the steps—feathers in hand, barn door wide open—into grass that came up to his knees.

"Johnny," I choked, my breath pinned in my throat. "Get over here!"

He snarled at me in a manner that suggested he might be playing, like there might've been a smile beneath his snarl.

"Want another airplane ride?" I scrambled to my knees, offering him my open arms.

He roared again and continued through the grass, heading straight for the pit and the flames snaking out of it.

"No!" I screamed. "Johnny come back!"

I hurled myself in his direction. The lead he had on me was small, but his strides were large. He moved faster than I'd ever seen him move before.

"Johnny!"

Feet from falling into the pit, he stopped running, flung the feathers into the air, and turned to me. The smile I'd detected beneath the snarl spread across his face, ghastly as the deathly armadillo I'd seen on the porch, almost as ghastly as what I imagined the Takoda Vampire to look like.

"I'm an alligator!" he said.

Feathers raining around him, he dropped to all fours and sluggishly slunk backward in a reverse crawl, straight into the fire.

THIRTY-SEVEN

Louie

My thoughts revolved around the word *why*. Why had it happened? Why hadn't I run for water instead of reaching for him? Why was he still smiling at the bottom of the pit?

"Please," I begged God and the Great Spirit, whichever would listen. "Bring him back."

A blanket of blame wrapped around me, urging me to roll over in the ash. The guilt I felt was almost as heavy as Johnny when I'd grasped his hand and pulled. Even though I'd always been able to whisk him into the air before, I hadn't been strong enough to yank him from the flames, forced instead to wrench my hand away when the raging fire scorched the beer can cuff around my wrist and birthed blisters on my bare flesh. Johnny's immovable weight was an anomaly I couldn't comprehend. Worse, and far more confusing, was that he hadn't just been heavy, he'd been strong. I hadn't been able to pull him out, but he'd almost pulled me in.

I turned toward the trailer, expecting to find J.L. standing there with scorn in his eyes. I hadn't done anything wrong, yet I couldn't shake the feeling that I'd committed the greatest sin. J.L. wasn't there by the door. Despite my feeling that the world had changed, the trailer and the land around it looked drab as always. No sadder than usual.

I swallowed to wash away the sour, smoky taste at the back of my throat and choked down deep breaths to stabilize my trembling core. My nerves were shot. I couldn't stop shaking. A high-pitched giggle nipped my ears.

Tasting bile at the back of my throat, I glanced back at the pit. Nothing had changed there.

The trailer. The giggles were coming from inside. I staggered to the back steps, where I could see J.L. through the window. He had Noemi by the wrists, swinging her around and around.

"Jean-Luc!"

The giggles slowed, then stopped. Jean-Luc appeared at the screen door, Noemi in his arms.

"Leave her inside."

He set her down and stepped out. Looking past me, he said, "What the hell is . . . ?" as his suntanned skin took on the color of an over-cast sky.

"You were supposed to keep him inside."

"I never saw him leave." His voice sounded as hollow as mine until his defenses kicked in. "Are you blaming me?"

I shook my head. The motion made me dizzy.

"I was tryin' to help you, Louie. You're the one who gets paid."

"Jean-Luc . . ." I started, but I didn't have the strength to assure him that I wasn't trying to pass the buck. "Get help."

He stumbled inside. My own legs felt as dependable as toothpicks withstanding the weight of an eighteen-wheeler. I sank onto the grass. I don't know how long I sat like that, but, having thrown up by the time Luke arrived, I felt like I was ready to lie down and die. Grandpa appeared only a minute after Luke. Sam came on the scene seconds after that. Dazed, I told them what had happened, starting with

Johnny roaring out of the trailer and ending with my inability to pull him from the flames.

Sam did circles around the firepit, kicking once at the colorful feathers beside it. Grandpa stood with his hand on my trembling shoulder. I expected Luke to say that I'd have to go with him.

"Are you going to be all right?" he asked instead.

"Louie's strong," Grandpa answered for me. He squeezed my shoulder, perhaps testing to see if I would crumble. I'd never felt feebler in my life.

"It seemed like slow motion," I confessed. "How'd he get so heavy?"

"Shock will do that to you," Grandpa said. "It isn't your fault."

I supposed shock could dull physical pain too. I could see my singed skin, but I couldn't feel it.

Word, as always, spread fast on the reservation. Soon, it seemed that everyone had come to witness the tragedy. Grandpa helped me off the grass and into the trailer. The heat inside and the stench of smoke clinging to the buckskin of my pow wow outfit, a stench that only intensified behind closed doors, made it feel like a casket lid had been lowered over me.

"I need air." I pushed past Grandpa and escaped to the front porch steps where the foreign stares of people I'd known my entire life landed on me. Despite all who came to gape, Ma didn't take a single step beyond her bedroom door. My horror had yet to enter her world. Maybe it never would.

"Here." J.L draped the sheet from my bed around my shoulders and dropped down next to me.

"I'm not cold."

"You're shaking like a leaf."

"How's this real?"

"Accidents happen."

"It didn't look like an accident," I whispered.

I told J.L. everything as it'd happened. "He let out a single cry," I said. "Not one of pain or fear. He was mad because he couldn't pull me in."

Neither of us said it out loud, but I was sure we must have been thinking about the same thing. Miss Autumn. She said Fay had tried to pull her into the septic tank.

Worried rumblings rose from the crowd. So much tragedy in such a short span had us all on edge. I looked away from the gapers in the yard and saw a gap in the blinds blocking Ern's window. He kept himself silent and sealed up, but I could tell he was straining to be part of life in that moment of death. The way he hid heightened my unease. The frantic wail that drifted in our direction a moment later made me wonder if I should have followed Johnny into the flames. Massive and mournful, the wail trailed Rosie Deshautelle down the road like a breath of black exhaust pouring from the tailpipe of an old car.

If I'd had the stamina, I would have sought a place to hide until the worst of it was over. My legs, however, wouldn't move, and my heart was too heavy for me to just get up and walk away.

Rosie's wail stripped all words from the onlookers' tongues. Only her howl and the soles of her shoes slapping the earth filled the air. Miss Vicky lassoed Rosie with her arms to stop her from running into the backyard. Tear-streaked, soaked with sweat, and yowling despite being short of breath, Rosie clawed at Miss Vicky like a rat trying to escape the clutch of a feral cat.

"Don't look, sweetie," Miss Vicky begged.

"My baby!" Rosie swiped her red nails across Miss Vicky's face, which elicited a yip from Miss Paula, who just stood to the side, taking it all in. Miss Vicky winced, but she didn't let Rosie go.

J.L ran to Miss Vicky's side. "Let me help." He wrapped his arms around Rosie. "I've got you." His words birthed a spiteful thought. He didn't care about Rosie. He only cared about getting his hands on her. They slowly slid up her body, settling beneath her breasts. His torso pressed flat against her back, his muscles straining for her to feel their strength.

Miss Vicky pulled away and pressed a palm against the puckered scrape on her cheek, leaving J.L. to wrangle Rosie on his own.

"Get your hands off me!" she screeched. "My baby! I want my baby!"

Jean-Luc could have overpowered her. He could have pinned her to the ground to keep her from seeing what had happened to her son if he'd wanted to. Instead, he stabbed me in the stomach when he loosened his hold and said, "Okay, okay . . . just let me take you."

The words deflated Rosie's anger. She reverted to being hysterically distressed rather than desperately pissed. Her body fell limp against Jean-Luc's, and he, like a traitor, led her to the yard.

The wait was excruciating, but a soul-stripping scream came, causing colossal tears to tumble down my cheeks. My cracked world crumbled even more when I glanced up a second later and spotted a round form hobbling down the road. She moved faster than I'd ever thought possible, her cane digging into the dirt with each uneven step she took.

"You shouldn't be—" Miss Paula said, the instant Miss Doris was within range.

"Shut up!" Miss Doris snapped. Puffing like an old steam train, her eyes pierced me like hot skewers straight off the grill. "Is it true? For the love of God, Louie, tell me if it's true."

Her command that I speak was one of the worst things she could have demanded of me. Even as Rosie's telling cries floated to my ears, Miss Doris kept her accusatory and insistent eyes on me.

The two words I spoke in response were so crippling that I nearly slid off the step. "It's true." The words alone weren't what rendered me weak, it was the look of utter sorrow that overcame Miss Doris's doughy face.

"Little John." Her words were broken and drawn-out, like the last few notes from a music box in need of winding.

"I'm sorry."

Her state of sorrow didn't live long. Her jaw tightened and her nostrils flared. The cold glint of anger overtook her eyes. "How could you let this happen?"

Surrounded by Miss Vicky, Miss Paula, and all the others who'd come to gape, I told them exactly what I'd told Sam and Luke. I told them that Johnny had willfully backed into the flames.

"You couldn't stop him? You couldn't pick him up? *You couldn't lock him in the goddamn house?*"

The volume of her usually loud voice hit a level I'd never heard. "I . . . I . . ." was all I could say.

"My money says he wasn't watching the boy," Eaton Ballard said from out of the crowd. "I saw him and the kids in the road the other day. He was letting them run wild."

Snorting like a bull, Miss Doris cracked her cane against the porch railing before stomping to the yard. Miss Vicky and Miss Paula gazed upon me with sadness and uncertainty in their eyes. Neither offered comfort. They went after Miss Doris.

I pulled the sheet over my head, wishing I'd soon find myself waking from the grisly nightmare. I stayed that way, silently wishing, until a familiar hand fell on my shoulder again.

"Come," Grandpa said. His intention wasn't to take me inside. He wanted to return to the firepit.

"Why?"

"To show them you didn't do anything wrong. Liars hide. The honorable stand strong. Come."

Grandpa was right. It took more strength to face them than it did to disappear. I got up and followed him to the yard. The can tabs jangled around my ankles with each step I took. I couldn't have felt like a greater fool.

Rosie stood sobbing into J.L.'s chest, his hand moving up and down her back, fingers lingering over the clasp of her bra. I scowled at him, waiting for our eyes to meet, but he never looked my way. He just kept rubbing her back, making sickening soothing sounds, acting so unlike himself.

Chris hoisted a tiny bundle into the back of his station wagon, parked a few feet away on the grass. Miss Doris watched until Chris got in and drove away, at which point she turned and spotted me.

"I can't even look at you!" She directed her bloodshot eyes at Luke and asked, "Isn't there something you can do? Anything?" The way she spoke made it mighty clear that she'd already had words with him about me.

"I'm sorry, Doris, but it was—"

"Don't tell me it was an accident, Luke!" she spat. "He ought to be dealt with until he tells us the truth."

"He's not lying," J.L. said. "I saw it happen. I saw everything."

Miss Doris's jaw slackened. Rosie pushed against J.L.'s chest to look up into his eyes. He tightened his hold on her hips.

"How come you didn't say something earlier?" Luke asked.

J.L. shrugged. "I was tryin' to make Rosie feel better."

"What did you see?" Miss Doris whispered.

"I was in the trailer with Johnny. I chased after him when he ran outside, but the screen door slammed in my face. He was already down the steps and across the grass by the time I pushed the door open again. He went into the pit all on his own."

J.L. told the same story I'd told him and all the others, except it was true when it came from my mouth. It was hard to say why he lied. I wanted to believe that he did it to protect me, but when I thought about what Grandpa had just said, I wondered what J.L. might be hiding.

Miss Doris swallowed hard. The loose flesh around her neck quivered. "I think I need some water."

251

She didn't stop me from taking her elbow and helping her up the steps. All of us more than weakened by the sun and the sight it had illuminated, Grandpa, Rosie, J.L., Luke, Sam, Miss Doris, and I crammed inside the trailer for a rest and some water. I sat Miss Doris on the couch next to Noemi, so silent and still that she must have known something bad had happened. I gave Miss Doris a glass with every cube of ice we had left in the freezer, saving none for the blisters on my hand. I aimed the box fan at her too. Its spinning blades slowed when I moved it, then picked up speed once more. Miss Doris drank slowly. Sadly. She set the glass on the coffee table next to one of the feathers Johnny had been flapping with earlier.

"I'm sorry, Louie," she said. "I let the devil get into me. I never should have accused you of something so heinous."

"It's okay." I wished she'd stop talking.

"I'm drinking this." Rosie had found one of Ma's unopened cans. I told her to take it with a flick of my hand.

"Louie taught Johnny how to be a big boy," my traitor-turned-defender unexpectedly said. The sight of J.L. holding the training chair's basin, full of pee, augmented my dismay.

Miss Doris cried harder. Rosie slurped from the can trembling in her hand. It seemed like the moment might never pass, like we would be stuck in that stifling trailer in excruciating silence, punctuated by snuffles and sniffles, for the rest of our shitty lives.

"I'll take you home," Luke finally—mercifully—said to Miss Doris.

"That'd be good." She slowly stood and looked down at Noemi next to her. The sight of my niece nervously twisting her hair in her hands made Miss Doris moan.

The bedsheet still wrapped around my shoulders, I followed everyone outside.

"Sam?" J.L. questioned. "Can Rosie and me catch a ride with you? I wanna make sure she gets home all right." His arm was tight around

Rosie's waist again. Sam nodded. Luke drove away with Miss Doris in his cab. Sam followed with Rosie and J.L. in his.

"Awful," Grandpa said, his arms clasped around Noemi on the porch.

While they embraced, I crept around the trailer, remembering the bird that now seemed responsible for setting the noontime horror in motion. I staggered to the spot where the woodpecker had fallen beneath the window and searched for its body in the grass. I couldn't find it. The bird I'd seen die more than once had somehow taken flight.

THIRTY-EIGHT

Louie

Sweat soaked the downy barbs of the feathers protruding from my fist. My white shirt was sweat-soaked, too, the sleeves rolled down, the right one partially concealing the bandage wrapped around my burnt hand. How I wished the rusted old wagon were squeaking behind me with the babble of two three-year-olds drowning out the squeaks. My lonely feet, pretending they were unaccustomed to the walk, carried me slowly, wanting to turn around and run.

Miss Doris's trailer looked foreign when I came upon it, a blue ribbon holding a bouquet of wildflowers to the door. I locked eyes with Miss Tilly, Ray Horn, Miss Paula, and J.L. within seconds of stepping inside. All of them appeared to want an explanation, their doleful stares suggesting I was the reason they were there.

I averted my gaze, and it landed on the very thing I wasn't ready to behold. The casket. Tiny, plain, and sealed, it reminded me of a chest or, more disturbingly, a toy box. With Johnny's favorite things set around it, it could have been just that. A toy box turned inside out: a child that would never play on the inside, toys that would go untouched on the outside.

The sight, coupled with the thought, turned my legs into butter on a hot skillet. Dizzy, I fell into the nearest open seat, still warm from Miss Vicky, who'd gotten up to grab dry tissues.

"Louie." The whisper sucked the air from my lungs. I'd neither seen nor heard Miss Paula approach, but she was next to me with a pair of scissors in one hand and a small leather pouch in the other. "May I?" she asked.

I nodded, and she snipped a lock of hair from the side of my head. It fell straight into the pouch, already thick with black and gray hairs poking out of it. The cut hair represented the past, the time we'd spent with Johnny. It'd go into the ground with him. The hair that would grow in the cut hair's place would represent the progression of life, the birth of new things. I wasn't ready to think about what was to come.

My hands in my lap and my eyes on my hands, I focused on the feathers tight in my grasp. How I'd usher them to the table where Johnny's rubber ball and tiny toy trucks were set among other offerings—a stuffed bear, a rubber frog, a tiny drum—was a mystery to me.

"You look a little green," Mac Langdon leaned over and whispered in my ear. Green was exactly how I felt. Pea green. Swamp green. The green of rotten dead things. "You should get some air."

Obeying him the way a private would a sergeant, I bolted for the door and rested my spinning head against the railing outside. Gasping, I didn't realize I'd been holding my breath until the pressure in my chest diminished and the throbbing in my temples went away.

"Looked like you were gonna ralph in there."

I startled at the voice.

"You seen Rosie?" J.L. tousled my hair as if I were ten years younger than him.

"No." The word barely came out.

"I thought she mighta gone by your place."

"Why would she—?" I slowly righted myself.

"To see your sister. For support and stuff. You know how girls are."

I shook my head.

"Well, she ain't here. No one's seen her all day."

"She's gone?" I thought of Miss Shelby.

"Not gone. Just not here. Doris said Rosie split when Chris Horn showed up with the casket." J.L. leaned far over the porch railing and scanned the land, searching for Rosie in the fields. "I shoulda stuck around this morning, but I slipped out before Doris was even up. . . . Rosie told me to take off."

"You mean—?"

"Do I look different, Louie?"

Aside from his collared shirt, he looked no different from the day before.

"I should," he whispered. "I *got* some, Louie. Finally got some. She did me, man!" The corners of his lips curled. "With her mouth, too. It was good, man. So fucking good. I swear I made this trailer shake."

His revelation winded me. Partly because I remembered how destroyed Rosie had been and I couldn't imagine getting off on that; partly because I was envious even though I didn't want to be.

"So much for the pow wow." He laughed. "What'd you say about that stupid warrior dance turning boys to men? Look, Louie, this is the only dance you need to know. . . ." He thrust his hips back and forth. "I'm a real man now." He whooped. "I'm gonna see if I can find her. Come with me and I'll tell you what it was like."

"No." I stared at the sweaty feathers in my fist. "These are for him."

J.L. pulled a can of his dad's chew from his front pocket and shoved a wad in his mouth. My stomach churned at the sight of brown spit dribbling over his lip. He wiped it with the back of his hand. "Guess I'll tell you later." He tousled my hair again, then leaped from the porch to start his search.

I stepped back through the door, thinking things couldn't get much worse. Miss Vicky was back in her seat, preventing me from taking refuge there. My eyes collided with Miss Doris's. She waved me over to where she was sitting, next to the casket. I couldn't follow through. Though the lid was shut, it didn't prevent me from seeing awful things, like a smiling face in flames.

My stomach roiled and my throat clamped shut. Light-headed and sweaty all over, I felt myself slipping just as the trailer door banged open and Rosie stumbled in. Everything that followed happened so fast that I don't remember when I let the feathers loose.

"Ros—" J.L. said from outside, his feet pounding up the steps.

"Leave me alone!" She slammed the door in his face.

"Rosie!" Miss Doris rocketed to her feet.

"I want everyone out!" Rosie looked like a weathered scarecrow, like she'd lost all her stuffing in just one night. Her greasy hair whipped around as she surveyed the room. "What're you all looking at? He's my baby. He's mine!"

Miss Paula leaped to Rosie's side to soothe her. Rosie swatted her away like a horsefly, making Miss Paula yip.

"You never even asked me!" Rosie screamed at her mother. "You never asked if I wanted Louie to watch him!"

Miss Doris's lips quivered. Her left hand blindly reached for the cane to keep her from collapsing. "Johnny loved Louie," she said.

"*Haw!*" Rosie sounded deranged. "You're as responsible for this as he is!"

"Enough," Mark Bishop erupted from the kitchen. "We all know you're hurting, Rosie, but this is a time for reflection and respect. There's no one to blame." Despite his declaration, his eyes flicked toward me.

"You!" Rosie shrieked. "How dare you come into this house!"

I recognized something scary in her glossy eyes, something I'd seen all too often in the years before Ma had become like an apparition among us. It was fiery rage that had ignited in Rosie's glare, the same rage that used to burn whenever things didn't go Ma's way.

"He's dead because of you!" Rosie thrust an unsteady arm at me to point the finger of blame, apparently unconvinced by the story Jean-Luc had told.

"Rosie, I—"

She threw herself at me, going slightly askew. I jumped backward, landing within feet of Miss Doris and the undersize casket.

"I'll never forgive you for this!" Her dizzy movements suggested that if she were speaking at her normal rate, she'd be slurring all over. "Never ever ever!"

"Rosie, if I could—" I started, another apology on my tongue. My voice had the same effect on her as gasoline on a lit match. She was on me before I knew it, digging her nails into my neck. I fell back, the hard exterior of the casket scraping up my spine.

"Rosie!" Miss Doris, along with a handful of others, cried.

The casket wobbled on its stand. Rosie and I tumbled to the floor, my back pulsing with pain. We made a crash when we landed. So did the casket.

"I hate you, Louie! I hate every single . . ." I could see Rosie's lips moving. I could see the fire in her eyes and the fury in her flushed cheeks, but though I knew she was screaming at the top of her lungs, I stopped hearing her voice. Only the relentless *ta-ta-ta-ta-ta-ta-ta-ta* of the woodpecker filled my ears.

My head fell to the side in time to see the casket's lid shut, having bounced open when the casket crash landed. It didn't stay shut for long. While the invisible woodpecker continued to hammer inside my head, the lid lifted. Horrified, I watched the seared thing inside sit up and turn its head toward us.

THIRTY-NINE

Noemi

I didn't want to believe it, just like I didn't want to believe the news about Roddy. Uncle Louie hadn't looked at me once while telling me about the boy I barely remembered, my old friend. He kept his eyes on the street, the glistening blood drops still comprising a consistent trail, seeming to lead us farther away from safety and warmth.

Arms crossed, I startled when my phone vibrated against my ribs.

I'm in!

It took a second to make sense of Sara's text. I'd been so consumed by Uncle Louie's gruesome memories that I didn't immediately know what she meant. Then it hit me. Roddy's iCloud account. She'd cracked the passcode.

Find anything yet?

Still distracted, I tucked the phone back beneath my arm. "Johnny sat up and looked at you?" I asked.

Uncle Louie swallowed a few times in between licking dry lips. "You have to believe it if any of this is going to make sense."

Suddenly, I was the one struggling to swallow. "Don't tell me it gets stranger."

Uncle Louie shifted his phone from his right hand to his left, the phone's light still aimed at the street. He wiped his sweaty palm against his pants. "So much of what happened that summer revolved around you."

"Really? How? And why didn't you tell me about it before?"

"I buried it," he said.

I couldn't blame him for not wanting to relive what he'd just described.

"I should have said something," he went on. "It's your life. You have the right to know. We were always together back then. Since you were born, really. We were close."

"*Were*," I echoed.

He heaved a heavy sigh, allowing uneasy silence to take over.

"It's not your fault," I said after a while, both because it was true and because he didn't deserve to be punished by me.

"I shouldn't have left."

"You did what eighteen-year-olds are supposed to do," I said, thinking about how young that sounded now. I'd been less understanding at the time. Only five when he flew the coop, I cried for days. "At least you visited. For a while."

He grimaced. "You deserved better."

"You were thirteen when I was born. You didn't owe me a damn thing."

"Not just from me."

Of course, I knew what he was getting at, referencing things I'd tried to bury myself, things that just might have made me what I was: a fuckup. If only I'd felt secure as a child, life might have been different. It took me a while to realize that—maybe too long. The reason I'd clung to Roddy, and Ben before him, and a slew of others before Ben, was because I feared abandonment. I'd experienced it over and over as a kid, and always when I was just getting comfortable. It wasn't just Uncle Louie who'd left me, it was Grandma, then Grandpa, and my own father before that. Even Johnny had been ripped away. And now Roddy, taken just when I was starting to think I had the future figured out.

"How'd it make you feel when he'd wink at you?" Uncle Louie asked.

A smile bloomed on my face. "The best. Special, because he chose me."

"Didn't you choose each other?"

"Yeah, but Roddy could have been with anyone. He was handsome. Talented. Funny. He chose me."

"That's not why you loved him, is it?"

The question wiped the smile from my face. "I loved everything about him. He saved me. I'd probably be in a ditch if he hadn't come along when he did."

"Were things that bad?"

I decided I might as well tell him everything. "I wasted most of my thirties and all my money on Ben, my ex. By the time I left him, I had nothing. Not a hope."

The blood trail ended without a carcass in sight. Stumped for a second, Uncle Louie jogged back to the cross street a few feet behind us. Sure enough, he found the trail again. The coyote had changed directions. The fact that it was still sticking to the streets made my skin crawl.

"Ben wasn't a bad guy," I said, rubbing my arms. "He just thought too much of himself. We were driven by different things. To him, success was money. He wanted a lot of it without having to work for it. He was always looking for the next big trend he could capitalize on. . . . If only I hadn't told him about my trust fund."

"You actually saved it?"

How irresponsible did he think I was? "You're the one who told me not to blow it all on a car and clothes or whatever else a dumb kid would want."

"I told you that?"

"Yeah, you did, which is why I kept most of it in savings. Until Ben finally broke me. Usually I could resist his *brilliant* ideas."

"What was it?"

I cringed with embarrassment. "Froyo."

"As in . . . frozen yogurt?"

"Fucking froyo!" I hid my face behind my hands. "Hear me out. It made sense at the time. It was taking off everywhere. People loved it. They were making Insta posts showing the different mixes they were making with all the different flavors and toppings—getting to make your own was a big deal. Not to mention that summers here are hot as hell. It sounded like it couldn't fail, and it *did* do well for a while, but in the end it was just another fad. Ben was supposed to pay me back everything I'd given him to buy into the franchise. I'm still waiting.

"Point is, I walked away from that relationship broke,"—I didn't bother bringing up the Jeep, an impulse purchase meant to make me feel better, but which I was still struggling to pay off—"well beyond the average age of a first-time bride or a first-time mom, and with nowhere to go other than my old bedroom at home. No one would want me. I was sure of that. But Roddy did, so I guess I wasn't dealt the worst hand in the world." Somehow, I had to believe that.

"Maybe not," Uncle Louie agreed, "but if life were a game of five-card draw, would you keep the cards you were dealt, or would you exchange them for new ones?"

I didn't answer. I didn't need to. We both knew that each of us would gamble for something better if given the chance.

"The Sauciers lived here when I was a kid." He ground to a stop and turned away from the road ahead of him. I saw nothing but darkness beyond where he stood until he redirected his flashlight, making a trailer appear. "George, June, and their son, Horace," he said.

Like other abandoned homes on the rez, the trailer looked like it might wash away during the next big storm.

"Horace was murdered years before you were born. Kids like me used to believe that a vampire got him." The beam of his flashlight slid to the right, coming to rest on a patch of overgrown grass. "I thought it could get me, too. Or *us*. I remember feeling like I had to protect you, like you were mine as much as you were your mother's. I didn't have that feeling again until Jill was born."

"You said she moved to Boston?"

The beam of his flashlight fell. "Before the pandemic."

"What does she do there?" I had a painful desire to know how much better my little cousin was doing in life than me.

"She's a sous-chef at a seafood restaurant. Long hours. Grueling work. She says she loves it." He found the blood trail with his light and recommenced walking. "As long as she's happy," he muttered.

"What about you?"

"Huh?"

"Are you happy?"

He chuckled and grabbed his chin with his free hand, clearly uncomfortable. "I'm fine. No need to worry about me."

I wasn't worried about him until he spoke those words. "You can tell me anything," I told him. "I'm grown now. You don't have to protect me anymore."

FORTY

Louie

My intestines quivered at the sight. Rosie, her hands still around my neck, squeezed tighter, burying her nails deep into my flesh. Her lips stopped forming words when she saw what had become of her boy. Strong gusts of horror-infused breath poured past them instead. Still, I could only hear the drumming of the derisive woodpecker. Weakened by what I'd seen, I stopped struggling. My body went limp. My head hit the floor, and my eyes ventured into the spiral of color beyond Rosie's right shoulder. The feathers I'd brought for Johnny floated down on the air.

A pair of brawny hands—Mac's, Mark's, or Ray's—pulled Rosie off me. She looked like an ireful cat being yanked away. Her mouth hung open mid-yowl, and her fingertips stayed hooked like claws. I didn't try to stand after the hands pulled Rosie away. I just watched the commotion unfold from the floor. Chairs toppled as bodies sprang out of them. Miss Doris heaved her hulking frame right over me, her cane touching down between my legs. A feather, black as ash, landed on my chest.

I saw only the trailer's ceiling after the feather touched down. The hammering in my head disconnected me from everyone else. I might as well have been alone in the trailer with the thing in the box.

I don't know how long I lay there, but when Grandpa appeared and placed a hand on my forehead, his touch did something that rearranged the signals being received by my brain. The maddening pecking stopped. Something far worse took its place.

Johnny's voice.

"No!" I screamed.

His words burrowed into my bones.

Frightened chatter followed Johnny's declaration. Screams rose above the gentle shushing from mouths of level-headed people like Grandpa trying to restore order. Rosie continued to curse me out in between questioning God about what she'd seen. The solid thud of the casket closing sounded once more.

"Easy, Louie," Grandpa said.

Bolting upright, I clumsily found my feet. "Did you hear it?" I bellowed. "Did you hear what Johnny said?"

"I want you to go sit outside. Catch your breath and wait for me."

"But did you hear it?"

Grandpa pushed me toward the door. "Wait outside."

Rosie collapsed on the kitchen floor. I staggered out onto the porch and squinted against the glare of the sun. Wondering eyes met me there, but I didn't hang around to be questioned by their stares. I teetered down the steps and ran into the knee-high grass, cutting across the field to get to the road rather than taking the longer route down the dirt drive.

"Wait up!" J.L. called after me. "Louie, what happened?"

I didn't cease. Didn't even slow. The words that Johnny spoke were too fearsome for me to stop and explain.

"Shit, man. What's with you?" J.L.'s rustling strides came closer. His shadow gained on mine and then his hands got ahold of my sweat-soaked shirt. He yanked. The shirt tore, spitting buttons at the ground. I spun around, landing on my ass.

"Stay away!"

"Is that blood?" he said.

My fingertips returned red from my neck. "Rosie . . ." I hopped to my feet. "I have to go home."

J.L. spat a brown wad into the grass. "Is Rosie all right?"

I pushed him away and ran.

"Louie!" Grandpa shouted from the top of Miss Doris's steps. "I told you to wait. Louie!"

I didn't look back. I just ran, desperately trying to outpace the unknown evil lurking among us. Heavy hopelessness hitched a ride on my shoulders. It added miles to the road that stretched out before me, and it turned up the temperature of the sun's heat. My throat dry like overcooked meat, inhaling each breath became a battle, like choking down fistfuls of sand.

I pressed on, passing the listing shed where George Saucier had held his son's heart in his hands. My sprint had diminished to a desperate jog by the time home came into sight. I felt like death, and I must have looked like it too.

"Louie." Ern's voice drove my teeth into the tip of my tongue. "Come over. Bring me somethin' to eat."

I would have nailed his window shut if I could have. My own front door was the only barricade I could put between me and him. I slammed it, then locked it. Bloody, sweaty, disheveled, and scared, I resembled the lone survivor in a horror film, only I wasn't so sure of my fate. Lula yelped at the sight of me. Noemi covered her eyes.

"It's coming!" I roared.

"What the hell, Louie?" Lula hopped off the couch. "What's coming?"

I didn't know what *it* was. I only knew that I had to fight it. I rushed through the living room and kitchen, closing and locking the windows on my way.

"You'll make us melt in here." Lula, already glistening, reopened the windows as soon as I closed them.

"Leave them shut!"

"What's wrong with you? You're scaring Noemi." The quaver in her voice indicated that she was scared too. "What's coming?"

"*It!*" I shoved her aside so that I could lock the windows once more. "We have to seal this place up!"

"Louie!" She hit me hard with her weight. I tottered backward, landing on the arm of the couch. Lula's uneasy eyes danced over the tear in my shirt, the blood on my neck, and the streams of sweat flowing down my temples. "Tell me what's wrong!"

My lips wiggled like worms, unable to produce the words that would make her understand. I couldn't tell her what Johnny said.

"Hold her." I pointed to Noemi, who still hadn't uncovered her eyes. "Hold her tight and don't let go."

Tears beaded along Lula's black eyelashes. "Tell me why, Louie."

"Aubrey, Fay, *Johnny* . . ." I said. "You have to hold her. Keep her safe." I took Lula's trembling hand and led her to her daughter. In the silence that followed, Noemi finally lowered her hands from her eyes. They narrowed upon spying the blood on my neck.

"Ouchie," she said.

"It doesn't hurt." I couldn't feel the scrapes any more than I'd felt the burn on my hand. The pain would come later.

Lula sat behind Noemi and wrapped her arms around her. "Are we going to be okay?"

"Yes," I answered as hopefully as I could. I didn't have a fucking clue.

I swept the curtain away from the front window and squinted toward the road. Aside from the pudgy presence in my far peripheral view, there wasn't a soul in sight. Nothing moved. Not a blade of grass. Not a bird in the sky. Not even a fly buzzed around the window-pane. There was something sinister out there, though. Something like the vampire. I could sense it coming closer.

Shivering, I let the curtain fall back into place, Johnny's voice echoing in my ears. After Fay's wake and what had happened in the cemetery, I couldn't say if anyone else had heard the words that came from Johnny's mouth, but that hardly mattered since the message had clearly been meant for me.

Noemi's next, he'd said.

FORTY-ONE

Louie

The air inside our trailer grew thick. Oppressive. Swollen with mois-
ture that stuck in our lungs like mud each time we drew breath. The
air tasted grubby. Swampy. Stagnant. The humidity dampened the
carpet and our clothes. Our home had become a marsh. A bayou. We
were nothing more than crawfish in the rocks hiding from that which
would tear us apart. Tamahka don't chew.

Lula and I heard the truck in the drive and then the knock on the
door. Neither of us moved to answer it. Dripping in a way that would
have driven her crazy on any other day, Lula held tight to Noemi in
front of the box fan, rocking her, hugging her, protecting her despite
Noemi's persistent battle to break free. The heavy sheen on my arms,
face, and neck stood testament to the terror coursing through my
veins, terror that kept me from unlocking the door even though the
man on the other side would never do me, Lula, or Noemi harm.

"Let me in, Louie." The fuzzy outline of Grandpa's head bobbled
beyond the drawn curtains. "We need to talk."

Steadying myself, I unlocked the door and pulled him in.

"You didn't wait."

I twisted the lock back into place. "I had to get home."

"You heard something at the wake." His statement was almost a question.

I nodded. "You didn't, did you? Did anyone else?"

He shrugged. Something bulged in one of his pockets. "I don't think anyone heard what you did. You're the only one who ran away."

Gritting my teeth because I still didn't want to say Johnny's words out loud, I flicked my fearful eyes at Noemi. "Can we . . . ?" I pulled Grandpa to my room. "I'm scared," I admitted once we were alone.

"We all are."

"Can we come stay with you now?"

He considered my request this time. "I'm sorry to say it, but I don't think it'd make a difference."

I deflated even more, the question I'd asked him in Sam's duck boat still on my lips. "Why's this happening?" Expecting the response he'd given before, I didn't allow him time to answer. "Are spirits behind this? Is it God?" I remembered the prayer sticks and feathers alongside the crucifix in Fay's casket—old beliefs mixed with new ones. "Did we do something to make them angry?"

"It could be one or both, but I don't think it has anything to do with anger."

"Then what?"

"Balance, like I said before, Louie. Something's thrown it off. We won't have peace until it's restored."

"What are we supposed to do until then? We can't just sit around and wait."

"No," he agreed. "The question is what can we do?" He rubbed a palm against the side of his head. "I have a feeling the answer will come to you."

"Why do you say that?"

"Because you sense more than the rest of us." His body sagged. "I only heard Rosie screaming at the wake."

Feeling hopeless, we returned to Lula in the living room. Ma was standing like a specter outside her bedroom door when we passed through the hall. She appeared frozen despite the sweat on her skin.

"Ma?" I called.

She stayed still for a second, then staggered to the kitchen, using the wall to keep herself steady. I realized then that it wasn't just the shadowy hall that'd made her look less than human. Her eyes were deep black pits, except for the whites, which had turned yellow. Her skin was yellow too, her face nothing more than scabbed and bandaged flesh stretched over bare bones. Her clothes hung off her like laundry on a line.

I went to her and reached for her knobby wrist. She swatted me away. My impulse was to run in response to her touch. She struck me as something to fear. Keeping calm, I turned out a kitchen chair so she could sit.

"I'll make you something to eat," I said, my voice lost in my throat.

She took a few shuffling steps, but she didn't sit. She merely grunted and pawed at the stack of mail on the table.

"You shouldn't go back to work. You aren't ready yet." The blood stains along the edges of the faded shirt she wore—*Roscoe's Get 'n' Go* embroidered on it—seemed to agree. I reluctantly picked up a leftover sleeve of Johnny's crackers. "You need to eat. Rest."

"I need money." She flicked one of the bills toward me, FINAL NOTICE stamped on its envelope in big red letters.

"You can't work if you can't walk." The way her shoulders curved down around her chest suggested that she had no muscle in her back.

"I'm making money now," Lula said from the living room floor. "We'll be all right, Ma, until you get better. Do what Louie says."

"See?" I peeled open the crackers and filled a cup with water.

"Let them help you, Mae," Grandpa said. "Can you let them do that?"

I thought she wasn't going to respond. The pauses in her speech were getting longer.

"You've got some nerve. . . ." I counted the seconds that passed. *One . . . two . . . three . . .* "Sayin' shit like that."

My fingers crushed one of the crackers upon hearing the anger, maybe hurt, in her voice. "What do you mean?"

One . . . two . . . three . . . four . . .

"I've done everything for you . . . even let you keep your kid here," she sneered at Lula, her words slow and slurred, every syllable requiring effort. "Now you're gonna tell me I need help? That I can't walk . . . That I gotta get better . . . I've been working my whole damn life and I've never needed nothin' I couldn't get myself."

"We're just saying you could use a break," I tried to explain.

One . . . two . . . three . . .

"Take a break and then you're *broke*," she huffed. "I gotta get ready." She swiped her hand across the table, sending envelopes careening off the edge, then retreated to the bathroom.

I put the mail back into a stack with the most intimidating envelopes on the bottom. Lula, Grandpa, and I stared at the bathroom door after that, like children eyeing a chrysalis, hoping and waiting for a butterfly to break free, or, at the very least, for Ma to come out and say she'd changed her mind.

"There's one reason she goes to work, and it's not for money. She goes to buy beer," I whispered after a while. "I don't know how to make her see what she's become. I can't make her change."

Ma emerged just then, looking no better than when she went in. The bandages on her face were wet. One of them hung from her chin.

"Mae, something serious is happening," Grandpa said as he tried to get through to her. "It concerns us all. We need you in good health."

Ma glared for a few long seconds, then—in a tone so contemptuous it stripped decades from her age—said, "I'm already late 'cause you took my truck. I gotta go."

"Make her stay," Lula begged.

"If you'd gotten the bingo hall built by now, I wouldn't have to go,"

Ma said to Grandpa. "You make us live like dogs." Her accusation spoke more about her underlying pain than she ever had.

"A bingo hall wouldn't make you better, Mae."

One . . . two . . . She swayed. *Three . . . four . . .* Her eyes stayed shut for more than just a split second when she blinked. Her head nearly rolled off her neck. *Five . . . six . . .*

"Worry about makin' yourself better." She turned to me and Lula, and, after another long pause, said, "Don't let him fool you. . . . He's only good to you 'cause he was so bad to me . . . and Mom."

"Mae," Grandpa sternly said.

"Ma?" Lula questioned.

"Tell 'em," Ma said to Grandpa. "Tell 'em how many nights you never came home. Tell 'em how we went hungry and how we cried. Tell 'em how many women were more important than Mom and me. Tell 'em."

The words Ma spoke were like rocks against a window. They added another crack to my already fractured world. I feared it would shatter into a million little pieces.

Grandpa's face drooped like bad lettuce. I remembered what he'd said the first time I asked if I could live with him, that I couldn't leave Ma because she'd been left before and because the abandonment had led her down the hopeless road she was on. Never had I thought he was talking about himself.

"Stay away from my kids," Ma said. "You've never done 'em any good anyway." She struggled with the door, then hobbled out into the darkness.

No one went after her. Not even me.

FORTY-TWO

Louie

Grandpa broke the anguished silence after Ma left. "I brought something," he sheepishly said. His hand trembled upon pulling a white pillar candle from his bulging pants pocket.

"No fire," I muttered. I could barely look at the candle—or Grandpa.

"Candles are holy symbols," he said. "The unblemished wax represents Christ. Fire embodies God. The flame will be sacred. And small. It'll be safe."

New beliefs, I thought. "I don't want it." I couldn't stomach fire because I knew what I'd see in the flame. The thought of it made my hand throb.

"The fire spirit is one of the greatest protectors we have," Grandpa persisted.

Old beliefs. "But Johnny . . ." I said.

"I don't think the fire spirit killed him." Grandpa's head shook. "Not really."

"Then what did?"

"Something else. Something none of us has ever encountered before. Something that drove him into the flames, like you said."

"We'll take anything that helps." Lula, hands shaking like Grandpa's, took the candle and placed it on the coffee table atop a dish from the kitchen. "Light it."

Jaw clenched, I turned away as Lula passed Grandpa a book of matches. The scent of sulfur momentarily filled the air.

"I . . ." I heard Grandpa swallow. "I'll check on you tomorrow." His footsteps moved toward the door. "I'm sorry," he said on his way out.

"I won't be able to sleep." Lula locked the door behind him.

I wouldn't be able to either. Overloaded with thoughts about what had happened at Johnny's wake, the candle on the coffee table, Ma's bitter outburst, and the truth about Grandpa, my mind raced faster than a sinner seeking salvation on his final day.

"Put Noemi to bed," I said.

"What are you gonna do?"

I may not have been equipped to fix all our problems, but there was one I could at least try to make better. I burst into Ma's room and collected every beer can I could find. Empty or full, it didn't matter. They all went back into the brown paper bags—deflated, for once— that she'd left lying on the floor. When the bags were bloated and hanging from my hands, I stood in the bedroom doorway and saw the crushing sadness of a reality few would willingly face. It came in the form of a bare mattress, a balled-up, bloodstained sheet on the floor, paneled walls, cobwebs in the corners, dirty clothes that covered the carpet, a lamp without a shade, and a broken mirror. The sum of the sadness was worse than what I might see in the candle's flame. Worse because it was real.

The room was a wasteland. Small. Stale. Sweltering. I couldn't imagine what it'd been like for Ma to squander so many years in there, sheltering crippling feelings and shameful secrets. I realized that the room reflected her state of mind, not her state of being, but it was so much easier to look at that paneled piece of hell and think that if her lot in life had been different, she'd be better.

Desperate to get rid of the beer, I told Lula to lock the door behind me and to only reopen it after I knocked. The cool, clammy air that licked my flesh upon stepping onto the porch with Ma's booze felt as luxurious as ice-cold air-conditioning. I drifted down to the bottom step and took one of the full cans from one of the bloated bags. I bent its tab and began pouring its contents into the dirt.

"Don't waste it," Ern said.

I stood the can straight to preserve its golden yield, which really did seem invaluable to so many on the rez.

"It's not cold," I said.

"Don't matter to me. Come over."

I handed Ern the half-full can before heaving the heaviest of the bloated bags onto his windowsill. His blinds locked at half-mast, he'd lifted the window screen so that he could sift through the bag, proceeding to cast the empty cans straight onto the grass. "Have one," he said.

I waved him off and started back toward home.

"Sorry 'bout what happened . . . 'bout Johnny," he said between slurps.

"Me too, Ern." I kept walking.

"Guess you heard what Sam found in the river?"

The assertion stopped me in my tracks. As far as I knew, Ern still didn't know about the bone, only the muddy scrap of fabric. I couldn't bring myself to tell him that J.L. had actually found the scrap, and that Sam had found something more macabre. "Any idea what you're gonna do? Have you talked to your dad?" I turned to face him again.

"He's in Georgia now." Ern took a long slug. "He's makin' room for me to move in with him. That your grandpa who just left?"

"You know it was."

"Why'd he come by?"

"It's Noemi," I muttered. "Aubrey, Fay, Johnny . . . I'm starting to see a pattern here . . . people who can't really fight to save themselves . . . and Noemi . . . well . . . she fits in with the rest."

"Protect her."

"How can I, when I don't know what I'm protecting her from?"

"There's a lot out there that we know nothin' about." He finished the beer and cracked open another. "Our ancestors embraced the unknown because they never knew what blessings might be born of it. But as history has shown, that same unknown might just rob you blind, then leave you bloody and barely breathin'."

"What are you saying?"

"What I already said earlier. Protect yourself. Protect Noemi, too."

"There was nothing I could do to protect Johnny." Frustrated, my fingers sank into my hair. "Not a knife, a gun, or even a bomb would have protected him from whatever forced him into the fire with a smile on his face. If I couldn't save him, how am I supposed to—?"

"Agate mighta worked."

"What're you talking about?"

"Agate. It's a stone. . . . Certain stones absorb certain energies. Agate's supposed to protect children. Put an agate stone in Noemi's pocket. Maybe it'll help."

"Where can I get one?" I asked, nodding.

Ern looked like he might inhale the can in his hand, his beach-ball-size head thrown back to collect its final drips. "Bet you didn't know that agate's the official gemstone of Louisiana." He belched.

He was right. Who, other than he and Miss Shelby, would know something like that?

"Look for it in the gravel beds around the river. Agate's different from regular stones . . . translucent with bands of color."

"I've seen some like that before!" My feet started back toward my trailer. "I'll find one tomorrow for sure."

"In the gravel beds," he said again, holding another can out the window. It glinted in the darkness. "Keep bringin' the full ones out. And somethin' to eat next time."

I ran the rest of the way across the field and beat on the door until Lula let me in. We hunkered down that night, just us with our fears and the white candle burning in the living room, part of me wishing the old box fan would do me a favor and blow it out.

Whether the candle kept the fearsome unknown from getting us that night, I'll never know, but I can say that it didn't keep the wood-pecker from trying to get in. The bird returned during those dark hours. The damned thing hammered outside my window all night long.

FORTY-THREE

Noemi

The flashlight's beam flicked up at the sky as if it might illuminate something flying by. Uncle Louie steadied his wrist, brightening the blood trail again.

"So," I persisted with the question I'd asked before, "are you?"

"Happy?" He didn't hesitate this time. "Can't in all honesty say that I am."

"How long's it been?"

He thought for a moment. "Since after the divorce. I might have been happy then. For a minute."

"Then what happened?"

"Things went back to normal . . . a new normal."

"Does that mean the divorce didn't help?"

"Not the way I thought it would."

We listened to our footsteps against the sticky pavement for a while after that, me wondering if I should apologize, if I'd dug too deep. Sara rerouted my line of thinking.

I might've found something

Why couldn't she just say what it was?

?

A photo

Of?

The toe of my left shoe caught on a rock. I stumbled, nearly drop-ping the phone. Uncle Louie shined his flashlight on me to help me see what I was doing. Regaining my footing, I walked blindly ahead, my eyes glued to the screen before me. An image sent by Sara popped into the conversation a second later.

I studied the woman in the photo. Mid- to late twenties. Happy, posed, beaming in designer clothes. The sassy tilt of her head re-minded me of the mean girls I'd dodged in school. The sparkly cruci-fix hanging from her neck suggested that she'd reformed. Still, her self-satisfied smile said a lot about her self-worth. Surely she thought she was something special because of how blessed she'd been, with looks, familial wealth, luck in general, and now the engagement ring on her finger, weighed down by a diamond the size of a big fat blue-berry.

Who is she?

Brandy

Brandy who?

Chapman

The name wasn't clicking.

Roddy's ex

I scrolled back to the photo and blew it up on my phone, zooming in on the face. I'd known that Roddy had had significant relationships in the past, just as he'd known that there were lovers I wanted to forget, but we'd never shared photos, stories, full names. Neither of us had seen who we were following. I stared, wondering why Sara had sent the photo. I assumed Brandy's flashy ring had something to do with it.

What's ur point?

"Everything all right?" Uncle Louie looked over his shoulder at me, his flashlight aimed at my feet. I hadn't realized that I'd stopped walking.

"Sorry." I hurried to catch up.

She sent it two days ago. To tell
him she's engaged

I needed no assistance to put the pieces together after that. The distance increased between me and Uncle Louie again, my mind weaving a web of *what-ifs*.

What if Roddy hadn't stopped talking to Brandy after they split?

What if he'd never stopped loving her?

What if he'd secretly hoped to win her back?

What if she'd thought the wink was for her?

What if he'd been crushed by her engagement?

Bottom lip clenched between my teeth, I skipped to catch up with Uncle Louie, telling myself not to jump to conclusions.

How'd he respond?

He wrote: Congrats!

Anything after that?

No.

I breathed easier. Maybe things weren't what they seemed. Still, there were details I needed to know.

How long between their last
text and the pic?

Were they in constant communication, or did Brandy's announcement come out of the blue?

Did he send her pics in return?

How much had they been sharing with each other?

"It's moving slower." Uncle Louie drew my attention back to the trail. The blood drops were coming quicker now, meaning the coyote wasn't covering as much ground between each drop.

"More bad news?" he prodded. He motioned toward my phone when I looked at him.

"I don't know," I said, my eyes stinging. I didn't want to think the worst about Roddy. My heart couldn't take it. I felt guilty for letting the doubt-inducing possibilities creep in. "It's just hard. . . ." I was breaking down. "It feels like everyone's saying he did something I don't think he would have done."

"Your reasoning?" he asked, as if I were one of his students.

"Well . . ." I shrugged. "We didn't tell anyone, not even Mom, but we were gonna get away from here. Not far . . . just off the rez . . . a place where we could leave the past behind. We were gonna get tattoos, too. Matching ones. Not identical, I mean, just a set. An antique key for him. A lock shaped like a heart for me. Because they go together."

"He must have been looking forward to it."

"Yeah," I said, glancing down at my phone. There was nothing new from Sara. "That's why none of this makes any sense." I wiped my eyes. "I'll still get the heart. As a memorial, you know? It'll remind me to be strong and self-assured. And happy. All the things that Roddy made me."

"That'll be nice," he said.

"Nothing like a new tattoo to distract you from your problems." I tried to be funny. "I'll look like the front of a Lisa Frank folder before you know it."

"Lisa Frank?"

I shook my head, *never mind.*

"Biggest problem with problems is that they never just go away," he said. "You can run from them, but they'll be waiting for you when you get back. Believe me, I know."

"Like Jean-Luc and Rosie?" I said, barely thinking.

"Something like that." He picked up his pace.

FORTY-FOUR

Louie

Sunlight through the gap between my curtains woke me from the small spell of sleep I'd slipped into after the woodpecker left. The light propelled me from my bed in search of the stone I hoped would fortify the barrier of protection around Noemi. I checked in on her before heading out. Wrapped in Lula's arms, she looked safer than on most mornings when Lula went to work and left her all alone.

I knew exactly where I wanted to search for the agate. A short distance downriver from where J.L. and I spent most of our time together was a slight twist in the waterway where buckets of gravel washed up on shore. J.L. and I had found enough fishing lures there over the years to fill an entire tackle box. I found a watch there once that didn't work. J.L. found a silver dollar that we spent on fries at the Blue Gator. For all I knew, it could have been the very spot where Horace found the trade bead Ern told me about.

I hopped over a rotted log and into mud to get to the river's edge. Just enough light twinkled through the trees for me to see the markings on the glistening, wet rocks. Most were black. Some were brown. None looked translucent to me.

I crouched low and duck-walked along the shore, sweeping my

hands over the rocks in search of one that fit Ern's description. My head low, I barely noticed the swift movement of something in the river, something larger than the rushing waves.

I scrambled backward, fearing it was the gator I'd seen when searching for Miss Shelby. Looking closer, I realized that something much more familiar was in the water. Human hips and the rounded arch of a broad, bare back, golden in the early morning sun. The rest of the figure's limbs were beneath the water's surface, its hands busy with a submerged stump sticking just a few inches out of the water.

"J.L.?" I said, only half certain because I couldn't see his face.

I must have startled him as much as he'd startled me. Whirling around, his jaw dropped and whatever he'd been holding between his teeth—a stick or a pilfered cigar—fell into the river.

"Didn't mean to scare you," I said. His jaw hadn't just dropped, a gasp had leaked out, audible over the gurgling waves.

"Louie!" He forced a smile atop the discontent that had crept across his face. "What are you doing here?"

I wondered the same about him, standing there in the water with his arms beneath the surface. "Looking for a stone," I said, expecting him to explain what he was up to in return, or, at the least, to ask why I needed a rock that was different from the thousands all around us. He, however, just went right on smiling, his ass in the air and his arms out of sight.

"What've you got there?" I asked.

He shrugged, hands still underwater. His uncomfortable smile turned crooked, telling me he was trying to cook something up on the spot.

"Wanna know what it was like bangin' Rosie?"

"Sure." I was curious. "Come over here."

The corners of his mouth wavered. He squatted in the water, leaving only his head above the waves. "Meet me at our usual spot, all right? Just gimme a minute."

I didn't retreat. He didn't persist. He turned his back to me and carried on with the submerged stump, only to climb ashore on the opposite side of the river once he was done.

"It's nothin'," he said in response to how I stared at the stump. I knew the statement wasn't true because I could see something stuffed into the stump's hollow center. The object was white in contrast to the rotted, old wood.

Grandpa's words rang in my ears—*Liars hide*—making me wonder what J.L. didn't want me to see. Not just in that stump, but behind the smile he could barely maintain.

"You never used to lie."

"I'm not lying."

His words propelled me into the water faster than a frog trying to outjump the snatch of a child's hands. I dove into the shallows where J.L. had been standing. Water filled my sneakers and weighed down my clothes. I reached for the stump as J.L. launched into the river.

"Don't!" he hollered. I latched on to the secret he'd stuffed into the stump. He clamped one hand around my neck and grabbed hold of what he'd been hiding with the other.

I had to pull hard because he'd fastened it beneath the water, but I realized what it was the instant I wrenched it free. It was the yellow-and-white-striped pillowcase from his bed, stuffed with something much harder than fiberfill.

J.L. dragged me into deeper water, his prune-like fingertips digging into my throat, still sore from the damage Rosie had done. I choked. He tore the pillowcase from my hand and flung it onto the shore.

"Get off!" I grunted.

Three inches taller and twenty pounds heavier, J.L. easily pounded me into the mud beneath the waves. I gasped and flailed, landing blow after worthless blow against the muscle ensnaring me. Gritty water blurred my vision, stung my nose, and filled my ears. My breath all but gone, panic welled within me. I thought I would drown. I thought the gator would get me. I watched the last of my oxygen float from my mouth, the bubbles bursting at the water's surface a foot above my head. My desperate lungs drew in water, cold and excruciating in my chest. My body wilted. J.L.'s grip tightened around me. One second he was pushing me deeper into the mud, the next he was heaving me toward shore.

"I'm sorry!" he cried.

I gagged and inhaled and prayed my lungs would stop hurting. My trembling limbs carried me up the riverbank so that I wouldn't be swept back in by the waves. The pillowcase lay just a few feet ahead of me. Some of what it carried had spilled out onto the ground.

"You owe me, Louie!" J.L. hollered, running up the shore. He frantically refilled the pillowcase, but it made no difference by then. I'd already seen what he was trying to hide. The bones looked a lot like the one Sam had pulled from between the rocks at the riverbend.

My mind cycled through animals from which the bones could have come: raccoon, wildcat, gator. But there was no denying the jawbone that'd landed atop a flat river rock.

Human.

"You?" I gasped, coughing water from my lungs. "You dug up the graves."

He got all the bones back inside the pillowcase and tucked it deep into some brush. "I didn't want you to see because you won't understand."

I staggered to my feet, teetering in front of him. "Why'd you do it?"

"I just wanna be like the tamahka," he said.

"What?"

"You won't understand, Louie. But you owe me, so you can't say anything about this to anyone."

"Jean-Luc . . . what the fuck are you doing with those bones?" I was confused and cold, slightly sore and bruised all over.

"I just wanna be like the tamahka," he said again. "I just wanna be strong."

"You're not making any sense."

"The tamahka, Louie. Look how strong they are. I wanna be strong too."

"What do the bones have to do with the tamahka?"

"I didn't hurt anyone," he insisted. "They were already dead."

Baffled by his reasoning, I turned to the water and looked at the spot where J.L. had been bent when I surprised him. Something had fallen from his mouth. I thought of all the times I'd heard him chewing. Crunching.

"I wanna be like the tamahka."

"But you're not like the tamahka," I whispered. *Tamahka don't chew.* "You can't be like them."

"I thought that since they eat their own when times are tough . . . and since they're so strong . . ."

"My gram . . ."

J.L. wiped mud off his abs. "She was a good woman. She took care of you and look how you turned out. Your great-grandfather was strong too. He was one of the best leaders our tribe's ever had."

I grabbed a nearby branch to pull myself out of the sludge.

"Try to understand, Louie. They can live on inside me. I can feel their strength."

I didn't know what to say or do. My hands curled into fists, though I didn't feel the impulse to throw punches. I almost felt sorry for him. I almost feared him too. Was he the same person I'd always known? Were we even friends? The sight of the lumpy pillowcase was like an eraser scrubbing out our past. The tussle and what it revealed had happened so fast that I couldn't make sense of what I was feeling in contrast to how I thought I was supposed to feel. J.L.'s next words were dumb enough to make me want to forgive him for being so stupid, yet so sordid that I wanted to sling mud in his eyes.

"There's not much of a taste." He snagged the pillowcase from the brush and peeked inside. "It's mostly texture . . . like gnawing on rocks and sand. . . . The water helps—"

"*Shut up.*" I breathed deep. "And Horace? Why'd you have to dig him up?"

"Just to see." He shrugged. "He's got teeth marks on his sternum."

"Teeth marks . . ." My vision dimmed. Something splashed in the water.

"You can't tell on me, Louie. You owe me."

"Owe you?"

"For Johnny. If I hadn't backed up your story, everyone would be blamin' you for burnin' him alive."

"It wasn't a story," I insisted. "I didn't ask you to lie for me."

"You didn't stop me either. You owe me, Louie."

Gutted like a fish sliced up the belly, I slumped away from the river without the agate or the friend I'd always had. J.L. stayed on the shore with the bag of my grandparents' bones, begging me not to tell.

FORTY-FIVE

Louie

Empty and dented, I might as well have been an old can upon return-
ing home from the river. The mud clinging to my body reeked of
earthworms and snails, and it gave me the appearance of a monster
that'd risen from the earth. Thinking about what J.L. had done gave
rise to invisible fingernails scraping my sternum, tearing it apart, providing passage for ruthless fingers to reach in and squash my heart. I
wondered where my anger had gone. I'd wanted to break whoever had
disturbed the graves when Grandpa told me that Gram had been unearthed, but now that I knew the truth, I didn't want to hurt J.L. I just
wanted to know how someone so close could suddenly seem like a
stranger. I flaked mud from my arms and face, then started up the
porch steps.

"Louie," Ern croaked from behind his blinds.

I craned to see through my living room window. Noemi was on the
carpet, scribbling over an already scribbled-on page in her kitten coloring book. The white candle, half its original height, burned on the
coffee table above her. Everything at ease inside, I ambled to Ern's and
stood among the crushed beer cans beneath his window. The air-
conditioning that leaked out made me feel a bit better.

"Bring me some coffee." He drew the blinds up to his nose. His bloated jowls looked puffier than usual.

"You all right?"

"Payin' the high price for the low life," he said. "Coffee."

"I'll make a pot." I flaked away more of the mud. Ern didn't ask about it or the stone I was supposed to find. I turned back toward my trailer, then stopped. Something I hadn't expected to say tumbled off my tongue. "I don't think your ma fell into the river. Not by accident, anyway."

The blinds sank. "Why not?" he grumbled.

"Because there's something strange happening here." After seeing how Johnny had been drawn to the fire and how J.L. had been so quick to pound me into the mud, I knew there was something greater at play. I felt like we were all fighting an invisible force with our backs against a wall. "I know you see it, Ern. Even behind your mask, you see everything."

"Didn't see what happened 'round the firepit. Didn't see what happened to your ma when she had her accident."

"I'm not just talking about what you see with your eyes. It's a feeling. A sense of knowing. Something made Johnny crawl into the fire, just like something made Miss Fay and Aubrey do what they did. And your ma . . . how many times has she walked over the bridge? She wouldn't have just fallen into the river. You know that, Ern."

"Accidents happen, Louie." I wondered if he'd heard J.L. say the same words to me. "My ma musta slipped off the bridge just like yours musta swerved off the road when she crashed the truck."

"Nah, Ern, there's a difference. There's a logical explanation for my ma's accident. There's not one for yours. There's barely one for Fay's, and Johnny . . . he wasn't just playing when he fell into the fire. If Noemi—"

"Did you get the agate?" he asked.

"It'll take more than that." I shook my head. "My grandpa says we're off balance. What do you think about that, Ern?"

His blinds dropped all the way down again, making it look like I was talking to myself out there in the sun. "Your grandpa's probably right. He usually is. If we're off balance it's because one energy has overpowered another . . . good over bad . . . bad over good. We all know there are spirits in the world, all around and everywhere. Some work with us, some against us. That's the way it's always been."

"But why?"

"'Cause we wouldn't appreciate the good if we didn't see it next to the bad, and we'd never feel accomplished if we were never challenged."

"Last night you told me there's a lot we don't know about."

"My head hurts, Louie."

"Come on, man. You're not telling me everything. You just said some spirits work against us. Tell me about them, Ern."

The blinds riffled. Ern's fingers crept beneath them, lifted the screen, and popped a leftover can—crushed like a puck—out onto the lawn next to the others. "You really wanna know?"

I stepped closer to his window.

"There's one spirit that used to scare me bad," he said. "More than any other."

"Tell me."

His chest rattled with breath, his voice a low rumble when he spoke. "The Meli Omahka." The blinds shuddered. "Black evil . . . Ma said it can wriggle out of the deepest, darkest depths after breakin' free from the earth spirit. Aboveground, it can do all sorts of awful things, but only 'til the sky spirit rains on it, washin' it back into the void from which it came. Balance, Louie."

"*Meli Omahka*," I gasped.

"I'm sure Ma was just tryin' to keep me on my best behavior." His voice cracked in an uncharacteristic way. "She said the more I misbehaved, the stronger the Meli Omahka got, enablin' it to break free. She said if it found its way to me, it'd make me wish I'd never been bad."

"Why?"

"'Cause the Meli Omahka can get in you, obliterate your brain, and make you do bad things."

Bad things, I thought. "Like stepping into a septic tank or crawling into a fire?"

"Always assumed it'd make you do bad things to others."

"You said Aubrey hurled boiling water at Jeannie before he died. That's bad, right? And that's where all this started, isn't it? With Aubrey? Do you think the spirit made him do it?"

Ern wheezed. "Spirits can do all sorts of stuff, Louie, like keep us happy, warm, and fed. You know that already."

"Yeah," I said, thinking. "I just don't get it. . . . Let's say the Meli Omahka got inside Aubrey. Maybe it made him do what he did. But wouldn't it have been cast back out after he died? Wouldn't it have been washed back into the earth? It rained buckets after Aubrey's wake, remember? Before anything ever happened to Fay and Johnny. If the Meli Omahka gets washed away, why are bad things still happening?"

"Maybe things aren't as simple as Ma's stories made them out to be. Think about it, Louie. Whatever evil is among us isn't necessarily our own. We didn't create it. It's not spawned by our upset ancestors in the ground, like some movies might make you think. We give it a name and say the rain washes it away because it helps us make sense of our world, our pain, but it could have one hundred other names and one hundred other remedies in one hundred other places. The evil spirit we refer to might be someone else's demon, someone's afreet, someone's boogeyman. Consider the jinn in Islamic mythology. La Llorona in Mexican lore. The baku in Japan. The jumbee in the Caribbean. Butzemann, Sack Man, Baba Yaga, Beelzebub. Each takes a feared form, dictated by history and culture. Like the spirit Ma told me about, many are meant to keep us in line, to make us *think* before we *do*. We may be the ones hurtin' now, but no one knows who's next.

The restoration of our balance might give rise to sufferin' someplace else. Evil never really goes away. It just searches for its next opportunity to spread and possess and steal all our light. It relocates."

"Maybe," I said, "but we can't just ignore it. We have to stop it."

Ern raised the blinds to half-mast so fast they made a slicing sound. "You can't stop the Meli Omahka, Louie. Can't stop any spirit." His voice was faint, and I got the feeling it wasn't the brown bottle flu making him whisper. "We can only wait for the scales to tip back in our favor."

"*Wait?* That's not enough," I said. "Someone else could die."

Ern's hulking shoulders became one with his nearly nonexistent neck, as though he were condensing himself into a gigantic ball. "All spirits have ears, Louie. If somethin' evil is afoot, it could be listenin', and it won't like what you're sayin'. . . . Or maybe that's just my childhood fear of the Meli Omahka speakin' for me the same way the Takoda Vampire always speaks for you."

"I just want to bring peace to our people."

"Be careful, Louie," he went on whispering. "You never know when the unknown will creep up on you."

I shuddered and looked to my left, ever aware that the unknown had countless places to hide in the fields around us. "I'll start that pot of coffee."

Ern nodded. His shoulders sank beneath the window frame again.

"One more thing," I said. "Have you seen a redheaded woodpecker around lately?"

As I'd suspected, his answer was no.

FORTY-SIX

Noemi

We were finding blood drops every two feet now, maybe less than that. The coyote was losing speed, its blood trail leading us close to home.

"It's dying," I said. My icy regard for the animal began to melt. I didn't like what it'd done to Roddy, but I liked what Jean-Luc had done to it even less. I began to imagine the animal's horror, its pain. Could it sense us on its trail? Did it think we wanted to finish the job?

Uncle Louie didn't waver. Eyes locked on the trail, his gait hadn't slowed one bit. I couldn't get a read on what he was thinking or feeling, and I still didn't know what, exactly, he hoped to find, only that he suspected the coyote might somehow tell us if Roddy's death was intentional or not.

"Yeah, but for the first or second time?" Uncle Louie eventually muttered in response to my remark about the animal dying.

It took me a moment to figure out what he meant, but then an image of the coyote on the street only seconds after Jean-Luc had shot it flashed in my mind. It looked dead. I'd thought it was. I would have argued with anyone who said it was still alive. Another chill ran down my spine.

"Do you think I'm crazy?" he asked.

"No." I'd been so eager to find evidence that backed what I believed that I hadn't questioned his state of mind upon following the coyote. I was curious, though, and now I had to wonder . . . if he was crazy, what did that make me?

"Your mom thought I'd lost it once." He swatted something on his face. "I almost thought I had as well. It was during the same summer as . . ." He heaved a heavy sigh. "You used to call me *Douie* back then."

"Really?"

"Yeah. Until . . ." He lifted his gaze. Our trailer was nearly in sight.

"Until what?" I reached over and grabbed his shoulder, forcing him to slow and to look at me. Dread gleamed in his eyes.

"I buried that too," he said. Turning from me, he increased his pace again.

"I'm scared," I admitted, immediately waking the phone in my hand so I could see colors and light, wondering how much digging I'd have to do to get him to unearth the parts of the past he'd interred deep inside himself.

Uncle Louie came to a sudden stop where the street met the mouth of a gravel driveway. He shined his light at the rocks. I saw the glint of blood, a tiny speck only a foot from my shoe.

"Why would it come here?" I said.

Uncle Louie took a slow step forward, raising his light as he went, shining it farther along the driveway. Gravel crunched beneath the weight of a few more footsteps. I think we both stopped breathing when his light landed on the furry heap near the end of the drive. I don't know how long we waited, but I'm sure we were waiting for the same thing: for the coyote to move.

"Is it . . . ?" I ventured.

Uncle Louie pressed forth, not going directly toward the animal but giving it a wide berth. His bright white light gave it an unnatural hue, making it look more blue than gray. I followed Uncle Louie closely, nearly stumbling into him when he stopped again just a few feet from the coyote.

"It isn't breathing," I said after a while. It wasn't moving at all. Uncle Louie didn't react to that. I shuddered. His response to my earlier remark about the coyote dying hit me harder than before.

"Stay back." He cautiously closed the gap between himself and the coyote. Close enough to kick it, he dropped into a squat, his light making the blood glisten on the canine's coat.

"Don't . . ." I tried to stop him from touching it.

His fingers passed over wayward hairs, making them waver. And then, as if to take it by surprise, he snatched the coyote by the scruff and yanked its head up.

I gasped, sickened by the thought that bits of Roddy might be inside that furry bag of bones.

Its eyes were slits and its mouth was open wide, its tongue hanging over its teeth. Uncle Louie turned the animal this way and that, its head flopping from side to side on its sagging body. I saw where the bullet had broken its skin. The fur along its neck and down its chest was wet and red. Uncle Louie let it fall.

I took a step closer, the top of my phone pressed to my chin. "It's not what you thought it was, is it?" I asked, having witnessed some— but not all—of the stress dissolve from his face, making his brow smoother and his lips less tight.

"Maybe not." He shook his head and hopped up. "Let's just . . ." He put a hand on my back and led me away from the coyote.

"Why'd we follow it? You can tell me now."

"Just a minute." He ushered me to the mouth of the driveway where we stood facing the field on the other side. Again, I don't know how long we waited, only that I had plenty of time to wipe my sweaty face, realize how badly I needed to pee, and check my phone for the text that would tell me if Roddy and Brandy were still close.

"What are we waiting for?" I whispered. Uncle Louie and Sara were putting my patience to the test.

"Just . . ." He raised a finger and sucked his bottom lip between his teeth.

A car came upon us, its headlights making it impossible to see who was driving or if anyone was in the passenger seat. It passed us slowly, and I turned to keep my eyes on it, watching until the taillights winked out in the distance, the sound of its rumbling exhaust replaced by the clatter of gravel being kicked about. Uncle Louie no longer by my side, I turned to find him darting back toward the coyote, looking lighter, freer, relieved that the animal hadn't gotten up again. He hopped into the overgrown grass along the drive and reappeared with a wide and wieldy rock. He placed it atop the coyote's body. I wasn't sure if he was trying to commemorate the animal or weigh it down.

"What for?" I asked, catching up to him.

He shrugged. "Might not matter." Despite his doubt, he didn't just look lighter, he sounded less tense. "There's a Sioux legend about Coyote and a rock," he said.

"Must be a lot of legends about Coyote."

"He's an important figure in Native lore. Smart and silly, he's a clever buffoon. He can be unpredictable, too, stirring up trouble, singing songs, seeing what he can sink his teeth into. I know the story I told you earlier wasn't all that funny, but Coyote's a trickster who loves to make us smile. He reminds us that laughter is necessary for survival. . . . It's something our people have always needed."

"Try me, then," I half-heartedly said.

"Okay . . ." He turned his flashlight off. "Try to see it in your head." He cleared his throat, then started the tale. "Coyote was walking with a friend when they came upon a rock. It was big with lines all over it. 'I think it has power,' Coyote said, proceeding to take off the blanket he wore, which he draped over the rock to keep it warm.

"'You are in a giving mood,' Coyote's friend said. 'The blanket is the rock's now.'

"The pair carried on and soon it started to rain. The rain turned to hail, and the hail turned to slush. Coyote got cold and wet. Teeth chattering, he said to his friend, 'Go back and get my blanket. The rock doesn't need it. It's gotten along without it for years.'

"Coyote's friend went back to retrieve the blanket, but the rock wouldn't give it back. 'What is given is given,' the rock said.

"Upon hearing this, Coyote returned to the rock. 'You're bad,' he said. 'Don't you care that I'm freezing to death?' He snatched the blanket back and retreated to his friend. The two began to eat, and as they were eating the friend said, 'Do you hear that?'

"'Hear what?' Coyote asked.

"'Rumbling. Like thunder.'

"They looked about and spotted the rock rolling toward them.

"'Run!' the friend said. 'The rock means to kill us!'

"Coyote and his friend ran into the pines, but the rock rolled right over the trees, reducing them to splintered pieces. Soon, it was on Coyote's heels. And then it rolled over Coyote, flattening him. Saying again, 'What is given is given,' the rock took the blanket and rolled away.

"A man came along a little while later and found flattened Coyote. 'What a beautiful rug,' the man said. He took Coyote home and placed him in front of the fire. Though he was flat, Coyote wasn't dead. He took all night to find his feet, but in the morning the man's wife said to him, 'Your rug just ran away.'"

Uncle Louie turned the flashlight on to see my smile. "I guess it worked," he said.

"A little," I admitted.

He aimed the light at our coyote again, perhaps to ensure that it hadn't found its feet. And though he kept his relief restrained, I had a sinking gut feeling that the coyote's death was bad news for me and Roddy. "What—?"

"Do you hear that?" he asked, stopping me from prying.

I strained to listen, wondering if he was trying to be funny himself. Rather than a rolling rock, I heard small yips and squeals.

"There." He redirected his light to the dilapidated steps of the abandoned trailer at the end of the driveway.

I stayed a few feet back, watching him approach. His shoulders slumped when he got a glimpse of what was beneath the steps.

It was a den full of three gray pups, all of them snuggled together.

"She just wanted to make it home," I said, glancing at the dead coyote.

Uncle Louie turned his flashlight off and rounded the steps so that he could sit. I joined him as my phone vibrated in my hand.

> Doesn't look like Roddy had been
> talking to her. No other texts
> since 2020

My heart swelled, still desperate for something hopeful to cling to. If Roddy and Brandy hadn't spoken in three years—if he really had moved on from her—then her engagement text might not have propelled him over the edge.

"You all right?" I asked Uncle Louie.

"Just thinking," he said, chewing a thumbnail.

"What about?"

He hesitated. "How I'm like that coyote over there. We both ran, both of us trying to escape danger, fear, and the unknown, both of us trying to find someplace safe." He shrank even more on the steps. "It didn't make it."

"You still have a chance," I assured him.

He worked to swallow. "I didn't just run from Jean-Luc, Rosie, and Holly," he said. "I ran from you and your mom, too."

I took a breath and held it, remembering five-year-old me standing by the window, wondering why he'd gone. What I said next was as much for me as it was for him. "Maybe. But you came back."

FORTY-SEVEN

Louie

I turned my back to Ern in his window and squinted across the way.

"No!" I started to run. "What are you doing? Get inside!"

Lula, the screen door propped open against her shoulder, didn't budge from our porch. She just pulled her hair away from her face and tilted her head to catch the breeze. "It's so damn hot in there."

I leaped up the steps. "Use the fan."

"It doesn't work."

I darted past her and plucked Noemi from the doorway where the tips of her toes were just barely touching the first porch plank. Hustling inside, I socked the box fan to get it going. "There. See?" I panted.

"So we're supposed to stay inside all day while you're out at the river?" Lula sniped, eyeing my mud.

"You okay?" I asked Noemi.

"Don't act like I wasn't watching her!"

"You're funny, Douie." Noemi scratched dried mud from the tip of my nose. "You need a bath."

I laughed for her sake, playfully threatening to wipe some mud on her. She squealed. I set her on the kitchen counter so that she couldn't run out the door. She reached for the box of cookies next to her as I lunged for the open living room window and slammed it shut. The candle on the coffee table kept my eye while I ran about the trailer, sealing it up. The pulsating flame atop the little lump of wax mocked me. Torn, part of me wanted to blow it out while another part hoped it really was doing us good.

"You can't take risks," I said to Lula, forcibly trading places with her on the porch.

"You're overreacting." She swatted me as I shoved her inside. "Louie!" I jammed the door closed and grimaced at her through the living room window, commanding that she stay put. "What are you doing? How come you get to go out and I have to stay in this freaking box?"

Rounding the trailer, I pressed a finger to my lips. Lula followed from window to window. I wasn't inspecting to see if the trailer was secure. I already knew it was as penetrable as a roll-back can of sardines; the same key used to reveal the little fishies would have unlocked our front door. I just had to see if the noise I'd heard the night before had been real or if it'd only been in my mind.

"I'm gonna come out there if you don't tell me what you're doing, Louie!"

I squinted at the siding around my bedroom window. Dozens of dimples dented the aluminum frame. The pocks proved that the woodpecker had been trying to get in.

"We can't take any chances," I said, heading back inside. "Noemi's at risk."

A look of alarm flashed across Lula's face and then she balked, her eyes rolling to the back of her head. "I don't know why I let you scare me yesterday. Look around, Louie. We're fine. Noemi's fine. Just because something bad happened to Johnny doesn't mean something bad's gonna happen to her. You're paranoid. Guilty! That's why you're so obsessed with keeping Noemi caged in the house."

"Guilty?"

"For not watching Johnny as closely as you should have. Now you think nothing bad will happen to Noemi if you keep her locked up."

"What?"

"Sorry to bring up a sore subject, but it's true. You fucked up with Johnny—*big!*—and now you're scared it'll happen again."

"Grandpa—" I started, intent on reminding her of his concern.

"He was reacting to you," she said. "You scared him as much as you scared me. All because you made a mistake."

"It's more than that. You weren't there at the wakes. You didn't see what I saw. You didn't hear what I heard!"

"Neither did Grandpa or anyone else. It's all in your head."

"I just talked to Ern. He told me about a spirit that—"

"Oh, bullshit, Louie!" Her eyes rolled again, so embellished that her head went back, her big hair bouncing. "Bullshit. *Bullshit.* You know those old stories are nothing more than myths. Why would you take anything Ern says seriously? He's a weirdo who sits around stuffing his fat face all day, and who knows what else? I know he watches me when I walk to work. His hungry eyes make me feel like a piece of meat. He's a creep!"

"Believe what you want. But trust me. I'm doing what's best for Noemi."

Lula threw her hands in the air and stomped into the kitchen to take Noemi off the counter. She took the box of cookies from Noemi too.

"Mine!" Noemi said, clinging to the last cookie she'd wrangled from the box.

"Believe me, I know how hard it is to accept your mistakes," Lula said. "But if you man up, you'll be able to move on. You can't blame what you've done on something you can't even see."

"Grandpa says the spirits are out of balance."

"Grandpa's from a different generation. He's superstitious and so are you. You're both stuck in the past. How is it that this whole damn tribe believes in spirits, talking alligators, and vampires? I've gotta get off this reservation."

Noemi scurried into the corner to finish her cookie. I made sure the front door was locked.

"You used to believe in him too," I said.

"Who?"

"Horace. And the Takoda Vampire."

"I never—"

"You did! When I was eight you said you saw Horace by his shed. You said he tried to hit you with one of his rocks."

Lula burst out laughing. "*If* I said that, it was only to scare you." She brayed. "You practically pissed your pants anytime anyone mentioned Horace or the vampire. You've always let your fears get the best of you. You're still so goddamn gullible."

"No," I said, denying that my childhood fear had been a joke to her. Lula had to believe in the vampire as much as I did. She had to know I wasn't crazy. "Why'd you want Grandpa to light the candle if you don't believe in any of this?"

"Because you were raving last night. You still are." She wiped tears borne of laughter from the corners of her eyes, leaving small black smudges on her skin. "Go ahead, blow it out. I don't care." She laughed some more. "All I know is it's turning into a decent day out there." She eyed the blue sky through the window. "There's even a breeze. We oughta get out and enjoy it. Lord knows we don't get to enjoy much around here." She shot a glance at Ma's closed bedroom door. Undaunted now that she'd rationalized my fears, she grabbed Noemi's hand and made a move for the exit.

"Wait!" I stopped her. "Let's make a deal. Keep Noemi inside while I clean myself up." The humidity in the trailer had revitalized the mud on my skin. Dark streaks dripped down my flesh. "I'll watch her all day after that, and you can do whatever you want. Go out. Have fun. Whatever."

"If you call consoling Jeannie and Rosie fun," she murmured.

"Please?"

Lula sent a stream of breath up into the air, making her overblown bangs wave. "Okay," she agreed, "but only because I owe the girls a visit. They've been through hell, and I haven't even called them because I don't know what to say."

I showered. Lula left. The candle continued to burn on the coffee table. Despite my initial resistance, I couldn't blow it out, just in case Grandpa was right about its power.

Noemi and I built a couch cushion fort, then started construction on a matching building-block castle. Carefully balancing one block on another, I was as carefree as I was likely to get, all things considered. That was until Noemi, a block clutched in each fist, asked, "Johnny?"

Hearing her say his name washed away the happiness I'd tried to feign like throwing a bucket of water onto a vibrant chalk mural.

"Not today." I realized that Rosie and Miss Doris must have buried Johnny that morning while I was at Ern's. I also realized that we were playing with Johnny's blocks. I quickly put them away.

"Tomorrow?" Her cheeks got chubby with a hopeful smile.

"Sorry, Pink Feather."

Question marks glinted in her eyes. She'd seen the sorrowful faces in our trailer the day Johnny ran out into the yard, the last time she saw him. No one, though, had told her anything about what had happened to her friend. Or that he'd never be back. My eyes watered.

"Don't be sad," she said, then pinched me the way Johnny had pinched her, her hands like claws. I laughed. It was either that or cry.

We ate a quiet lunch of PBJ sandwiches. Noemi ate half of hers;

the other half ended up in clumps, stuck to her fingers and face. I picked at mine. She insisted on a story when I tucked her in for a nap. I read to her about a giant with stinky feet and long toenails. She slept, I stood guard, interrupted by Grandpa, who called to check up on us like he said he would, though I'm sure he would have come in person if it hadn't been for the secret Ma had spilled. Noemi wanted to play with her dolls on the porch after she woke. I talked her into making them dance on the kitchen floor instead. A thorough conversation about the different kittens printed on the pages of her coloring book brought the early evening to an end. Noemi liked the kitty she'd given purple eyes to best.

"Pretty eyes like Grammy's." She tried to show the drawing to Ma when Ma emerged from her room later that night. Ma's head dipped in the direction of the open coloring book, but she didn't say anything about it. Noemi, already accustomed to Ma's lack of interest in anything other than what she brought home from work, appreciated the meager head dip more than I ever could. She scampered back to the couch, grinning from ear to ear.

Ma headed for the door. "Be careful," I said. It wasn't what I wanted to say. I wanted to beg her not to go. I wanted to help her and to tell her about everything that had happened. I wanted her to know that somehow, someway, I was going to restore our balance. More than that, I wanted her approval and support.

"Ma, if you stay, I'll—"

"If you go in my room again . . ." She cut me off with the first half of a threat. "Stay out. Don't touch my shit."

I followed her to the door, knowing nothing I could say would make her stay. I had to let her make her choice, because it was a choice. At the least, I wished I could erase the scabs on her face or smooth her tangled hair. Even with the brilliant sun dipping toward the horizon as she set off on her walk to work, she looked sick and sad. The radiant orange glow made the dusty dirt road look like it'd been paved with gold, but it couldn't make Ma look any better than she was.

I watched until she was gone, then looted her room again. I couldn't stop her from going to work or from buying beer from the mini-mart at the end of her shift, but I could reduce her consumption of it, even if it meant she'd be mad at me. I searched Ma's space and collected all the alcohol I could find, from beneath the bed, behind the dresser, buried in the pile of dirty clothes. Since I didn't want to go outside—or even open the trailer door—to give Ern the beer, I stashed the cans in the backpack I'd stowed at the back of my closet for the summer. Ma would never look for them in there.

"The bunny and the duck," Noemi said from the living room. She'd settled on the floor between the couch and the coffee table, a stack of construction paper next to her and dozens of crayons in a colorful pile.

"It's past your bedtime," I said, yawning, hoping the woodpecker would let me sleep.

Noemi shook her head and pointed at the TV. "Cartoons," she said. "The bunny and the duck."

"Sorry, Pink Feather, they're not on now." I clicked through the channels so she could see for herself. Nothing but the tiresome tones of the nightly news filled the living room as the remote began to slip from my hand. Next thing I knew, I was bolting upright, my heart in my throat, my eyes on the closed curtains, concealing whatever had hurled the rock at the window.

"Easy," I whispered to myself, unsure now if I'd heard a harsh clack against the glass, or if I'd manufactured it in my mind. I took a deep breath and rubbed my tired eyes. Aside from muted tones of awestruck voices hawking a crazy contraption meant to melt pesky pounds from hips and thighs, the trailer was quiet. And then Noemi spoke.

"Louie," she said. "Louie."

I turned the TV off and swept my gaze from one end of the trailer to the other. A thin line of yellow light glowed within the gap between the floor and the closed bathroom door; Lula was home. The candle continued to burn on the coffee table in front of me, just a wick in a puddle of translucent wax. One of Noemi's feet, sticking up in the air from the floor, swayed beside it.

"Louie," she said again.

"How are you still awake?" I muttered, pushing myself forward on the couch cushion. "Come on. Bed."

"Louie . . . Louie."

I realized then that she wasn't really calling me. She was just saying my name. I leaned down to see her, lying on her stomach, scribbling on a piece of paper.

"Louie. *Louie* . . ."

I blinked some more. And then it hit me. The way she was saying my name. Though she was pronouncing it right for once, it sounded wrong coming from her, like the wind when it whispered, or Ern when he commanded me.

"Noemi?" I reached for the foot sticking up in the air. She rolled out of range, putting the coffee table between us, and stood with her drawing in her hands.

"Louie," she said. "Louie!"

"Is that me?" She'd crayoned a bunch of brown and green squiggles. Using a little imagination, I could see a silhouette.

"Louie."

I thought she was going to give me the drawing, but she didn't put it in my hands when she extended it over the coffee table. She held it over the candle's wick and let it burn.

"No!"

She smiled, giving me something to scream about. Her teeth! No longer were they boxy and cute. They'd grown long and sharp.

I jumped to my feet amid billowing ash. Cinders fell from Noemi's hands, revealing fingers that had shrunk into fleshy, clawlike nubs.

"Louie," she said, right when the candle winked out in its dish.

I screamed again, torn between wrapping Noemi in my arms and running away from her.

"What is it?" Toothbrush in hand, Lula burst from the bathroom, white foam around her mouth.

"Look at her!"

Noemi's lips pulled back from her gums, showing off glistening, pointed teeth. Her stubby nose flattened on her face, turning into two reptilian slits. I leaped over the coffee table and made a grab for her. She swiped one of her half-human claws at me. I slipped to the side like a boxer dodging a punch, then lunged at her and swept her into the air, keeping her at arm's length. I foolishly thought I might be able to shake her back to normal, as though she only needed waking.

"Louie, stop!" Lula screamed.

Noemi's limbs swung this way and that while a terrible, snakelike smile spread across her face. Head striking forward, she sank her jagged teeth into my right arm, right above my burn.

Blistering pain surged through my body, forcing me to drop my niece-turned-monster to the floor. Her head hit against the edge of the coffee table on the way down.

"Noemi!" Lula shrieked. She chucked her toothbrush at me on her way to her daughter.

"Her hands! Her teeth!" I ranted. "Don't touch her! Do you see? *Do you see?*"

Noemi's appearance didn't faze Lula a bit. "Shut up," she said.

Produced by pain, Noemi's wails injected me with guilt, like a killer in church. As Lula lifted her, Noemi—a bloodred rose blossoming on her temple—looked at me through confused and frightened eyes. She didn't understand why I'd done what I did. I didn't understand what I'd seen. The razor teeth. The stumpy fingers. The absent nose. They'd gone away, and if it weren't for the bite mark on my arm, I might have believed that my haunted mind had been playing tricks on me.

"There's something *really* wrong with you, Louie!" Lula stomped to her room. "Come on, baby. I won't let him hurt you anymore."

The fear I saw in my niece's eyes hurt ten times worse than a kick to the crotch. Much worse than the bite's lingering sting. Blood streaked down my arm from the tiny holes left by Noemi's teeth.

"Look!" I brandished my arm so that Lula would see the strange bite mark. She slammed her door without ever looking back.

Exasperated, I swatted the dish holding the remains of the candle from the coffee table. Warm wax splattered across the carpet. The dish shattered against the wall. Desperate and alone, I reached for the lock on the front door, but I didn't have to turn the bolt. My careless sister had left it unlocked while I was asleep. I threw the door open, thinking I'd go to the river in search of the agate again. It was the only hope I had left.

"Never brought the coffee," Ern said.

I took one step onto the porch and froze, finding the rotted and worn corpse of the redheaded woodpecker at my feet. Its back was featherless, bald. Only a nub remained of its beak.

I drew my leg back and sent the damned thing flying into the field. It crash-landed in the grass as I staggered back into the trailer, locking myself in once more. What was I thinking? I couldn't leave. Not after what I'd seen. Not with the evil already upon us.

I reeled about the space, clutching my heaving chest, feeling helpless and doomed. My arm continued to bleed, and Noemi continued to wail in the other room. Between her cries and the rapid beating of my heart, I felt done for, doomed.

"Breathe," I whispered, forcing slow and steady inhalations. Once I could stand without the threat of toppling over, I washed the blood from my arm and bandaged the bite. I went back to the living room and picked up the largest piece of the broken dish I could find, the closest weapon at hand. Wrangling the lawn chair, I set it in the hall outside Lula's door and stationed myself in it. I had no idea what we might be up against, but whatever it was, it'd have to get through me first.

FORTY-EIGHT

Louie

My arm burned, my eyes blurred, my chin sporadically dropped to my chest. Staying alert had been easy at first. Noemi's cries, combined with inky shadows crawling across the wall, had kept me on edge. It was during the subsequent eventless hours that I succumbed to sleep. Rather than rocking me in a merciful embrace, however, it thrashed me from one side of the rickety lawn chair to the other, filling my head with awful images that couldn't be real, but which seemed undeniable in the dark. I saw serrated flesh, rows of unending teeth, and rivers of blood. Upon breaking from sleep's spell, I wasn't sure if I'd really been dozing or if I'd been swept into a lightless hole occupied by dreadful things. My watery mind, my stinging arm, and the bitter taste at the back of my throat prevented me from making sense of my surroundings. I felt lost and confused, different, dizzy, and starved.

Head spinning, nausea swelled within me. Certain that I'd be sick, I sprang up, sending the lawn chair tumbling backward. I staggered outside to escape the trailer's stifling air and hung my head over the porch railing. I heaved. Nothing came out. I had nothing in me. My hunger surged, demanding more than the boxed macaroni and cheese in the cabinet or the frozen waffles in the freezer.

"Louie," Ern called.

I reeled into the shadows and gripped tight to the railing there, desperate to deny the sudden and sickening urge compelling me to find out what Ern's insides tasted like. I wanted to rip. I wanted to tear.

Tamahka don't chew.

"No," I scolded myself, though no amount of grit or self-commandment could overrule the need. I retched again, sick and ravenous at once.

"Louie," Ern kept calling.

"Shut up!" The need commanded that I do frightful things. It made me wonder if Lula's blood was as red as the lipstick she wore. My hold weakened. I'd be in trouble if my hand fell from the railing. So would Lula. So would Ern.

And what about Noemi?

My stomach gurgled.

"Please." I pled to God and the Great Spirit, whichever would listen. Neither offered any relief. The hunger gnawing on my insides called to mind the Takoda Vampire. I thought of Horace, who'd been feasted upon, and J.L., who'd feasted in his own way. With that last thought, I found what I hoped would grant me relief. J.L. had had a hunger I couldn't explain, and he'd turned to the cemetery to satisfy it. Maybe I could too.

I fixed my bare feet in the direction of the road and released my hold. Though the hunger begged me to inflict pain upon the potential victims at hand, I bounded down the porch steps, leaving the trailer unlocked as I sprinted straight toward the cemetery, bypassing the listing shed and the yellow tape outside the Lavergnes' house on my way.

I blazed across the bridge and past the pow wow grounds, whorls of fog twirling within the dance circle there. I might have been a springing deer or a black vulture soaring through the sky. I didn't feel like myself. Something essential had been stripped from me, my essence altered, my ability to reason reduced. Instinct ruled me, ordering me to rip and tear, turning me into an animal that scurried on the ground.

I didn't realize I was on all fours until I darted past Sam, asleep in his truck, and found myself feverishly clawing at the fresh grave of somebody I once knew. The stench of decay grew stronger as dirt rained all around, bringing me closer to the body below. It wasn't until I descended beneath the earth's surface that I realized more than my appetite had changed.

My hands and feet weren't right, and yet they didn't register as wrong, just different—armored, webbed, more effective for digging.

"Louie." I pressed my nose to the box beneath me. "Come out of there." It was a woman calling to me. From above. "You don't want to open that coffin."

"Who's there?" I growled.

"Climb out and see."

Shaken from the frenzy I'd fallen into, I clambered out of the pit and peered past the ridge of dirt.

"I thought you were dead," I said.

Miss Shelby loomed before me. Thin as Ern was fat, her graying hair hung around her shoulders and her thoughtful eyes sparkled in the darkness. Hands clasped, she stood only a few graves away.

"I know what you're up to, Louie. I know what you think you want. There's something inside you. Fight it!"

My mind flickered. Did I want to fight? "How?" Uttering the word was as tough as confessing a long-held secret.

"Do you know our origin story?"

"Yes," I huffed. "My grandma taught it to me."

"Tell me."

"You know it."

"Tell it anyway."

Preferring to savor the delicious stench surrounding me, I willed the story past my lips.

"It is said," I panted, "that the Takoda people were born from a sacred hole in the ground. Blocking the hole was a bayou, and blocking the bayou were two alligators called tamahka. One was red. The other was blue. The Takoda leader said to the tamahka, 'Let us leave this hole. Let us know the land, the sun, and the water in which you swim.' The tamahka approved because our people were pure of heart and their souls were sincere. Our people were born without weapons or ill intent. But, the tamahka warned, should our people become sneaky like the snake when it soundlessly slithers behind its prey, or callous like the bobcat when it kills for its own amusement, then the red and blue gators would swallow our people whole, for alligators only use their teeth to shred and to tear. Tamahka do not chew."

"You know the story well," Miss Shelby said, nodding.

"Why'd you have me tell it?"

"So that you'll understand what I'm about to tell you." Miss Shelby didn't seem afraid of me. Couldn't she see how hard I was straining not to lunge at her? "Do you know the story about the alligators and the anoles?"

I shook my head, heavier than ever.

"Listen and learn. Then do what's right."

My body quivered. A waft of putrid flesh tempted me to turn my attention back to the welcoming hole.

"Long ago, Louie," Miss Shelby started, stopping me from diving into the grave, "there were no small lizards. There were only tamahka that kept watch over the land, the water, and our people. But one day the tamahka, whom we were supposed to trust, turned on us. They swallowed six of our people whole. Six people who had done no wrong. In response, the tribal elders gathered and decided that our warriors would have to do something to keep the tamahka from turning on us again. The warriors gathered their spears and sharpened their rocks, then faced the red and blue tamahka in the night, which is when the tamahka preferred to hunt. The warriors said, 'We have never acted with ill will, yet you swallowed our people whole. We cannot allow this.' So the warriors cut the red and blue tamahka into tiny pieces, but they did not kill the tamahka because that would have been wrong. Each tiny piece of the tamahka grew a head, four little legs, and a tiny tail, turning into little lizards called "anoles." The anoles understood why our warriors had done what they did, and, unlike the tamahka, the anoles could do our people no harm. That is why now, in the shadows of night, every anole can look like an alligator, and every alligator can be turned into an anole. It is the same tonight, Louie."

"What does that mean? What do you want me to do?"

"Go," she said.

"Can't you tell me—?"

"Go!"

"Where?"

"Just go!"

I staggered backward, my eyes snagging on the coffin's moonlit lid.

"Run, Louie!"

I resisted the temptation beneath me. Desecrating graves wasn't what my invader wanted anyway. It wanted me to do something more. Something worse. I retreated from the cemetery, leaving Miss Shelby without ever asking where she'd gone or why she'd left.

My transformed feet didn't feel capable of supporting my weight as I ran, yet I refused to get on all fours. Scrambling like an animal in the cemetery had only made the awful urge worse.

My mind a blizzard of desperation and awful impulses, I couldn't make sense of what Miss Shelby had said, and I didn't know where she wanted me to go. Able to think of only one person who might understand her message, I ran straight for his trailer. I needed to tell him that his mother was alive.

FORTY-NINE

Louie

I could smell Ern before I could see him. I could hear him too, baying like a hound each time he howled my name.

I ran faster, my mind growing less my own. The reprieve granted by Miss Shelby's appearance in the cemetery had expired, forcing my will to war with the ugliness that had settled inside me. Hard as I fought, my invader took the lead, though I still had enough sense to know the difference between right and wrong. Even so, that didn't guarantee how I'd act. I salivated in pursuit of the easy prey wailing in the window.

"Raise the blinds!" I shouted. "I wanna see your eyes, Ern. Raise 'em up!"

The blinds stalled midway, then rose. The expression on Ern's fat face morphed from one of mild confusion to an overblown grimace.

"Louie!" he screeched. "What the hell are you doin'?"

I fell to all fours and picked up speed.

"Louie, stop!"

The fat face came closer. A frantic hand fiddled with the cord that controlled the blinds. I scrambled up the porch steps, leaped onto the railing, and lunged at the window.

"Stop!"

I latched onto the windowsill. Confined to the couch, Ern couldn't cram his massive figure beneath the window frame. He turned his face away, powerless to conceal the ridge of his mountainous back. I slammed my open mouth against the window screen. It gave way, creating a barrier between my teeth and the meaty roll hanging from the right rear side of Ern's rib cage. My mouth struggled to take a bite.

He yowled. I thrashed. Ripping. Tearing.

Tamahka don't chew.

"Son of a bitch!" Ern cried. He jolted upright and craned his stumpy neck. The mouthful of fat, shielded by the window screen, didn't come loose, but I could taste the blood seeping through the wire, making it more metallic. I swallowed and sucked, trying to draw out more, oblivious to the crusty steak knife Ern pulled from the pile of dirty dishes next to him until the blade was in my face.

"Back off, Louie!"

I fell from the window, the taste of blood on my tongue and a stinging slash in my nose. The pain broke my invader's trance, leading me to choke on the stench of death. I could smell it stronger by Ern's window than I had at the cemetery.

"Your ma's not dead."

The grimace on Ern's face faded. A doleful wheeze streamed out. His muscles slackened, and the knife fell from his trembling hand, landing beneath the window.

"I saw her," I said, through teeth that wanted to tear. "She spoke to me in the cemetery."

Ern paled. "What'd she say?"

"She said I've been invaded. . . . The Meli Omahka, don't you think? She told me the story about the alligators and anoles. She said in the shadows of night every anole can look like an alligator, and every alligator can be turned into an anole. She said I would understand what that means, but I can't make sense of it. Help me, Ern. Tell me how to put an end to the spirit inside me. You're the only one who can."

"Already told you I don't know how to stop a spirit."

My toes burrowed into the ground, searching for roots that would prevent me from attacking him again. "There must be a way to get it out of me. She must have told you. Think!"

"She never told me that, Louie! But I think I know how you can subdue it."

"How?"

"You *know*."

I glared at him.

"You gotta calm it by doin' somethin' bad . . . *really* bad. . . ."

"*Bad*," I echoed, feeling the weight of the word. I felt hopeless, too. Was there no other way?

Wincing, Ern reached for the wound on his back. "You didn't just wanna make me bleed, did you?"

"What if I won't do what it wants?"

He shrugged. "Then I guess you'll always wanna lunge at me the way you just did. You'll wanna lunge at everybody."

The truth strengthened my craving. I needed something struggling between my teeth. Wiping the blood from my nose, I noticed that my fleshy fingers were gone, replaced by scaly appendages with claws.

"What's happened to me, Ern?"

"What do you mean?"

"I look different."

"Only thing different 'bout you is that bloody grin."

He couldn't see my physical transformation. Only I could. And only I'd be blamed if I did something bad to Ern.

"You could let the spirit solve your problem, Louie," he said. "Let it consume the person who's consumed you."

"Who?"

"The person who keeps you up at night. The one who haunts you deep in your heart. The one who's on her way home right now, earlier than usual."

I turned and saw her staggering down the road, a bloated brown bag hanging from each hand.

"No!" I screamed at her and then at Ern. "You're mad! How could you say that?"

I kicked dirt into the air as I ran from him, heading for the road, then the river, thinking the waves might wash away my hunger. If the water didn't help, I'd sink my teeth into frogs and fish. Or—I ruthlessly thought—maybe I'd find J.L. there, holding his bag of bones. He deserved my invader's fury for what he'd done.

Ma and I crossed paths on our respective ways. If she sensed me charging at her, she didn't let on, and I didn't let on how easy she would have been to kill. Racing past, I stripped the two brown bags from her hands. The sound of the tearing paper melded with her disgruntled scream.

"Bastard!"

The force with which I'd snagged the bags spun Ma in a half circle. She tottered like a buoy on water, then fell. Leaving her in the dirt, I focused on my throbbing nose, hoping the pain would prevent me from turning my mind over to the intruder inside me, so that it wouldn't do what Ern said it could—*obliterate your brain.* Intoxicated by the collective scent of sludge, water, and dead things decaying in the ground, I tossed the brown bags away. I smelled the rot of dead fish, too, their dried-out gills making them look like they'd been throat-slit on the shore.

Having arrived at the spot where J.L.—absent now—had been with my grandparents' bones, I collapsed on the river's edge and roared. The water called to me, fog swirling above its surface. I bent to peer into the shallows and screamed at what I saw.

The spirit had taken hold, just as it must have taken hold of Aubrey, Fay, Johnny, and Noemi. The bite mark she'd left on my arm was gone, both it and the bandage replaced by textured skin. I didn't doubt, though, that the bite had transferred the evil into me, leaving me with an elongated snout, beady eyes, pointed teeth, and an alligator's smile.

FIFTY

Noemi

We left the coyote sandwiched between the gravel and the rock, its hungry and restless pups growing louder beneath the Mire trailer's steps. Mom's car was out front at home. The living room light was on.

"I was about to call again," Mom said when I keyed the door open. "Where'd you two run off to without paying your tabs?"

"Nowhere, really." Uncle Louie reached for his wallet. Mom motioned for him to sit. He dropped onto the couch, his elbows on his knees and his head in his hands. I used the bathroom, then fell into the barrel chair by the window. Mom pried the cap from a bottle of beer and sat beside her brother.

"Some night." She took a swig, turning to me. "You were right. He never showed."

I swiveled around to face the windowpane. Reminded once again of how rare Roddy was, I felt sorry for Mom because she'd never had a man like him. The curtains were open, but I couldn't see out into the yard. All I could see was the faint, dark image of a woman looking back at me. My gut reaction was to swivel around again, to get away from the woman watching me through puffy eyes, but I forced myself to stay put, to assess the creases and lines on her forehead and around her eyes, the slightly sagging skin at the corners of her mouth, and the thin cheeks that weren't as robust as they once were. She wasn't ugly, just hard to accept, though others had accepted her, and loved her too.

"I don't know what to think," I muttered, keeping my eyes on the glass.

I heard Mom swallow. "Sometimes you have to let your brain idle."

I thought of the joint in my pocket, probably all bent and broken now. "It just hurts." The woman's glassy eyes got even glassier, shiny and wet.

"It's going to hurt," Uncle Louie said. "For a long time." He sighed. "Can I suggest something that might help?"

The eyes of the woman in the window dropped. I studied the pink feather tattooed on my forearm. "What?" I asked.

"Don't let yourself go with Roddy."

"What do you mean?"

"You've lost him." I heard him shift on the couch. "What you're going through is the worst. . . . It sucks. But it sounds like you've tied your worth to Roddy. The way you talk about yourself in relation to him—as if you're only worthy of whatever he bestowed upon you because he *chose* you—strips you of value and esteem. Whatever he brought out in you, whatever he made you think was possible, whatever flaws you thought he fixed . . . none of those things go away with him. You're still you."

There was sense in what he said, I just didn't think it was possible to separate myself from my man like that. I ran a finger over the feather, feeling only flesh. "Roddy . . ." My throat stoppered up. I swallowed to clear it. "He didn't wanna get a tattoo. I pressured him to say yes and nagged him until he swore he was looking forward to it. I don't even know if he'd have kept the sessions we booked." I'd thought a couple's tattoo would be romantic. Short of a ring, I thought it would make me his and him mine. "Maybe he didn't have the same feelings for me that I had for him."

"Maybe he was just being himself," Uncle Louie said.

I looked at the woman in the window again, wondering if I could possibly love her, and what it would take to make her see that whatever Roddy had or hadn't done, it was a reflection of him, not her, and that she was no less vital now than she'd been when he was alive.

"You can make things easier on yourself, too," I said, swiveling to face Uncle Louie on the couch.

He lifted his head. "You're right."

"What are you two talking about?" Mom asked.

"Does she know?"

"Not all of it," he said.

"Know what?" Mom wondered.

Uncle Louie breathed deep. "The summer Johnny died. You remember?"

She took two long sips. "How the fuck could I forget?"

"You blamed me."

"I did not!" She slammed her beer onto the coffee table with such force that white foam erupted over the bottle's rim.

"You said I made a mistake, that I was guilty."

"Louie, I—"

"It's okay," he said. "Let me get it out. Whether I was to blame or not, you were right. I was guilty. I *felt* guilty. I thought I'd let it go over the years, but I'd just blocked it out, like moving a piece of furniture over a wine-stained rug. The guilt came back after Jill turned three. I tried to ignore it, did my best to shove it aside. It worked for a while. Being a husband, a father, and a professor kept me distracted, but Johnny . . . he just kept coming back. The older Jill got, the more I thought about him, wondering what he'd have been like at ten, twelve, sixteen, twenty-one, wondering what he'd have done, if he'd have been like a brother or a son. . . . But he wasn't the only who one who came back."

For a moment, it looked like he was going to grab Mom's drippy bottle of beer, or maybe the bong still perched like a vase at the corner of the coffee table. His jittery hands went up instead, combing through his hair.

"I started hearing rocks against my bedroom window." His revelation threw me for a loop. "It started after the divorce. I still hear them now."

"Rocks?" I asked.

"There was a rumor when we were kids." Mom proceeded to explain what Uncle Louie was referring to, telling me about the mythic vampire Uncle Louie had mentioned on our walk. I didn't think things could get stranger or scarier, but they did after that. I couldn't face the window again.

"I'd thought the vampire was gone after the summer of eighty-six," Uncle Louie said. "Even had reason to believe it'd never existed . . . not the way I'd thought, anyway." His head started to shake and it didn't stop. "The vampire's been with me—*draining* me—all these years. And not just as a bad memory. Some nightmares transform you. Some become a part of you. Some do both."

FIFTY-ONE

Louie

I peered deep into the black eyes of the monster—me. Gnashing my teeth, I dove into the water, shattering its glassy surface. A thick tail steered me beyond the shallows into the sweeping current that whisked me toward the spot J.L. and I once regarded as our own. Yielding to my unsettling urge, I snapped at a smallmouth bass slumbering along the riverbank. The fish clamped between my teeth, I climbed ashore, bass blood dripping into the dirt. The droplets called to mind what J.L. had done in that very spot when he'd thrown my scab into the mud, mixing my essence with the earth. He'd talked about tradition, the pow wow, and the warrior dance.

The fish flapped in my mouth. I swallowed it whole. What had Miss Shelby been trying to tell me? What did she need me to understand?

In the shadows of night every anole can look like an alligator, and every alligator can be turned into an anole.

Staring at my hideous reflection, I pondered words and memories that spun in lopsided circles inside my invaded head. Alligators. Anoles. Blood. Mud. The pow wow. The warrior dance. Tradition.

I grew hungrier by the second.

Aubrey. Miss Fay. Johnny. I remembered the last thing he'd said. *I'm an alligator!*

"So am I." My belly grumbled.

Blood. Mud. The pow wow. The warrior dance. Tradition. What I'd become. Those things went together. Somehow, they did.

Aubrey. Miss Fay. Johnny. *I'm an alligator!*

I faced my reflection again, both horrified by what I'd become and by the sudden urge to tunnel into the mud, to sleep, to let my invader finish what it'd started inside me. It'd be easy. Probably painless, too. I'd just have to let it . . .

"No," I said, focusing again. Images of Ern and Miss Shelby, the cemetery, and the myth of our tribe's boogeyman creeping out of the mud sped through my mind. I thought about the warrior dance and how it brought us face-to-face with our opponent. I thought about the tamahka in our origin story and how they'd become our enemy before we'd turned them into anoles.

The warriors gathered their spears and sharpened their rocks, then faced the red and blue tamahka in the night.

I replayed those words over and over, and slowly something started to take shape. A realization. Like a Polaroid picture developing, foggy until it isn't. My body had already been changed and my mind was well on its way to being altered forever. I wasn't powerless, though. I could be the warrior or the gator. I could give in or fight.

Snatching another unsuspecting fish from the water, I tore it to pieces between my teeth. I'd have to go home to do what needed to be done, and I'd have to resist the temptation that would swell inside me there. Turning from the riverbank—death on my tongue—I stood on my hindlegs and ran back to the trailer.

Lula was shuffling from her bedroom to the bathroom when I burst through the door. She narrowly avoided tripping over the up-ended lawn chair I'd left in the hall, only to fall after I pushed her aside on my way to my room.

"Louie!" she shrieked. "What the fuck?" Like Ern, she couldn't see what I'd become. Whimpering on the floor, she had no idea how easy she would have been to devour.

I slammed my bedroom door, locked it, and whipped open the closet. My pow wow outfit hung there, untouched since the day Johnny had backed into the flames. I tore my tattered clothes off and—tugging, stretching—pulled the pow wow outfit on over the muck from the river that'd dried to my skin. The pants sat low in the back, below the tail hanging from my waist. The vest bulged against the scutes of my reinforced flesh. The supple buckskin, however, stretched to accommodate my new frame. I squeezed the metal cuffs—one shiny, one singed—around my wrists and fixed the can-tab janglers around my ankles. A surge of real power filled me the moment I fit the bustle on my head. It made me think I stood a chance.

"What the hell, Louie?" Lula said, pounding on the door. "What are you doing?"

Noemi started to cry in the adjacent room.

"Stay away from me." Knowing I couldn't leave through the front, I whirled toward the window and saw the glint of the antler-handled knife Grandpa had given me. I grabbed it from the shelf above my bed, threw the window open, and slithered outside. Landing hard in the grass, I remembered the woodpecker that had dimpled the aluminum around the window's frame. My bloody snout led me to the dead bird in the yard. I clutched it with my free hand, resisting the impulse to take it between my teeth, and hightailed it out of there.

Racing back to the river, I slid to a stop in the rock-riddled mud along the shore. My reflection sparkled on the water's surface. Half alligator. Half man. An animal with feathers standing straight up on its head. A killer dressed in warrior's clothes.

Though the night was now dead, shadows loomed in the early morning darkness. I stuck the knife into the trunk of a nearby tree and dropped the woodpecker into the mud next to the water. Gentle rolling waves licked it.

I scowled at the reflection bobbing by my feet and locked eyes with the monster that had overtaken me.

It wanted me to cause pain. It wanted me to murder.

I wanted to cause pain. I wanted to murder.

The spirit was doing exactly what Ern said it could and more. The evil didn't just compel me. It *was* me. I had to kill it. But would killing it kill me?

Hungry, determined, and afraid, I stared into the black eyes of the reflection I wanted to erase. Could I?

"It's trying to trick you," I whispered about my doubt. Whatever the risk, I had to accept it. I had to do what needed to be done. The woodpecker on the ground between me and my alligator image glittering on the water's surface, I commenced the traditional warrior dance.

In mud that yielded to my weight, I worked harder than ever to perfect the motions that would mark me as a warrior standing up to my enemy. The moves felt nearly impossible on my alligator legs, but I didn't quit. I couldn't. Keeping my muscles tight, I hopped and bobbed, turning in semicircles, always facing my enemy. The sounds of a steady drum and chanting voices floated through the trees from the pow wow grounds. The drumbeat propelled me to dance harder. Fiercer. The reflection slowly started to change.

The alligator snarled and snapped, gnashing its gleaming teeth, trying to stop me from separating from it. I hopped. I bobbed. I swept my arms and plunged my feet, keeping my eyes fixed on my enemy. The gator sneered and scowled, clapping its jaws, trying to keep me in its grasp, trying to swallow me whole.

My hair sprouted from the top of the gator's head. My left shoulder popped through beneath its neck. The more I danced, the more of myself I saw reflected on the water. My pallid right hand clawed free.

Dirty toes budded from the gator's webbed ones. We were becoming two, but still I felt its desire to shred, to tear.

Tamahka don't chew.

The decision was mine to make, a decision denied to Aubrey, Fay, Johnny, and the woodpecker because they hadn't known that they had a choice. I could rip and tear others. I could rip and tear myself. Or I could rip and tear the evil within me.

My human hand snatched the knife from the tree where I'd stuck it. Miss Shelby's words echoed in my head. I had to be certain.

Every alligator can be turned into an anole.

Ma's beer-can tabs jangling around my ankles, I raised the knife. My eyes still firmly fixed on the reflection grimacing in front of me, I gritted my teeth and slammed the blade into the alligator's heart. The hilt thunked against my chest. I gasped, winded though no pain tore through me. The alligator writhed. Despite the split-second expression of defeat that flashed across its ancient face, it remained standing, its angry eyes trained on me. The single stab wasn't enough. The gator was strong, ravenous for us to remain one.

More of Miss Shelby's words thundered in my mind.

. . . the warriors cut the red and blue tamahka into tiny pieces . . .

I withdrew the knife from the gator's chest and raised my hand high to bring it back down again. The Meli Omahka sensed what was coming and funneled some of its energy back into the woodpecker at my feet. The dead bird flapped in the mud. My gaze wavered. I lost sight of my enemy.

The gator seized the opportunity to reclaim its hold of me the instant I looked at the bird. It ripped me away from the water and slammed me into the mud. The knife fell from my grasp upon hitting the ground, and, as my invader took control, I didn't feel the urge to retrieve it.

The Meli Omahka's power swelled. It stiffened my body from snout to tail, readying the gator to rip me away from my true self the same way gators in the wild rip prey apart by performing the death roll, a dizzying maneuver of repeated rotations, their jaws clamped tight around a head or a neck. If it rolled me, I knew I'd never escape it.

I willed my hand to reach for the knife. My fingertips grazed the bloodied blade. The gator started to turn. Straining, I slithered forward. My fingers wrapped around the antler handle. I turned the blade toward myself, an act as painful as breaking my own arm. The gator tossed me on my back, slamming me hard against the ground. Grunting, I brought the blade within inches of my face. A second from burying it in my forehead, I stopped, a realization creeping in.

Ern had been looking at me when he sank his steak knife into my nose, making me bleed. He'd seen me, not the gator. If I wanted to spoil the spirit, I'd have to see the enemy I was fighting. Mustering my will, I wriggled inch by inch until I glimpsed the water. The gator's head appeared, thrashing, striving to gain momentum that would throw us into an all-out spin. It slammed me down again as I drew the knife over its snout. It bellowed. I grunted, straining with all my might, pressing hard, digging deep. The gator's upper jaw came free. It sank beneath the waves like an old boot thrown into the water. My own bloody nose and upper lip replaced it in the reflection.

The spirit, weakened by the damage I'd done, stopped trying to turn. My strength surged. I stood. Squeezing the antler, I vowed not to remove my eyes from the reflection again.

Once more attuned to the music in the air, my tired feet found the rhythm that would pit me against my prey. The knife dug deep beneath the gator's thick scales. The beast's armored body quivered as strips of its flesh drooped like tassels from its frame. I sliced piece after piece of the scaly skin away, reducing the tamahka to chunks of bloody flesh that floated on the water, reflecting more of me now where the alligator once stood.

The gator's lower mandible flapped. A feeble hiss came from our collective throat. My hand kept slicing, casting more of the gator away, slowly draining its desire to slam me down again.

"For Aubrey. Fay. Johnny." I cut a piece of the gator away with each utterance. "For Gram. Grandpa. Lula. Noemi. Ma."

Soon, it was I who stood stronger than the invading spirit. The alligator pieces created a bloody stew in the water. My springy feet came to a stop in the mud at the exact instant that the age-old music evaporated into the air. I no longer needed the dance to mark me as a warrior. I was one.

The knife fell from my hand, and I sank to my knees. The swirling gator pieces rushed toward the riverbank, converging upon the wood-pecker just barely sticking in the water. I jumped back. The dead bird pulsed in response to the bloody pieces trying to possess it, but it would never peck or fly again. The defeated pieces bobbed in the shallows of the riverbank. I hoped they would sink and be gone for good. Instead, they swirled some more, making the water whorl. The pieces jiggled and jerked, becoming thinner and longer as the blackish-red hue of death upon them brightened into vibrant shades of green.

My mouth fell open. My body shuddered.

Each tiny piece of the tamahka grew a head, four little legs, and a tiny tail . . . I heard Miss Shelby's voice precisely as the pieces sprouted the impossible appendages.

The harmless anoles that the gator had become scrambled onto shore and scurried toward me. I closed my eyes and crumbled into an exhausted heap. The last thing I felt before I passed out was a parade of tiny reptile feet stamping wet footprints all over my face, painting my flesh black with mud, like the war paint warriors wore after victory in battle.

FIFTY-TWO

Louie

I came to on the shore beneath the midday sun. Its warmth blanketed my battered body. Stiff, sore, and scraped up from the tips of my toes to the slit in my left nostril, I sluggishly stood, my mind murkier than the fog that sometimes rolled in off the river. Looking down, I saw prints impressed into the mud—four webbed toes amid human-shaped soles. The tattered scraps of my buckskin outfit, each no more than a few inches wide, littered the ground along the water's edge. If not for the mud and blood smeared over my body, I'd have been as naked as the anole clinging to the tree beside me. He puffed out the bloodred fan beneath his throat in a territorial display, then skittered into the safety of the leaves.

My nakedness and the buckskin scraps, stained by small drops of dried blood, clouded my mind with confusion. I bent to pick up a piece of the outfit and came face-to-face with the rotted woodpecker, reeking of death. My stomach turned. I remembered what I'd done.

My eyes swept over the waves before me. A handful of feathers floated upon them, next to a familiar reflection. Streaks of mud aside, it was the reflection I was used to seeing in the mirror each morning. I was whole again. A warrior, too.

I collected my knife and turned away from the river, only to turn right around after taking two small steps. The woodpecker. I couldn't just leave it there. It deserved better than what J.L. had done to it, better than what it had endured as the Meli Omahka's puppet. Using a flat river rock, I dug into the dirt a few feet from the river's edge and placed the woodpecker into the hole, giving it back to the earth from which it came.

One spirit laid to rest, I headed home, thinking about the other spirit that had haunted me for the better part of my youth. Recalling the tremendous hunger I'd struggled to suppress the night before, I finally understood how hard it was for Ma to deny her thirst. Assuming it was as strong as the appetite I'd had, she'd have quite a war to wage against whatever was weighing her down. It'd be her war to win, but I'd be by her side through the battles.

Ern watched me plod up the drive at home. I scaled the side of the trailer and crawled in through my bedroom window. The knife, crusted with blood, went back on its shelf. I looked longingly at my bed. Soft cries from the other side of the bedroom door prevented me from lying in it, compelling me to pull on a pair of shorts and a sweat-stained shirt instead.

"Louie?" Lula's voice trembled through the door. "Are you there?"

"Everything's all right now." I joined her in the hall.

"It's . . ." She shuddered at my bloody, muddy appearance. "Oh, Louie . . ."

"What's wrong?"

She pointed a nail file toward Ma's room.

Ma looked the same as always, silent, still, and partially wrapped in a sheet atop her bare mattress. She didn't reply when I whispered, then hollered her name. Sickness slithered into my stomach. I forced myself to approach the bed, each step a struggle with quicksand. I struck like a rattlesnake jabbing her shoulder upon reaching her side. Otherwise, I wouldn't have had the courage to touch her.

Ma was dead.

"I heard her choking," Lula sobbed. "The door was locked. By the time I pried it open . . ." She could barely contain herself. ". . . it was too late."

Stunned and sorrowful, I lurched away from the bed. It couldn't be. I'd robbed Ma of her daily stash on my way to the river, and I'd cleared the beer from her room the day before that. This wasn't supposed to happen. She was supposed to get better. But Ma hadn't crumbled overnight. She'd been eroding for years. She'd been the problem I couldn't fix, the knot I couldn't untie. I'd believed she'd change, that she'd find what she needed, that she'd stop destroying herself and destroy her invader instead, that she'd finally love me the way a mother is supposed to. Her cooling flesh and the vomit on her lips blew every hope I had to smithereens.

Lula rested her head on my back and hugged me from behind. The two of us cried until we were empty inside.

"We have to get Grandpa," she said.

I wiped tears from my eyes. "Not yet."

"Why?" She kept her face buried, unable to look.

"I need you to help me with something first."

"What?"

I pulled free from my sister and yanked the stained sheet off the bed. "Make her beautiful," I said.

FIFTY-THREE

Noemi

Mom took another bottle of beer from the fridge. "Noemi?" she offered.

"No thanks," I said.

The bathroom door creaked open precisely as she popped the bottle's top. The sound of Uncle Louie's footsteps followed a second later, only he didn't reappear in the living room. I shifted in the chair beneath me, craning to see as he bypassed the two bedrooms on his left, one of which used to belong to him. He stopped outside the door that dead-ended the shallow hall and placed his hand on the knob. Mom took a couple steps out of the kitchen and followed my gaze.

"You can open it," she said to him.

He glanced back at her, his face pink and glistening, freshly scrubbed. I heard the *click* of the latch. The bedroom door swung open. I don't remember what the room looked like when my grandmother slept there, but I knew what he'd find inside: a bed too big for the square footage, furniture, mirrors, and lamps that made the space look like a hotel suite, and the night's rejected outfits strewn all over the place.

Uncle Louie filled the doorway, then slumped against the right side of it. His shoulders heaved. Mom, blinking fast, met him at the end of the hall where she stood on her tiptoes and put her chin on his left shoulder.

"It's not just Johnny and the vampire," I heard him say, voice thick, his words running together. "She haunts me too."

"She had struggles we knew nothing about," Mom said. I could tell she was straining to keep it together. "We were kids. What could we do?"

"I took her beer from her, and who knows what else."

"You were trying to help."

"I hurt her," he sobbed. "She died."

Mom's chin slipped from his shoulder. Her eyes took its place. "Ma caused her own death. It isn't your fault. It never was."

His head shook and his hands moved to his face. My eyes sought a place for me to hide. I felt like a trespasser in their moment of renewed grief.

"It was my fault," Uncle Louie argued. "I didn't know it then but—" He faltered. Turning his head away, he pressed his brow against the doorframe. "She was dependent on the alcohol, Lula. Her brain had become so accustomed to it that she couldn't function without it. I—"

"She couldn't function *with* it," Mom corrected him. "Don't you remember what she was like?"

"I've read about it," he said. "When a dependent alcoholic is forced to function without booze, the body and brain struggle to work without it. Sudden withdrawal can cause horrible consequences. Anxiety, irritability, the shakes, disorientation, headaches, blackouts, seizures . . . *vomiting.*"

Mom struggled to wrangle him around, to make him face her without spilling the beer in her hand.

"Don't, Louie!" She looked him in the eyes. "You can't do this to yourself."

It was clear, though, that he'd been punishing himself since long before he returned to the rez.

"If I hadn't—" he blubbered.

"If *she* hadn't." Mom cried just as hard. "She did this to us!"

Uncle Louie pulled the bedroom door closed and stormed down the hall. I swiveled in the chair so that I wouldn't have to face him.

"You're doing it now, too, aren't you?" He picked up the bottle that had foamed over onto the coffee table and threw it into the sink a little too hard. Shards of broken glass exploded over the basin and onto the counter.

Mom ran up behind him and tossed the beer in her hand into the sink as well, just not as hard. "Listen to me, Louie." She took his face in her hands. "Ma drank every damn day. Every night. You haven't been around. You don't see me. I do it once a month. *If that.* I'm not like her."

His eyes slid toward the bong, but he didn't say anything about it. "I'm sorry," he quickly said.

"I understand," she assured him.

"I thought by coming back I could finally say goodbye and bury all this shit for good . . . the pain, the sorrow, the guilt . . . but—" He pulled his face from Mom's hands.

"But what?"

He dissolved onto the sofa again. "I don't think I can. I don't think I want to. Everything here is a part of me. Grandpa tried telling me that long ago. Bad as some of it hurts, I can't let it go."

"You can't keep punishing yourself either," Mom said.

"No," he agreed. His gaze shifted from her to me.

"We both need help," I said.

"I feel so hopeless," he murmured.

I moved from the chair and squeezed in next to him. "You have to wake the warrior within you," I told him. "Help me become one."

"How?"

"It's all about the enemy, isn't it? Once you lose sight of it, it swallows you whole."

He nodded.

"Sounds like we've both lost focus."

FIFTY-FOUR

Louie

Braids woven with wildflowers I'd plucked from the field replaced the knots in Ma's hair by the time Chris Horn came to take her away.

"Come with me," Grandpa said, eyes swollen and red, after Chris's station wagon pulled out of the drive.

I shook my head. I had to stay. For the time being, at least. Lula went with him. She took Noemi and a bag of their things and silently sat beside Grandpa in the old Ford.

I lingered on the porch before going back inside. Everything looked the same, but nothing felt the way it had the day before. It never would again. I showered and opened the windows to let out the gloom. I picked up the pieces of the broken plate and did my best to scrape the dried candle wax from the carpet. Standing in the doorway that'd so often been blocked, my heart pounding so hard I could hear it, I wondered about the decisions Ma had made and why she'd made them.

I parted the curtains in her room, letting in light for the first time in years. A single can fell from the windowsill and glinted in the sunlight. Empty and a bit dusty on top, I took the can in my hand, crushed it, and made a promise to myself. I pulled the tab from the top and shoved it deep into my pocket to serve as a reminder, then collected Ma's untapped stash from where I'd hidden it in my closet.

Backpack on, I set out across the field to sit with Ern one last time. Part of me felt low for doing it, but when I thought about what he'd done, my intent didn't seem so bad.

"Thought you might want this." I hoisted the backpack through his window. The screen was gone, destroyed by me the previous night. He didn't bother with the blinds. He hadn't said a word when Chris came to take Ma away, and he still didn't say anything upon taking the backpack and slowly unzipping it. He pulled a can from the bag and bent the tab forth.

"You didn't hurt me too bad last night," he said, between noisy sips. He cast a glance at the wound on his back. "Just gave me a deep bite. . . . Sorry 'bout your Ma."

I sat on the bottom step outside his door. I didn't want to be too close. "I guess we really do have the same awful thing in common."

Ern's slurp sounded like a question to me.

"Both our moms are gone now. Dead." I didn't look at Ern when I said it, but I could tell he didn't like what I was getting at by how fast he started to swallow. "I told you I saw your ma in the cemetery last night. Now that I've had time to think about it, though, I know she's not alive."

Ern drank faster. He finished the beer in his hand and scrambled to open another, never questioning me about what I'd seen among the graves.

"Our stones sink after being tossed into the river, and we go into the sky with the star spirit to watch over our people at night," I said. "Isn't that how the story goes?"

He didn't speak.

"I think the star spirit let your ma walk the earth last night to help me. What do you think about that, Ern?"

"I know how bad it hurts," he said, "but did you come here just to make me hurt even more?"

I shook my head and let him drink for a while, waiting for his sobriety to melt into something messy, like chocolate in the sun. Short of telling me to get lost, drinking was pretty much all he could do. And while I don't think he wanted me there that afternoon, I don't think he wanted to be alone either.

"You gonna stay in the trailer without her?" he wheezed.

I didn't answer. I was still thinking about Miss Shelby in the cemetery and all the other strange things I'd seen. Ern cracked another beer. He tossed the empty can alongside the others on the grass. The knife that had sliced my nose rested among them.

"My ma wouldn't want me to leave," he said. "She'd want me to stay."

"With her?" I asked.

"She took care of me."

"So then why'd you kill her?"

Ern tossed the second can from the window. Another chirped open. "Thought you'd understand," he said.

"Understand?"

"We've got the same awful thing in common, don't we?"

"I didn't kill my mom," I said through gritted teeth.

"Then who did you kill?"

"No one."

"I didn't either." Tilting his head as far back as it would sit on his neck, he poured the beer down his throat. "Neither of us killed our moms."

"I smelled death," I said. "When I lunged at you last night, I smelled death inside your trailer stronger than what I smelled in the cemetery."

Ern made another can chirp. "I saw you stagger home today. Streaked with blood . . . like you'd just taken a life . . . and like you were 'bout to take another. Looked like you were on a mission."

"Not to do what you think I did."

"I didn't tell your grandpa or Chris Horn 'bout any of that," he said. "Didn't tell 'em that I saw you sneak around the trailer naked, or that you had a knife in your hand. I coulda. . . . Still can."

"It doesn't matter." I shrugged. "My ma doesn't have a knife mark on her. No blood either."

Neither Ern nor I said anything for a while after that. I was scared. Sad. Life felt like it hinged on that eternal moment. Though it eventually passed, as all moments do, it seemed like it carried the weight of the world, like everything would crumble once the truth was known.

"Ern." I couldn't stand the silence any longer. "Just say it. Admit what you did." I looked directly at him, stabbing him with my eyes.

"Haven't done anything, Louie." His voice quaked. So did his massive frame. "I'm trapped. Can't you see that? I'm trapped here. There's nothin' I coulda done to anyone."

"You're lying, Ern. You deserve to be trapped for what you did."

"What I did . . ." he muttered.

"You killed your ma. Why'd you do it?"

"I didn't," he said, instead of trying to make me understand.

"She's in there with you now, isn't she?"

"Luke searched every inch of this place after she went missin'. Your grandfather and the tribal council watched him do it." Ern's voice was like a river rock, flat and cold. "My ma's not here. She left the day of Aubrey's wake and she ain't been back."

Ern could insist all he wanted. I remembered what I'd smelled the night before, the scent that had intensified my desire to shred and to tear, wafting on his extra-cold air-conditioned air. Sitting there on the bottom step, I could still smell that scent, just not as strongly as before.

"Did Luke make you stand when he searched inside?"

"What?"

"Did he make you stand up?"

"Shut up, Louie."

"Did you stand for him or not, Ern?"

"Why you doin' this to me?"

"Because I know what you did, and I know how you hid her. You didn't stand up, did you? You killed your mother, Ern. How could you kill your ma? She loved you. She took care of you. She never left your side. *You* killed her."

Ern gasped. I thought he'd issue another denial, but the sob he'd been trying to suppress broke free instead. "She was the only one I thought was safe. The Meli Omahka must have gotten into me and—"

"Stop lying, Ern. It wasn't a spirit, a demon, the boogeyman, or a vampire that made you do what you did. You tried too hard to hide it to make me believe that. You lied about everything, didn't you? You lied when your ma went missing. You lied about the scrap of clothing we found in the river. . . . I think it belonged to my grandmother," I said, not bothering to explain. "You lied when you said you didn't know what led Aubrey, Fay, and Johnny to do what they did. It started with you, Ern. *You* threw the reservation off balance.

"You told me that doing bad things strengthens the Meli Omahka, allowing it to escape the earth spirit. But you also told me that there's no point blaming vampires or Voodoo for our mysteries. You said everything comes down to people. And I think this comes down to you. You chose to do what you did, and in doing so you unsettled all of us. You killed your ma before Aubrey reached for that pot of boiling water, didn't you? She must have been dead at least two days before you told us she was missing . . . and only because you got hungry."

The way Ern poured another beer down his gullet told me I was on the right track.

"Why'd you do it?"

"She's the only one I thought was safe," he said.

"What are you talking about, Ern?"

"Never thought I'd hurt her."

"Are you saying you thought you'd hurt others?"

His pause chilled my blood. "I did . . . hurt others."

"Ern?" My throat had gone dry as salt.

"That old story about Horace and the Hensleys . . ." His body quivered. His narrow eyes began to cross, the beer taking hold. "It wasn't Horace who threw the rock at Gus's windshield. It was me. Albert Picote found Horace starin' at the carnage from the side of the road, but that's only 'cause I ran before Albert got there. I told Horace to lie, and since I was the only kid his age who'd ever been nice to him, he did.

"The Meli Omahka came out of the ground after that," Ern said. "When it reached the earth's surface, it crawled into me. I told you last night that to subdue the spirit you gotta give in to its demand . . . and that's exactly what I did."

"Ern?"

"I had to satisfy it," he said, as if defending himself.

"How?"

"Horace."

"What are you saying, Ern?"

He took a deep breath, then uttered the words I never thought I'd hear him, or anyone, speak. "I'm your vampire, Louie."

The drunken admission didn't hit me the way it should have. It didn't seem possible that he, the lump in the window that'd always been there, watching, could be the one who'd filled my childhood with fear.

"Horace said he couldn't keep my secret any longer. He said he was gonna tell everyone that I threw the rock. Since the Meli Omahka was restless within me, I did what was best for me and for it. I satisfied its hunger. I protected myself."

I let that sink in. Tried to, anyway. Knowing what *the vampire* had done to Horace, however, indicated that Ern had gone to ghastly extremes that superseded self-preservation. "What'd you do with his blood?" I heard myself ask, morbidly curious yet not so sure I was ready for his reply. "After you drained it?"

Ern's response came in the form of a long, cold stare. It didn't answer my question outright, but it damn sure made me not want to ask again.

"You enjoyed it." I supposed that to be true. "All of it."

His face slackened. "Maybe you're right, Louie. Maybe all this does come down to me. Whatever made me wanna throw that rock at Gus's windshield is what made me wanna throw another one. But I'm not all bad. I wouldn't have caged myself in this trailer with the one person I never thought I'd hurt if I was. You don't know what it's like to live like this. In this body, in this box. I'm trapped, Louie. Dead and buried for the last ten years, as far as the rest of the world is concerned." His beer-soaked breath spilled self-pity onto his air-conditioned air.

I didn't feel sorry for him. "Aubrey, Fay, Johnny," I muttered. "Why do you think the spirit went into them this time and not into someone like you?"

"Maybe it wasn't strong enough yet," he said. "I did a bad thing by killin' my ma, but killin' all the Hensleys at once was worse. The Meli Omahka musta broke free with mad strength after that. Maybe children and people like Aubrey and Fay are easier for it to inhabit in its weaker state. . . . Like you said yesterday, they couldn't fight to save themselves."

"And animals," I said, thinking of the rattlesnake outside the Forstalls' front door, the armadillo that had appeared on my front porch, and the woodpecker J.L. had shot down by the river. They hadn't been capable of battling the spirit the way I had. "Did you ever look in the mirror when the Meli Omahka was in you?"

"Don't think so. . . . Why?"

"Just wondered."

A belch rang out. Another beer can flew from the window. "How'd you beat it?"

His words were slurred, and I'd already said everything I needed to say to him. Still, I stayed there on his step. Just Ern, me, and Ma's beer. When he asked again how I'd fought the Meli Omahka, I told him the one truth we both knew well.

"Tamahka don't chew," I whispered. "Tamahka don't chew."

FIFTY-FIVE

Louie

A long blade of grass drooped from between Jean-Luc's lips. He spat it on the ground when he noticed me by his dad's wood stack, about thirty feet from their dilapidated house. Straddling an old wooden bench, he had a bucket beside him, a fillet knife in one hand, and a catfish on the bench before him. He eyed me for a few seconds, then turned his attention back to the cat.

He put a hand on its big flat head to hold the fish on its side, its tail and body feebly flapping up off the bench every few seconds. The knife, thin and narrow like an elongated razor blade, slid straight through the mottled skin over the cat's rib cage, making it flap some more. Cartilage popped and something squelched inside the doomed fish. Pink fluid seeped out onto the bench as J.L. turned the blade and swiftly drew it along the fish's spine, producing a crunchy scraping sound. The knife emerged at the base of the tail, looking almost as clean as when it'd gone in. J.L. flipped the fillet off the body so that it landed skin-side down against the bench, then turned the fish—likely dead, though still feebly flapping—over to repeat the process on the other side. He held the carcass up by the head, innards hanging down, as if admiring it when he was done, then tossed it into the bucket.

"My ma's dead," I said.

He paused for a second, his hand hanging in the air, before snagging another frightened fish from the bucket. He slammed it onto the bench, his knuckles white around its head. I listened to him saw through it, gritting my teeth the entire time, then watched as he cut the catfish's whiskers off for no apparent reason.

"Aren't you gonna say something?"

He cast the remains into the bucket. I heard another fish flap against the plastic imprisoning it and cringed. The stench of death filled my nose again.

"Sorry about your ma," he said, his eyes on the whiskers. He didn't ask what had happened to her, but he probably didn't need to. I supposed nobody who knew her would be surprised by the way she went.

My feet carried me closer to the bench. J.L. stood and wiped his hands against his shorts, already streaked with mud. "You could probably stay for supper," he said, peering into the bucket. "Dad caught enough."

It'd been more than a year since I'd eaten at his place, hot dogs wrapped in white bread, his father chewing tobacco as if it were a side dish, spitting into the old coffee can next to the mustard and relish.

"I've got something to do." I took another step closer. He stooped to move the fillets he'd already cut onto a paper plate that'd been weighed down by a rock on the bench behind him.

"Guess you gotta plan the funeral."

"Yeah, but—"

"Hang on." He went into the house. The crooked screen door slammed behind him. I moved toward the bucket and though there was nothing I needed to see in there, I couldn't stop myself from looking. My skin crawled at the sight of the dead and the dying. Jean-Luc returned with another paper plate. "Dad's frying potatoes to go with 'em."

My appetite was long gone. It wouldn't be back for weeks. "Why

351

are you pretending?" I asked, thinking his behavior was just another lie.

"Pretending what?"

"Like everything's normal." Like we were still friends.

He bent to pluck another blade of grass, stuck it in his mouth, and chewed. "Did you come here just to tell me about your ma?"

I almost said yes. Almost turned around and walked away. Did he care at all? "No."

"So?" He chewed some more, then grabbed the fillet knife again, his free hand dipping back into the bucket. I looked away as he hoisted the last living fish from within, his fingers stuck inside its gills.

My eyes, searching for something soothing, something that would help loosen the knot in my belly, landed on the messy rock garden, overcome with weeds, to the right of the door. I almost didn't notice the turtle shell mixed in with the rocks. Nearly black, it was weathered and roughly the same size as the rocks, each a bit bigger than my fist. A memory surfaced.

Jean-Luc and I were five when we first met by the river.

Wanna see something cool? he'd said.

Happy to be away from home all on my own, I'd nodded and chased after him as he ran up the riverbank.

Look! He'd pointed down at something nestled in the grass, something moving in a weird way.

What is it? I'd realized what it was a second after asking. It was a snapping turtle, upside down, the round dome of its shell against the ground. Its legs were flailing, thrashing the grass around it in a desperate attempt to turn itself over.

Caught it right out of the water with my own two hands!

Cool! I'd bent low over it, even touched one of its webbed feet, knowing to stay away from its mouth because a snapper had taken half of Sheila Hensley's left little toe when she'd been sitting with her feet in the water. *You're gonna let it go, right?*

Yeah.

We'd made mud pies, swung from tree branches, and cupped grasshoppers in our hands, some of the greatest fun we'd ever had. Promising to meet him in that very spot the very next day, I'd left when the sun started to set without ever seeing him flip the snapper over.

The knot in my stomach tightened. The turtle shell blurred in my vision. It couldn't be, I thought, but that was because I didn't want it to be. In all likelihood, it was.

The final fish carcass splashed into the bucket.

"Earth to Louie," Jean-Luc said.

I turned back to him. He spat the blade of grass from his mouth. It landed on the bench, the blade's wet end ravaged.

"So why'd you come?" he asked.

I scratched a mosquito bite on the back of my neck. "Where is it? The pillowcase?"

He plopped the fresh fillets onto the paper plate. The fillet knife bowed when he pressed the tip against the bench.

"You didn't tell." His eyes on the knife, he moved his hand up and down, angling the knife from side to side, making the blade bow to the left, then to the right, again and again. "You didn't, did you?"

I'd called Luke to tell him about Ern, but I hadn't told anyone anything about Jean-Luc's bag of bones. "You'll have to do that yourself." I didn't think that he would. Still, I hoped to see him change. "Did you hide the bones by the river?" I was afraid he'd say he'd done something worse with them.

"What do you want 'em for?"

"They're not yours," I said, thinking about more than just the bones. The woodpecker. The snapper. What else had he unjustly taken? "Were you always like this?"

He stopped playing with the knife. I hardly recognized him when he looked at me, his eyes dark and dull. "Like what?"

"Remember trying to surf on the river when the current was

strong?" We'd used broken plywood in place of an actual surfboard. It hadn't worked. "And racing bikes around the pow wow grounds? Climbing trees in the fields? Firing rocks at tin cans and glass jars? Wrestling in the mud? Driving the truck into town without an adult around, our feet barely able to reach the pedals?" I could feel my lips wanting to smile.

"Yeah."

"We had fun."

He stabbed the tip of the knife into the bench again.

"I won't forget," I said.

"What do you mean?"

I didn't explain. "So where'd you put it?"

He made the blade bow some more, then plucked it from the wood and used it to point at a pillar of old tires next to the wood stack. I found the pillowcase tucked in the hollow center and pulled it free.

"Later," he called as I turned toward the street.

I crossed the yard, keeping my tired eyes ahead. I almost didn't glance back. "Later," I said before there was too much distance between us, wondering when and if *later* would ever come.

The screen door slammed again, and he was gone. I went on my way, already missing him and Ma and what might have been.

I didn't untie the knot holding the pillowcase shut when I got to the cemetery. I didn't have to sneak among the graves either. Sam, having hurried off to assist with Ern, had left the grounds unsupervised. I took the shovel from Ray Horn's shed, the same shovel Tom had used to exhume Miss Fay, then forced myself to face the damage I'd done the night before. The open grave gaped at me. Dirt sat in a ridge around it. I lowered the pillowcase into the hole, then shoveled the dirt in on top.

No sound came out of the ground. Only I cried.

FIFTY-SIX

Noemi

Grace Hebert didn't work Saturdays. She met us at the Resource Center on the reservation anyway, after Mom called in a favor. After an hour of talking about what had led us there, the weight on our shoulders, and how we were coping at that very moment, Uncle Louie and I walked out side by side, pamphlets in hand, feeling nervous, vulnerable, a little scared, but lighter and hopeful, too, both of us committed to coming back.

"That was better than expected," Uncle Louie remarked about the experience. "Easier."

I hummed my agreement, tucking the pamphlets into my bag. We walked in the opposite direction from which we'd come, the two of us sluggish and sleep deprived. The sadness that had settled within me hadn't lessened overnight. In fact, it was sturdier now, firmly rooted and holding my heart on a spear. Grace had validated my grief. She said the grieving process could bring up unexpected feelings in the coming days, weeks, and months, but as long as I didn't try to banish them to the dusty, dark corners of my mind, there was a good chance I'd come out stronger on the other side. I'd told her how happy I'd been with Roddy and realized while listening to myself speak that you can be the happiest you've ever been and still not feel like it's enough. Because, like Uncle Louie said, I couldn't expect Roddy or anyone else to keep me content. I had to be happy with myself first.

We came upon the Blue Gator Grill, quieter now than it'd been the night before, its lot nearly empty. It looked different in daylight, rundown and in need of fresh paint.

"Is that . . . ?" Uncle Louie said, jerking his head toward the lot. Neither of us said anything about the bloodstain on the side of the street. It was bigger than I remembered, and it made me wonder if I might have had an easier time accepting what had happened to Roddy if the coyote—and even Roddy himself—had been compelled by something sinister, like the spirit that had compelled the woodpecker from Uncle Louie's past, and which I now knew had compelled me as a girl, if only for a few minutes.

I glanced in the direction Uncle Louie had indicated and noticed the man bent beneath the raised hood of the black Dodge Challenger, striped with red, parked in the Blue Gator's lot. I'd seen the car plenty of times. It'd been speeding all over the rez for ten years or more. "That's him," I said.

We were nearly past the watering hole when Uncle Louie decided to stop.

"What are you doing?" I called as he approached the Challenger. He didn't explain, and I didn't pry. I just trailed after him, leaving plenty of space between us.

"J.L.," he said, sounding self-assured.

Jean-Luc, still wearing the tattered tank top he'd had on the night before, the rings of sweat now twice as big beneath his stringy arms, popped his head up. The bulky jug of coolant he'd been pouring into the radiator sagged in his hands. The way he glared, as if he were the one who'd been on the other end of his revolver, suggested that he had unfinished business with Uncle Louie. Or, at the very least, that he had a skull-splitting hangover. The old friends stared at each other until Jean-Luc spat a green wad on the ground.

"Yeah?" he said.

Uncle Louie riffled the pamphlets in his hand. "Just wanted to say thanks."

"For what?"

"For saving my life."

Jean-Luc smirked. Brown teeth appeared. "Fuck off, Louie," he said, bending to finish filling the radiator. Uncle Louie lingered a moment longer, then took a step back and slipped the pamphlets he'd taken from the Resource Center into the Challenger through the open passenger window.

"Think he'll read them?" I asked once the Blue Gator was behind us.

"Hope so," Uncle Louie said.

We didn't speak again until the tribal police department was in sight. Crybaby Cain, otherwise known as Chief Fisher, must have taken pity on me despite how I'd treated him back in high school. My Jeep was parked in front of the station, the spare tire that'd been bolted to the back of the vehicle now swapped with the one that'd blown.

"Breakfast before you have to head in there?" Uncle Louie asked. We'd been too uneasy to eat before meeting with Grace, both of us nervous about what a mental health therapist would ask of us.

I glanced at the clock on my phone: 10:27 a.m. My stomach gurgled. "You're going to the pow wow's opening ceremony later, right? How about lunch? I'll meet you over there. We both deserve some fry bread."

He smiled. "Deal."

I turned to look at the doors in front of me, hesitating just for a second.

"I'll stay if you want me to," Uncle Louie offered.

"It's all right," I said, shaking my head. "I can handle it." I didn't think there was anything conclusive I could tell the authorities that would help them make sense of how Roddy ended up dead—I assumed Sara had already told them about what she found in his sock drawer and on his phone—but I wanted to help in any way I could. And I wanted them to uncover the truth, no matter how painful it might be, though I knew his manner of death might be labeled *undetermined*, lacking clear evidence to call it an accident or a suicide.

I gave Uncle Louie a hug, promising to meet up with him as soon as I answered all the official questions. Hands in his pockets, he set off toward home.

A pair of yelps rang out when I pulled the police department's door open, one from me and the other from the startled individual on her way out. The invigorating air-conditioned air that'd washed over me from inside fell victim to humidity the instant I backed away.

"Sara," I gasped, reaching for the railing beside the door.

Her haggard expression and the puffy purple skin beneath her eyes indicated that she hadn't slept. Despite the rising heat, she was still wearing Roddy's blue button-up shirt.

"They're expecting you," she said.

I took a deep breath and nodded. She gave me a tight-lipped look of understanding—compassion, maybe—on her way past. I grabbed the door again.

"Noemi."

I turned to face her. She looked so frail.

"Thanks for being there for my brother," she said. "He told me how much he loved you."

My eyes clenched shut. I couldn't stop the sobs that racked me. And then her arms were around me, and we held each other like sisters, which we might have been.

"We'll help each other through this," I said.

Her head nodded against my shoulder. "If you ever want to talk . . ." The offer meant a lot coming from her. I didn't want to let go.

"Take it," she said when the embrace broke. She slid out of Roddy's shirt and handed it to me. "It still smells like him."

Clutching it to my chest, I watched her get in her car and go, waving once as she drove out of sight. The baggy shirt hung from my frame when I put it on, the same way it'd hung from Sara's.

Needing a moment before I went inside, I leaned over the railing, opened the music app on my phone, and scrolled down to my favorites, searching for our song, the one we first danced to at the Landry wedding. Its irresistible riff. Its jaunty rhythm capable of brightening bad days. Its reflective lyrics so full of happy memories from a short-lived love affair that they somehow made you sad. Together, they created the soundtrack of our love and life together, bringing back flashes of moments I never wanted to forget—a smile first thing in the morning, singing in the car, brushing our teeth side by side, daring each other to see who could handle the hottest hot sauce, cuddling on the couch, his warm body slick against mine, cooking Sunday supper, falling asleep on the patio furniture, teasing Mom behind her back, hugging extra tight when it was time to say goodbye. The memories poured in, and I felt myself go slack, relying on the railing more than before upon realizing that there were so many things Roddy had shared with me and no one else, things the TV audience never got to see. All those things meant more to me than ever now as I remembered the whirlwind of our love and the way things were when he belonged to me and I belonged to him, his brown-eyed girl.

Burying my nose into the loose fabric hanging around my chest, I drew a deep breath in.

FIFTY-SEVEN

Louie

Cries rose on the wind the instant the shovel pierced the earth. I put my foot on the shovel's step, driving it deeper, turning up dirt and roots. The sound of metal scraping against gravel in the ground competed with the woeful cries, hurting my ears, my heart.

I squeezed the handle tighter, my concentration broken as the hairs on the back of my neck prickled, making me shiver.

Building for our future, Grandpa Joe had said, sinking a shovel of his own into undisturbed earth. I'd been beside him during the groundbreaking ceremony, clapping as he heaved that first shovelful of dirt over his shoulder, his words to the delight of everyone who'd gathered to see the start of something big, expecting the venture to solve big problems, never considering that bigger ones might be birthed.

Like the cries, mournful now, the Grand Nacre rose out of the earth, not just a high-stakes bingo hall but a full-blown casino and resort, its shiny glass doors officially sliding open in October 1994, two months after Grandpa Joe's stone sank. Considering what he'd told me about the hungry fish and the fish that have fed, I'm not sure he believed what he said when he set the construction into motion, but I do think he had hope.

I'd had hope, too, as I'd climbed my old porch steps for the first time in twelve years, the thumping bass line of an unfamiliar song seeping through the windows of the trailer I barely recognized. The siding's not metal anymore. The windows are new, as are the AC units jutting out of them. The porch is bigger than it used to be, bedecked with a grill the size of my boyhood bed and an outdoor bar, littered with ashtrays and bottle caps.

I peered out across the way after climbing the steps. Ern, it seemed, should have been there. I could almost see him in the darkness of his old window when I squinted against the setting sun. No one's occupied the Mire place—rotted now—since Luke and Sam, aided by Mark Bishop and Mac Langdon, hauled Ern out and into the back of Luke's pickup to take him away, his belly full of Ma's beer. I'll never forget the words Luke spoke after he'd ordered Ern to stand from the couch. I'd been watching from outside the door as Ern arduously took to his feet.

You ate our food. You did this, and you still ate our food.

They found Miss Shelby beneath the couch cushions, wrapped in blankets and crammed among deflated filling and flattened springs, her body evening out the impression Ern's weight had created over the years. He never explained how, though the medical examiner determined that Miss Shelby had suffocated to death. He never said why either, but I knew the truth. He did it because he wanted to.

Mark used his Sawzall to widen the trailer's door. He cut through the metal like a tin can, freeing Ern from one prison just to deliver him to another. Ern didn't utter a word when Sam and Luke took him away. He just glared at me with empty eyes from the bed of the pickup, his drunken gaze so cold I knew he'd take my life if given the chance.

Noemi was right, I hadn't immediately recognized her when she opened the trailer door, maybe because I was still thinking about Ern, wondering what had become of him and if he had any hope to hold on to.

I glanced back at her after leaving her outside the tribal police department. Eyes on her phone, she was crying and smiling, the worst and best of life colliding in a way that'll either break her into smaller bits or rebuild her.

The cries intensified as the hole widened at my feet. Alone, I wiped sweat from my brow and sucked my lips between my teeth, my eyes sweeping the expanse as if something were approaching, as if it would let me see it if it were. My unease dropped me into a squat, the tall grass masking my face, reminding me of Ern again and the days when the Takoda Vampire was something in the night rather than an ailment inside me, before I knew how easily balance can be broken.

A high-pitched cry hung in the air longer than any of the others before it. It called me to my feet, telling me to dig. I didn't have much deeper to go. Scraping the surface had been easy, but digging deep is always hard. You never know what you might uncover from the burial ground within. Could be guilt for not being able to fix someone who never knew how to fix herself. Or secrets you've kept for a friend you once called "brother." Or strength instilled by someone respected yet flawed, just like the rest of us.

The cries around me turned frantic, hungry, and sad. I looked toward the rotted steps I'd sat on while talking with Ern, now sheltering three pups in their den, at least two months shy of self-sufficiency. Listening to their yips, I thought of Lula, Noemi, and me, not all that different from them, huddled close when times got tough. Glancing back at the trailer across the field, Lula inside, I wondered if the pups would find a way to survive. I hoped they would. Hadn't we?

The final shovelful of dirt rained down onto the mound beside me. The wind gusted again, redolent of rot, carrying cries for the dead, of the dead. Maybe. I wondered if I'd always hear them, like persistent clacks against the glass of my bedroom window.

Bending, I lifted the wieldy rock beside me, the corpse beneath it rigid now, its lips pulled back, baring teeth. I grabbed it by the scruff and lowered it into the hole in the ground, and into the one within me, not too deep this time, having experienced that things we bury sometimes resurface, far uglier than when we laid them to rest.

EPILOGUE

Noemi

I parked the Jeep in the shadows of the Joseph Broussard Pow Wow Grounds, named for my great-grandfather before the start of the new century, when I was sixteen years old. Hands on the wheel, I breathed deep, knowing this year's festivities wouldn't be easy to endure. Nothing would be for a while, not with the nagging notion that I was supposed to be with Roddy, here and everywhere. I tilted the rearview mirror toward my face. Subtle lines around my mouth and eyes, puffy skin, and blotches of red filled the reflection. I wasn't comforted by what I saw, but I felt no impulse to bat the mirror away. Denying the state of things wouldn't make them, or me, any better.

I sat for a while, the Jeep's interior growing hot beneath the midday sun, reminding me that I ought to take the top down for the ride home, to let the wind put tangles in my hair. Car doors slammed around me. Excited voices rang out. Life went on, and so it goes.

I got out of the Jeep and took off the button-up shirt that was making me sweat. My nose buried in its folds, I took another breath before tying it around my waist and proceeding to the pow wow's entrance. Mom and Uncle Louie were waiting for me there, looking tired yet sturdy. They'd withstood a lot. I was lucky to lean on them.

"All right?" Mom asked, giving me a hug.

"Yeah." The ground beneath my feet felt firmer than it had over the last sixteen hours. I knew it'd go spongy again in the days ahead, but I wasn't afraid of falling. Not anymore.

Hands reached in our direction as we navigated through the crowd. Well-intentioned whispers met my ears. The dozens of men, women, and children wearing regalia around the dance circle lifted my spirit. Adorned with traditional feathers, porcupine quills, ribbons, buckskin, beads, and bone, they wore modern artifacts as well— military tags, heirloom jewelry, bandannas, patriotic patches, sports medals, buttons, and cum laude cords—each reflecting their individual past and present, the objects signifying important parts of their lives, like the shirt tied around my waist.

We made our way past stands selling arts and crafts, T-shirts and hats, following our noses to where patties of dough bubbled in oil. Uncle Louie ordered three, and soon we were holding the hot bread in our hands, oil leaking through the paper wrapped around it. Uncle Louie squeezed honey onto his. Mom slathered hers with butter. Cinnamon sugar was the only way for me.

One bite and I was whisked back to days that lived as carefree memories in my mind, back when I was a kid and Mom and Uncle Louie would chase me around the pow wow grounds, though I know now that we'd never truly been carefree. We'd withstood our troubles then, and we'd withstand them now, together.

"Will you stay past the weekend?" I asked Uncle Louie. "For a little while?"

Louie

I licked honey from my fingertips. The fry bread revived feelings and memories I'd thought were gone, making me realize that they hadn't really been lost; I'd just let myself drift too far from the past.

"Can I?" I asked Lula.

"Stay?" she said.

"The hotel's too cold for me." Everywhere I went within the casino and resort was so frigid that I had to wear sleeves. Though it was within walking distance of my old home, I felt worlds away within its walls, the same way I felt when I escaped up north. Home was humid. It always made me sweat.

"You'll have to earn your keep." Lula smiled, butter glistening on her lips. I didn't bother reminding her that she still owed me for all the free babysitting I'd done.

"Come on." We found a spot on the bleachers where we could watch the opening ceremony, solemn and exciting, consisting of prayer, the Eagle Staff, the grand entry led by veterans, flags from all the nations in attendance, and dancers ready to honor sacred traditions—and maybe win some money, too.

Lula waved to Rosie, sitting next to Jean-Luc in the bleachers across the dance circle from us. I waved as well. Rosie didn't wave back. I didn't blame her, but I hoped that one day she would.

"I missed this," Lula said close to my ear.

The hot sun beating on our backs. Vivid colors all around. Fairground odors. Rhythmic music. Feelings of pride, awe, and assurance that our people and our ways would go on and on. I'd missed it too.

"Are you gonna?" I asked when the emcee opened the dance circle to all, Native or not, to join the communal celebration.

"Next year," she said, making me smile. She always said that.

The pow wow of 1986 had gone on that summer as planned, and, lacking buckskin, feathers, and beads, I'd danced in it with as much purpose as when I'd danced on the river's edge.

Thinking of Ma, Noemi, Lula, Roddy, Grandpa, and Horace, I stepped into the dance circle again today, knowing that there will always be an enemy to keep at bay. The drum beat loud, reverberating in my chest. The singers started their song. I began my dance. I'm better at it now.

ACKNOWLEDGMENTS

Since you've read this far, I want to thank you first. Connecting with readers since my debut, *Sisters of the Lost Nation*, came out last year has been a unique and rewarding experience. A privilege, too.

Indian Burial Ground is a story that's been with me for a while. I wrote the first draft in 2015, though I didn't know back then that it would turn into *this* story. For that, I have my editor, Sareer Khader, to thank, and for helping me see that the first draft was only half complete, and that there was a lot more story to tell.

For endless hard work, keeping me on track with media and events, and producing another beautiful book, hats off to the incredible team at Berkley, including Yazmine Hassan, Lauren Burnstein, Ivan Held, Christine Ball, Jeanne-Marie Hudson, Claire Zion, Craig Burke, Jessica Plummer, Hillary Tacuri, Emily Osborne, Christine Legon, Megha Jain, George Towne, and Hannah Gramson.

Much gratitude to my agent, Amanda Orozco, for so meticulously handling all the things that would overwhelm or confuse me, and for working with my best interest in mind. A mountain of thanks to Tanen Jones as well for picking me, and for being a voice of wisdom and reassurance, always when I need it most.

A great deal of gratitude goes to my family and friends, for continuous encouragement and support, and for being my biggest fans.

Finally, I'd like to acknowledge the two horrific and heartbreaking themes that run through this book—suicide and alcoholism—specifically in regard to their prevalence among Native and Indigenous peoples. While it isn't easy to provide clear-cut answers and explanations as to why Native and Indigenous peoples experience higher rates of suicide than all other racial and ethnic groups in the United States (according to an analysis from the Centers for Disease Control), it's highly likely that limited health care resources, high levels of poverty and unemployment, and a lengthy history of historical trauma all play a part. Compounded, they create hopeless circumstances.

The same reasons, in addition to lower education attainment, housing issues, violence, mental health issues, and loss of connection to culture, are attributed to binge drinking and alcohol use disorder among many within Native and Indigenous communities (as indicated by the Substance and Mental Health Services Administration).

Regardless of your background, if you or someone you know is struggling with alcoholism or suicidal thoughts, please seek assistance. For substance abuse treatment and mental health referrals, contact the Substance Abuse and Mental Health Services Administration's National Helpline at 1-800-662-HELP. For suicide prevention, dial 988 to reach the Suicide and Crisis Lifeline.